KU-449-475

Kate Muir is the author of *Left Bank* and *Suffragette City*. She writes a weekly column in the Saturday Times, and has worked as a foreign correspondent in Paris, New York and Washington DC. She was born in Glasgow and now lives in London with her husband and three children.

Praise for *Left Bank*:

'Muir writes a subtle and untouristy Paris, whether depicting a café or a piece of cheese. Her characters are similarly nuanced, at once self-examining and hopelessly deluded. Elegantly and ironically, she both celebrates and satirises the French love affair with philosophy, food and love affairs themselves' *Daily Mail*

'Vivid observational wit . . . Muir has a talent for conjuring up people and atmospheres in a few wry sentences. Hearts break, egos come crashing down, and Muir's gallop through the salons of the terminally pretentious is hugely entertaining' *The Times*

'*Left Bank* is the kind of novel you can really immerse yourself in – Kate Muir's characters leap off the page' *Heat*

'Extra compelling' *Prima*

'[A] seamless comedy of manners . . . Adult entertainment on a plate' *Independent*

'This arresting mix of passion, fashion and Parisian chic is magnifique!' *Company*

'Excellent, witty entertainment' *Woman and Home*

'Addictive . . . starts as a light tale of angst and adultery in the wealthy *arrondissements* of Paris, but develops into a meaty tale of morality and responsibility . . . the Parisian setting is wonderfully evocative' *Easy Living*

By Kate Muir

Suffragette City
Left Bank
West Coast

Non-fiction
Arms and the Woman

West Coast

Kate Muir

headline
review

Copyright © 2008 Kate Muir

The right of Kate Muir to be identified as the Author of the Work has been asserted
by her in accordance with the Copyright, Designs and Patents Act 1988.

Extracts from *Lanark* and *Unlikely Stories Mostly* by Alasdair Gray,
first published in Great Britain by Canongate Books, 14 High Street,
Edinburgh EH1 1TE

Extract from *On the Road* by Jack Kerouac, (Penguin Books, 1972)
Copyright © Jack Kerouac 1955, 1957. Reprinted by permission of
Penguin Group (UK) and Penguin Group (USA) Inc.

Extract from *Scottish Journey* by Edwin Muir.
Reprinted by permission of Mainstream Publishing

Extract from *The Testament of Gideon Mack* by James Robertson (Hamish Hamilton
2006). Copyright © James Robertson, 2006. Reprinted by permission of Penguin
Group (UK) and Penguin Group (Canada), a Division of Pearson Canada Inc.

Extract from 'To a Fat Lady Seen From the Train' by Frances Cornford
from *Selected Poems* (Enitharmon Press 1996).
Reprinted by permission of Enitharmon Press

First published in 2008 by HEADLINE REVIEW
An imprint of HEADLINE PUBLISHING GROUP

First published in paperback in 2008 by HEADLINE REVIEW
An imprint of HEADLINE PUBLISHING GROUP

1

Apart from any use permitted under UK copyright law, this publication may only be
reproduced, stored, or transmitted, in any form, or by any means, with prior
permission in writing of the publishers or, in the case of reprographic production, in
accordance with the terms of licences issued by the Copyright Licensing Agency.

All characters in this publication are fictitious and any
resemblance to real persons, living or dead, is purely coincidental.

Every effort has been made to fulfil requirements with regard to reproducing
copyright material. The author and publisher will be glad to rectify any omissions at
the earliest opportunity.

Cataloguing in Publication Data is available from the British Library

978 0 7553 2504 7 (B-format)
978 0 7553 4709 4 (A-format)

Typeset in Sabon by Avon DataSet Ltd, Bidford on Avon, Warwickshire

Printed and bound in Great Britain by Clays Ltd, St Ives plc

Headline's policy is to use papers that are natural, renewable and recyclable
products and made from wood grown in sustainable forests. The logging and
manufacturing processes are expected to conform to the environmental
regulations of the country of origin.

HEADLINE PUBLISHING GROUP
An Hachette Livre UK Company
338 Euston Road
London NW1 3BH

www.headline.co.uk
www.hachettelivre.co.uk

For Magnus and Kate Macintyre

'I do like Scotland. I like the miserable weather. I like the miserable people. I like the fatalism, the negativity, the violence that's always just below the surface.'

The Devil in *The Testament of Gideon Mack*,
James Robertson

'Work as if you live in the early days of a better nation.'

Alasdair Gray (after Dennis Lee)

Contents

Glossary

Bar-L – Barlinnie prison
bevvy – drink
biscuit toes – holed shoes
blootered – drunk
bogie – go-cart
boke – vomit
bowffin – pungent, stinking
bridie – meat pasty
bumfled – crushed up
burn – stream
carnapcious – irritable
close – hallway
cludgie – outdoor toilet
crabbit – grumpy
crapper – coward
cutty sark – short shift (Burns)
doatery – old, unsteady
doo-lally – crazy
dreich – damp, rainy
droukit – soaked, damp
dunted – butted
dwam – daze
eejit – idiot
face is tripping you – you look mournful
feart – afraid
flitting – removal

gallus – great
get beasted in – eat up
gies – give us
girn – whine
gless cheque – refundable bottle
greetin' face – crying face
gutties – gym shoes
havering – raving
hoaching – packed
honking – stinking; also drunk
humphed – carried
jammy piece – jam sandwich
jings, crivens, help ma Boab – expressions of surprise
lochan – small loch
manky – dirty
midden – rubbish pile
minging – smelly
miroculous – drunk
mockit – dirty
ned – thug
numptie – idiot
oxter – armpit
P45 – redundancy note, also to chuck someone
plook – spot
Radio Rental – mental
raining stair rods – heavy rain
rain-mate – a transparent plastic tie-on headscarf
ran dan – razzle
shoogle – shake
skelping – smacking
sleekit – cunning, sly
smirr – light rain

spindrift – spray whipped by the wind
stank – a roadside drain
teuchters – Highlanders
thrawn – contrary, tough
up to high doh – hysterical, stressed
wacky backy – dope

Prologue

2000
'Once in a Lifetime':
Talking Heads

Charles's long-nosed, long-in-the-tooth sportscar swerves insanely from lane to lane in the darkness, causing fear and loathing all along the Marylebone Road. Loads of people won't even take a lift off Charles, but Fergus is calm, cradled in the old leather of the Karmann Ghia's passenger seat – one of the few places where he can relax. Speed comforts him. He likes planes, too. As they drive, Fergus skims through Charles's music selection which is famed for being crap, and therefore requires an ironic touch. He comes across Leo Sayer's 'When I Need You', and tanks up the volume.

'Oh for God's sake,' says Charles, taking a hand off the wheel to punch Fergus, and the eject button.

'I wasn't the one who purchased *Singalong Hits from the Seventies*,' says Fergus in a mock-pious Scottish voice. He scrolls through the CD holder, shaking his head in despair: 'Years of mediocrity here. And you were never even a punk, were you?' He narrows his eyes at Charles's

1

yellow waistcoat and fat silk tie, and laughs. 'You big prissy Sloane, you. Anyway, I'm dead fond of this song. Reminds me of Burnoch at its worst.' Fergus sings along in a falsetto. 'D'you remember Leo Sayer's bad hair? And that clown suit?'

Charles gives his full attention to speeding up. He's only happy at the front of any line. 'I won't be ignored,' says Fergus. 'Answer, or I'll put on Enya, final proof that your taste is minging.'

Fergus finds a barely acceptable track – why should Charles's unerring taste fail in this one area of his life? Charles is talking away about the deal they're doing tonight, but Fergus has already taken some coke, and he enters that semi-floating state where Charles's words have rhythm, but no meaning. If Fergus half closes his eyes, the car lights blur into a river of red ahead, and a river of white across the road. The two colours flow sedately past each other. Suddenly a police car rips across the junction in a blue flash. The pattern of light jerks Fergus into a memory of home: of standing on the hill listening to the sirens in the distance, watching the red tail lights of the police car and the white headlights of the ambulance meeting on the loch road on the night he left. He remembers colours the way other people remember anecdotes; he has a photographic memory. That's his job.

'Anyway, genius has always been a commodity,' continues Charles, still deep in conversation with himself.

Fergus surfaces from his trance to glare at him. 'What d'you mean commodity? The commodity here is your humungous commission on my work. The genius is quite separate,' says Fergus, not modestly.

'If I may quote Baudelaire . . .' begins Charles.

'If you fucking have to,' groans Fergus.

'As Baudelaire said, in the nineteeth century: "To create a trademark, that's genius. I must create a trademark," ' says Charles, grinning over at him. 'So stop moaning about the commission and being compromised. You're just lucky you've become a trademark, an international brand, and you've got me there ready to dirty my hands so that you can cash the fat cheques while remaining the high-minded, working-class son of—'

'Watch out! Fucking pay attention to where you're going.'

Charles clips the wing mirror of a car and yatters on, uncaring, 'We're the first generation where artists have become true businessmen and felt neither shame nor pain. Look, they've even taken pleasure in it, in simultaneously exploiting and exposing commercialism. Why does Emin invert and embrace celebrity? Why does Sam Taylor-Wood spend so much time with Elton? Why does Hirst make so many versions of the same top-ten works? Why else is there Jay Jopling and a vast machine behind him, and me behind you? Why are you wearing that bespoke suit?'

'Because you prostituted yourself for it. But thanks anyway,' says Fergus, lifting a lapel to luxuriate in the orange silk lining and butter-smooth worsted wool. Charles grins and dives without signalling into a faster lane. A blonde in a humungous black Range Rover Vogue makes a wanker gesture at them. She's all bones and bling. Charles zigzags madly before they roar off right in front of the four-wheel drive, leaving it honking furiously. They're hooting with laughter too.

'What are you on tonight?' asks Fergus. It's a rhetorical question. Drink and cocaine have become a drug in their own right for Charles, who balances and mixes them expertly, like an alchemist. His mood is perfectly chemically calibrated. He never makes mistakes. He is always charming. But Charles pretends he hasn't heard Fergus. Instead he gives his friend a strict, schoolmasterly look. 'I tell you, Fergus, the evening's only going to get worse, and you'd better be on your best behaviour.'

'Charlie m'darling, I'm always on my—'

'Bollocks.'

'. . . best behaviour. It's you that's cruising round like a heidcase. I've been up working in the studio since six this morning. My eyeballs feel like they've been through a shredder. I'm knackered.' Fergus cracks his knuckles.

'Or hyper. All that's predictable is your unpredictability. Best behaviour, I mean it. This contract's international, penetrating a whole new market, and even the dinner's costing three hundred pounds a head, so—'

'Three hundred quid for sushi? At Ebi? Each? You're bullshitting.'

'Nope,' says Charles, looking peculiarly smug, even for him. He skids the car to a stop on the icy road and tosses the keys to a man in uniform.

'Mr Wentworth, good to see you and your Karmann Ghia again,' says the valet parking man, staring lovingly at the blue car, which has the body of a Porsche, the engine of a souped-up Volkswagen Beetle, and the reliability of a Trabant. In the Mayfair of jerks with Mercs, it is a thing of almost archaeological wonder.

Charles nods grandly and turns back to Fergus. 'You'll

enjoy Ebi tonight. There's no one in the world better equipped than you, Fergus, for this moment. You have all the right appetites. And *they*'ll think dinner is performance art,' he adds, thumbing derisively at the two Russians who have been following in a car behind them. Their chauffeur looks beige and shaky after the inexplicable race through central London.

Fergus glances at the Russians, gives a smile which borders on a sneer, then slaps Charles round the shoulder. It's the best sushi restaurant in London, so he can't complain.

'You're the man.'

They go over to greet the Russians fulsomely. The Russians leave their chauffeur ticking over on the kerb and follow Charles and Fergus downstairs into a dim basement of such exquisite minimalism some might think it plain. The restaurant chatter and clatter is muted to a rounded hum by Ebi's grey felt walls, and the waiters glide back and forth across white polished concrete to the stone tables. Cocooned in pools of soft light, their sushi carved from the most exotic of sea urchins, lobsters and jellyfish, the diners look up when Charles strides across the room stinking, as the rich do, with confidence.

The diners also stare at Fergus MacFarlane, but they've no idea why. His suit is well cut, not flashy. He is barely five foot ten, hardy and sinewy. His face is nondescript until animated. There's an edgy energy about the man, not much else of note. On closer inspection, the diners spot the jaw, as nicely defined as that of any in Hollywood, the darkish hair, and something disturbing in the eyes: a raw, aggressive blue. Do they recognise him? Is he someone important? He walks as though he's important. He's cocky.

Trotting behind, the two Russians look, well, American, in their casual, buttoned-down clothing and loafers. (They are trying their very best to blend in – they have only managed to divest themselves of those uniform long leather coats in recent years. But in some suspicious way they still seem to have no necks.) The audience's interest returns to its hand-rolled seaweed wraps and miso-blackened halibut.

The four men go down a long white concrete corridor, which has a sheet of uplit water pouring down one expensive wall.

'They should fix that fucking leak,' growls Fergus, somehow embarrassed, his hands twitching the change in his pockets. Sometimes he hates doing this, selling himself. But like Charles says, genius is a commodity. He snorts. The Russians look at him nervously.

'Now we're entering the tunnel of love,' says Charles, sardonically. Fergus gives him a withering stare. The Russians – Mikhail and Yakov – are increasingly excited. Yakov, the overweight agent from St Petersburg, who is here to be seduced into a deal, says: 'I have heard that this restaurant has very high Zagat ratings, yes?' Yakov feels more secure when he knows he's somewhere fashionable.

'Oh, my, I see it has also got a Michelin star,' adds Mikhail, a pert gallery owner from Moscow, dealing in London and desperate to be truly European.

'We're not really here for the food,' says Charles.

Peculiarly, Charles takes them through the wine cellar, where a waiter bows low and ushers them through a door into a small, dimly lit room with leather-upholstered chairs surrounding a marble table on which lies . . .

'It's a fucking human sacrifice,' says Fergus.

'This is not for real,' says Yakov, delighted.

'This is dinner, gentlemen. Do sit down,' says Charles, nannying.

'Some fish supper,' says Fergus, more Scottish than usual.

On the table, with her eyes tight shut, but breathing softly, is a naked Japanese woman covered in tiny, carefully arranged slices of raw fish. In some way it reminds Fergus of a Roman mosaic: the little rectangles of pale oranges, reds and creams scattered on her flesh.

'Drinks, gentlemen? The sake is very good, but I shall be having the house citrus Martini – lemon vodka, Cointreau, and lime juice.'

Fergus grins and shakes his head at Charles carrying on as though nothing was happening, as though they are not about to use a woman as a plate. Charles has obviously been here a lot on business, and Mikhail and Yakov are in drool-filled heaven. Fergus wants to laugh, because they think this is dead sophisticated. But who cares, because Yakov has the big money now the Russians want their chunk of British art. Those who traded in gas, oil and arms now trade in artists. Of the premier league, howlingly famous sort. As the twenty-first century opens, the fresh-in Moscow–London elite wants something abject, freaky and profound – but above all, likely to appreciate – on its walls, and a Fergus MacFarlane photograph ticks all those boxes. Or, as Charles once put it, 'Once London's investment-fund managers are frantically bidding for you as their new portfolio, you know the rest of the world will dumbly follow.'

Fergus sits down, cracks his knuckles again, knocks back the Martini, and stares at his dinner in silence. The Japanese girl is exquisitely lovely, and the arrangement of sashimi is artfully done. She appears to be entirely naked, but for a thong which is naffly covered with fresh rose petals. The only sign of life is her chest rising and falling almost imperceptibly, and a blue vein pulsing at her temple. Fergus wonders if she's bored.

'Ahem,' interrupts Charles. 'The maître d' just asked me to politely mention that you should always use the chopsticks provided. This *course* should last for half an hour, and then, sadly, we will move on to more mundane fare.' At this, he languidly stretches out his chopsticks, lifts a morsel of yellowtail from the woman's right thigh, and eats it with theatrical relish.

'Delicious,' he says. 'She is delicious, isn't she?'

Yakov is pacing round the slab, unable to decide which lovely little titbit he should pick from the girl's soft creamy-brown skin. He gives a barely suppressed roar of excitement. Charles raises one ironic eyebrow at Fergus. This is not the first deal he has sealed here on a napkin, Fergus guesses. He wonders if Charles has helped his clients eat sashimi off pretty young boys here too: Charles prefers boys, Zagat and Michelin rated.

The slab has something of the mortuary about it, thinks Fergus, and the girl is scarily still, her hair fanned out black on the white marble. She smells of nothing. No perfume or soap, but beautifully clean. A waiter refills his Martini. Mikhail is picking delicately at some wafer-thin slices of scallop, a faraway look in his eye. Yakov pounces on a morsel of smoked eel, nestled in the girl's cleavage. Fergus wishes he had his camera, because it's a moment of modern *hommage* to Allen Jones's forniphiliac sculpture of a woman as coffee table, half nude, on all fours, with a sheet of glass on her back. Plus there's the added dissonance of a red-faced preppy Russian, aroused in all his greed.

Fergus sighs. It's dreadful and disgusting, weird and wonderful, this place where feminism appears to meet cannibalism. It makes him jumpy. The use of humans as furniture – or in this case crockery – is a wee bit freaky, even for him. Yet he knows these wasabi-wouldn't-melt-in-my-mouth girls from the front restaurant – all PhD students and actresses, earning a bit on the side. Undoubtedly, everyone is getting their money's-worth here at Ebi. Everyone is happy with the arrangement. There are worse arrangements, Fergus knows.

He lifts some fresh sweet shrimp from the girl's belly and slides it into his mouth. The cortex of his brain tingles as it always does when he eats raw fish. It's the only meal that makes you feel better, not worse, afterwards, thinks Fergus. Then soft scallop, a little warm from her breast, slides down his throat. Charles lets loose his shark grin. Everything is going according to plan. While the businessmen sit down to talk numbers, timescales, limited editions, percentages, Fergus, the artist, walks round the subject and begins to enjoy himself.

Wrapped round the girl's rosy nipples are tiny hand-rolled cones of seaweed, filled with slivers of tuna so rich they turn into cream in your mouth, and do not require chewing. The salmon roe are like tiny orange marbles in her perfect little belly button, strangely arousing. Fergus lets his fingers trail on the girl's skin. Her eyes flick open for just a second and then close again. He is repulsed and attracted.

The waiter bustles in and invites them into another private dining room for the next course. So they will never see the girl move. She will remain nothing but a platter for them, *nature mort*. Fergus lingers behind, but the other men are shouting and laughing cheerily, perhaps in some relief. Their drinks come strong and fast – they share a secret now, they are a brotherhood. Fergus moves on to the water, silent. Charles must be doing a lot of coke to drink this much and remain sober. But he doesn't miss a beat: Charles is selling Fergus to the Russians, over a body, for a lot of money. He sold Fergus long ago to the Americans and the Europeans. But new and unexpectedly lucrative markets are opening up all the time. All that Gazprom share money with nowhere to go. It's lovely. There's plenty of currency in Britart or, in this case, photography. And Charles has become quietly lax over how limited the limited-edition prints are. The Russians go into a lengthy hymn of praise for Fergus's work – its iconoclasm, its daring, its sinister core. 'I'm just a regular snapper,' he shrugs, charming them, his voice rapid, 'with an overworked subconscious.'

Charles has always known, from the day he discovered Fergus, that he was in some way infinitely saleable, though sadly not malleable. At about the same time, it dawned on Charles that the human rather than the divine was going to be more important in the art market. His client's saturnine character has provided a certain interest, and his soft West-

Coast accent has also proved helpful – why, after all, do television advertisers and telemarketers use the Scots to sell washing powder and life insurance? There is a down-to-earth authority and magnetism to Fergus's voice, particularly in England where being Scots renders one conveniently classless.

There are risks, costs and benefits in being associated with Fergus MacFarlane at this time in his life, as he enters his thirties. He is not what you would describe as a responsible man. As a father, as a lover, as a husband, and as a friend, Fergus is unpredictable, capricious, perhaps intentionally so. You never know who or what is next. Even in his work, Fergus always seems to be proceeding in a sensible, lucrative direction, and then something dark rips him apart from within, and spins off somewhere else. He is always running from something: boredom, ordinariness, or the shadow of death. He remakes himself, and returns. Fergus may be Charles's best friend and biggest-earning client, but Charles doesn't trust him one fucking iota.

'Hey, friend!' says Mikhail when the deal is cut. 'Now you have sold your soul to me, Fergus.'

'I sold that a wee while ago. Somewhere else,' says Fergus. 'Don't feel bad.' He shakes Mikhail's hand, and his contempt goes unnoticed. The Russian's face floods with pleasure. Mikhail, with his pale skin and empty blue eyes, reminds Fergus of a peeled lychee. Fergus laughs alone.

Charles gives Fergus an exasperated look. Fergus grins wolfishly and fiddles with the cufflinks on his red cotton poplin shirt from New and Lingwood, and straightens his Richard James bespoke jacket, worn without a tie. Mikhail looks longingly at him, trapped in the aspirant hell that is Lacoste and Ralph Lauren. 'I wish you'd take me down Savile Row with you and show me—'

'One day.' Fergus is irritated. They've cut the deal. Why waste any more time with these tossers? His thin fingers start drumming on the table. He pushes his drink aside and starts texting someone on the phone which he never normally turns on. He deletes half a dozen missed calls from his wife Athene which he always refers to derogatorily as 'domestics'. He bites a ragged thumbnail. Charles recognises the signs, and calls over the Maître d'. Charles pays for dinner in cash, red £50 notes, and the sleaziness of the transaction is confirmed.

As they leave the white concrete tunnel, shoals of creepy salary men fresh from whisky and karaoke pour in, gibbering in anticipation of their fishy woman on a plate. Fergus scowls at them. He feels tense, frustrated, crass. The Russians are removed by their chauffeur into the icy night, and the Karmann Ghia is brought round. Fergus grabs his Puma sports bag from Charles's car and suddenly shoots inside the restaurant. 'Wait a minute.' He emerges in trainers, a vest and shorts. Charles stares in horror.

'Oh, not again. It's midnight, you fucking idiot. It's midwinter, for God's sake. I'll give you a lift to Belsize Park.'

Fergus tosses Charles his bag and suit. Charles crumples them into the back seat in exasperation. He checks his phone. 'Athene's texted me twice, trying to find you. Again.' Fergus nods.

'I'll get her at home. Thanks, Big Man. Another good job well done. I'm away off.'

'Ghastly Russians,' says Charles, cheerfully slapping him on the back.

'Ghaastly,' says Fergus smiling, imitating Charles's old Harrovian accent. 'Seeya.'

Fergus starts running into the blackness and frost, trying to pound the tension inside him deep into the pavement. It's four miles home to Belsize Park, a nice, easy distance for clearing the head. He speeds up before hypothermia catches him. The vest was not a good idea, but by and by, as he heads up through Mayfair towards Baker Street, he feels the hot patch of sweat grow on his back. He's flying, still high on the remains of the alcohol and the joy of speed. Teenagers waiting for the late-night bus stare at the half-naked madman, his muscles taut, his eyes looking inside, not out, his breath white in the darkness. He pounds on, sleaze falling away, commitments falling away, millions falling away, until he is left with the raw residue of his own self, his needs, desires, ideas; the real stuff that matters. Anyway, it's better that he has this run at midnight rather than going straight home and fucking Athene again when she's exhausted.

He turns into Regent's Park, plotting a crossways trajectory which will come out at the far side of the zoo. The trees are skeletal and black, and the formal flowerbeds are all dead. Yet Fergus is not afraid of the shadows of the park at night, and all the strangeness it contains. He'd take anyone on, but no one seems to bother him, ever. It must be some pheromone, a warning he gives off. Tonight he sees no one, not like it is in the dogging dog days of summer. Even the zoo animals are indoors, their peculiar captive moans and sighs muffled, the camels' foetid smell occasionally breaking through the crisp air. Fergus is mesmerised by his own trail of footprints across the perfect lawns, the grass dusted with icing, the tiny satisfying frost-crunch beneath his feet which he hears between his own hot breaths. There's an extraordinary pleasure in wiping the hot sweat from his forehead, then letting the beads fall and become ice. The stars are all out, as much as you can see them in the orange fluorescent city: Orion's Belt, the Plough. Fergus suddenly misses the big night skies over the water in Burnoch, their emptiness and clarity. He hasn't been back to Scotland for years.

Then he's leaping the park gates, over the road, loping up and over Primrose Hill like a hare, stopping for barely a second to glance back at the superior views down to the lights of the London Eye and the silhouettes of the Gherkin and Canary Wharf. He no longer feels an outsider here. In fact, he's almost proprietorial nowadays. He has taken this town, quite possibly for a ride. He smiles to himself. He's relaxed now, almost euphoric. He rolls on into the wide avenues of Belsize Park, past those huge white stucco houses with their pillars signifying the monetary and social successes of their owners now and then. He loves the grandeur of the fronts, those tall bow windows that open out in summer, the high ceilings. Fat, foie-gras houses.

He walks up through his own pillars to his own front door, painted the sort of matt architectural grey which signifies: *we are in the know*. He takes his phone and the keys from the satisfying little zip pocket inside his shorts, opens the heavy door, and flicks the downstairs alarm before it goes off. Fergus stops for a moment inside the hall, and sucks up the warm silence of his house, his prime property in a sought-after street, which safely holds his wife and two sleeping children. His beautiful wife. His beautiful house. And he wonders how he got here. Sometimes he is still stunned by it all. He hums a bit of the Talking Heads song, 'Once in a Lifetime', as he goes down into the kitchen. He takes a bottle of Hildon water from the silver fridge, drinks it all, and stares up at the double-height sheets of glass in sliding steel frames that have replaced the back walls, over two of four storeys. The polished concrete kitchen worktop runs seamlessly from inside to outside, miraculously through the glass. The architect also built the exquisite slate wet-room shower with the glass roof that slid back to let in the stars, or the warm summer rain. Fergus has known leaky roofs that cost less.

Moonlight floods down through the glass walls, and the warmth of the underfloor heating beneath the limestone floods up into Fergus as he kicks off his trainers. He pads up through the vast living area, with its balcony over the kitchen, its elongated modular sofas, and limed oak shelves specially calibrated for his oversized art books. He only has one of his photographs in the living area, but it covers most of the longest wall. He just started properly collecting his own photographs when he discovered Charles – his dealer, for God's sake – was quietly buying one out of every limited edition 'as an investment for my retirement'. His wall photo is one of a series of seven-foot-high blue Tennent's lager cans, like the Lager Lovelies of Fergus's youth in Scotland, and on the side of this can is a life-sized woman in an open-necked orange-checked seventies' shirt with a long pointed collar. The model should, by rights, be an ordinary centrefold, a proper girl-next-door Lager Lovely. Instead, she's photographed from directly above, cruelly flattened by the lens. Her eyes are huge, and she's turning round abruptly, as though terrified by something. Nostalgia is ripped apart by unease.

Fergus hums as he climbs the stairs (with their custom-woven Roger Oates runners, £90 a metre, in case you're counting. Fergus still is.) On his way he looks in on Raphael, in his white-carpeted room with the tropical rain-forest mural Fergus had painted for him, and on Hannah, his second-born, his baby daughter in her cot. They're soft skinned, oblivious, breathing gently. He feels a rush of joy. He feels good. So good, so wealthy, so happy, so full of exhilaration that he needs to make love to Athene. Still. After all that exercise, at one in the morning, and she's probably just fed the baby.

'A man's gotta do what a man's gotta do,' says Fergus to himself, grinning. He imagines Athene deeply asleep upstairs in a field of her own long red curls on the white sheets. When he comes in late on nights like these he likes to watch her dreaming: achingly beautiful, serene, milk-smelling. Once he's made love to her, Fergus knows he will relax and sleep deeply, his demons exorcised and his energy excised for a few hours if he's lucky.

In the dressing room, he throws his running clothes on top of Athene's, her long, long leggings and sweatshirt discarded on the velvet armchair, which is odd because she's usually obsessively tidy. For a moment, Fergus stands and looks at himself naked in the long mirror. He feels the muscled strength in his legs; he is satisfyingly anchored in the earth. He's thinking of something Burns wrote. Fergus has an unspoken affinity with Burns – his grasp of Scots and English, his knowledge of rich and poor, his furious shape-shifting, and, of course, the fact that he was a prodigious shagger. These words of Burns – part of a letter, or some poem – are very funny, but they express his mood exactly:

> I have fuck'd her till she rejoiced with joy unspeakable and full of glory.
> I gave her such a thundering skillade as electrified the very marrow of her bones.
> Oh what a peacemaker is a good we'el willie pintle.

The Burns will either wake her up, make her laugh, or have its desired effect on desire, thinks Fergus, as he opens the bedroom door.

Athene is sitting stiffly upright in the bed, a livid white corpse that seems to have risen from the death of sleep. Words issue from her like staccato spikes: 'Where the hell have you been? Why didn't you answer me? I called you six times. Six times.' She starts screaming at him. 'Why didn't you answer?'

'Well, I was having dinner with Charles and we were doing a deal with some—'

'You don't give a fuck, do you? Do you know what happened to me?'

Athene starts bawling. She covers her face with her hands and her shoulders are shuddering.

'Athene? What is it? What did I do to—'

'It's what you didn't do. You weren't here. You're never . . .' but he loses what she's saying next in a flurry of hot tears and hysteria. Then some words emerge, clear.

'I got attacked today. Nearly killed. And you weren't—'

'What? Why didn't you—'

'Because your fucking phone was turned off as usual. Because you never tell me where you are. Because you need your artistic silence – or maybe it's licence . . .' Athene's tears have been sucked back in by her anger. Her cheeks are glowing red, and her voice is squeaking. She's yabbering right in his face.

'Fergus, a man came up behind me when I was running on the Heath this morning, on the path in the woods behind the ponds, and he threatened me. He had a knife, Fergus, he had a flick knife.'

Fergus holds her tight, trying to pull her down from the peak of hysteria. He knows, he feels the sudden nausea, he's seen it in the evening papers: London Fields, Finsbury Park, now the Heath – the rapist. Athene's gabbling, almost incomprehensible.

'I could hear him in the bushes, running parallel to me. I could hear him breathing and crashing about. I just knew . . . something made me alert, and then he came at me with his hood up, holding the knife. I just froze. He blocked me in on the path, and he was smiling. I wanted to scream, but nothing came out. And then a wave of blind fury, a wave . . . a wave of adrenaline came over me. He said, I think he said, "You just keep your fucking mouth shut and you'll be all right." He put one hand over my mouth, and the other was holding the knife near my throat and I don't know why, but instead of running away, I bit his hand until I could taste the blood and I grabbed his wrist above the knife. And then I kneed him in the balls.'

'Oh my God, Athene. Oh Jesus, you should've—'

'Should've what? Let him kill me? Rape me? He wasn't a big guy.' Her eyes are bulging with something like excitement. '*I* wanted to kill *him*.'

There's something twisted about her reaction, Fergus thinks. 'Shit. I'm so sorry. What did you do?'

'He was shocked. Shouting. He dropped the knife. I don't think he was expecting to be attacked. And I put my hands round his neck and I started to strangle him. He went down on the ground, choking, red in the face, and I kept pressing for a long time on his windpipe. He made a strange wheezing sound and I let go. He started retching and I ran away and shouted to some other people walking, and they called the police.' Athene is panting with urgency. 'We went back but he was gone, so I picked up the knife with a Quavers bag – to keep the fingerprints.'

Typical of Athene to be so well organised, to remember about fingerprints, thinks Fergus. Athene sits on the edge of the bed, with her back to Fergus, her head in her hands. Her shoulders, white in a white nightgown, occasionally shudder. He kneels before her, puts his hand under her chin, forcing himself into her field of vision.

'And what happened, darling?' he says, quietly. 'Did the police catch him? Did you go to the station?'

'No. He's still out there somewhere. I filed a report, did an identikit thing. It took hours. Where the hell were you all day? Where the hell were you when I needed you?'

Fergus sighs. He feels deeply ashamed of ignoring all those domestic calls. 'That doesn't matter now. What matters is you're all right.' He tries to squeeze her hand, but she pulls it away. He feels hopelessly inadequate, a man who has failed to protect his woman.

'No,' says Athene, mad eyed, hair everywhere like a fire round her head. 'That's not what matters.' Fergus feels a sudden chill, without knowing why.

Athene stands up, facing him. Facing him down. 'I found out something today. I suddenly understood what you're doing to me in all your irresponsibility, your selfishness. You're sucking life out of me and pumping lives into me, but you're not giving anything back, are you?' Her voice goes low. It's ugly, almost hissing. 'Because when I fought back against that man, I found I had this awful anger in me and it came flooding out. The harder I pressed his neck, the better I felt, punishing him.'

Her jaw is set tight, determined, satisfied. 'The worst thing about it is this, Fergus: every second that I was crushing that man's throat, I imagined that he was you. I was punishing you.'

Chapter One

1978

'The Wombles Theme': Mike Batt

This is the story of Fergus MacFarlane, born in the early seventies in the Scottish fishing port of Burnoch. Back then, Fergus had not developed his extraordinary eye and rapacious tastes, and his steely ambition was as imperceptible as the proverbial iron in Irn Bru. The young Fergus went almost unnoticed in his wee itchy grey school jumper, leading a life which was average by the standards of the time. His father was averagely drunken, averagely violent, and worked for an average wage at the fishing. His mother had been a teenage bride, for all the usual reasons. The MacFarlanes' home was an ordinary two-room-and-kitchen rented flat in a sandstone tenement on the seafront.

There on the West Coast, Fergus's father Gordon trawled for herring, and then as the herring ran out, prawns and langoustines, which he pronounced 'lang-goose-tins' in case folk thought he was soft, talking French. The locals wouldn't touch the fancy shellfish – it went to the hotels in Glasgow – and Fergus's mother bought proper

Bird's Eye fishfingers from the Co-op supermarket along from their flat. Fergus was fond of fishfingers.

The Co-op had a monopoly on Burnoch's food supply, and the shop's blacked-out windows on the tenement front belied the fact that it was the all-seeing eye of Burnoch, the place where all information was exchanged. For instance, everyone knew the history of Fergus's mother, Isla, a tall, smart, bitter woman who'd nearly made it out of Burnoch to secretarial college in Glasgow. Then, just before her seventeenth birthday, she fell pregnant by Gordon MacFarlane and was dragged back by the town's gloomy undertow.

There's a local saying: 'It's a lucky man in Burnoch that ken's his ain faither', a reference to the town's exceptionally high illegitimacy rate, caused by the heavy bevvy sessions and winter darkness that falls at three in the afternoon – plus the efforts of the visiting yachties in summer. So, in a sense, Fergus was one of the lucky ones, for a time. He knew his father.

Mr and Mrs MacFarlane did not have the greatest of relationships, although Fergus felt it was marginally better when they went drinking together than when his father drank alone. This meant that his mother did not sit up till midnight on Friday and bait his father as he staggered in with a cut lip from a fight, or, on calmer nights, a fish supper wrapped in newspaper in his oxter. Mrs MacFarlane would issue a guilt-inducing sigh, and one sharp word: 'Well?' Then there was sometimes another fight, which usually involved traditional, old-fashioned phrases like 'Where's your wages, then?', 'Fuckin' hoor!' and the sound of the fish supper or perhaps an item of china hitting the floor. Anyway, if his parents went out together to The Hop and Anchor – the 'e' of hope had been missing the last twenty years – Fergus got babysat by his Auntie Margaret and Uncle Jim up the road, and they had a big colour telly and Mint Matchsticks. You could lie there on the floor, in front of the coal-effect electric fire, and just lose yourself in the *Generation Game* and the brown shagpile. Uncle Jim could always remember all the stuff on the conveyor belt, down to the toaster and the cuddly toy. It was dead brilliant.

His parents' raucous evenings at the Hop and Anchor were short lived. When Fergus was eight and in Primary Four at Burnoch School, his father drowned at sea, trying to save another fisherman who – and this was not unheard of then – couldn't swim. They both died on a pouring, howling, black Thursday night, dragged apart by panic and cold, and sucked deep under the Kilbrannan Sound somewhere west of Arran. The bodies were never found.

Fergus has a searingly clear memory of his father's funeral in the severe, grey Church of Scotland overlooking the bay. It was May, a nice time of year there with all the garish yellow gorse showing through the church windows, suggesting a tropicality that was far from the case. Mrs MacFarlane was all in black with a big hat she'd got that morning reduced in Smart But Casual, the town's finest clothing shop. The hat added to her troubles by constantly sliding down her clammy forehead. Mrs MacFarlane held Fergus's hand so tight that for hours afterwards he could see the four red crescents her nails had left in his skin. His mother said nothing to him during the funeral except when he started picking his scabby knee, and she hissed, 'Sit at peace!' In Scotland, that meant 'sit properly', but nowadays Fergus longs to do just that, to sit at peace.

The service continued. Gordon MacFarlane was a fine father and husband, and he died a hero, said the minister. The congregation nodded, pleased to have a good word to say for the man at last. 'Oh hear us when we cry to Thee/For those in peril on the sea,' they sang. Even at the age of eight, the hymn seemed wrong to Fergus, and he knew what peril meant, because of Beryl the Peril in his *Beano*. The cries of his dad in peril had been ignored. God was deaf, or blind, or something, and the label of Fergus's school blazer was prickling his neck and he didn't dare move. It was unfair – why had God rescued the minister in peril on the sea, but not his dad? The minister knew all about nearly drowning, because he'd been a purser on a MacBrayne's ferry which went down, leaving the crew and the cargo of sheep swimming desperately across the moon-lit loch to shore. The minister's blinding conversion occurred as he and twelve other lambs of God found themselves soaked but safe on the beach.

Looking round the church, with its brown-painted pews and Calvinist lack of decoration, Fergus was suspicious. There was no coffin to see, not like when his grandmother had died last year in an orange-varnished box with cheap brassy handles and a wreath of sweetie-pink carnations. There was no body, just the word of the minister and the boat's skipper to go on. His dad was twenty-six. Surely you had to be a grandpa to die? Fergus wasn't sure whether his father really had drowned, until he looked up at his mother and saw her eyes, all glassy and empty under the too-big hat.

'You carry within you many fine memories, Mrs MacFarlane, which will be of great help in your task of rearing your child,' said the minister at the door. Isla looked at him, genuinely puzzled, and then nodded out of politeness.

They walked out into the sun and the yellow gorse. After his brother's funeral, Uncle Jim patted Fergus on the shoulder, unable to speak, an agonised rictus on his face. Auntie Margaret took Fergus, wrapped him in her huge soft bosoms, dunted his head with her bifocals and stated officially: 'The Poor Wee Thing'. Fergus burst into tears, for the second time in public since his mother had told him the news two weeks before. Auntie Margaret – pronounced Magrit, locally – squeezed him with one arm while with the other she dug deep into her clasped handbag and found, beneath the lint, old prescriptions and a spare pair of American Tan tights, two mint Pan Drops. 'There, son,' she said, and put them in his hand. It was funny the way people always called him son, even though they weren't his mum. He stared at the two big white sweeties, and for a moment he thought they were the dead man's eyeballs, but then he popped the Pan Drops into his mouth. The mint seared his tastebuds and stung him awake and alive. Something clicked into place in his mind.

'Two Missing at Sea' said the headline on the *Burnoch Gazette*, and there was a picture of Gordon MacFarlane and Bobby MacKay, the man he failed to rescue. They were standing cheerily on the harbour, raising a pint to celebrate the new boat, the *Dalriada*, bought by the skipper two years ago. But with that headline, it looked like Gordon and Bobby were celebrating their own deaths.

Mrs MacFarlane put the paper in the bin, saying, 'I can't stand the sight of that thing.' Fergus waited until she was watching *Charlie's Angels* on television, crept in his pyjamas into the kitchenette in the wall recess behind her and retrieved the paper from the wet tea leaves. He put it beneath his bed, in his Clarks size 2F shoebox from his new black funeral shoes.

Over the next few months, Fergus sometimes woke up at night, panicking, unable to breathe, sweating, his thoughts screaming: 'Something's missing! There's something gone. I've lost something. What's missing?' And as consciousness flooded down upon him, his throat would tighten in recognition of the coming pain, and the voice in his head would say flatly, 'My dad. My dad's missing.' Then it was quite helpful to put on the little metal spotlight by his bed, get the shoebox out, and look at the tea-stained picture. He hated Bobby MacKay for killing his dad, for dragging him down until the dark water closed over his head.

Fergus would tunnel into his own darkness in the small hours, under the pilled orange nylon sheets with his stuffed brown dog. In this safe place, he would try to remember his father's face, the real one, not the one in the newspaper. He would conjure it up and recall a series of smells – the oil of the boat's engine on his dad's navy jacket, the fish on his hands, the smoke and bacon grease secreted in the wool of his jumper. And then there was the fishing boat. Fergus liked thinking about the boat, freshly painted blue and red every season, a fifty-footer with a Kelvin engine, hydraulic crane, winches, sonar and an echo sounder. Sometimes he'd wander alone along the harbour and stand staring at the *Dalriada* if she was docked, waiting for his father to come back from the dead and wave from the wheelhouse. Fergus only got a chance to go on the boat a couple of times with his dad, but he remembered Munro, one of the fishermen, frying up bacon, eggs, tattie scones and square sausage for them all on the tiny galley stove. Fergus left the fried tomato, though, and played with it on his plate because he didn't want to finish and be sent back home. He sat rocked by the waves in the dim, smoky fug of the cabin, and felt like a proper man, like his dad.

As a proper man, Gordon MacFarlane wasn't one for kissing or hugging much. Indeed, much of his physical contact with Fergus had been a skelping for giving his mother some cheek, or not coming home for his tea on time. The lines between affection and violence were not at all well drawn in the MacFarlane household, up there on the fourth floor of the tenement with its panoramic harbour views obscured by mangy net curtains. As Fergus's mother explained, 'Your dad's sometimes working a twenty-hour day and he needs a bit of peace at the weekend after being at the fishing all week'.

Peace mainly took the form of bed and bevvy. There were good reasons why Burnoch had thirteen bars despite its very small population. Mr MacFarlane referred to his evening activities as 'going on the ran dan' which would result in a state he graded the morning after as either 'guttered', 'blootered' or 'miroculous'. On returning from the pub on both Friday and Saturday nights, Mr MacFarlane would make his presence loudly felt, cursing all locks, keys, furniture and persons that stood in the way of his glorious, arcing, midnight piss. The sound always woke Fergus up, because his room only had thin plasterboard walls – the bathroom had been cut out of a corner of the bedroom when the outdoor cludgie was abandoned. After the piss, came the aforementioned argument, during which it was safest to get right beneath the sheets. Next up was the annoying banging on the opposite wall, right next to his bed, just below his Rangers poster. Thump, thump, thump-thump-thump. Thump, thump, thump-thump-thump. It usually lasted about five minutes, until his dad gave out a big howl, and then there was silence – until the snoring started.

The only time Fergus got to sit on his dad's knee was while he watched the Rangers or Hearts match on telly on a Saturday afternoon. (Mr MacFarlane's team allegiances were always Protestant.) Fergus liked the sing-song way the presenter read out the football scores afterwards: 'Albion Rovers nil, Greenock Morton two. Partick Thistle one, Celtic three', and would loll happily against his dad's pullover. Mr MacFarlane always had a six-pack of Tennent's lager by the side of the mustard velour settee, and participated volubly and garishly in the match commentary, occasionally sending Fergus flying when he rose up to berate the referee for blindness and stupidity. Fergus treasured these moments. He collected his dad's used Tennent's cans, which were pale blue with photos on the back of half-clad women called Heather, Sally, Sylvia and Lee. Heather was Fergus's favourite and displayed her assets to advantage in two different can pictures – one in a tight brown shirt, and the other in a pink top. Heather had what Fergus's best friend Fat Al called 'sexy boobs'. Fat Al

– Alan to adults – was nine, a year older than Fergus, a farmer's son and very advanced on many fronts, including height and weight. He liked Sylvia best. There were eight different Lager Lovelies in the series, and Fergus kept the cans along the window ledge in his poky bedroom until Auntie Margaret came in one day and said that wasn't right for a wean and put them in the bin.

Mr MacFarlane never drank on the boat. He said that you always had to be on the ball at sea. And Fergus's picture of his dad on the water is very different from that on the land. It was as though he became a different species. Reptile to amphibian, or something like that. One morning, the summer before he died, Mr MacFarlane shook Fergus awake at four in the soft July dawn. He handed him his jeans and said: 'C'mon, son, we're going fishing.' Munro was already on the *Dalriada*, and Bobby MacKay, and the skipper. Mr MacFarlane tossed Fergus across to Munro, and jumped on himself. The engine boiled and grunted and soon they were on the flat mirror calm of the loch, heading down towards the Clyde estuary. Even out on the water, Fergus could smell the blooming heather, the ferns and the pines in wafts. Seagulls followed the boat, and then his dad quickly pulled him over to the rail and pointed out three porpoises flipping and diving beside them. Fergus held on to the side of the boat, mesmerised.

Munro, who was old and beardy, had a half-pint mug of tea in his hand, and came out to lecture Fergus on the herring, the silver darlings, the fish that was no longer fished. 'You detected the "burning", aye, that show of phosphorescence in your wake.' Fergus didn't know what phosphorescence was. 'The water turns silver when the plankton gets disturbed by the fish,' said Bobby MacKay. 'It's a strange sight.'

Suddenly there was a great commotion on board. Mr MacFarlane was everywhere, stripped down to his vest, twirling winches, paying out the net. The muscles bulged on his arms: the net was heavy, with steel boards attached to it, designed to dig slightly into the muddy seabed where the prawns or langoustines lurked. 'If it digs down too much you get mud balls,' said Fergus's dad. 'We call the mud balls spuds, you know, like potatoes.'

The fishermen spoke a strange language: the scary red jellyfish were scouders. Even dead and dry in the net the scouders could still give you a horrible sting. And Mr MacFarlane kept talking about catching wombles. 'Like on the telly, Dad? Like Bungo and Tomsk? Wombles aren't real. You're having me on.'

'No, wombles is just a nickname for the prawns. Or they call them beetles.'

Fergus laughed. It was just one more good reason to be a fisherman when he grew up.

And then, a year later, when the downside of fishing was made all too abundantly clear to Fergus, he only had that long summer day to cling to, with its glassy clear water and creatures with silly names: silver darlings, wombles, beetles, scouders.

Throughout the empty summer that followed, the summer without his dad, Fergus ran wild. His mother didn't seem to want him about the flat – she watched telly all the time in her pink dressing gown – and she sent him outside every day, unless it was pouring, with a jammy piece and a poke of crisps. Like all the other children of Burnoch, he roamed the park, the shore and the streets on his bike. Fergus liked to be busy all the time – it took his mind off things. His speciality was scouring the bushes in the park and the bins on the seafront for empty lemonade, Irn Bru and Vimto bottles, 'gless cheques' which could be exchanged for a five-pence deposit at Nairns, the newsagents. Often he made twenty or thirty pence a day. Plus there were all sorts of other interesting things in the bushes – women's tights mysteriously thrown away, a lone white high-heeled shoe, and sometimes a dirty magazine, which he could examine and then sell on to Fat Al, who kept a collection of pictures of lassies with big tits in a Rover biscuit tin nailed to the back of his bogie.

Sometimes among the group in the playpark, when they were running up the big metal slide to annoy the girls trying to slide down, Fergus would see Karen MacKay. She was Bobby MacKay's daughter, a runty wee thing. Karen still had stabilisers on her bike, and was the teacher's pet, so was beneath contempt for many reasons. Just seeing her made Fergus feel sick; she reminded him of the drowning. So he gave Karen as wide a berth as you can in a very small town. But one slightly rainy, coldish afternoon at about five, when he was cycling home for his tea, Fergus had to go past Karen's house, and he saw her with her big sister making a dead complicated camp with cardboard boxes, polythene sheets and old deckchairs on the grass. (Karen had a new council house with a lawn and bumfled silky curtains with bows. Her mum had loads of ornaments in the windows.) Fergus was studying Karen's tent village so carefully he hit a stank and went flying over the handlebars. He banged his head, slid across the wet gravel and shredded all the skin on his knee. He sat there dizzily holding his leg, watching the blood bubble out of the grazes through his ripped jeans, trying not to cry. The big sister ran into the house, but Karen stood staring at him over the wall, expressionless, like a doll.

'Here, son, c'mon in and we'll get you a plaster,' said Mrs MacKay, appearing at the gate. 'Oh it's yourself . . .' she added, a look of worry coming across her face. 'How're you doing, Fergus? Is your mum managing?' Her voice sounded tight.

'Fine,' said Fergus, feeling tearful and angry. He didn't want to be here. It made him think about his dad. And he was embarrassed. Mrs MacKay sat him on the big Bendix washing machine in her kitchen and wiped the bits of gravel out of his bloody knee with cotton wool which she took out of a glass display jar of pink, blue and yellow cotton balls. Karen picked her nose and watched the first aid with deep interest, particularly when Fergus winced in pain at the TCP.

'Karen wants to be a doctor one day, don't you, Karen?' said her mum as she slapped a big plaster on his knee. 'I'm going to call your mum to come and get you, Fergus. You're a bit wobbly,' continued Mrs MacKay, and she sent them to sit in the living room. Fergus found he was shaking and cold. He kept his anorak on and sat with his back warming at the Gas Miser fire, with its surrounding horse brasses. Karen's big sister came in and tossed a six-pack of Tunnock's caramel wafers at them.

'Here. That'll get rid of your greetin' face,' she said, and left.

Karen opened the packet and divided the spoils fairly – three chocolate biscuits each. Fergus snuggled into his anorak – his mum had bought him a new one from C&A for the start of the school term next week and it was blue with an orange lining in the hood. He licked all the melting chocolate off the biscuit, and then ate the wafer. Karen did the same. Fergus stared at her. She had her greasy hair in two bunches tied with elastic bobbles that looked like Dolly Mixtures. She took a Pet Rock out of a box in her pocket, and set it between them on the rug.

'They Pet Rocks are rubbish, total rip off,' said Fergus.

'My dad gave it to me.'

'Oh, right.' Fergus squirmed.

'Do you miss him?' she said.

'Who?'

'Your dad.'

'Uh huh.' Fergus opened his second biscuit.

'Is your mum dead grumpy all the time? Mine is.' Karen was watching him through her long brown fringe.

'It's shite,' said Fergus, trying to sound tough.

There was a funny smell in the room, a chemical smell, as they started their third biscuits, both feeling slightly sick. Karen jumped up.

'Eeww, look, your anorak's melting!'

And so it was, a blue patch of goo was bubbling in the plastic at the back nearest the fire. Fergus calmly took off the anorak and let it cool.

'Your mum's goin' to kill you and that,' said Karen, and just at that moment, they heard Mrs MacFarlane arrive. Fergus quickly pocketed his third biscuit.

'Seeya,' he said, shrugging.

'Seeya.'

His mum was holding the bike, which Fergus now saw had a burst tyre. 'C'mon. Let's get you home,' she said. Fergus's knee was stiff, and he tried not to limp.

About a hundred feet down the road, Mrs MacFarlane noticed the melted back of his anorak, which had now gone hard and slightly crispy. She grabbed him by the collar and started shouting, right in his face.

'I just bought that this week and you go out and ruin it! That's supposed to last you all year at school. You stupid wee eejit. Do you know what I paid for that? Well, you'll have to wear it anyway. For fuck's sake!'

She looked like she was going to cry. Fergus didn't want to see her cry. All that fuss over an anorak. He pulled away and pushed the bike ahead on its flat tyre in the rain. He didn't mind that his anorak was ruined. He wore it all year, a scar on his back.

𝔅urnoch 𝔊a𝔷ette
May 12, 1978

TWO MISSING AT SEA
By Alan McWhirter

Two Burnoch fishermen are missing, presumed dead, according to Argyll police. The men have been named as Bobby MacKay, 28, and Gordon MacFarlane, 26, both crew on the Burnoch-based trawler, the *Dalriada*.

The accident happened last Thursday during a Force 10 gale in the Kilbrannan Sound, west of Arran. The *Dalriada*'s captain, Martin Gillies, said that the storm blew up around 10 p.m. and Mr MacKay was swept overboard as the boat was engulfed by huge waves.

'Bobby was paying out the nets when he suddenly disappeared into the darkness,' said Mr Gillies yesterday. 'Gordon came running to tell me at the wheel and we threw a lifeline to him, but he kept coming up and going under. Then Gordon dived in after him.'

Mr Gillies, 42, who was clearly distressed during the telephone interview, said he saw neither man again, despite patrolling the area for four hours and calling in the coastguard.

A spokesman for the Clyde Coastguard said that by the time their boat arrived, there was nothing to be done: 'This is a terrible tragedy for all concerned, and our thoughts are with the crew and the fishermen's families.'

Mr MacKay, of Westwood Avenue, Burnoch, leaves a wife and two daughters, and Mr MacFarlane, of Harbour Road, leaves a wife and a son.

Chapter Two

1978

'When I Need You': Leo Sayer

In the months after the drowning, a tremendous lethargy came upon Isla MacFarlane. Her thin legs felt as though they had elephantisis – she had seen that on one of those Africa appeals on the telly – and the huge flares of her jeans put up unexpected wind resistance as she forced herself along the seafront past the ironmongers and the school to the Co-op. There the supermarket staff dispensed comfort and comfort food: tins of Ambrosia creamed rice, Golden Wonder crisps, Walnut Whips, Vimto, Milanda loaves. Demanda Milanda, went the advert. The wifies at the checkout kindly failed to ring everything up at the till, quietly slipping things into her bag. 'How're you doing, hen, awright? Still signing on?' they enquired. She was the talk of the town, even before she'd got out of the shop door. 'Aye, it's terrible and that. She's looking peaky, isn't she no'? A mother at seventeen and a widow at twenty-five . . . it makes you wonder if there's a God,' was their general assessment.

Isla was too exhausted to wonder if there was a God, and too exhausted to even make chips, which previously had been their daily bread. Instead she sent Fergus down to Catani's chippy in the evenings with some change while she remained walled into the tenement. Isla got spotty, the flat got dirty, and she often forgot to wash Fergus's drip-dry school shirts. Unread *Daily Record*s piled up in the hall, and the bath was a zebra of different tidemarks. The bin stank. Isla and Fergus stopped eating up at the table in the kitchen recess, and sat on the mustard three-piece suite in front of the black-and-white telly with trays on their knees watching *Nationwide*, *Tomorrow's World* and *Top of the Pops* consecutively without moving. They even reverted to Heinz chocolate puddings for babies and ate directly with teaspoons from the tiny blue tins with a rosy-cheeked infant on the label.

During the dreich autumn days while Fergus was at school, Isla lay down on the settee and fell asleep, her body made from some heavy metal. She slid in and out of hot, slimy dreams where Gordon appeared walking silently out of the sea mist, his eyes a terrifying red, his skin pale. Her addiction to this half-sleep was so bad that in the month after Gordon died she even went to the doctor's and got a pregnancy test, because the last time she'd felt this sluggishness and stupor was when she'd been carrying Fergus. The test was negative. Now it was the weight of the dead, not the living, holding her down.

She put on Leo Sayer at full volume on the record player, that song they used to play all the time on the jukebox at the Hop and Anchor, 'When I Need You', and cried her eyes out again, until she was almost whooping as she gasped for breath. She felt so fucking sorry for herself. So fucking sorry. It was fine for Gordon, relieved of all this, relieved of the burden of bringing up a wean by himself on the dole. No, Gordon was away on the ran dan as per usual, away from this shite life. More tears sluiced down. She'd even stopped wearing her favourite blue mascara, because of the bother of getting it off her cheeks after the crying. What a waste. What a waste of her life, her chances. She should have left this crap town. She should have left school before Burnoch sucked her down, and drowned her in its tedium. 'You can all fuck right off!' she shouted at no one.

As Isla lay there on the settee, in the damp, putrid afternoon, the yellow and brown flowered wallpaper on all four sides seemed to move towards her, like something from a psychedelic horror film. She felt shivery and hot. Her head was throbbing. The walls were crushing her, and she rose up against them and started peeling the paper off in huge sheets, ripping it viciously upwards. She would strip it bare. Isla started to enjoy the noise of tearing and destruction, and soon the carpet was covered in a layer of curled paper, while the walls revealed layers of the pink, grey and ferny history of the flat's previous occupants. She put on the Abba album with 'Knowing Me, Knowing You' roaring out at full volume, and ripped down more wallpaper.

She didn't hear when Fergus came home from school and rang the bell. Puzzled by the loud music and the silence from his mother, he let himself in using the house key he kept on a string tied inside his schoolbag for emergencies. He stood at the living-room door and saw that his mother's long brown hair was full of strips of wallpaper, and her eyes were wide and mad. She looked like a witch. She wasn't aware of him watching until he spoke.

'Mum! What're you doing? Look at the mess you're making.'

'I always hated that paper.'

'But it's brand new. Dad put it up.'

'Uh huh.'

'It was *wipe-clean* wallpaper, Mum!'

Fergus burst into tears, but he didn't know why. His mum wasn't being grown-up, and he hated it.

Isla didn't notice. She kept on tearing with her nails at the pattern on the walls, looking wildly delighted when a strip of washable polyvinyl zipped cleanly all the way up to the ceiling, as Abba blared on. Suddenly there was a thunderous banging beneath their feet. Then came some shouting, then the repetitive bang-bang-bang again. A dog started barking.

'Oh shite,' said Isla. 'That'll be Mrs McGinty down-stairs, hitting a broom on her ceiling to complain. I better switch it off. She's a right cow. She'll go complaining to the landlord and everything.' And as soon as the record player was switched off, Fergus's mum became completely calm, as though she herself had been unplugged.

'Gie's a hand, Fergus,' she said, smiling at him oddly.

Fergus started picking the shreds of rubbery wallpaper out of the sink, peeled them off the greasy cooker, off the carpet and the settee, and put them all in the bin. In fifteen minutes they had cleared the room and Isla went round with the Hoover for the first time in months. Then they sat together on the settee, staring at the messy walls. Fergus got up and started collecting samples of other people's wallpaper: the ferns, the pink, the grey stripes, the damp-mottled yellow, the bumpy woodchip, and their own flowery vinyl. He carefully stored them in the shoebox under his bed. He liked the idea of the layers of lives. He wondered what else had happened long ago in that room.

'I'm no' sitting here on my bum all day looking at that. Let's get out of here. I'm going down the pub,' said Isla jumping up, suddenly resolute and cheerful.

Fergus changed out of his school uniform into jeans, his anorak, and his old white gutties. Isla emerged from her room with her face all orange with bright blue eyelashes, her hair brushed clean of paper and flicked back with hairspray. She had on a purple bomber jacket with a fake furry collar, and her best jeans – the new drainpipe ones, not the flares. She took Fergus's hand as they walked down the stairs, and for the first time in months he felt things were normal again. He squeezed her hand and smiled up at her. He thought she looked beautiful. On the stair landing below, their ancient neighbour Mrs McGinty came out in her hairy fawn dressing gown with rollers in her hair ready to complain as per usual about the noise.

His mum was all polite. 'Awfy sorry, Mrs McGinty. Got a wee bit carried away doing the cleaning, but we're all done now. We're off out so you should have a quiet evening.'

'Off out, are you?' said Mrs McGinty looking disapprovingly at Mrs MacFarlane's garish make-up. 'To the pub, is it?' In her day, mind, widows wore black and stayed in for at least a year. She herself hadn't been in the pub since Mr McGinty passed away five years ago.

'Aye, to the pub,' said Mrs MacFarlane looking her neighbour hard in the face. Mrs McGinty's ratlike dog – which had only three legs due to a very slow run-in with a milk float – growled and tried to nip Fergus's fingers. He leapt back.

'The dog doesn't like weans,' observed Mrs McGinty sourly, and slammed her door as they headed down the close.

Outside, a wind had got up and cleared the damp heaviness in the air. At five thirty the streets were filled with people hurrying home for their tea, and the rigging of the boats was whistling in the breeze in the horseshoe of the harbour. Coloured flags snapped back and forth on the masts beneath a pale bluish sky. In the distance, far across the sea, you could see grey humps, the outlines of far-off islands, and the squarish red and black Caledonian MacBrayne ferry puttering out. The smell of coal fires wafted by, as Burnoch settled in for an evening in front of the telly. Local folk nodded to them as they walked jauntily along the seafront: 'Isla, Fergus, how're you doing?' Mrs MacFarlane hadn't been anywhere much apart from the Co-op for five months, although there was one grim trip on the bus to What Every Woman Wants in Glasgow for Fergus's school uniform (and her new drainpipes).

They headed for the pub, past the chandlers and the fishermen in overalls loading boxes of prawns on to lorries going south, past the original painted fishermen's cottages that were there before the tenements and the warehouses. The Hop and Anchor was not as rough as some of the drinking establishments in town; fights only occurred there on a Friday or Saturday night, and it had a proper lounge for the ladies. The dark wood bar smelled of bacon rather than piss and stale slops, and was famous for its colossal breakfasts for the fishermen. Fergus was always fascinated by the way his feet stuck to the pub's greasy tartan carpet. As you walked it made a slurping noise, only audible to dogs and small children. In a certain sense, the Hop was a child-friendly pub, in that all the kids sat outside on the dry-stone dyke at the front opposite the water, while their parents went drinking inside.

'I'll have a pint of lager and lime and a bag of peanuts for the wean outside,' said Isla to Tommy the barman.

'Nice to see you out and about again, Isla.'

'Aye.' There was an embarrassing silence. What was there left to say? 'And I'll have twenty Consulate.'

Isla preferred menthol cigarettes – she thought they were more sophisticated and they also made your breath smell better. She lit one and exhaled the clean mint through her nostrils, letting go at last. Soon a cheery bunch of women in their twenties, who worked at the fish factory, called her over to their table by the fire. Isla sometimes worked a few casual shifts there when they had a rush job, and she'd been at school with most of girls, as they still called each other. In fact, everyone had been at school with everyone else in Burnoch, except for the incomers and the English. The upside was that you were never alone; the downside was that everybody knew your business. But tonight Isla felt warm and befriended; a burden lifted off her. She got in a second round for the girls, and lobbed Fergus a bag of KP peanuts out the pub window. 'That'll have to do for your tea for the now.'

Fergus was pleased. It was a change from chips. He hopped off the wall, where he'd been sitting fantasising about different ways of killing Mrs McGinty's dog: poisoned Kennomeat, an accidental fall down the stairwell, a shot from the tenement window with an airgun, and the like. He shouted over as his mother turned away.

'Can I go up the woods to see if Alan and all them are at the swing? It'll no' be dark for a while yet.'

Isla told him to be back in an hour. Fergus set off along up the path which started where Burnoch Burn came out to the sea. The path was a green tunnel at this time of year, before the nettles, bracken and brambles died back with the first frosts, and he took a stick to beat the prickles into submission as he walked along, humming between handfuls of peanuts. He never felt afraid when he was alone in the wild; it was only in the house that his stomach tightened up with fear of the unknown and his newly unpredictable mother.

In the distance, he could hear screams, shouts and the occasional splash. About a quarter of a mile upstream the burn opened out into a deep pool between two high banks, and there Fat Al and the other older boys had managed to throw an old tow rope over a branch in the middle of the water. The bottom of the rope had a giant knot for sitting or standing on. It was, Fergus felt, the best swing anyone had put up in Burnoch so far – the high banks created a speedy drop; you could trail your feet or hands in the water as you crossed; and there was, thrillingly, the chance of failing to flip up on the opposite bank, whereupon you were left dangling pathetically midstream, unless someone held out the big boat-hook which was used to pull the swing in.

'Hiya,' said Fergus, and he was acknowledged by the gang: Fat Al, Derek, Roddie and Kenny.

'Awright, Fergus?'

'Awright.'

At nine, Fergus was a year younger than most of them, but his insane lack of fear gained him respect. He had also been able to supply the gang with two cans of spray paint for graffiti – one silver metallic – which he had nicked out of Uncle Jim's garage. They had a brilliant time decorating the concrete tunnel under the town bypass. Fat Al, a pinkish boy with red hair whose looks belied his wild tendencies, was always the ringleader in these dangerous schemes – glue sniffing, graffiti, ringing doorbells and running away – but today they were just mucking around. Al had, however, thought up a riskier variation on swinging which involved jumping out of a high tree on the bank with the rope between your legs. This meant there was a sudden, terrifying jerk when the rope went taut over the water. Al went so fast he slapped into the branches on the opposite side.

'It's gallus,' he said as he landed back again, his cheek bloody with scratches.

'Bagsy me next,' said Derek, reaching out towards the swing.

'Naw me,' said Fergus. 'I just got here, but. Gies a go.'

He pushed past Derek and went to an even higher branch than Al, just to show him. The rope jerked hard, but then he swung out over the clear water, making a Tarzan yell. He turned his back so the sharp branches wouldn't cut him, and then swung over again hanging his head down so low he could feel the peaty water splashing on his face as it came over the rocks. The rope was holding nicely.

'Fucking magic,' he said, and passed the rope to Derek, who stood up on the knot instead of sitting to outdo

Fergus. Then it was Roddie's turn. He started climbing and then paused, nervous, high above the bank.

'You're not feart, are you?' said Fergus. 'We all jumped from the tree no bother.'

'Roddie Woddie's a crapper . . .' sang Al. Following their leader, they all took the mickey out of Roddie as he stood frozen and pale. There was no choice but to jump or lose face. Roddie was a big, clumsy, blubbery boy (his mother ran Catani's chip shop), and when the rope jerked suddenly taut, he took fright and lost his grip. He crashed into the water midstream, and hit his head on a rock.

'Fuckit,' said Al. Roddie wasn't getting out of the burn. They ran down the bank and started to pull him into the shallows. Fergus was puzzled by how heavy and wobbly Roddie had become. Had he drowned like his dad? The shoe-cleaning stuff dissolving on Fergus's gutties made a long white trail in the water, next to a red one pouring from Roddie's cut head. Red and white mingled to make a pinkish stream. Fergus stood frozen in the water, staring at it, as the others laid Roddie on the grass. Roddie suddenly turned his head to one side and was sick all over Al's new Adidas trainers.

'Oy, you manky wee bastard! Are you all right?' said Al, simultaneously annoyed and worried.

'Ma head hurts.'

They tried to raise Roddie to his feet, but he was grey-faced and floppy, and there was blood in his hair.

'Go and get his dad from the chip shop,' said Al. 'Quick, Fergus, run.'

Fergus ran as fast as he could through the whipping undergrowth along the burn, his shoes squelching, humming: 'I'm a human ambulance. I'm a human ambulance. It all depends on me.' He was proud Al had chosen him. He could run faster than all the boys in Burnoch Primary, even the eleven year olds. He was at the chip shop in five minutes, but it took Mr Catani a lot longer to lumber back through the woods.

'C'mon, Mr Catani,' said Fergus, agitated. 'He's down there on the bank.'

In the growing dusk, he could see Roddie propped in an odd position against a rock, Al crouching beside him. Mr Catani ran down and checked Roddie over, before heaving him unsteadily to his feet.

'You fucking wee eejits!' Mr Catani was the same livid red he turned after a night over the deep frier. 'What possessed you to put a swing up over the rocks? And don't tell me it was Roddie's idea because I know what you lot are like. And I'm taking him for an x-ray at Kinloch, and see if I find he's cracked his skull I'll have the police on youse. Now go home to your parents. Away with you.'

The boys followed, a safe distance behind Mr Catani and Roddie, in a small subdued bunch. Fergus felt horribly guilty for asking Roddie if he was feart, for starting the teasing. He kept thinking about the blood and the white shoe cleaner mixing in the water. He was shivery and frightened. Frightened of accidents, of falling, of water.

The sky was black when Fergus got back, his shoes squelching as he walked through the town, where the warm lights of houses, the houses of proper families, had started to dot the curve of hills around the harbour. He ran to the Hop and Anchor to get his mum. 'Children aren't allowed in this time of night,' said the barman at the door.

'I know, but . . .' Fergus slipped past the barman and poked his head into the lounge. It was hoaching and the smoke nipped his eyes. His mother and the girls from the fish factory were roaring with laughter, empty Babycham bottles littering their table. Then Isla noticed him staring.

'Where've you been, Fergus? You're soaked. I said an hour and it's nearly nine o'clock.' Isla was staggering over to the pub door, her speech slurred. Fergus had a feeling she'd completely forgotten about him until then. He told her what had happened to Roddie. 'What if he's injured, Mum? What if he's not right in the heid? What if it's our fault?'

'Och, don't be daft; if he can walk and talk he'll be fine,' said Isla, but Fergus felt that as a grown-up, she should be the one doing the worrying. Instead, he was literally supporting her. As they went unsteadily round the cobbles of the harbour towards home, Isla sometimes grabbed Fergus's arm.

'They heels are a liability,' she said, peering down at her boots when they reached their flat. 'Still, maybe I'll get a new pair. Hey, Fergus, I'm away tomorrow to try for a job in the shoe shop, in Saxon's. One of the girls says there's one going, and you get a staff discount on all the shoes. Twenty per cent.'

'Do they have Adidas?' asked Fergus. He envied the other boys' fancy trainers which weren't forthcoming while his mum was on the dole.

'No, proper shoes. It's not a sports shop.'

'Oh,' said Fergus, disappointed. 'My gutties have got biscuit toes, you know . . .' He pointed down. 'Biscuit toes' was the term used by the local children when they grew out of their gymshoes and holes appeared at the front which could potentially be fed biscuits.

'Well, if I get the job, the first pair of shoes is yours, out of my wages.' Isla hugged him and put him to bed.

'D'you think Roddie will be awright?' said Fergus, once he was in bed and holding his brown dog, which he generally considered himself too old for.

'Oh stop going on about it. I'm away to sort my clothes for the interview. Now go to sleep.'

At two in the morning, the screaming awoke Fergus. A bloody head had cracked open on the rock, and the sea was battering it, splattering it, again and again. It was his dad's severed head, rolling on the rocks. 'Muuum!' Fergus screamed. 'Muuum!' He was in the sea, wet all over. Maybe it was his dad's blood that was wetting his pyjamas. Isla switched on the centre light, and Fergus looked up at her in her nightie, her face puffy with drink and exhaustion.

'It's awright,' she said, holding him. Then she leaped up. 'You haven't wet your bed again, Fergus? That's the second time this week.'

Fergus immediately felt the cold, wet bed and realised his blue nylon pyjamas were covered in pee. His mum looked mightily pissed off, and half asleep. She shoved him in a new pair of pyjamas and then seemed to run out of willpower.

'Och, I can't be bothered changing your sheets, you'll just have to come into my bed tonight.'

Fergus followed Isla through to his parents' bedroom.

His dad had never been keen on Fergus coming into their bed, so he was interested in how big and different it was from his own. The pink candlewick bedspread had strange, raised leafy patterns on it, and he snuggled down under the sheets and blankets. His mum put an arm round him, and seemed to fall asleep almost immediately. She had on her St Michael satinette nightie from Marks and Spencers in Glasgow, and Fergus stroked its silkiness. It was like that lovely feeling you get when you run frogspawn jelly through your fingers. His mum's long brown hair smelled of Sunsilk lemon shampoo, and he curled up behind her, curving his shape round hers. Fergus felt warmth percolating him from his toes up, and an immense feeling of security, before sleep came.

The next morning, Isla woke too early, disturbed by the strange presence in her bed. The dawn was already breaching the thin curtains. When she had a job and money, she'd get proper lined curtains, and a nice polyester washable continental quilt like everyone else. None of these itchy blankets. Isla looked over at Fergus, his face inches away from hers, his breath warm and fresh. She stared at his lanky body, his long eyelashes, his slightly pouting lower lip, his strong bone structure. Suddenly she was shocked by the familiarity of that face asleep, of seeing a young Gordon MacFarlane alive again in her bed.

The same, but different. While there had been something slow and lugubrious about Gordon, except when he'd been at sea, Fergus awake was like a child on speed – tense, like herself. He was a weird, unsettled baby: he girned all the time, always red and kicking. He seemed angry, until he sat up at four months, crawled at five, walked at nine, talked at ten, and stopped crying completely. Gordon had been crewing for some rich boat owners during sailing week when Fergus was conceived. Gordon was living at home and Isla was still at school when they made love in a mahogany-panelled double cabin in a vast white cruiser, while its owners were having dinner in the hotel. The boat was gone on the Monday afternoon when Isla got back from hockey practice, but Fergus remained: conceived in grandeur, born into poverty. Isla smiled, shrugged, and wrapped her arms around him now, remembering that feeling of the sea on the yacht, rocking her back to sleep.

Chapter Three

1980

The Observer Book of British Birds

Fergus was trying on some of the ladies' eveningwear stilettos in front of the mirror. He particularly liked a red sandal with a diamante buckle, but his grey school sock was all bumfled at the front. He took his socks off, and paraded again in two sandals, one red and one gold. He sashayed from side to side, belting out 'Hey, Big Spender'. Fergus liked it when Saxon's big glass door to the street was locked, and he existed in a secret world in the shop with his mum, dressing up in the shoes to become characters from *Dallas* on the telly, his favourites being Pam and Sue Ellen. Such goddesses could hardly be imagined in bunion-filled Burnoch.

On Saturdays, Fergus always walked his mum down to open up Saxon's on Harbour Street. He wasn't supposed to get to Uncle Jim and Auntie Margaret's before nine in the morning, because Margaret liked her lie-in before she looked after him. Fergus waited in the shop while his mum got the till ready, opening little plastic bags of one, two and five pences into the little drawers. He was sitting wearing the stilettos and humming the *Dallas* theme tune when the door clicked open and closed his fantasy world.

'Hello there, Fergus, should you not be away down the road by now?'

Fergus froze. It was Stuart Meek, the shop manager, a self-satisfied man in Polaroid aviator-style glasses and a brown suit with a dusting of dandruff on the collar. He had one of those funny singsongy Hebridean accents.

'I've got three-and-a-half minutes yet,' said Fergus, eyeing the shop clock.

'Oh,' said Stuart, sounding slightly irritated. 'Well, mind you don't break those heels.'

'How come they're all left feet on display?' said Fergus, struggling to walk straight on two left-footed sandals.

'Stops people stealing them.'

'Except Catholics,' said Fergus, giggling to himself.

'What d'ye mean?' said Stuart.

'Catholics. Left footers,' said Fergus grinning.

Stuart narrowed his eyes. He wasn't sure if a child should be making such remarks. But as the spawn of the Wee-Free Church of the Hebrides, he was aware of the local obsession with the sectarian divide. He stomped off into the back of the shop and asked Isla to hurry Fergus up.

Isla was standing at the mirror putting her hair into a high ponytail, getting ready for the onslaught of customers, and she smiled at Stuart Meek's reflection behind her. Isla had risen swiftly in Saxon's, from salesgirl to supervisor in a year. You could track her ascent by studying her frequent appearances in the Employee of the

Month certificates hung in the so-called canteen, a windowless cupboard at the back of the shop containing a fluorescent strip light, a kitchenette and a couple of chairs oozing sponge stuffing. Stuart squeezed into the tiny room with her, panting slightly.

At twenty-seven, Isla had discovered she had a sharp mind for business, a mind temporarily dulled by her years at home as a mother, working occasional shifts in the fish factory. But now, she had traded the dole for independence, and widowhood for a new feeling of liberation. She liked to be on show, clacking efficiently round the shop in her high heels, tight pencil skirt and silk blouse, cashing up and cashing in. As Employee of the Month, Isla was particularly good at selling 'sundries', largely useless waterproof sprays, suede cleaners and insoles, which added a few quid to every sale. 'It all mounts up,' said Stuart. 'Look after the pennies and the pounds will look after themselves.' That was the sort of thing Stuart was fond of saying.

Stuart was notoriously mean: despite his fat manager's salary and lack of dependents, he bought a six-pack of meat bridies every week from the Co-op and heated one up each day for his lunch in the Baby Belling stove. He also nicked the employees' newspapers, teabags and milk, and was slippery about buying rounds in the pub on Fridays. He seemed, however, to have enough money for a brand-new maroon Talbot Horizon car, which he proudly wax-polished every week in the car park behind the shop.

The folk of Burnoch had little choice but to patronise

Stuart's establishment, there being no other shoe shop in town except the ironmongers which sold wellies. Even when shoes didn't fit, Stuart had trained his staff to stretch the leather, or offer insoles. So Burnoch limped around in discomfort, with blisters and rubbed heels, and Saxon's sales targets were met. Stuart's method of operation was to be oleaginous to everyone at the front of the shop and unpredictably cruel to the employees round the back. He lurked behind the towering shelves of shoeboxes in the storeroom, and slid out when you least expected, like an adder from under a rock. He gave Fergus the creeps.

Fergus wandered the shelves and wondered who christened the shoes: they all had names on the boxes, sandals called Leila and Kathy, or men's chunky shoes called Trucker and Clint. The colours were numbers, which Fergus thought was stupid: 00 was black, 01 was brown, 06 was red. Fergus watched his mum finish up, putting the shoes back on the displays. He wanted to go up and give her a hug, but felt too embarrassed in the shop. She bustled around looking dead smart, and all day long she wore a pair of shiny high heels called Janine, in 00. Stuart was also watching Isla from his station at the till, and biting the red skin round his nails. Stuart wore slip-ons called Colin in 01, and maroon socks.

'A wee word in your ear,' he said beckoning to Isla. Stuart put his hand on Isla's shoulder in a proprietorial way, and Fergus felt slightly queasy as he left the shoe shop and started walking along Harbour Street to Uncle Jim's to go birdwatching.

*

Fergus's mum appreciated the free babysitting while she worked on Saturdays, but she laughed at Jim and called him a 'twitcher', which to Fergus seemed a stupid word for the deadly serious business of tracking, watching, spying, hiding and then pouncing with the camera. Jim didn't merely have to watch the birds – he had to capture them in a perfect shot, close up. If he could take a picture of a bird with eggs, feeding its young, or in some mating ritual, so much the better. He put up hides and sat in them for hours armed with the telephoto lens and jelly pieces. Fergus liked being under the green-and-brown plastic-leafed camou-flage net in the cramped hide with Jim. They breathed in the fug of hot, damp grass and maintained the vigil in near silence, waiting for time to go by, watching the birds fly back and forth from their nests. Fergus's job was to have the next roll of film waiting to load, or to pass the spare camera and the tinted lenses. He also had to have *The Observer Book of British Birds* at the ready, in case any unknown species flew by.

Uncle Jim was dead fussy about his tea when he was out on the hills. First, he had to get a nice hollow in dry, sheep-cropped grass, or shelter behind a rock where the primus stove wouldn't blow out. The search for the correct spot took ages, because it also had to be near a spring or burn. Then he'd heat the peaty water in a small kettle he kept in his rubbery-smelling canvas rucksack. 'It has to be boiling properly – I canny stand tea from a flask. Tastes of hot plastic. It's bowffin'.'

He would toss in the two Scottish Dividend teabags – practicality had pried him away from his caddy of loose tea, which Fergus used to shake like maracas. The mugs were chipped enamel, topped up with two teaspoons of sugar from another metal caddy, plus milk from a Tupperware container. But you had to admit it was a fine, fresh cup, worth all the palaver.

Once the tea was made, if there was the slightest glimpse of sun, Jim would go bare chested – he liked to keep up his tan. Fergus would copy him, shivering right into the autumn as they rubbed Ambre Solaire tanning oil into each other's backs. It felt great, and the foreign-holiday smell lingered for days. Jim had his hair slicked back with Brylcreem. Fergus liked the smell of warm sun on the Brylcreem too and was fascinated by the red pots of it that opened upside down and lived in the bathroom cabinet at his uncle's house. He put his fingers in the luscious white goo and wanted to slick his own hair back, but his mum had got him a skinhead number two cut at the barber's. 'That'll last you a proper while, and save us some money,' she said, practically. But Jim liked his hair longer, with the side parting just so.

Some might have called Jim pernickety, and perhaps in another time and place he might have allowed himself to be gay. He and Auntie Margaret had no children. Fergus's mother said that was 'a sorrow' to them. Jim was his dad's older brother, but there were ten years between them. Jim always said Gordon had been 'an afterthought'. Fergus didn't know quite what that meant, but he felt it had something to do with the hereafter, which the minister talked about sometimes: the place where his dad had gone.

Jim's resemblance to Gordon – in particular their tendency to a dark mono-brow – was comforting for

Fergus. If he narrowed his eyes, he could imagine Jim was his dad – except that Gordon had been taller and beefier, with a burgeoning beer belly. Jim was more energetic and lean, knacky with his hands, and ran his own garage. The sign up the back of Colquhoun Street said 'MacFarlane Motors – MOTs. Crypton Tuning'. Jim also had two petrol pumps, so there was a big orange Gulf sign. He always gave Fergus and Isla the current free gifts that came with the petrol – a set of bubbled-glass tumblers and an inflatable Gulf beachball. Jim worked hard during the week, wielding spanners lying on his back on a rolling platform beneath the jacked-up cars. 'You look like the man painting the ceiling in the Sistine Chapel,' Fergus once said to him. Jim popped his oily head out from under a Hillman Avenger, astonished. 'I seen a drawing of him doing it in the library,' explained Fergus, except like everyone else there he pronounced library 'ly-bry'. Jim was fond of Fergus, in small doses. He liked the unexpectedness of him.

During the week, Jim worked hard, a fact which was reflected in the comforts of his home – he and Auntie Margaret had just got a Betamax video player (hers) and a self-warming Hostess trolley (his). Jim loved cooking. He also had all the latest glossy car magazines which Fergus pored over while Jim fixed up some romantic wreck of a vehicle in the back shop. On Saturday, though, Jim believed in a day of rest, and he was always out on the hills or shores, birdwatching. Around Burnoch, there was no shortage of birdlife: by the shore there were wagtails, gannets, red-throated divers, oyster-catchers and lanky herons. Two golden eagles nested most years high on the cliffs of the rocky islands nearby. Buzzards wheeled high above the bracken, suspended in hot-air pockets for what seemed hours to Fergus, and hawks hung nonchalantly in the sky until they suddenly dive-bombed. In their hide, the invisible birdwatchers were also regularly dive-bombed by Tornadoes or F16s, fighters out of RAF Macrihanish or Lossiemouth. The warplanes buzzed the contours of the land, busting the sound barrier, the boom of their engines disjointed from the sight of the dark wings. Fergus simultaneously hated and was excited by the fighter jets: they were messengers from an outer world, where everything was faster, more dangerous.

Up on the moors, Jim and Fergus escaped the narrow walls and narrow minds that oppressed them in Burnoch. Not that they would say that, because they didn't talk much to each other, and what they did discuss was mostly of a technical nature, concerning apertures, lenses or species. But Jim was quietly aware of Fergus's rabid curiosity about the world, and Fergus was aware that Jim was in some way different from everyone else, in the depth and seriousness of his obsessions, be they photography, cooking or mechanics. What mattered to uncle and nephew was that from almost everywhere up there on the high moors you could look out over the ocean to Ireland, almost to America. And even when the sea was out of sight over the hills, you could feel it in the salty wind, the endless expanse of it beyond.

Jim told Fergus endless stories about St Kilda, the island on the edge of the world, a two-day sail out from Oban, past the Hebrides, to the last land before America. St Kilda was a ghost island, the grassy top of an extinct volcano poking out of the Atlantic. The last remaining inhabitants had been taken off St Kilda in 1930, and all that was left was the church and the ruined stone village. And the seabirds: forty thousand pairs of puffins, plus gannets and fulmars and bonxies, clinging to the sharp rocks that rose vertically out of the Atlantic. A pilgrimage was in order, said Jim, to the Mecca for twitchers. They would go together one day.

While they dreamed and roamed, it wasn't just birds they saw. By the hill lochs, stags would appear, and in certain seasons these were pursued by rich, heavily armed people in Land Rovers and silly hats. Then Jim and Fergus retreated for safety towards the rocky shore where they spotted adders, mink and otters. (Jim never photographed wildlife without wings – he was a specialist – but he'd stop the car for Fergus to get an animal photo for himself on Auntie Margaret's old Instamatic from Boots.) On the single-track roads, they often saw feral cats crossing, and once they found a couple of tourists doing what Uncle Jim described as 'winching' in their car in a lay-by. Fergus rolled down the window and snapped that as they went by, and Jim clouted him on the ear.

On rainy Saturdays, of which there were multitudes, Fergus and Jim would hole up in the bathroom. To Auntie Margaret's irritation, she was banned from coming anywhere near the room as the windows were carefully blacked out and the bath covered by a board to create the perfect darkroom. Trays were laid out for the developer, stop bath, and fixer, and Fergus learned about timing, accuracy, and making white ghosts and dark shadows. He realised then that photographs were not reality, but images that could be manipulated and twisted. He loved being in the hot, tiny, chemical-smelling room, concentrating on a contact sheet in the red light, beneath the damp tights and vast Playtex cross-your-heart bras and photographs pegged on the washing line.

When Fergus was ten, Jim's photography met with some success – he won the Birdwatching Magazine annual competition with his colour photograph of a red-throated diver feeding her young. This was the finest moment of his life. An exhibition was soon held of more of Jim MacFarlane's photographs in a tourist gallery in Oban, and Auntie Margaret took Fergus up there in their car. Fergus felt proud to be related to Jim. He thought it was cool that the photos all had matching frames and were printed in poster sizes. He also clocked the price tags.

Soon after Jim's exhibition, Fergus's Primary Six class went on a school trip to the Art Galleries and Museum in Glasgow. Fergus had never been to a big museum before and they got crisps and Panda Cola on the coach down. The Art Galleries were huge, marbled and Gothic, like nothing Fergus had ever seen before. They smelled of rich wood polish and musty death. Just walking through the high-ceilinged halls sent him into a pleasurable dwam. He floated away from the rest of the class, their voices fading, and found himself standing before a huge painting at the top of the gallery stairs: Salvador Dali's *Christ of St John of the Cross*. It was uncannily real, the cross looming out of the blackness and bulging ominously over the watchers below. Below Christ's feet was a sunset over a fishing boat in a rocky blue harbour which looked exactly like Burnoch on a good day. Christ was painted from above, so you could only see his shoulders and the back of his hair. He was faceless. He could have been anyone. He could have been Gordon MacFarlane, crucified and dangling in the eerie light.

Fergus felt the nails through his palms, the feeling of his heavy body swaying forward, away from the cross, his head falling. He stood there beneath the psychedelic Jesus for fifteen minutes, awed by the power of the image, until Miss McNicoll, his teacher, found him and dragged him away to look at saggy stuffed animals with glass eyes. Miss McNicoll was a bitter spinster who once described Fergus in his school report as 'an obnoxious little character who thinks he knows all the answers'. Downstairs in the mammals' galleries, there were pathetic tableaux of lions, zebras and seals, all moulting and mockit in their dusty glass cases, and of absolutely no interest to children raised in the Attenborough age. Fergus was fascinated, however, by the peculiar language of the yellowing display labels, half in Latin, and last done by the Victorians.

He kept the labelling in mind when Auntie Margaret developed his latest roll of thirty-six pictures. The Instamatic had unchangeable focus which meant close-ups blurred, and in far shots the birds were tiny blobs. After a few disasters, Fergus soon realised his bird photographs were going to be a sorry sight compared to his uncle's telescopic-powered ones – until he could afford the proper equipment, of course. Only larger wildlife, such as deer or the citizens of Burnoch, came out properly in Fergus's shots. Fergus always had plenty of time for photography, especially now his mother was working at Saxon's and some days didn't get home until a quarter to six. On wet days he let himself into the flat and watched *General Hospital* and *Crossroads* while he did his homework, and on dry days he hung out with Fat Al and made potions, fires or waterbombs, or wandered round town with his camera. No one noticed him much – another skinny brown-haired kid in an anorak, cycling by – so he was able to get quite close to his prey. He moved silently round the port like a wraith, sucking in other people's lives, his shutter barely audible. Behind the camera he felt powerful for once, sitting in judgement upon those he knew.

When Auntie Margaret gave him the paper wallet of his new photographs, Fergus ran home, shut the door and spread them out on his bed, breathing in the chemical smell. He felt tight inside his stomach, nervous. He got out his collection of white shoebox lids from the discards at Saxon's, and began carefully framing and captioning the best photographs. Two hours later he had the big cardboard box ready containing his exhibition, and lugged it round to Jim's garage. His uncle was the only mechanic left at the end of the day, and was under a car changing an oil sump.

'I'll be out in a minute, son,' said Jim. 'Oh shit. Here, Fergus, get under here and put that basin below the sump. We're going to have to drain it.' Fergus took off his anorak and wriggled underneath the car, passing screwdrivers and a new sump to Uncle Jim. Then he took the basin off to dump the used oil in a drum. While waiting for Jim to finish up, Fergus decided to make a display of his photographs on the long tool bench. Jim appeared, hot and sweaty in his vest. He wiped his hands on a greasy rag, and stared. Under the stark fluorescent lights, Fergus's photographs had taken on a horrible garish quality, the colours brighter than the dull reality of Burnoch. But it was the labelling, in magic marker, which freaked Jim out.

Lesser Spotted Teenager said the first picture, a portrait of Fat Al's big sister and her unfortunate skin. Next came *Tracey Irvine at the Playpark with her Young*. Tracey was smoking, her red-rimmed eyes vacant, and her kids were out of focus behind. Then there was *Pie-Eyed Farmer*, one of the farmers from up the Oban Road in town for the sheep sales, staggering out of the pub, blootered. Further along, inevitably, there was *Bald Old Bird* (Mrs McGinty taken from above in *Christ of St John*-style, using half-light of the close, with her thinning hair patchily hennaed). Last came *Plumed Lady in Shoe Shop* – Fergus's mother photographed through the reflections of Saxon's window, wearing her new feather and bead earrings from What Every Women Wants and kneeling as she fitted someone's boots. Jim reached the end of the display along the workbench, and then rocked back and forth on his heels. He found it disturbing, though he couldn't quite say why. He lit a cigarette.

'Did your mum see these already?'

'Naw.' Fergus waited, expectant. It mattered to him what Jim thought.

'You're a sleekit wee thing, aren't you? You just don't know what's going on behind that face of yours. Aye, well, I think they're very funny, the bird-book-style captions. And you've taken the pictures at the right distance. Get too near and that camera's rubbish.'

'Get too near and people spot you.'

'Oh, it's Candid Camera, is it?'

'That's the idea.'

'Well, maybe we can get you a better camera secondhand, and you can try for more bird photos after all that practice. I can see you worked hard, thought about it a bit. They're no' holiday snaps.'

'That'd be pure dead brilliant, Uncle Jim – the camera, I mean. But I like taking people even more than birds. This isn't practice.'

'Oh,' said Jim, feeling slightly disappointed. 'You're very decisive for someone of ten and a half.'

Fergus grinned at him. Jim gave Fergus a friendly push.

'Get away home with you, and take that so-called exhibition of yours with you. We don't want the whole town seeing what they really look like, do we?'

Fergus took this as a compliment, Burnoch being a place where compliments did not come as easily as criticism.

He ran excitedly home, hugging the cardboard box. Isla was sitting on her bed smoking a cigarette and carefully painting her toenails a vampirish red, something Fergus had not seen her do before. He started unpacking. 'It's my exhibition of *mounted* photographs,' he announced proudly, and Isla smiled, though she was thinking of something else entirely.

Her reaction to the exhibition was not what Fergus expected at all. He made her sit on the settee while their boil-in-the-bag Vesta chicken curry was heating, and showed her the pictures one by one, like a magician. Isla laughed at the first photograph of Mrs McGinty on the stairs, but as more landed on her lap, she became agitated, until her own portrait appeared.

'You been watching me? Spying on me round at the shop?' she snapped. 'What else have you got in there? That's not nice, Fergus. That's mean and nasty what you're doing. Laughing at people. It's not right, poking your nose into other people's business.'

'But Mum—'

'Is Jim helping you with this? I don't know what he thinks he's doing. I thought it was birdwatching you were—'

'Jim didn'y help. I did it myself. On my own initiative.'

Isla thought there was something freaky about the long words Fergus would suddenly use. 'Initiative?'

'Aye, it was my own idea.'

'I know what initiative means, Fergus. Don't be cheeky.'

Isla stabbed the plastic Vesta bags with some scissors, and splurged the yellow curry and rice on to two plates. They clattered down on the coffee table in front of the settee.

Fergus was close to tears. 'I only came once to the shoe shop, when I was waiting for you. I wasn't spying. I thought it was a beautiful picture with those feather earrings.' Isla looked at him closely, to see if he was telling the truth. She was never sure these days.

They ate without speaking, Fergus squirming in silence as his mother's jaw chomped noisily and the gas fire hissed. After dinner, he slunk off to his bedroom, and lay for a long time on the bed clutching his cardboard box, feeling mournful and resentful. His battery alarm clock ticked. His sheets smelled fusty. The electric fire was broken and the room was cold and damp. He'd slept in his mum's bed for a couple of years now, so he hadn't stayed the night in his own room for ages, not since he'd been loaded with the cold and his mum had said he was too snottery to share hers, coughing like a drain all night, and he'd been shoved off into the single bed. The Benylin cough mixture was still on his bedside table beside the metal spotlight and an empty bottle of Lucozade which had left a sticky ring. Fergus took a big glug out of the Benylin bottle. It buzzed in his throat, and felt rich and comforting in his stomach. He didn't really care what his mum thought of the photos. He finished the bottle.

'Get your pyjamas on and you can come and watch *Dallas*,' shouted Isla outside, conciliatory. She didn't mention the photographs again. Fergus's pyjamas were blue nylon, and a bit short at the ankles, but just putting them on made him feel sleepy and dizzy after the Benylin. He snuggled up on the settee next to Isla, thrilled himself with Sue Ellen drunkenly screaming at JR, and almost sleepwalked as he went to bed an hour later. He crashed out while his mum read *Cosmopolitan* under the bedside light. He felt warm and contented curled up beside her. Everything was back to normal.

Except that it wasn't, because a month or so later, Stuart from Saxon's started coming round for his tea every Friday. The third week, despite his famed thriftiness, he brought Fergus a set of three Matchbox toy cars.

'There y'are, son. There's a police car there and everything.' Stuart puffed out his chest proudly, as though he'd done some heroic deed. He adjusted the comb-over that covered his balding patch. Isla looked on fondly.

'Now what do you say, Fergus?'

'Thanks. Thanks, Mr Meek.'

'Stuart,' said Stuart smiling cheesily. 'Aye, it's not easy for a man to step into a ready-made family.' Then he ruffled Fergus's hair. Fergus's spine froze in pure horror.

Within days, Fergus had sold the Matchbox cars, in pristine-box condition, to a Primary Two for fifty pence and a packet of Wrigley's Juicy Fruit.

'Why does Stuart think I still play with cars?' he said later at home alone with his mum. 'That's for five year olds. For Pete's sake, I changed an oil sump with Uncle Jim the other week. I can jumpstart an engine. I know all about real cars.'

Isla scowled at Fergus. Then her voice became persuasive.

'Stuart doesn't know many children or what they like, Fergus. Poor man, he's a *bachelor*, no one to look after him. All his family are far away on Lewis, you see,' said Isla. Fergus didn't say anything, but he suspected the worst. The sudden presence of paper napkins at dinner was a giveaway. Plus, he'd been sent over to Jim and Margaret's a lot on Friday nights over the last few months.

'If he's a *bachelor* he could eat Batchelor's Cock-a-Leekie soup alone instead of coming here,' sniggered Fergus.

'You being disgusting? You being cheeky again?' Isla narrowed her eyes at Fergus.

'No.' He tried to look as bland as possible. But no way was Stuart coming round for his mother's cooking, so it had to be something else, reasoned Fergus. Isla could not cook at all. Yes, she could transfer orange-breaded objects from the freezer compartment to the pan, and make chips.

Her veg ran out after frozen peas and baked beans. And he did like the tins of golden syrup pudding, but surely Stuart could do all this too? Fergus certainly could. In fact, he was taking cooking lessons off of Jim to save the household from the dire repetitive fare of the Co-op, where his uncle said the Burnoch wifies kept buying sagging yellow broccoli instead of green because they didn't know any better. Jim had been particularly upset when red peppers at last came to Burnoch, and the shopkeepers wrote prices on the skins with black magic marker, not realising the outside was edible.

Jim said he was Burnoch's only cordon-bleu chef, whatever that meant. Indeed, the other night Fergus's uncle had excelled himself with 'Asparagus Roulade', which were spears of tinned asparagus (a long, green pointy vegetable that made your pee smell funny) wrapped in rolls of thin pink ham, with cheese sauce poured on top, and then baked in the oven. It was magic, and stayed warm on the Hostess trolley while Jim served sherry and whisky to his guests, Mr and Mrs Catani, who appreciated foreign food. Fergus was allowed to bring in the pudding he'd helped make: Black Forest Trifle, using a whole tin of black cherries in syrup and fresh whipped cream, not the UHT stuff. Fergus knew all this knowledge would be useful in the future. He had started cooking for his mum, trying to have something nice ready for her after the shop closed at five thirty. He began experimenting a little, watching Delia Smith's *Cookery Course* on the telly, and scribbling down her recipes. Effie at the library had also let him take out some adult cookery books on his children's ticket. But he needed scales. They didn't have scales. Or freshly ground black pepper. Where would you find freshly ground black pepper in Burnoch?

But Fergus did not cook on Fridays. The sight of the maroon Talbot Horizon parked proprietorially outside the tenement sickened him. Instead, with his mother's tacit agreement, he disappeared with the other boys over the back walls of the closes into the concealing dusk. There were dares, of course, and attempts to jump from the highest walls and from first-floor windows. One of Fergus's favourite games was the long-distance pissing competition, which took place as they all stood in a row on the back wall of the school, and had the added attraction of a potential raid by the janitor in mid flow.

The gang roamed the streets, broke into the abandoned fish-processing factory, and sometimes slipped on to the pleasure boats in the dark, nicking small, almost unnoticeable items – a few fags here, some cash there, a fancy torch – from the yachties who never thought to lock up among simple country folk. Although the boys would never have stolen from the shops of Burnoch, (shops where they'd once been parked outside in their prams) there was an unwritten rule that when the idle rich swept in on their yachts and cruisers in the summer, they were fair game. The sailors colonised the harbour, braying outside on the hotel terrace in the evenings in their gold-buttoned navy jackets and rugby shirts, injecting a temporary class divide into the port. Fergus eyed them, fascinated by their ease and wealth, puzzled by these waterborne creatures from another world.

When pilfering became too risky, after complaints to the police from the boat owners, setting fires became the new obsession of the gang. Fat Al was going through a pyromaniac phase, following his porn and graffiti phases of the previous year. The fires were above the port, exactly where the early Scots had placed their beacons to warn of Viking raids up and down the coast, and the views went on for ever. Al favoured burning huge truck tyres on the waste ground. The smoke was thick, treacle black, and ripped your throat out, but the fire was solid and long lasting even on a rainy evening. Plus it kept the midges off. All the boys helped, humphing old mattresses and wood on to the pyre with other rubbish. Fergus loved watching the way the shapes of objects morphed in the fire; the mattresses bursting from flat blackened slabs into a series of glowing orange metal corkscrews. Sometimes he even brought his camera and documented the disintegration in the flames. The gang also burned pork sausages and ate them with their middles still deliciously pink and raw. In the embers they cooked potatoes in tinfoil, but they always remained frustratingly hot and hard. You could often still see the fire afterwards from Fergus's mum's bedroom on the other side of the harbour, an orange signal that waned slowly during the night.

One evening, however, Fergus had been up at the fire for about an hour, and Fat Al was demonstrating his new trick – melting plastic bags of different colours on the end of a stick. He swung a flaming bag dripping molten white plastic around and around his head, so it looked like a firework. Suddenly a long trail of burning plastic flew off and stuck to Fergus's bare arm.

'Ey-yah! Ey-yah, bastard!' screamed Fergus in agony, trying to shake the searing plastic off. The other boys ran to him.

'Put something wet on it. Here.' Someone was pouring a cooling bottle of Barr's lemonade over his forearm. The plastic went brittle and he picked it off, but a long strip of his skin had peeled off too, and the arm was raw-pink and weeping below. It reminded Fergus of the undercooked sausages.

Fat Al took his arm and looked at it closely. Somehow Al never got injured or caught himself.

'Fuck, that's a right bad wan. Better get yer mum to see to that. Might need some cream or something. But don't say you got it with us, right?'

'Right,' said Fergus. His loyalty to the gang was paramount. 'I'm away, then. See youse later.'

He didn't cry until he was out of sight, walking down the hill. The burn was a new kind of agony for him, one that went on and on, stinging with the same intensity and never going away. The incessant pain somehow caused a slide show in his mind of all the accidents that had happened since his dad's drowning: skinning his knee on his bike, his anorak melting with that same molten plastic stench, Roddie cracking his head on the swing, the blood in the burn, and now the burning. Little accidents that would be part of any normal childhood, except Fergus was so sensitive to them, he felt he was being stalked by misfortune.

It was getting dark by the time Fergus walked up the stair of the close to the flat. It smelled of piss from Mrs McGinty's incontinent dog. He was back earlier than usual, but the nights were drawing in. He let himself quietly into the hallway, his arm still throbbing. The lights were off, and the living-room door was half closed, emitting just the flicker of the telly. Maybe his mum was out, but Stuart's car was still parked outside. Then Fergus heard a muffled, grunting, wet-slapping noise, and it made him move stealthily. He knew even before he looked that it was not going to be a good sight. He knew that they were probably, in Fat Al's words, 'sexing' each other. Yet all Fergus saw when he peeked round the door was the high back of the settee and Stuart's polished 'Colin' slip-ons abandoned on the floor, next to his mother's 'Janine' stilettos. Suddenly, over the arm of the settee, two big feet appeared wearing maroon socks, and joggled steadily back and forth.

Fergus backed away, slipped out of the door, down the stairs, and managed to make it to the front steps before he was sick everywhere. He knelt there in the dark until the retching stopped, and then walked unsteadily across to the harbour. There he sat on a bollard for a long time, and watched the black skeletons of the rigging and thought of the books he'd read about running away to sea, about pirates and tropical islands and ten-year-old cabin boys like him. He tried to slip away into his imagination, to leave the place, but there was a lingering bad taste in his mouth. He turned his head away from the open sea and forced himself back into the closed world of Burnoch.

Fergus took a drink from the public fountain beneath the Warm Emorial, which is what the kids always called the monument to those citizens of Burnoch who died in the First World War. He plunged his stinging burn into the cool basin of water beneath the names of the dead. He was puzzled when the pain was numbed for a moment, yet he still wanted to cry. Then he realised his sore arm would go away, but he would never get his mum back, not like before.

Fergus took a deep breath, and walked up the empty backstreets to Jim and Margaret's.

'Aww the pet,' Margaret said, when she opened the door and saw his arm. 'The wee pet.'

Chapter Four

1985
'Heaven Knows I'm Miserable Now': The Smiths

When Stuart Meek left Stornoway for the mainland long ago to immerse himself in ladies' footwear, his mother crocheted him a spare toilet-roll cover in the shape of a white poodle with a blue satin bow. The fact that Stuart had kept Mrs Meek's handiwork and given it pride of place in the bathroom with its avocado suite told Fergus all he needed to know about his new home. He had moved to Stuart's bungalow on the hill above Burnoch four years ago when Isla and Stuart got married. The managing director of Saxon Scotland came to their wedding. 'Manager-of-the-Month marries Supervisor-of-the-Month in Wedding-of-the-Year!' Stuart wore a powder-blue ruffled shirt and a beige suit, Isla got howling drunk, and Fergus refused to take Stuart's name.

'I give you a proper home, and that's all the thanks I get?' said Stuart, astounded that Fergus didn't want to be Meek. 'Mark my words, you'll regret that.' Relations with his stepfather deteriorated further after this. Fergus, an uncomfortable fifteen, mainly lurked in the bungalow's chilly, hardboard-floored loft, which was reached by a retractable ladder and trap door.

Fergus became increasingly fond of the retractability of the ladder one day when he ventured into Stuart's golf bag in the garage after noticing his stepfather furtively stuffing a magazine down among his clubs. From the bowels of the leathery-smelling bag emerged the creepy and inevitable news that Stuart was a shoe fetishist. There were many glossy, mildly worrying photographs of weedy men in bondage leather sucking the high-heeled patent toe of a dominatrix, along with a variety of shoe spankings. Fergus leafed through the magazines, staring at sights far worse than anything he'd come across in Fat Al's extensive library, and felt a visceral wave of disgust and hatred for Stuart. He couldn't bear the idea of him touching Isla. He kicked the golf bag over, so the clubs and the magazines spilled out for all to see. But perhaps his mum knew already. This thought made him nauseous. Anyway, Stuart was now proven to be a complete and utter tosser. And no wonder Isla kept complaining about her corns with all those stilettos she still wore to work every day to keep him happy.

Aside from his monomaniacal fetish, Stuart was a paragon of dullness. His monotonous voice irritated Fergus to the point of torture, and Stuart's constant state-ments of the bleeding obvious were increasingly hard to bear. The bungalow felt like a vice round Fergus's head, its low-ceilinged rooms crushing him: he wanted to punch holes in the plasterboard walls to let in the air. It was a bought house, not a council one, and instead of a number it had a name: *Marbella*. Stuart had once been on a half-board SunSpot package holiday from Glasgow airport to a half-built hotel in Marbella, and had never forgotten it. Fergus would sometimes fantasise about having a new nameplate for their house specially cast in the same curlicued wrought iron: *Shithole*, *Purgatory*, *Dullsville* – he'd just stick it up instead and see if anyone noticed.

In the winter, Fergus increasingly spent hours at school or in the warmth and light of the local library afterwards so he didn't have to go home. Or he hung out at Al's farm so often that Al's family started referring to him as 'the lodger'. In Burnoch library, he was often the only visitor left before closing time, and Effie the decrepit librarian took an interest in him – he was, after all, one of the few people who didn't request the latest Catherine Cookson. Effie imposed her own eclectic taste upon Fergus, ordering piles of books up from the central library in Glasgow: *Catch 22*, *One Day in the Life of Ivan Denisovitch*, *The Rachel Papers*, *One Hundred Years of Solitude*. And Fergus read non-stop to escape into worlds that were not so small, with better weather.

While *Marbella* was a prison for Fergus, it was a palace for Isla. After the draughty tenement, the bungalow was a comfort and a joy, with its leak-proof roof, brand-new bathroom and central heating. Isla enjoyed her Advocaat and lemonade on the Naugahyde settee with Stuart on a Saturday night after work. She at last had the possessions which she'd always deserved. She loved her ruched sateen window blinds (known locally as 'hoor's knickers'). She sang when she washed the dishes in her new kitchen with its view over the neat back lawn and the plastic rotating umbrella for drying clothes. And she was someone about town: Mrs Meek, a married woman, a shop supervisor, respectable again. Isla had been brought up in Burnoch by two truly miserable Presbyterian parents, who had passed away some years ago in a cancerous fug of Players' untipped and Kensitas Club. Before their untimely deaths, a year apart, they taught their children not to expect too much, not to have hopes that could be dashed, not to take risks, and, above all, not to have too much fun. This resignation had percolated the very core of Isla, Fergus thought. What else could explain her happiness in this wholesale embracing of the limits of her own life, this embracing of a stingy pervert with a greasy comb-over, for God's sake?

One Saturday evening in June, Fergus gave a mock lecture on the subject of *Marbella* to Fat Al, who was lying on the loft floor of the bungalow listening to Talking Heads' 'Stop Making Sense' and smoking a pathetically thin joint.

'We're in a different world, Al, a different time zone here in *Marbella*,' began Fergus.

'Aye, it's the dope. Slows you up.'

'No, you'll find that here in this bungalow the hours always stretch and sag like one of your dad's prolapsed sheep. There's no stopping it, no cure. You cannae try to rebel – it'll do no good. No, you've just got to sit there and let it pass. When I was wee, I used to call it Cabbage Time, when everything went into slow motion. Cabbage Time happened around tea time, five thirty p.m., and we'd be having salty mince with bits of carrot chopped up in it, and mashed potatoes with those sickening surprise lumps, and cabbage. And my mum and Stuart would talk small talk, about nothing, nothing that mattered in the world, and then she'd discuss, in some detail, *cabbage and wind* and how she wasn't "taking" cabbage any more. The consumption verb here in *Marbella* is "take", not "have" – why, I don't know, but you'll take a cup of tea, and you'll take a custard cream. Given all that monotony, you'd think there would be more time to think, but it turns out there's fuck all to think about.'

'I think "Psycho Killer" is the best track, don't you, Fergus?' Al took a Woodpecker cider bottle off the floor and peered into it to see if there was any left. He sucked down the hot, flat remains and puffed out his chest in his black T-shirt in front of Fergus's bedroom mirror. He flexed his muscles, Popeye-style, until Fergus rose from the floor to throw an empty beer can at him.

'Ooh, it's not Fat Al, it's *Homme Fatale* now, isn't it?' said Fergus, teasing. He could see Al didn't quite get the joke – he had opted for woodwork rather than French – but Al was attractive, no longer fat in that puppyish way. At sixteen, he had turned out braw and broad-shouldered, muscled from humping sheep and sacks on his dad's farm. Al's hair was still red, but he now had a shadow of brownish moustache, which made him look like he hadn't washed.

'D'you think I should grow a moustache?' said Al, still preening, mostly to annoy Fergus.

'Nah. No one'll ever shag you again,' said Fergus, grinning.

'At least I've had a shag.'

Fergus sighed. He was bony and boyish still. He

attempted to pump up some muscle next to Al in the mirror. 'I look like Johnny Rotten with anorexia,' he said.

'Don't worry,' said Al, 'it's not your fault. I'm on the case. Tonight, we will break your duck, I guarantee it. Your target tonight, should you choose to accept it, is Fiona Robertson. She's just broken up with Billy and she's dead good in bed.' Fergus wasn't sure whether this recommendation referred to Al's own experience, or the general opinion of Burnoch's youth. He nodded.

Al was full of sensible advice: 'You don't want to aim too high the first time, not one of those blondes wi' the big tits like Jenny Munro – indeed, I might have a dab at that myself tonight. Naw, it's easier with someone younger than you. You want tae build a reputation. Fiona's a bit peely wally looking,' said Al, wrinkling his freckly nose a little. 'But she's more likely to be impressed.' He suggested ways of impressing Fiona, which seemed a bit too complicated for Fergus, whose grasp of the subject was based on the occasional magazine and Desmond Morris's highly technical descriptions of the male and female orgasm in *The Naked Ape* which had come free with *The Nineteenth Hole – Great Golf Jokes* from Stuart's Reader's Digest bookclub.

After Al had talked about nookie, Fergus tried to talk about nihilism, a new concept which he thought might explain his state of mind every time he entered the bungalow. He put on The Smiths' 'Heaven Knows I'm Miserable Now' as accompaniment.

'Uh huh. Like I was saying, when nothing happens here, day after day, it makes you wonder what it was like for people in the Gulag, or prisoner-of-war camps, that had to live a life in their head to avoid every day being the same, to survive all that dullness dreeping all around them . . .'

'Gulag? Whit?' said Al, lost. He wondered if Gulag was Glaswegian slang for Barlinnie prison, the Bar-L, but fortunately he was too stoned to care. It was just Fergus, wittering on again.

Fergus looked all intense, frowning: 'What about those prisoners who write poems in their heads line by line, day by day, and memorise them for publication years later when they get out? But how did they keep the colours, the words in their heads, how did they hold on to the pictures before the grey seeped in and drowned everything? Before everything went flat and grey. Like Burnoch.'

'I don't know who you're on about as per usual but I think I know the feeling,' said Al. 'You know when I was working late last summer in the kitchen of the Burnoch Arms cleaning pots?'

Fergus nodded and took a drag on the joint. Al continued.

'I kept trying to have a laugh with the other guys, or to think about some bodacious birds, or owning a big yacht, but the pots got bigger and bigger and heavier and heavier with more burned-on shite. Like your mince, all floating in scummy, greasy water. I wanted to boke all the time. All I could think about was chundering. Couldn't fantasise about anything at all.'

Fergus looked sympathetic. Al had famously saved £400 that summer, and had bought himself a secondhand dinghy with an outboard motor.

'George Orwell, he worked in the kitchens of Paris and got a book out of it. You got a boat. It's the unpaid boredom here that gets me.'

'C'mon,' said Al, a little unsteady from the dope. He pulled on his denim jacket. The loft floor seemed to have tipped up at a strange angle. The retractable ladder was challenging. 'Let's go down the harbour and Alka Seltzer some seagulls. Cheer us up.'

The feeding of Alka Seltzer to seagulls was a fine Burnoch childhood tradition. Obviously, with the hangover rate in Burnoch, Alka Seltzer was as common as soap in local bathrooms. The technique was to take some white bread down to the water, and toss it up so the seagulls would fight over it. They soon got skilled at catching in mid air, so when the Alka Seltzer went up, hidden in a lump of bread, they gulped it down. Five minutes later, it was said, the seagull would fizz as it flew over the harbour and then explode.

As Al and Fergus sat on the seafront on some fish crates, waiting for one of the poisoned seagulls to detonate, Fiona Robertson and Karen MacKay came along. Actually, they sashayed, because they'd both been practising swaying their bums in high heels and skin-tight jeans in front of Fiona's bedroom mirror for the last hour. Karen was famous for being the class swot, so it was dead weird seeing her all tarted up for the night. The girls were also wearing lurid make-up and striped legwarmers they'd got reduced at Smart But Casual. The boys stared.

'You got ants in your pants or something? You're walking awful funny, the two of you,' said Al, always forward.

'I don't know what you mean, Al,' said Fiona, pretending to be insulted. Her cherry lipgloss was so thick Fergus thought it looked like car axle grease. A great waft of cheap matching perfume came from the girls. Fergus staggered backwards, doing a mock-asphyxiation routine. Al frowned at him. Fiona continued, oblivious. 'Anyway, are youse going to the disco and that later?'

'Dunno. If we can get some voddy, maybe,' said Al. 'Are youse?'

'Yeah,' said Fiona. 'Seeya.' And they bravely continued sashaying.

This was a fulsome invitation by Burnoch standards. Al said it totally confirmed that Fiona was on for shagging Fergus. Al himself had higher plans for Jenny, one of the Fifth Years. The youth-club disco was in the Scout Hall, and though no one attended the Scouts any more, it still had strict regulations against alcohol. You had to hide a bottle of vodka in the toilet cistern and take turns to go in to neck it or go outside for some dope. Still, it was as close to entertainment as they were going to get, especially if none of the seagulls exploded. A big bird plummeted out of the sky like a stone and disappeared under the water.

Fergus shook his head in disappointment and stood in front of the Tourist Board information sign on the harbour. Under 'What has Burnoch to offer? Possible Activities:' he wrote 'FUCK ALL' in giant letters with a felt pen from his pocket. Then they went over to get some chips at Catanis and Fergus subbed Al who managed to buy a half-bottle of Smirnoff from someone he knew at the offsales at the Burnoch Arms.

It was eight, but the sun was still laying long, warm stripes on the stone of the harbour wall and the water was Mediterranean-blue as Fergus and Al walked along to the Scout Hall, not noticing the exquisite landscape, the port with its brightly painted houses cradled in the green hills. They only saw the commercial world as all that Burnoch had to offer: the rundown bars, the café and the Crafty Caledonian with its gruesome hand-knitting, carved crooks and crap Celtic jewellery for the tourists. Nobody in Burnoch would be seen dead in that stuff. Then there was the Empire Cinema, unchanged since 1920, reeking damp and carpeted with sticky Kia-Ora. Further along, the filling station, the butcher's, and the Argyll Hotel, followed by Fleming's with its Fancy Goods and sherbert lemons, Saxon's shoe shop, the agricultural and veterinary supplies, and the frozen shellfish exporters. Plus the barber's, where they still sold condoms in the traditional manner.

'Something for the weekend, sir?' Al reminded Fergus as they passed the closed sign on the barber's beneath the striped pole and the window's faded photographs of David Cassidy-style feathercuts from the seventies.

'Huh?' said Fergus, but Al just took a packet of Durex from his pocket and silently handed him one.

'Oh shit. Are you saying I've got no choice?'

'It's the Scout motto. Be prepared,' said Al.

Fergus giggled, but he was suddenly incredibly uneasy, having to prove himself.

'Thanks, Big Man.'

Fergus felt a weird adult thrill of excitement as they entered the Scout Hall. Someone had blacked out the windows – local skin conditions were such that no one wanted bright light – and Elvis Costello's 'Accidents Will Happen' was playing. Some of the girls were dancing in 'Frankie say RELAX' T-shirts – fashion always came late (but considerably discounted) to Burnoch. Al discreetly poured vodka into their Cokes, and everything began to go brilliantly. Fergus and Al danced with Fiona and Karen and their mates Eileen and Sharon, but mostly they observed the action. There was a hierarchy of behaviour: on benches round the walls, a few thirteen year olds locked jaws and sucked the enamel off each other's teeth. The fourteen year olds tried to plant lovebites on each other, to provide opportunities for a slagging at school on Monday. The older kids danced indifferently, and gossiped as they smoked dope outside the hall door, evincing contempt for those inside. They were acutely aware that there was nowhere else for them to go. By ten o'clock, all pretence at sophistication was gone, and everyone was desperate to get off with someone. Fergus wandered inside to find Fiona again. He could just imagine his hands round her bum in those too-tight jeans, the axle-grease lipgloss coming off on his mouth, the grinding, slow dances before . . . he patted the condom in his pocket. Unfortunately, Fiona was nowhere to be seen in the darkness. Then Fergus realised she was crashed out full length on the stage behind the DJ, going at it tonsil to tonsil with Al. This was all wrong. This was not according to plan. Then Al had the temerity to give Fergus a thumbs-up sign behind Fiona's back as he passed by. Fergus's life and stomach hit rock bottom together.

He moved in on the less-desirable Eileen, his second choice for the evening, but as they were dancing, she kept staring over his shoulder at someone else she fancied. Soon Fergus walked desultorily out into the long summer night and sat on a rocky outcrop, kicking the grass behind the hall. Instead of blackness, there was a strange browny-grey glow, a middling light that could go either way towards dawn or dusk. And it was balmy, warm enough for a T-shirt. The lights of the houses across the harbour were coming on, and the sky was executing all the pastel clichés of an Impressionist painting, while the bass notes of Pink Floyd thrummed grimly on.

'You wouldn't know it was a shithole to live in, would you? Looks like a brochure from the Italian Riviera or something.' Karen had sat down next to him on the rock. She pronounced 'Italian' in the local manner as 'Aye-talian'. Fergus gave her an offhand nod.

'Blue Nun?' She pulled the half-drunk bottle from a purple shoulderbag.

'Oh Jesus, that stuff's disgusting. Awright, then.' Fergus took a slug of the Blue Nun and gagged. 'Tastes like sweeties stewed in petrol. Worse than your Buckfast Tonic Wine.'

'Nicked it from my mum's drinks cabinet. Desperate I was.'

'Desperate I am,' said Fergus, grinning mournfully.

He looked over at Karen. 'Thought you were going with Andy the night. Saw you dancing with him.'

'Naw, he's nice and all that, but he's got a face like a dartboard.'

'Mmm.' Fergus nodded. Acne had cruelly pitted Andy.

'Thought you were going with Eileen.'

'Naw, she's got a face like a melted welly.' He was laughing.

'Or a face like a burst couch,' she finished. They were hysterical now, playing with the school vernacular.

'Oh c'mon.' Karen slid across the rock closer to him.

Her voice sounded a bit slurred. 'Fiona had it all planned for ages – she's gone off with Al, you know and—'

Fergus started kissing her, for that seemed to be the only dignified way out, given the circumstances. Trust Al to leave him the leftovers. Still, they needed no reheating. A few minutes later, Fergus had reassessed them as choice morsels. He'd not gone near Karen much before because she had a reputation for being a bit boring and offhand at school. But this definitely had potential, so he suggested they leave the very public environs of the hall for the discreet quiet of his old close and the walled back green behind the tenement nearby. Arm in arm, they slipped quietly away from the crowd and staggered down the street clutching the Blue Nun.

Fergus led Karen into the tenement, and kissed her up against the close's cracked and crackled Victorian tiles patterned with strange green and purple leaves, stamens and open-mouthed flowers. Karen's face was warm against the cool tiles, and her touch was relaxed, a world away from the desperate, grubby gropings he'd experienced with girls before. Fergus opened his eyes for a moment, watching Karen intently until her brown eyes rolled back into her head and she closed the lids. That was surrender, wasn't it? I am right in there, Al, thought Fergus, just like you said. Karen had treacly hair, an interestingly long tongue, and too much orange pancake make-up. (At school she was usually so pale you could see the veins in her temples.)

'You're beautiful,' Fergus told her, coming up for air. Al had told him to say that.

'Oh Fergus,' she said. She sounded squeaky like she was going to cry and Fergus wasn't having it. In the last few minutes his jeans had grown so tight that he thought they would burst. He pressed himself against Karen, between her legs, but she'd got tight jeans on too, so he couldn't fathom what was going on down there. He was desperate, though. Shaking. The close was cloying and smelled of piss.

'C'mon and lie on the grass with me,' he said, pointing out to where the moon loomed over the bin sheds in the twilight of the drying green.

'But what if someone sees and—' she began. She was drunk enough not to care. Fergus took her hand and pulled her down the back steps of the close. A door slammed above and there were heavy steps and patterings. It was Mrs McGinty dragging her three-legged mongrel Archie downstairs for a last walk. Fergus and Karen hid, one flight of stairs below her, compressed in the shadows against the wall, trying not to laugh. The dog barked in their direction, but Mrs McGinty towed him, unheeding, out on to the street. 'Stupit dog. Get on wi' it!'

Karen was immobile with fear, and Fergus thought he would take advantage of the enforced silence to unzip her jeans and slip his fingers in for a fiddle in the soft front bit – well, that's what you said, Al, thought Fergus, and you were right. About two minutes later Karen went into some kind of meltdown.

'What do you want me to do? Is this good?' Fergus whispered, manoeuvring around.

'Archie! Come at once!' shouted Mrs McGinty.

'I'm going to come at once too, if I'm no' careful. You're

so gorgeous,' Fergus told Karen. She was shaking with silent laughter and pleasure – and fear of discovery by Mrs McGinty.

Karen's got nice thin legs, thought Fergus, surprised by his catch of the day, and a lovely pair of little tits. He'd breached her top by the time Mrs McGinty's slippers slowly slapped up the stairs. The dog limped behind, and the door slammed.

Fergus kept one hand down there in Karen's jeans, his fingers inside her, and he pulled her slowly down on to the still-warm ground, which gave up the scent of crushed grass all around them.

Hold back now. Al's advice was still being followed to the letter, so Fergus didn't let her touch him. He pushed her hand away from his jeans. He had a local reputation to build here. He kissed her and stroked her and asked her where and how and how soft and how hard and how often, just like Al said, and in a not very long time she went all shuddery and peed a tiny drip into his hand, and Fergus assumed she'd come, hadn't she? Had to be, or she wouldn't be crying like that and saying 'Oh Fergus' and unzipping his jeans.

'Here we go, here we go, here we go,' sang Fergus in his head. Then he slid his hand into his pocket for the condom, and it wasn't there. It had gone awol somewhere between the Scout Hall and here. And after all that practice putting them on.

'Shit,' he said. 'I've lost the condom.'

'You didn't think I was gonnie let you?' said Karen, genuinely surprised. 'I'm fourteen, I'm a virgin, and I'm staying that way for a while. Even with you, Fergus.'

'But . . . but, everyone says—'

'Who gives a flying fuck what everyone says? Do you believe they're all getting it? They're not.' Karen looked hard at him, but she was also smiling. 'Mind you, there are ways round the problem.'

She wriggled further down into the grass and got Fergus's cock in the lovely tight ring of her middle finger and her thumb. She slipped the tip of it into her mouth and soon he was the one with his eyes rolling back into his head.

'Oh Karen,' he said. 'Oh God, oh Karen, oh God.'

Well, it was a semi-religious occasion for him, his first one like this with a girl. He just wished he was inside her though, and not out here trailing spunk on the grass beneath the tenement. But doing it with Karen felt so different from being alone; it was bigger, rounder, more complicated, and thrillingly out of his control. And now his mind was warm and emptied of all worry. He existed only in this moment, and it felt good.

Karen was lying beside him, face to face with him. She was stroking the hair back off his forehead. 'Thanks, Fergus,' she whispered. 'That's the first time a man's ever . . . a boy's ever made me . . .' and then she laughed. They were embarrassed, suddenly. It was too man-and-wifey lying there. And they were all but naked, beneath Mrs McGinty's lighted window, attracting the midges. They pulled on their clothes and sat on the stone tenement steps sharing a fag. Karen leaned against the banister, and Fergus against the wall, their legs and feet entwined. He let out a long-held sigh. There was orange pancake make-up on his new white T-shirt. Karen was looking at something above his head. He stared too.

'See they tiles up there, Karen? You'd never notice them normally, but they look like flowers – but then again, like something else. They look weird . . .' and he started giggling. 'They look sort of beautiful . . . and dirty, don't they? I lived here all that time and I never noticed, never knew enough to notice.'

'Yes,' she said. 'You're right. I was thinking that too. I saw paintings just like them in a book once. I'll show you it sometime.' Fergus pulled her to his side of the steps, and kissed her again, wondering about her.

'It's eleven . . .'

'I'll walk you home,' said Fergus, his face buried in the silkiness of Karen's hair, smelling it, remembering, because the rest of her was perfumed with artificial scent but this was her essence. As they walked along the waterside, he knew there was an indefinable shift in his head, as though he had developed a new sense, beyond the five obvious ones.

Karen was more prosaic: 'I feel like we're glowing like the Ready Brek kids in that advert, and everyone can see us, and knows what we've done.' Fergus smiled.

Last orders were simultaneously over in twelve of the port's bars and the streets were hoaching with noisy, blootered humanity. One of the troubles with Burnoch was the tendency of its more distant residents to drink-drive home, there being no other form of transport. Fortunately, the police were in a lock-in at the Mason's Arms on most Saturday nights, including this one, so discretion was assured. Still, the stench of Eighty Shilling and whisky-soaked breath was incredible, thought Fergus, as they dodged through the crowds and the cars on the waterside as they walked by the sea. The moon fought to reflect on the indigo water, which still seemed to hold the daylight, close to the summer solstice.

They heard it first behind them, a great metallic creak and scraping sound, and then a splash, as a car tipped slowly over the harbourside and plunged, cartoonlike, into the water. The drowning-car situation was almost an annual spectator event in Burnoch – there were parking spaces all along the front, and no wall. Someone was always dumb enough to leave their handbrake off, particularly the tourists and the incomers.

This car didn't go under straightaway, but floated, a bubble of air in metal, half in and half out of the water, with its headlights miraculously on. A crowd rushed to the edge of the harbour, someone calling: 'Anywan in it?'

A roar came from the crowd, and people started panicking. A man was taking his shoes off. Fergus and Karen ran closer. Then Fergus clearly saw that the car was a maroon Rover, the same as Stuart's new car, which he often drove to the pub. At that moment, the car's lights fused and went dark, and the front started sinking.

'Fuck, it's my mum's car!' shouted Fergus and jumped off into the murky, oily bay. Karen started screaming. The tide was out and it was about five feet deep and Fergus ripped his leg open straightaway on something rusty and sharp under the dark water. The adrenaline was hammering so hard he hardly noticed, and he half swam, half walked on the slimy mud to the car. Only the roof was fully visible, but through the submerged windscreen he could see Stuart's jowly pink face shouting in the air pocket inside the car, his body writhing, his hands scrabbling at the door. Isla wasn't there. Stuart was alone. Fergus felt a surge of relief.

He ducked beneath the surface and tried to open the car door from the outside under the water. A big man, one of the volunteer firemen, joined Fergus in the water, tugging at the handle, but it wouldn't budge.

'Pressure's too great from the water outside. Have to wait until there's a bit more water in the car and then it'll open,' said the fireman knowledgeably.

Fergus was still freaked out: 'But he doesn't know that. He's . . . look!' Through the blurred windscreen, as though in a faraway film, Stuart seemed to be having a seizure or a heart attack. The water was up to his waist and his red mouth was open, gasping for air, and you could see all his grey metal fillings.

'I'm going to smash the side window, let the water fill faster, get him out,' said Fergus, diving under to pull a stone from the sea bed. Undersea, everything was calm, womblike, timeless. The shallow June water was almost warm, and the shouting of the crowd was gone. There was just the lapping of the waves. There was no need to panic, thought Fergus, as a shoal of tiny silvery fish came by him. Stuart will have had the usual three pints, won't he, and the water is beautiful. Fergus's hand closed on a big, rounded stone in the mud. He floated gently up. Take your time, laddie, said a voice in his head, why don't you just take your time?

𝔅urnoch 𝔊a𝔷ette
June 8, 1985

CALL FOR HARBOUR BARRIER AS CAR SINKS IN LOCH
By Alan McWhirter

Burnoch Parish Council last night called for a metal crash barrier to be installed on Burnoch Harbour, after another car rolled off the quayside into the loch.

The latest incident – the second this year – occurred last Saturday at pub-closing time. The car's owner, Stuart Meek, was in the vehicle at the time when it fell. He was trapped in the car for a few minutes as it went under, and was rescued by his stepson Fergus MacFarlane, and Pat Monaghan, a volunteer fireman.

Mr Meek, 37, who manages Saxon Shoes in Burnoch, was taken to Kinloch Hospital suffering from shock, but was discharged the next day. He was unavailable for comment.

Another supporter of barriers on the quayside is Jessie Henderson, 54, of Bute Street, whose car sank in the harbour last year. Mrs Henderson said: 'I was putting my shopping bags from the Co-op in the boot when the car started moving. I must have left the handbrake off. All I could do was watch as the car sank into the loch and my loaves floated away.'

Anne McGinty, a parish councillor, said: 'This is the eighth time a car has gone over that harbour in living memory, and something should be done about it. We will be writing to the Roads Department.'

Chapter Five

1986

On the Road: Jack Kerouac

The nearest tattoo parlour to Burnoch was on the Kinloch caravan site, and run by Dougie Morrison who had a sideline in carving rocks and tombstones, so his tattoos were more monumental than tasteful. Parlour is perhaps too fancy a word for Dougie's establishment: you sat on an old armchair in the trailer down by the burn, and tried to look out of the tiny window at the beeches jostling so as not to see what was happening to your upper arm. There was a smell of mildew and rotting carpet; Dougie hummed in competition with the buzz of the multi-needled tattoo machine as he drilled a chain of Celtic knots into the skin round Fergus's bicep.

The pain was excruciating. Why does no one tell you that about tattoos, wondered Fergus. It was a punishing half-hour trapped beneath a heavy-duty sewing machine, a human-leather punch, and even by Monday the weekend's tattoo still felt hot like a ring of sunburn beneath his school shirt and blazer. Dougie said doing the outline was the most painful, before the endorphins set in. Fergus's first tattoo was cushioned by his arm, a warm-up for the swirling triangular Celtic knot that he'd drawn up for transposition to the thin layer of skin along his vertebrae. For this pleasure, you paid Dougie cash – the parlour wasn't exactly licensed. On the other hand, the fishermen of Burnoch had gone there for years, to no ill effect. Fergus went every Saturday, since he could only afford to pay in instalments. It was easier in small doses, given his epic plans for adornment.

In Burnoch, Fergus felt every sting of the needle had pushed him further from conventionality, and he luxuriated behind the bathroom door in the secrecy of it, until Isla came home unexpectedly from Saxon's one Saturday with an upset stomach and found him slobbing in his boxer shorts in front of the telly. One of the rough-hewn tattoos was still bloody.

'Oh Jesus! You know you'll have that for life?' she screamed.

'That's the idea,' said Fergus, deadpan.

'They tattoo needles are infested with Aids and everything,' Isla said.

'Naw. I went to Dougie. Dad got his tattoo there twenty years ago. Dougie remembers him. Remembers the dragon down his arm.' Fergus switched channels and continued to eat a family pack of crisps.

'That's it! I'm not giving you any more fucking money to destroy yourself,' said Isla, clattering into her bedroom and slamming the door, realising afterwards that her role seemed to be the more teenage one. She felt completely drained. Any time she challenged Fergus, he tried to bring his dad into it, knowing the damage it instantly caused to Stuart in comparison. Isla lay there on the duvet, smoking, staring at the Artex-textured ceiling and tried to fathom why, day in and day out, you could cut the atmosphere in *Marbella* with a knife. She put it down to the night the car sank last year: she guessed that Fergus in some unsaid way regretted rescuing Stuart, and in return Stuart silently loathed being indebted to Fergus. The balance of power, adult-to-child, was lost. Isla was torn; she floated between her two men in a dwam, unpredictably favouring one and then the other. Resentment and jealousy fermented in the bungalow along with Stuart's watery homebrew, which he'd started in an attempt to limit his drunk driving from the pub. Over the months since the accident, Isla had become quiet and watchful, even a little depressed, and had made it her business to expect the worst. And wouldn't you, when the sea persisted in dragging your men down like that?

It was the elements she feared most. The slightest storm would have Isla up to high doh, and that spring there were many. The overflowing waves left seaweed like hanks of hair in the trees by the loch. The lightning exploded electricity poles, and once it hit the house, making the telephone wires spark and jump like live snakes. The power was often out for hours, the television died, and Isla carefully had all the household electrical appliances tested by Uncle Jim after each tempest. Meanwhile, she railroaded Stuart into buying a secondhand Volvo – reinforced with Swedish safety – and he sulked because he could not find one in maroon. Mindful of her own fate as well as that of her men, Isla dreamed of death and cancer, and her fantastical ailments became, she knew, infamous in the doctor's surgery. She walked carefully on her high heels, fearing a twisted ankle at any moment.

Stuart's rescue had the opposite effect on Fergus. He seemed unleashed by it, and Isla knew from the late nights and early mornings when Fergus staggered in smelling of God-knows-what, having been with God-knows-who, his pupils tiny, that the days of parenting were numbered. The girlfriend situation was no better. Isla had approved when Fergus had been going steady for a few months with Karen MacKay – a sensible girl, hard working, respectable – but suddenly they'd started arguing all the time. She had listened to them through the thin floors of the loft, Fergus swearing and cajoling, and then there had been no sign of Karen again. Fergus was foul tempered for weeks and wouldn't talk about it. After that there were just the used condoms in his bin, left for anyone to see, left for Isla to clear up, and half Fergus's class passing through half the night. Everyone knew everything. There were Fergus's photographs to prove it: no need for a mother's intuition.

Sometimes Fergus didn't come home at all at the weekends, claiming he was staying with Al. Isla tried to impose late-night curfews upon him, and when those failed, she wept. At sixteen, Fergus was now taller than Isla, and stronger than the flabby, cowed and irritable Stuart. He had, Isla felt, no respect for them. Their only real hold over him was money, which is why Fergus started work on the very day his exams finished in the summer.

Fergus and Uncle Jim were perhaps the only folk in Burnoch who had faith in the new Fyne Delicatessen. It was whispered that the owner was Jewish, which was considered most exotic in a white-bread Protestant town which had taken ten years to get over the Sikh family running Nairn's the newsagents. The Fyne Deli had opened on the front at Easter, and after an initial inquisitive scurry through the front door, the local populace had backed off, shuddering at the prices and the dangers of foodstuffs from heathen lands.

Fergus liked the surreal food. He used a bright, colour-saturated film to take a photo of the wifies of Burnoch in their rain-mates and hairy coats staring into the huge, chilled shop window filled with psychedelic food combinations: lobsters displayed with strawberries and sliced kiwis – wee furry brown fruits which were bright green with black spots inside. Burnoch was also astounded by the honking, bowffin cheeses kept *warm*, for Pete's sake, on a board covered with dirty straw. Single Austrian marzipan sweets with Mozart on the wrapper cost fifty pence! A slice of salami was daylight robbery. Boarding up and closure were surely only months away.

Tourists were suckers for the obvious smoked salmon and shortbread; anything with a tartan ribbon on it. At first Uncle Jim and the Catanis from the chip shop were the only regular local customers; Jim came in for wild boar pâté and olives, and the Catanis for Italian specialties that lurked in their genetic memory. They even bought sliced Mortadella – electric-pink meat with white cubes of fat embedded in it, which local rumour said was made from donkey. More suspiciously, the only Catholics for miles around, the nuns from the Notre Dame convent in a distant village, appeared with their tiny van on Saturdays and filled up with quiches, salamis, sun-dried tomatoes and expensive dessert wines that had no role whatsoever in Communion.

For Fergus, the sights and smells were gloriously un-

Presbyterian. There were marble counters, and globe-ball lights and fresh dusty-rose paint on the old shop front. Shelves went to the ceiling. The place had an aura of decadence; even the owner, Sam Green, a gangly man with wild hair and bottle-cap glasses, looked like he came from some Mitteleuropean fable or university, although he was, in fact, from Glasgow.

'You'll be wanting an assistant over the summer, then,' said Fergus, walking in one day. 'When the yachties all come.'

Sam appeared in a blue-striped apron from behind the counter. He hopped, a little tensely, from foot to foot. Wordless, he offered Fergus a fat circle of orange-red sausage on the end of a knife.

'I've seen you about. You're the one that takes the photographs. Jim's son.'

'No, he's my uncle.' Fergus liked the sausage. It was hot and spicy, with a dark taste of blood, and of something exotically far away from the watery pink rubber version in the Co-op.

'What's this?'

'Spanish sausage. León chorizo. Rich smoky aroma. Leaves your taste buds in a frenzy. Moist, meaty, paprika-laced.' Sam sounded like an advertisement.

'León chorizo,' repeated Fergus, awed, hoping for another slice which was not forthcoming.

'I'm not paying much. Business isn'y exactly booming yet.' Sam peered myopically at Fergus, and his nose twitched when he saw Fergus's black-rimmed nails. 'And y'might wantae scrub up a bit.'

'Aye. I was painting my bedroom.'

'Black walls?' But Sam smiled and gave him the job, recognising there was something about Fergus that did not quite fit into Burnoch.

The Fyne Delicatessen paid a good deal less than the wages everyone else in the class was earning at the fish packing for the summer, and the hours were long, because Sam only had a part-time assistant – Susan from the now-defunct greengrocer's. Yet although Fergus's feet hurt by six o'clock every day, the delicatessen unlocked dormant areas of his brain related to smell and taste and sheer pleasure.

'Taste it, taste it. Or you'll be no use to me,' Sam would say in his persuasive voice, when something new came in, like tiny tins of foie gras, or dried trompettes de mort mushrooms. Fergus had to try everything, so he could spread the good news among the folk of Burnoch, translate it into their language. He tried to draw a line at cheese that pooled on the counter and smelled of ripe oxter and damp dog, but Sam forced him on. Great mysteries were explained – olive oil came in many flavours, virginal being the most popular, and it was a far, far thing from Mazola.

Fergus was a quick learner, deft and instinctive, with an eye for display. His only mistake was at the end of the first week when he sliced the expensive Parma ham for the first time on the electric machine, in sensible slabs, and the English yachtsman he was serving said, 'No way, mate. You'll have to do that again. Thin like paper, yeah?'

When Sam saw the discarded fat slices of ham, he started screaming hysterically at Fergus, shaking and swearing and threatening to dock his wages. Fergus realised from his over-reaction that there was something not quite normal about Sam, but he couldn't quite put his finger on it. All he knew was that it was a bizarre scene – a hissy fit that seemed to be about to end in a head butting. But another customer came in, interrupted Sam's raging and saved Fergus's bacon, so to speak.

By the end of the day, a now-calm and conciliatory Sam took Fergus back to the huge, whirring electric meat slicer, put it at the thinnest setting, stuck in the chumpy leg of Parma ham, and with his hand on top of Fergus's, showed him the exact pressure to make almost-transparent slices, and how to lay them out in lines on single, layered sheets of greaseproof paper. Fergus felt strange beneath the arch of Sam's long fatherly arms at the machine as he was taken, literally, under Sam's wing. He wanted to lean back against him, and rest, but he didn't.

'Gonny let youse off this time,' Sam said in the guttural accent which belied his extremely delicate sensibilities. He shut up the shop for the evening and took Fergus into the back kitchen, where he'd whizzed up the discarded slices of ham with chilli oil and was serving it on pasta. He piled the pasta high on Fergus's plate. 'Get torn into that,' he said. 'The thing about you, Fergus, is that you've got aesthetic instincts. You get it: food, art, photos and that. But I don't know where you get it from.' Sam gestured in the direction of *Marbella* and its mundane inhabitants. 'I don't know where. You're like a hearing child born to deaf parents.'

'Stuart's no' my dad either, you know,' said Fergus, and explained the story to Sam. Sam listened and asked for more. Fergus was suddenly aware that Sam might be lonely. He had not made many friends in Burnoch, despite his regular appearances at the bar of the Argyll Hotel. (It was felt locally that a man – especially one who lived *alone* – should not be quite so interested in food and cooking.) In the back shop, after closing time, sitting opposite Sam in the dim light beneath a bank of pickled herring jars, Fergus felt that he was talking to the first adult who really understood him, more than Uncle Jim, and also that there was something exciting here, an undercurrent of the exotic. To Sam, Fergus was both amusing and fascinating, overflowing with half-chewed ideas and quite unaware of his own, remarkably spotless perfection.

They drank unsaleable Japanese beer with ripped labels and talked about books and music – although Sam with his mad professor look seemed a million years old, he was in fact only thirty – and how Sam had been a lawyer before he discovered that food could be a way of making sense of the world, and that a personal passion could be made commercial. He had sold the first proper delicatessen in Glasgow at a profit, and come up to start another in Burnoch.

'Why?' asked Fergus. 'Why are you here? There's nothing here.'

'There's the sea. There's the cheap rent. There's space. There's a new market,' said Sam. 'And Glasgow was suffocating me. It was too much, I'm trying to get away from all that. And I broke up with my wife. So there was no reason to stay. Besides, maybe one day a beautiful woman will walk into the shop here . . .'

'Oh.' Fergus stared at him, his eyes screwed up. Escaping the wife, he could understand, but not to Burnoch. 'Nah,' he said shaking his head. 'How could you leave the city for here? I think about nothing else, about leaving Burnoch, *the place that time forgot*,' he said, imitating a cheesy American voice. 'The place where time stopped, in cabbage time.' Sam looked puzzled, but Fergus continued. 'They're only half alive, people here. I've been reading *On the Road*, you know, and Kerouac says that bit about "The only people for me are the mad ones, the ones who are mad to live, mad to talk . . ." '

' ". . . mad to be saved, desirous of everything at the same time, the ones who never yawn or say a commonplace thing, but burn, burn, burn like fabulous yellow roman candles . . ." ' continued Sam, laughing at Fergus. 'Yeah. Everyone reads Kerouac when they're a teenager.'

'Not here they fucking don't.'

'I remember that feeling,' continued Sam. 'I remember thinking the same. I'll show you a video I taped off the telly about him one day, when I unpack all my stuff.' Fergus waited, desperate to hear more, but nothing was forthcoming, and Sam had begun to look edgy, as though he wanted to go. Fergus lovingly sopped up the last of the pasta sauce with a piece of what Sam said was ciabatta, and stuck the plate in the sink.

They locked up and Sam went over to his car, a secondhand Saab. He lived somewhere out of town, in an old shepherd's house in the hills.

'Thanks for the dinner,' said Fergus, waving and walking on. 'I'm away,' he called over his shoulder. 'The girlfriend's parents are out the night . . .' He winked.

'Fuck!' said Sam. 'I've lost the car keys.' His hands were now shaking. Fergus offered to go and look on the floor of the shop, but he found nothing there or on the counters. They searched the road. Sam was becoming frantic. He

103

tried to call the port's only taxi, but it was miles away. After a few minutes waiting, he became rigid with tension. 'I need to get back now . . .'

'Here,' said Fergus. 'I'll hotwire it for you. Have you got a screwdriver and a pair of pliers in the shop?'

'No. What do you mean, you know how to hotwire?' Sam narrowed his eyes.

'My uncle Jim at the garage. He showed us. He's teaching me to drive and all. I'll run over and borrow the tools. Just stay there.'

Within a few minutes, Fergus had returned with Jim. No one locked their cars in Burnoch, so they'd soon pried off the dashboard cover behind the steering wheel with the screwdriver. They found two sets of wires, one for the dashboard lights, and one for the ignition.

'Dead simple,' said Jim. 'Because the car's old, the ignition wires are both red, but it's when you get yellow, black and blue that it's harder. Just twist they two red wires together until the engine turns over. Undo them when you stop.' He handed Sam the pliers, and left the engine running.

'Thanks,' said Sam smiling. He was pale and sweating, but clearly relieved. He drove off far too fast.

Jim and Fergus stood on the front together, staring after Sam's polluted trail.

'Odd man,' said Fergus. 'Gets weirdly excited and upset by stuff.'

'And he needs a new exhaust,' said Jim. 'Where are you off to the night then?'

Fergus explained he would be visiting Jennifer Gilles that evening on the new Barratt housing estate. He didn't explain that her parents were away: he couldn't talk to Uncle Jim about those things in the way he could with Sam. Fergus and Jennifer's coupling up had been caused by a serendipitous remark by Joe Robertson at Burnoch High a few months before. Joe had ventured, within the hearing of a bunch of the girls, that Jennifer Gilles had 'been around so much it's like fucking a Co-op bag.' Fergus, who at that time was merely a friend of Jennifer's, had felt an unexpected anger at this patently unfair remark, and had taken Joe out with a single, sharp headbutt to the nose. As Joe lay bleeding in the playground, Fergus's social standing rose (he was no longer considered peculiar despite his earring and predilection for New Romantic-style eyeliner at the weekends) and Jennifer was alerted to the fact that Fergus fancied her. She was dark, pale skinned, pretty; a big-boned girl originally from Northern Ireland. She was into Goth stuff, so the two of them started taking the bus down to Glasgow at weekends to go to tattoo and piercing shops, and to Flip, a store which sold American surplus clothing. They were desperate to go to clubs, but there was no way to get home. On the last bus in the evening, they'd share a copy of *The Face* magazine, which Fergus would keep for the photographs.

Now that Fergus was working weekdays and Saturdays in the deli, the trips to Glasgow were over, and he mostly met Jennifer in her bedroom, where they conducted furtive and experimental sex. For Jennifer it was true love; for Fergus it was something less profound: a friendship where the participants were often naked. His relationship with Jennifer wasn't all consuming; it wasn't the profound passion he'd read about in books. Indeed, he almost found it more romantic hiking alone up into the moors for hours on end, marching into exhaustion, towards some kind of exorcism.

As he walked along the ridge of hills above the loch, he sometimes met up with Jim. But their days of birdwatching together were over – a sixteen year old couldn't admit to being a twitcher. Jim took Fergus for driving lessons, though, talking as they drove for miles into the wilderness, and then they'd come back to go round the only roundabout, and through Burnoch's single traffic light, over and over.

On the rare summer nights when Jennifer, Jim or Al weren't around, Fergus began to go bathing in the dusk, alone in the loch off the shingle beach behind the harbour. He would swim out into the dark water, the endless depth beneath him, into the moonpath if there was one. The shallows were warm from the Gulf Stream. He would float and paddle there for almost an hour in the salty, buoyant loch, waiting, thinking about the thin line between life and death, above and below the water. Both were tempting in their own way.

The return home, to the bright carpets and brittle arguments, was all the harder after that. Not that Stuart was violent or anything – just malignant. The place stank like a brewery, with big white plastic dustbins of lager festering in the kitchen. It also smelled like an ashtray, for there were cigarette butts everywhere, even on a plate at the side of his mother's bed. You would think that having two parents die of cancer might give you some pause for thought, thought Fergus, but clearly Isla was too terrified and tense to pause for anything.

Every time Fergus put his key in the door of *Marbella*,

a heavy weight settled upon him. He hated himself, and his unquenchable energy coiled bitterly in on him. His chest felt as though it were starting a cold, filled with the phlegm of home, which somehow had to be expectorated.

So the deli became a cure and a refuge, a place of light, the big plate-glass windows reflecting the ever-changing waters of the harbour. Fergus's friends would come by at lunchtime and hang out, and their presence made others curious about the shop. Uncle Jim came in for a special kind of rice called Arborio, cited in an Italian recipe book Mr Catani had given him. Even Karen came in one day, to buy one of Sam's dark-chocolate cakes for her mum, and Fergus greeted her cheerfully and then dropped all her change on the floor as he served her.

'You're just an accident waiting to happen, Fergus,' said Karen. She looked irritated. Fergus felt guilty and somehow despondent, but it was hardly his fault that she wouldn't go to bed with him. What did she expect? And you had to try to stay friends. It was difficult in a small town to avoid someone, especially when they were often in the same classes. Karen gave him a piercing stare, and then walked off with the cake in her hand and her head high. Fergus went into the back shop and gave the freezer a good kicking.

But then something amazing happened. Mrs McGinty – his old neighbour – tied her yapping, three-legged beast up outside the door, and came in, still in her slippers. Fergus was astounded when she bought a single slice of honey-roast ham wrapped in paper, which she put carefully in her old crocodile handbag, snapping the clasp shut as though protecting a fortune. The next week, Mrs McGinty did the same again, and again. Sam was overjoyed and said this was the best local advertising he'd ever had.

The yachties were the most annoying customers, asking for silly wee portions of cheese and always wanting their lobsters dead, so Fergus had to keep a pot on the boil in the back shop, where crustaceans could scream in private. The local poachers brought in pheasants for a few quid a bag, which Sam hung grandly in the window and sold back to the landowning classes at a huge premium. The yachties and tourists were impressed that the deli sold Cornish Yarg (gray backwards), a cheese from the Duchy of Cornwall's estate. Fergus was good at spinning a tale, giving out tiny bites of cheese and wild boar pâté for customers to taste, and he hit on the idea of sticking the rock-hard round of cold brie in the microwave for a few seconds, so it was perfectly runny for the rush of customers on a Saturday. 'Genius,' said Sam.

One evening, in the July Glasgow Fair fortnight, Sam announced from the till that their takings were the highest ever. He locked them both into the shop to clear up. He handed Fergus a Biro casing, with the ink cartridge missing, and said: 'There's a wee bonus for you tonight in the bathroom.' Fergus realised the pen was used as a straw, so he was not surprised when he found a line of white powder on a tile by the washbasin. He was delighted. He hadn't tried cocaine before. Speed, yes, but not cocaine. Bit out of his price range, and not easy to come by in Burnoch. He sniffed, numbing his nose, and noticed very little change. Except that he felt better, more together, and he was moonwalking. Discreetly.

It explained a lot about Sam Green: his amazing energy,

his tension, his agitation – and perhaps his local income before the deli took off. Fergus floated into the front shop.

' "Somewhere along the line I knew there'd be girls, visions, everything; somewhere along the line the pearl would be handed to me",' announced Sam dramatically, grinning at Fergus from behind his bottle glasses. Fergus looked puzzled. 'Kerouac. Your man. Thought you'd recognise it.'

From then on, Fergus was aware of layers of business going on in the shop. Though he couldn't be sure exactly when Sam was dealing cocaine as well as ciabatta, he saw everything with new eyes, while still enjoying the regular bonuses after work. Susan, the other assistant, was quite unaware of anything. She just yabbered about her boring kids all the time. So it was Fergus who was cashing up on a Friday night, when what can only be described as a caricature wee Glasgow ned knocked on the glass doors. Sam shouted to Fergus to let him in, and ran out of the back shop to greet the shorn-headed man with a time-battered face. While Sam finished a phonecall in the office, the man lurked around the till chatting to Fergus, staring at his black clothes. As Fergus sorted the change into small plastic bags for the bank, the man peered closer, his breath wafting beer.

'Whit are they?' He was pointing at a bag of twenty-pence pieces.

'Twenty ps. What did you think they were?' The man made Fergus twitchy.

'When did they come out?'

'I dunno. Maybe five years ago.'

The man nodded sadly. 'Aye, that'll be it. That's when I went in.'

'In where?'

'Barlinnie, of course. The Bar-L. Did Sam no' tell you? Got out on Wednesday. Gie's a slice of that game pie there, will you?'

Fergus thought it was sensible to make no further enquiries about Barlinnie or its former prisoner. The man had put down some equipment from the chandlers, and was sitting on the marble worktop in his grubby jeans, ripping into the pie. Fergus threw the takings into a bag and handed them to Sam, who grinned at him as he left.

'You talked to our local pirate, then?'

'Aye,' said Fergus, and disappeared up the street, wondering if the coke came in – or perhaps out – by boat. Best not to ask, he thought.

Of course, Fergus's complicity with whatever was going on merely served to bring him closer to Sam. In Burnoch it was hard to find likeminded people your own age – there were only thirty-one pupils in Fergus's year at school – and Fergus was happy to make the cross-generational leap. Sometimes they went to the pub together after work and chatted up some women, with Sam buying the drinks because all the barmaids tended to know who was still at school. Not that they minded you drinking; they just minded being caught serving you.

Fergus was in the lounge bar at the Argyll when Sam pushed a fusty-smelling, yellow-paged paperback across the table. It was Alexander Trocci's *Young Adam*, a grim piece of existentialism set on the industrial canals around

Glasgow in the 1950s. 'Your kind of book,' said Sam. 'Take it.'

Young Adam was like Kerouac without the sunlight. It fitted Fergus's edgy mood perfectly, with its descriptions of the coal barges on the canal, in the last days of Scotland's industrial power. The book was bursting with images that kept Fergus awake. He was finding it harder and harder to sleep anyway, so in the early hours before work, he wandered down on to Burnoch's desolate docks which had once been filled with pair trawlers, herring, creels and boxes of smoked kippers, in the days before quotas and over-fishing killed the industry. In the sepia morning light, he took a series of photographs of the bleak detritus that remained: the empty quays with strange rusting hulks of winches, and the signs from a lost time: 'Fishing Boats. Motor Launches. Scottish builders of the "Stella" class yachts,' it said on the rotting wooden skeleton of the shed which had once been Burnoch Boatbuilders. He broke into the oldest fish-processing factory, now closed with the redundancy notices still on the staff board inside, and wandered through the steel tables and a conveyor belt dripping rust in the salty air. On Friday evenings, when the dole cheques came in, he took photographs of the one-time factory workers and fisherman drinking in the pub. Even the *Dalriada*, his dad's old boat, was a rustbucket and only went out two days a week now. Fergus wondered how his father would have coped.

The photographs were eerily beautiful; a harbour film set and its abandoned cast. Fergus took them to the Burnoch Gallery and Craftshop, which displayed them in silvery frames. One day, while Fergus was at the deli, some toff came in off one of the big gin palaces moored in the harbour, and bought all twenty prints. The gallery rang Fergus with the good news. And could he have a new set of 'originals' printed up the next day by the way? Fergus suddenly had enough money for his third and final tattoo, and much more to spare. He started saving for the first time in his life, saving for a rainy day. He reckoned, it being Burnoch, that the chances were high that it would rain on the day he walked out.

Jim was delighted – and possibly a touch jealous – that the gallery had taken Fergus's photographs. He studied the second set of prints of the grim remnants of the fishing industry as they hung in the darkroom before Fergus took them over to the gallery on his lunch break from the deli. 'Burnoch is dead,' Jim said. 'Long live Burnoch.'

'What do you mean?' said Fergus.

'Well, the fishing's mostly gone, and this place is increasingly becoming a playground for the rich, for the tourists and their yachts, the Glaswegians and southerners with second homes. The sort of people who need delicatessens, not herring from the sea. Those are the new industries here. As for you, son, you're just nostalgic and old fashioned.' Jim grinned.

'Bollocks.' Fergus was irritated.

'You're the one that's still reading books from the fifties and taking photos of dying industries when you should be thinking about your future, about a proper career.' Fergus gave him the finger in a friendly way, unsure what Jim was telling him to do. 'Aye, and not in photography. No one makes money from that. Unless they do weddings,' continued Jim. 'Here. I'll drop you off at the deli.'

Sam shut up shop early that afternoon. There was a gale getting up, and business was paltry. The port smelled of autumn, of gusts of the leaves rotting in the damp and the first coal fires. Fergus lurked by the door of the deli, waiting for Sam to lock up, unable to face going home.

'Fergus?' Sam said. 'Why are you standing there like that, son? Your face is tripping you.' Fergus shrugged. 'Well, I'm doing nothing. How about I show you that Kerouac video? I found it the other night. I'll give you a lift home with me the now.'

Sam had already provisioned up with coke, beer and a bashed quiche rejected by the nuns of Notre Dame, and they sat on the sofa in his long white cottage overlooking the loch, isolated from everything. He still had no curtains. 'What's the point? There's no one to see in but the sheep.' Fergus found it disturbing, this openness to the wind-lashed night.

The documentary was in black and white, filled with anger and craziness and cars and landscape and long rolls of yellow writing paper and passion and all the things out there that Fergus longed for and could never express. At the end of the video, Kerouac's cracked voice played over views of the rail sidings in some lost town, the wires on telegraph poles, the endless road stretching away.

Fergus felt desolate and exhilarated at once. Sam looked at him, understood, and put his arm round Fergus's shoulder. Fergus let his head lie back against the wool of Sam's jumper. He closed his eyes for a while. Fergus felt the twitch of a hard on, but then that happened to him all the time anyway – around women, men, televisions, photographs and purple passages of prose. Fergus remained where he was, because wherever he was, was the opposite of normal, traditional and acceptable in Burnoch. There was one thing he could say for his upbringing in this small-minded world: it had given him all these negatives, all these opportunities for revolution, for which he was very grateful.

Chapter Six

1987

Rattlesnakes: Lloyd Cole and the Commotions

In formative moments, music maps your brain. Guitar chords connect along your synapses, lyrics silt up your memory, and your emotions are forever Pavlovian when you name that tune. The band destined to fill this role for Fergus was Lloyd Cole and the Commotions. The group was from Glasgow, lanky lads in dark shirts led by a philosophy student whose pretentious lyrics rhymed Norman Mailer with tailor, and namedropped Eve Marie Saint and Truman Capote. Their album *Rattlesnakes* was known in the *NME* as a 'student bedsit classic'. From the bungalow, with the album on a constant loop, Fergus could only aspire to the imagined glories of bedsit life.

Months before May 1987, Fergus had ordered two tickets for the Lloyd Cole and the Commotions concert at the Barrowland Ballroom in Glasgow. Rumour had it that the band was going to break up – so this was his last chance. But now, looking at the date on the tickets, Fergus realised the gig was a few hours after his Higher English exam, and the evening before his Higher Maths. Which was not good. Jennifer Gilles, who was not exactly a genius and needed two C grades to get into college, wouldn't want to be out on the town before her exams; Al had left school and was working late at the boatyard. Fergus was resigned to the fact that he'd have to go by himself. Then Karen MacKay rang him at home. 'Hear you've got a spare ticket to Lloyd Cole on Wednesday. Can I buy it off you?'

'What about the maths?'

'You either know it or you don't by now. So how much do I owe you?'

Fergus felt uncomfortable, but he couldn't say no. Jennifer would be pissed off with him. That was the trouble with Burnoch, the place where your sins and omissions will always find you out, where the same characters kept being recycled. For instance, at Jennifer's sister's wedding the other week, everyone knew that the bride had previously slept with the best man, and her bridesmaid had, over the years, shagged two of the four ushers, not out of promiscuity, but thanks to the limited roster of available partners. And here was Karen again, right in his face.

'I'll see you on the six o'clock bus to Glasgow, then,' said Fergus resignedly to Karen. 'I'm pretending to my mum that I'm round at Jennifer's revising.' He kept to himself during the hour and a half on the West Coast Motors bus, ostentatiously studying sheets of maths formulae. Karen was sitting across from him reading the *NME*, hunched in her denim jacket, her hair over her face.

She was wearing a Commotions T-shirt. She'd copied her *Rattlesnakes* LP on to a tape for Fergus before they had broken up.

They walked down towards Gallowgate from the bus station in near silence, but once they were inside the Barrowlands, pints in hand, Fergus's mood lifted with the sheer thrill of being there at the right moment, the only moment, in the cavernous dark space in the beer-soaked, hot, swaying crowd. He blended in among the skinny jeans, leather jackets and floppy hair; for once he felt part of a tribe. They roared and sang along to 'Perfect Skin', 'Forest Fire' and 'Charlotte Street'. Their stamping feet rebounded on the famous sprung Barras floor.

'It's hotter than auld nick's armpit, ferchrissake,' shouted a drunk man next to Fergus and Karen, and they laughed at him, and danced together, intoxicated.

They had agreed to leave early, to get the last bus at eleven, but how could they when the music of a thousand dull afternoons in their separate bedrooms was suddenly live, loud, and inside their bodies as they danced in the vibrations of the megaton speakers beneath the stage? As the last encore faded, Fergus realised that they would have to hitchhike home. He was so joyous from the music that he was quite unfazed by their lack of transport. They stood on the corner thumbing, falling around and giggling for twenty minutes, but no one stopped for two blootered teenagers by the Barras market.

'Shit,' said Fergus. Karen was starting to look worried.

'I don't know why you let us miss the bus. The morning one won't get us there in time for the start of the exam. And I'm no' standing here all night like a pun of mince.'

She folded her arms, but she seemed more angry at herself than Fergus. 'Fuckit,' she added.

The Barras was deserted now in the orange streetlights. The last stragglers from the concert were gone. The neon stars on the concert hall's front clicked off into darkness.

Fergus stared across the road at the plastic detritus in a skip on a building site, and a plan began to solidify in his mind. What if they were to borrow a car? Not steal, borrow. The police would tow it back to the owners. It would just be temporary. He put this to Karen.

'No way,' she said. 'Don't be an eejit.' Then after five more desultory minutes on the street corner she enquired: 'D'you mean that? D'you know how to hotwire a car?'

Fergus found a long piece of hard plastic from the demolition site and, with Karen as lookout on the corner, slipped round into a deserted side street and slid it down the side of a car window to click the lock on the door. Then he took out his penknife and swiftly fixed the ignition wires together, thanking Uncle Jim beneath his breath. He brought his new vehicle proudly to the corner. 'Get in quick!'

Karen was impressed. 'Could you no' have got us something fancier? A jag or something? I mean, a *beige* Escort? For God's sake.'

'I know how Fords are wired. No choice. Now concentrate on the route home. We don't want to get stopped.'

At first they were terrified of being caught by the police. Fergus's driving was jolting and erratic until he got used to the car. But once they were on the A82, heading down the empty side of Loch Lomond, they relaxed. Karen put on the radio. They drove on, sometimes singing along, for almost an hour.

'It's funny, wonderful really, having your own car for a few hours, having the freedom to go anywhere,' she said. Fergus grinned over at her, complicit, deliciously sealed in their dark box against the night.

Then everything stopped. Their hearts slammed into their ribcages and their necks jerked back. There was a scream, and everything went into slow motion: the dying deer slid down the bonnet and landed with a heavy crump in the ditch. The scrub oaks closed round the Ford Escort. A smear of the deer's blood trailed down the windscreen outside. Karen's face had smashed down on the dashboard. Liquid trickled from her head across the black leatherette.

'Karen?' Fergus said tentatively, and then he shouted, 'KAREN!'

She suddenly jerked into life. As her head sprang back, blood sprayed out from her pale forehead in the moonlight. A memory floated into his head, of the scene he had been writing about that morning in his Higher English paper, when Dracula rips open a vein in his chest with his nail and makes Mina drink the spurting blood from the wound.

'Oh Jesus, Jesus Christ . . .' he said, ripping off his T-shirt and holding it to her head. Fergus was suddenly so shocked his teeth were chattering and his knees were jerking involuntarily. Karen put her hand up into the bloody mess of her brown hair.

'Shit,' she said, staring at her wet red hand. Then she started screaming again.

'It's OK. It's OK. I've got you,' Fergus said, calming her.

Her screams terrified him more than the blood. 'It'll be all right, Karen, it'll be all right.'

He mopped at her forehead with the T-shirt and soon he could see the deep cut clearly, about two inches long and straight across. What was that white thing he glimpsed for a second in the opening of the cleaned flesh? Could it be her skull? He tore a strip off the T-shirt and wrapped it tight around her head.

An expensive black car screamed to a halt beside them. A middle-aged man in a suit got out. A banker, an accountant, something dull.

'You awright, son? You're in a right mess here. You need help?'

At this point it dawned on Fergus that he'd been drinking, nicked a car, crashed it, and injured the passenger. He was about to go to prison. He got out of the car but was careful to stay in the shadows. His brain raced into action. He suddenly developed a heavy Glasgow accent. His fringe fell over his face.

'Aye, my friend's got a wee cut on the forehead. She's awright, but, eh, Ah don't want to leave her. Could youse call an ambulance from a phone box? Is there a village somewhere down the road?' He knew perfectly well there was a village: Burnoch.

'No bother, son. Are you hurt yourself?'

'No, Ah'm fine,' he said ducking back into the car. 'We hit a fucking deer on the road.' He nodded at the man and gestured at the carcass. One leg poked out from behind the deer's head at a weird angle.

'Ah better stay with her till the ambulance comes.' He patted Karen, who gave the man a limp smile.

The man now seemed excited by his mercy mission, and leaped into his car in a dramatic *Starsky and Hutch* manner. Fergus watched his speeding tail-lights weaving wildly in and out along the banks of the loch.

The stolen car was oddly unscathed. The elastic scrub oaks had provided a sort of crash barrier on the bank above the loch. Fergus had flashbacks of Stuart's car tipping slowly into the harbour, but the Ford Escort had settled safely with two wheels in a ditch. Fergus also realised that the car wasn't going anywhere. He was trapped.

Karen was lying back on the passenger seat, pressing on her makeshift bandage.

'I'm going to have the world's biggest headache,' she said, and tried to smile again.

Fergus was relieved to see that blood was no longer spurting from the wound, and that Karen was properly conscious. The red stain on the front of the strip of T-shirt seemed bigger, though. Fergus held his head in his hands. He couldn't believe what was happening: Karen would go to casualty at Kinloch Hospital, and he would go off in handcuffs to the police cells. All because of a fucking deer. Talk about shite luck. He gave a ragged sigh. He slid across the seat and put his arm round Karen to reassure her. He tied the bandage tighter on her head. For what seemed hours, but was probably only ten minutes, he stayed there holding her, saying almost nothing. Through the open door he smelled the seaweed on the loch, the car-crushed grass and bracken, and beneath that Karen's scent, and fresh blood. Fergus was nauseous with fear. Then in the night quiet, they heard the faraway sirens, and the ambulance light swooping and disappearing again as it rounded the distant curves of the loch. It was nearly over.

A look of panic suddenly crossed Karen's face. She pulled away from him. 'Go! Just go, Fergus.' Her voice was high, frightened. 'Run! I'm all right. It's just a cut.'

'But you're—'

'They'll arrest you, for fuck's sake. Go! I'll say I was hitching from Glasgow, make up a name.'

Karen seemed very rational for someone who had a serious head injury, which gave Fergus a sliver of hope. Maybe it *was* just a cut. The sirens were almost upon them now.

Fingerprints, thought Fergus. He took the remains of his T-shirt and rubbed the steering wheel, gear lever, handles, key, and anywhere else he might have touched when he was driving or hotwiring the car.

'Get the hell out of here or you'll end up in jail.' Karen was shouting now. 'Fergus! Go!'

He had a few minutes. The ambulance was nearly there. He could see it following a police car round the far bend, the blue lights reflecting on the water. His body started moving, though his mind had made no decision that he knew of. Fight or flight, and there was no fight to be won here with the police. He grabbed his leather jacket. He looked at Karen, stricken. He put his hand on her shoulder. He kissed her tentatively on the head.

'Go,' she said again, through clenched teeth.

What was there left that he could do? The ambulance would take her now.

Fergus dived into the trees and ran. The forest camouflaged him almost immediately, sucked him into the foliage. It all looked the same, oaks and beech in every direction, then jam-packed with spruce higher up. He knew he must run uphill just until the sirens stopped, when his crashing footsteps might give him away.

It was hard to see in the dark green gloom, despite the moonlight. His feet were moving so fast that Fergus immediately became tangled in some briars and went face first into the mossy roots of a tree. He leaped up, panicking, and kept moving at such speed that the spruce trees rushed endlessly towards him, aiming for his eyes. He held his arm over his face but the sharp branches kept whipping his bare chest under the open jacket. The leafy ground shot away beneath him like a slimy treadmill, and he pounded on, until the sirens stopped.

In the clear and perfect silence of the night sound carried clearly. He could hear his own breathing, the slamming of car doors, the urgent voices. Karen's voice? He hoped so. He couldn't see anything down below by the loch, even though he was no more than two hundred feet above. Now Fergus slid his feet gently underneath the twigs that might crack, and wove his body slowly and quietly under the trees, like he and Jim used to do when they were birdwatching. He moved stealthily now, but always upwards. The doors slammed again and a siren started – the ambulance had gone north to the hospital, but not the police car. Far below, Fergus thought he could see torches through the trees, but he wasn't sure. He was shaking with suppressed adrenaline, and he couldn't break into a run or the sound would carry. He walked in agonising slow motion for what seemed like an eternity, until he heard the police car drive away far below. Then he sat down in the bracken and cried.

*

It was ten miles to Burnoch by road round the meandering lochside, but only five or so directly over the hills. There was no choice – he couldn't be found on the road by that police car. He just had to pray that Karen had kept her mouth shut, or else there wasn't much point in going home. Fergus started hiking and soon he was above the treeline, following the side of an ever-shrinking burn upwards to the rock- and scree-covered ridge. There was plenty to trip over, despite the moonlight, and he soon twisted his ankle in his new Doc Martens, and stood there recovering, looking down on to the white moon path across the loch out to sea. In the distance the hills were grey and the islands were like black lozenges on the water. He would miss the views. He would miss being in the landscape.

Fergus was only vaguely aware of the blisters forming on his feet as he slogged on. There was a forestry track he knew now, leading down through the dead-faced stone cottages of a village above Burnoch, abandoned long ago in the Highland Clearances. There were rustlings in the undergrowth, and he saw the disembodied eyes of a fox watching him. He shivered. But now as he went downhill, the trees were back, slashing at him, and the question of what to do next was unavoidable. He had to disappear.

Fergus zipped up his jacket and stiffened his resolve. But what of Isla, what of his mother? He could think only of himself, not her reaction to him leaving. He had a rush of memories, of when he was small, after his father had died. He was snuggling up behind his mum in bed, against her silky nightgown; he was walking along the harbourside with her as the yacht masts clinked in the wind; he was cooking a Delia Smith recipe for her. But that Isla was gone. She belonged to Stuart now, not him.

A huge roar filled the sky, and Fergus dived, terrified, beneath a tree. He'd thought it was a helicopter, searching for him, but then he realised it was a fighter jet screaming by, on a night mission, low over the mountain. He crossed the burn. When he cupped his hands to sate his thirst, he thought he could still taste Karen's blood, and bent down to wash his face and bloodstained hands in the cool water. It was a subject he'd recently covered that afternoon in Higher English paper II: Explain Lady Macbeth's descent into madness (10 marks).

Now it was about three in the morning, and he could see the lights of Burnoch in a horseshoe surrounding the bay. Soon he was walking stealthily along tenements on the front, and up towards the bungalow, where he slipped his key in the lock. Stuart was snoring away like the pig he was.

Fergus crept into the bathroom, stripped off his jacket, and looked at himself in the fluorescent-lit mirror. He saw a haggard face, with a fresh cut on the cheek, lank brown hair and disturbed, black-rimmed eyes. It was not a pretty sight. His chest was all scratched as though he had been flayed, punished by the trees. Fergus gave a long, shaky sigh, and climbed up the ladder to bed.

The alarm went off at eight. He lay still in the soft morning light, in the softness of his bed, frozen hard with guilt and fear. He tried to conjure up some telepathic message to Karen. Was she badly hurt, or was it just a couple of stitches? It's the hardest part of the head, the front. That's why head-butting works so well. But he should have stayed with her . . .

How could he find out what had happened? Where was she? No, he just had to start the day as normal. He couldn't ring anyone. He couldn't ask any questions. He closed his eyes as a precaution against any tears escaping and pulled the duvet over his head. This was not happening. This never happened. It was time for another ordinary day in the sleepy fishing port of Burnoch.

Isla rattled the bottom of the ladder, all cheery rise and shine, and shouted up to him.

'C'mon, Fergus. You were out far too late studying last night. What time did you get home from Jennifer's, for Pete's sake? I didn'y even hear you come in. I must've been asleep.'

Fergus only grunted from beneath the covers. His mum's head poked up at the top of the ladder. She never usually came up that far, fearing the avalanche of junk on Fergus's floor. She peered across. 'You look knackered, Fergus. I always said you never should've tried to take six Highers at once. Five would've been plenty. What exam is it this morning?'

'Maths.'

'Well, you better get on, then. It's at nine, isn't it? I'll make you some tea and toast.'

'Lazy wee shite,' Fergus overheard Stuart saying, as he wandered into the kitchen. Stuart was picking his nose behind a copy of the *Daily Record*.

Fergus pretended Stuart was invisible, beneath contempt, and grabbed some toast. He was particularly hungry this morning, and the idea of never seeing Stuart again gave him a warm feeling inside. He put on his school shirt and trousers, and quickly packed a small rucksack with his leather jacket, jeans, T-shirts, boxers, driving licence, two paperbacks and his camera and lenses. He put a note for his mother on his bed. She wouldn't find it until she got back from Saxon's.

'I'm away then, Mum,' he shouted. Isla came out of the kitchen, wafting bacon grease, and Fergus gave her a quick hug. She looked surprised. He hadn't hugged her for ages, and he hoped she'd just think it was nerves before the exam.

'Good luck with the maths,' she said, closing the front door of *Marbella* behind him.

Fergus thought he might as well sit the first maths paper, because there was nothing else to do until the bus for Glasgow left at one o'clock, and anything else would be suspicious. He smiled reassuringly at Jennifer, who looked flustered, but his eye was continually drawn to Karen's empty chair – only ten of them were taking Higher Maths. He felt sick, sick with guilt. No one in the class seemed to know yet. The invigilator had said nothing. He found it impossible to concentrate. Formulae merged and collapsed beneath his pen. The questions made no sense.

At lunchtime he went to the cashpoint and took out all his savings. Then stood in the playground with Jennifer and the crowd, listening to his friends wondering where Karen was and chatting about how hard the maths paper had been, until he couldn't bear to be there another second. He grabbed hold of Jennifer and hugged her hard.

'Hey, we're not supposed to get seen doing that in school,' she said, secretly pleased. 'Was your passion running away with you, then?'

'Something like that,' said Fergus. 'I'll call you.'

'What d'you mean? We've got paper two in an hour . . .' But Fergus had gone, out of the Burnoch Academy for the last time. That afternoon, two desks were empty in the school gym for the maths paper.

The bus ride to Glasgow in sheeting rain made him tense: they passed the spot where the Ford Escort had gone off the road, and was now being winched on to a yellow tow truck. The deer had gone, probably into someone's freezer by now. Fergus felt nauseous. He hadn't had any lunch, and the old biddy next to him kept offering him Murray Mints. 'No need to hurry mints!' she would add each time she spoke to him, her false teeth clacking. Fergus wanted desperately to hurry away from there. He considered strangling the old woman and adding to his crimes. Then he tried to take his mind off the journey by reading a paperback Sam had recently given him, but concentration was impossible with things so far wrong. Fergus felt worried and tender about Karen. At the same time he found himself wondering if her family was some kind of blight on his: every time a MacKay and a MacFarlane got together, there were drownings, sinkings and crashes. Fergus stashed the book in his rucksack, and looked nervously out the window, watching the raindrops merge and trickle on the glass.

By ten thirty that evening, Fergus MacFarlane was poised to flee the country. He was waiting at Buchanan

Street bus station in Glasgow, watching someone's hot steaming yellow piss travel slowly towards him from beneath an advertising hoarding for Tunnock's teacakes on the next stand. A tramp wanted fifty pence off him, but the guy was bowffin. He was getting nothing. Fergus screwed up his nose and turned away, fidgeting, shifting his rucksack from shoulder to shoulder, desperate for the all-night bus to come. He tried to look on the bright side: he was away to London for the first time, aged seventeen. He was wearing his black leather studded biker's jacket, which had never been near a motorbike and which normally made him feel brilliant. Plus he was a fugitive. Plus he was shitting himself.

Still, who was to say he'd be connected to the crime at all? He wouldn't be the first teenager to freak out and disappear after a maths exam. It all depended on Karen keeping to her story. He doubted she would last long, talking to the police. Fergus thought about calling Jennifer to find out what had happened, but he'd better wait until he was out of the country. Out of the country! He was going to England, to London for the first time. A layer of excitement covered his fear and exhaustion.

The National Express overnight bus opened its pneumatic doors, Fergus jumped on and smelled his future: a heady cocktail of diesel, new upholstery and old chemical toilet. More than anything, Fergus wanted to sleep. Sam Green, who had travelled a great deal in his youth, had once lectured Fergus on the all-important technique for getting yourself two seats to sleep across all the way down the motorway from Glasgow: 'You go up the back, put your bag on the other seat, and swear someone else is sitting there. Or just swear anyway. If it gets really busy, you kid on you've fallen asleep across the other seat. And if you think you're totally fucked, start talking to yourself. That always sends them away.'

The headlight eyes of the coach went on in the stand. Fergus took out a Co-op bag containing his camera, his other book, a cheese roll and a bottle of cider, and tossed his rucksack in the luggage compartment. Using Sam's patented technique, Fergus kept a steely grip on the seat beside him for twenty minutes; it was the last empty one on the bus. He was going to get a night's sleep, which he needed more than anyone. But then as the engine started snorting catarrh, a lassie in jeans and a biker jacket embarrassingly like his own jumped on and said: 'Is that wan empty?'

'Aye,' said Fergus, giving her a look like she was total scum.

'Oh thanks,' she said, in a silly wee voice. She stank of that perfume Jennifer used to wear, the orange one called Charlie. Fergus felt nauseated. He hated the girl beside him, quite unreasonably. She looked like she wanted to talk, so he turned his back on her. They pulled out of the bus station, up on to the start of the M8 as it went past the Necropolis, with its hundreds of Gothic tombs, statues, crosses and stone columns spiking the night sky. They left death behind, and the grim banks of high flats, the rusty gas tanks and all the concrete crap that poured out of the rear end of Glasgow. As they sped up, Fergus felt the mess and detritus he'd left behind in Burnoch receding. He was on the road at last.

The wee lassie next to him had the brass neck to try

starting up a conversation with him. 'Where are you from, then?' she asked.

'Oban,' he said quickly. He took out his copy of Martin Amis's *Money* and pretended to read. He had a feeling that if he said anything he might somehow incriminate himself. But she was unstoppable.

'Are you going to stay down there? This is my first time, I've never been before, I'm a bit nervous about getting the Tube underground and everything. I'm staying with my big sister's pal in Ealing and—'

'I don't know how long I'm going for,' said Fergus, cutting her short and narrowing his eyes. 'I'm busy reading just now,' he added, thinking, 'stupid cow'.

'Oh,' said the girl taken aback. 'Right you are.'

She sort of shrunk herself even smaller into the corner of her seat by the window, and got out a can of Irn Bru. She'd obviously shoogled it running with her bag, and it sprayed across the pages of his book when she pulled the ring.

'Fucking hell,' said Fergus.

She apologised and then tried to mop the pages with a tissue.

'Jesus. Just leave it be,' said Fergus, and turned his back on her again.

Fergus woke up at four in the morning as they pulled in for a break at a service station on the motorway somewhere in England. He'd crossed the border for the first time, without noticing. He realised he and the girl had curled up against each other as they slept. He had a stabbing moment of regret about his mum and Jennifer. He pulled himself away from the girl's warmth, and she jerked awake. He was starving. He sat alone in the fluorescent glare of the cafeteria and ate sausage, bacon, egg, tomato and fried bread. For some reason those tastes in a strange environment brought back visceral memories of breakfast with the fishermen on the *Dalriada* when he was seven. 'That was then and this is now,' he said aloud, and a man supping tea at the next table stared at him. Fergus was suddenly all too aware of being utterly alone, with no plans whatsoever, and nowhere to stay.

He climbed back on the coach, and the steady speed calmed his agitation. Fergus liked this feeling of riding through the dark, into the unknown, into Victoria Coach Station. He wanted to follow this path through the orange sodium streetlights to wherever it ended at dawn. And at that moment he knew that whatever happened, he wasn't going back. Not until he was rich and could tell them all to go fuck themselves.

𝕭urnoch 𝕲a𝕫ette
May 15, 1987

POLICE IN HUNT FOR CAR THIEF AFTER SCHOOLGIRL HURT
By James Keith

Argyll police have launched a manhunt for the runaway driver of a stolen car. The man, believed to be from Glasgow, crashed the car last Monday on the East Loch, and left his passenger – a Burnoch schoolgirl – bleeding in the passenger seat.

The car, a beige Ford Escort reported stolen in Glasgow, appeared to have hit a deer on the road before it crashed into the bushes. The driver disappeared immediately after the accident.

Police say the passenger, Karen MacKay, 17, of Westwood Ave, Burnoch, was hitchhiking home from Kinloch when the accident occurred on the A83. She was concussed in the incident, and was taken by ambulance to Kinloch Hospital. Yesterday, she was unable to provide a full description of the man, other than that he had dark hair and said his name was Steven.

A passing motorist, who drove to Burnoch to call for an ambulance, saw the driver and told police he had 'floppy hair and a Glasgow accent, but it was too dark to see more.'

The Ford Escort was stolen from an address near the Barras market in Glasgow. Police said no new fingerprints were found on the car. No traces were left by the runaway driver except a paper bag containing half a chorizo sausage. Police have asked anyone who was driving in the area around midnight to come forward to help with the investigation.

Chapter Seven

1987

Money: Martin Amis

Fergus was sitting breathing in the chip fug in the Burger Shack upstairs at Victoria Station. For an hour, he'd been watching two teenage boys at the Formica table in the corner, who also seemed to be waiting, sluglike for time to pass. One kid was maybe fourteen, runty, in tight black jeans, with gelled or maybe just greasy hair, and an earring. His skin was pale grey and he kept worrying a plook on his forehead. The boy had, Fergus noted, put four sugars in his tea, and he was now pouring another two into his mouth straight from the sachet. His hands weren't steady. The other kid was preppy, handsome in a button-down blue shirt, open at the neck, and clean white chinos. They looked wrong together. The older, preppy boy glanced over at Fergus now and then. He reminded Fergus of someone he couldn't place. The boy gave him a friendly nod across the greasy tables. They'd seen him killing time here yesterday. Fergus felt the inside of his stomach curl up. What the fuck was he going to do now?

'Better get started,' said the preppy boy, pointing at the wall clock, and his punkish friend shrugged resignedly.

They went down the escalator to the main concourse of the station. It was five thirty, and commuters were beginning to pour through. From the burger bar windows above, the passengers' ebb and flow was like a perfect dance: their swerves to avoid each other and their formations of lines at the platform gates. Fergus numbly watched: so many people, with so much money, with somewhere to go.

Fergus checked his pockets. He was down to £5.52. He stared over at the destination signs. He couldn't even get a return to the seaside, to Brighton, or Southampton, or Chichester on the train for that. Another cup of tea was about all he could afford. He sat down in the café again, and let the day stagnate around him.

Below, the two boys from the burger bar made too-long visits to the Gents, and then loitered, leaning against the photo booth, watching. An older bald man in a blue jacket with gold buttons came up and chatted to the boys, before walking off with the punkish kid, talking and gesturing anxiously. The preppy guy smoked a cigarette, then wandered off to the Gents again. Fergus took out *Money* and started reading. He felt flat, as though all his energy had been sapped just getting here. The book was all hard-ons, hand jobs, hangovers, massage parlours, slot machines, pubs called the Blind Pig and the Butcher's Arms and it starred a man named John Self. What had seemed on the far side of fiction in Burnoch, here began to have a documentary feel.

Fergus's mind was still in Burnoch, although he'd now been away for four nights. Just staying alive and finding somewhere to sleep safely in London had taken all his energy. But no one had arrested him; possibly no one cared, so he got up the courage to go to a phone box and ring Al to explain where he was. He desperately wanted to know whether Karen was all right.

'Six stitches in her heid, and a beamer, and someone said she missed her maths exam.'

'Aw shit,' Fergus said. He imagined Karen lying to the police and her family for him, and it seemed that he had the easier time, homeless and lost. No exams, no relatives. 'Can you tell her I'll write to her when it's safe? Can you tell her I'm really sorry for fucking up her maths?'

'S' your job to tell her, but I'll pass on the message for now. It's not exactly going to help her get to university and that, is it?' Al was irritated. 'Plus the police were apparently round the school asking people about you. And Jennifer's having a fit. And guess what? They're all hassling me because they think I know something. And now I do.'

'Fuck. I'm sorry.'

'As your mum might say, "sorry's not good enough".' Al laughed, but he sounded upset.

'Look, you tosser, I was worried about you.'

Fergus could only make a small noise because he had a lump in his throat. Al knew what everyone was saying, because although he'd left school to work on the boats, he still hung out with the same crew in the evenings. 'They said Jennifer was crying in class. But apparently Karen sat History yesterday, so that was OK. But what are you going to do, Fergus? Six Highers down the pan. And your mum's going Radio Rental.'

'Uh?'

'Mental. You haven'y been in London *that* long. You're losing it.'

The phone started beeping. Fergus felt relieved as his money ran out. He'd made sure Al would say nothing about the accident, but he didn't trust anyone else. Even Jennifer. He found more change and forced himself to call her. She was going doo-lally, wailing like it was the end of the world. The more emotional she got, the more reserved Fergus found himself becoming. He couldn't bear her hysteria. He said it was just a temporary separation. He blamed the exams and family trouble for his disappearance. He couldn't tell Jennifer the truth, though it must have been blindingly obvious to everyone, because she was the type, he knew, who would blab.

'You were with Karen. You went somewhere with her. Don't pretend to me. I thought we had a proper relationship . . . I thought we'd get engaged . . .' Jennifer's voice disintegrated into sobs. He tried to reassure her, but at the word 'engaged' he felt a huge surge of relief that there were five hundred miles between them.

The phone beeped again.

'I've got tae go. Don't have any change left,' said Fergus, and he detached himself from the receiver and his past with a click. He would miss having Jennifer around, but he wondered if he had anything really to say to her. What had they in common except the cloying intimacy of the town that knew everyone's business? He would not miss that.

Fergus posted an ambiguous postcard of Piccadilly Circus at night to Isla. He didn't want her sending out a search party or anything: 'No deid yet, Mum. Will call you soon as I'm sorted. Love Fergus.' He sat in the café staring at nothing and drafting a letter to Karen in his head, a letter which he never sent. He wondered if his mum would talk to the police. Stuart certainly would, the little shit. But London was a big anonymous place; he was old enough to leave school; and as far as anyone knew, he'd committed no crime.

'You finished that tea yet? You going to lick the cup or something?' A pug-faced waitress started clearing Fergus's table far too briskly. She looked at him in disgust. Fergus wondered if he was minging. He had passed one night on the moulded plastic chairs of Victoria Coach Station, feeling safest where he'd landed, but he hadn't made it through till dawn – it was warm enough all right, but some druggies were hassling him, and he'd walked up to Victoria train station. After all, the station had all mod cons: eating, washing, and even entertainment facilities if you liked trainspotting or reading porn or the *NME* free in W. H. Smith.

All the top tourist attractions in London were out there for the visiting, too. Yesterday he'd humphed his rucksack down to the river, and walked along to Westminster and Big Ben. Big deal, he thought. The buildings looked exactly like they always had on television: shuttered, empty, brown. The Thames was dung coloured and the sky was low and stormy. He'd felt the dull weight of Karen's fucked-up chances adding to his own. He'd lifted his camera, and then let it dangle flaccidly round his neck. Everything was just as it said on the map he'd often studied in Burnoch library and on the Monopoly board. The sights had given him a horrible feeling of déjà vu: he already knew where to turn to reach Trafalgar Square, then

Piccadilly Circus, and The Mall, which they didn't pronounce Moll. The only surprise was the raucous traffic, the sirens, the pollution, and that people sat outside at restaurant tables on the street and shouted over the din, eating dust in their dinner. The city was all throbbing, exciting, but he'd felt cut off from it, estranged. The wildly imagined London he wanted to embrace was closed to him, or perhaps it didn't exist.

He'd spent two foul nights in a shelter just by Victoria, which a homeless guy had recommended. It was a tall, red-brick, blank-eyed building: a human storage unit. There were six beds to the room, like a hospital, but with hairy moss-green blankets and a strong smell of midden overlaid with bleach. A scarily caring man with a beard and a faded Free Nelson Mandela T-shirt had filled out a form with Fergus's details. Fantasising that he was on some 'Wanted' list, Fergus had said his name was John Green and that he was eighteen. The bearded man had just looked at him and said 'Yeah?' resignedly.

The first night, Fergus had tried to sleep in his leather jacket, with his rucksack as a pillow. Old men had loomed in the shadows and the smells of sweat and beer slithered around him. Someone had hawked up phlegm from the rotting depths of his body, spitting it into a paper cup on the floor by the bed. By day, Fergus's only thought had been to escape from this hopelessness, and he had hitched on his rucksack and gone round some pubs and building sites, asking for casual work. He was twitchy, deathly pale, and unkempt: not a pretty prospect for employers, and he'd given off a stench of something – neediness or dirtiness – which merited rejection.

The second night in the shelter, the bearded caring man had threatened to find him a social worker. Fergus had slept heavily this time, however, with three nights of tortured sleep behind him. When he'd woken in the morning, his new Doc Marten's – placed beneath the bed – were gone.

Fergus stood in manky secondhand trainers – a donation from the shelter – on the balcony by Burger Shack above the station concourse, and took his mind off his feet and fortunes by experimenting with fast and slow exposure photographs of the human maze below, the clashes avoided, the individual atoms repelling each other.

'Hey, you. What were you taking those photographs for?' The preppy boy he'd been watching was standing aggressively above him outside the burger bar.

'Och, just took them for myself. For a project . . .' What was the guy's problem?

The preppy looked at him hard, and then relaxed and sat down. 'Thought you were police surveillance or something but they'd never use someone so young. Did you just get here?'

'Eh. Aye,' said Fergus, surprised.

'You look like you could do with a drink.' He gestured to the seat beside him.

'Thanks. Cup of tea.'

'So is that a Scottish accent?' The boy smiled. He had some kind of northern accent himself.

'Uh huh. From north of Glasgow. Came on the night bus on Wednesday.'

The guy went off to fetch the teas, whereupon Fergus

suddenly saw from behind that his chinos were unnecessarily, and perhaps intentionally, tight. This, Fergus thought, explained the fear of being photographed going in and out of the Gents. The interior of London was slowly revealing itself to him.

'Well, mate . . .' The preppy eyed Fergus, his drainpipes and his biker jacket thoughtfully. 'I've seen you around here a couple of times. Have you got yourself a place to stay?'

'S'pose maybe it'll be Centrepoint for a while – that night shelter round here is boggin'. Got my Docs nicked there,' said Fergus, gesturing wearily at his trainers. 'I'm Fergus, by the way.'

'Dave,' said the preppy. 'Pleased to meet you.' Fergus grinned. He was suddenly comfortable, on top of things again, though he couldn't say quite why. He felt, quite inexplicably, that accidents might happen in a good way here down south. That London was the magnetic opposite of Burnoch. Positive instead of negative. Dave and he sat and talked for a long while, about the station, about how Dave had a room in a house just across the river in Vauxhall, where he went when he wasn't busy (doing what, exactly, wasn't clear), about music – Soundgarden and the Screaming Trees, and about Fergus's plans to get a job in a bar or a deli, or maybe work for a photographer. The two of them recognised something in each other: that they were ambitious, looking for opportunities, and that they were both open to almost anything.

'Contacts. You need contacts,' said Dave, who couldn't have been more than a year older than Fergus, but was trying to give the impression of being a sophisticated man of the world. 'That's all that matters in this life.' He leaned forward and spoke quietly. His breath smelled of Tic Tacs. 'Everyone who is anyone passes through this station: businessmen, MPs, journalists, photographers . . . and then all the ordinary folk like taxi drivers and cleaners. You'd be surprised. It's busy, very busy. Specially at rush hour, know what I mean?' Dave raised his brow.

Fergus frowned at him, as though he was a bit deaf. 'D'ye mean you fuck them? For money?'

'That's not how I'd put it, mate,' said Dave, 'but you're spot on. I like to say we provide services, and it's mostly not fucking. That takes too long. Too dangerous these days.'

'Shit,' said Fergus in wonder. He'd kind of guessed that. It was like it said in the book he was reading. He felt both a knee-jerk repulsion and a fascination, reading the entrails of the big city, the stories, the characters. 'And is it lucrative, then?'

'Looo-crat-iv? Lucrative?' said Dave, rolling the word round his tongue. 'You mean what do we make on average? Well, discounting the 10p it costs to go into the Gents each time, it's £19.90 profit, and some regulars pay £30, depending.'

Fergus narrowed his eyes. That was more than he'd got for a day at the deli and it wasn't computing. 'Why's your wee mate in the black jeans eating the packets of sugar, then? Can he not make enough?'

'Oh no, Gary does very well. Looks so young and skinny, see. You wouldn't guess he was sixteen from the look of him. But he's got a habit and everything.'

'Ah. Aye.'

'Anyway, I'm away back to work.' Dave saw that

Fergus's face had fallen. 'You know, we'll be taking a break about seven thirty or eight to go to the pub until we get the late nighters nearer eleven. "Last-train-to-Chislehurst chaps!" ' Dave said, imitating a posh English accent and laughing. 'Yeah, before the punters go home to their lovely wives. You want to come for a pint, then? I'll stand you. You can pay me back when you have the money. Down at the Crown, round the back of the station.' Dave touched his shoulder as he left and a look passed between them that made Fergus both nervous and excited.

Fergus sat and sipped his now-cold tea. It was an offer you couldn't refuse, wasn't it? Especially if you had no other offers. He sighed, strapped on the rucksack again, and decided to kill some time walking out of the station along the endless barbed-wire-topped brick walls at the back of Buckingham Palace. The Queen had a big garden. Miles of royal trees. A fucking huge back green. Fergus suddenly remembered his dad, an enthusiastic Scots Nationalist and republican, singing to him when he was little: 'God save our gracious Queen/Long may she sell ice cream/On our back green.' He laughed out loud, and passers-by averted their eyes. Fergus couldn't quite get used to the fact that in London normal communication techniques like smiling and nodding were considered perverse between strangers.

The front of Buckingham Palace, with the gold winged statue, the clashing-coloured flowers and all that predictable stuff from the telly, was hoaching with tourists. They were dead ugly. Too brightly dressed, with broiled faces from the sun, their passports and money strapped to their bulging stomachs. Fergus wanted to slash the bum bags open, watch the tourists scream, watch the green dollars fly into the air. A scramble for dollars or pounds, like the scramble for coppers after a Scottish wedding. He slid among the fat waddling gawpers in shell suits and bright-white, box-fresh, bucket-sized trainers. Dumb Americans, he thought, all worshipping the royal family and the Queen, their piggy eyes bulging, their ice creams dripping. They looked too Technicolor to be real. Soon Fergus's camera was up and about and focusing close on the details: the overtanned skin, the lipstick gashes, the huge arses – no, a whole series of gloriously huge teal and purple nylon arses! – the money-clutching fear of foreigners. Everyone else had their cameras out too, taking pictures of the red guards in their stupid bearskin hats. Fergus realised he was even more invisible here than in Burnoch. He took what he wanted. Took the piss unnoticed with his telephoto lens. His London wasn't going to be a fake, tourist fantasy.

By the time Fergus got to the Crown to meet Dave and Gary, he was feeling elated and free, though why he didn't know: no money, no home and no job were only the start of his troubles. His new friends were rent boys, not exactly high society. Also, his shoulders were aching from the backpack, so he rested it against the bar and used the last of his fortune on a pint.

Dave and Gary came in, looking frazzled. 'Hi, mate. Police were about to raid the bogs again. Had to move it fast. Though why they fucking bother I don't know. We just go back to it half an hour later.' Dave flicked back his hair a couple of times.

Fergus nodded understandingly, though he wasn't quite sure what a raid entailed.

'I'd buy yous a pint, but I'm all out,' he said.

Dave appeared to have a roll of twenties in his pocket. He bought more drinks, peanuts and scampi and fries too. Fergus wolfed them down. After a pint, Gary wandered off somewhere, probably to score some smack, and said he'd be back at eleven.

'So,' said Dave, pulling up a stool next to Fergus's. 'Wasn't so long ago that I got off the bus myself. Six months ago. Mind you, it was a shorter journey. Manchester. But still. You need a plan of action, mate.' He sipped his pint and eyed Fergus like a prospector, smiled, and flicked back his hair again.

Fergus realised who Dave reminded him of, when he'd first seen him: it was, worryingly, George Michael from Wham! – but a younger version. He liked Dave with his wide-boy chat – the kindness of strangers and all that – but he realised that there had to be some kind of payback.

Dave continued. 'We're self-employed here. No pimps or anything, but we all look after one another. It's safe in the station, but when you take the risk of going home with a john, or you get an S and M freak, well, you know . . . anyway, another pint?'

Fergus nodded gratefully. He felt a huge sense of relief, just at not being alone any more.

Dave sounded like he wanted to convert him: 'See, I do a clean, preppy, classic look but there's guys catering for all tastes: muscle boys and indie kids like Gary. You'd be an indie kid, skinny like that.'

'I'm not applying for a position.' Fergus grinned. He could feel the alcohol relaxing him, comforting him, letting him to float along with fate and chance. He swayed a little. He hadn't eaten anything proper since breakfast. Fergus smiled at Dave again: 'I'm no' against it. It's just that where I come from you don't. Not if you don't want your heid kicked in. And then there's Aids now and all that.'

'Yeah. And there's Trojans.'

'Trojans?'

'Durex, you know. Blowing them's dodgy, but you can't go wrong with a quick hand job, cash on the nail, set you on the road to fame and fortune. Or at least buy you a burger, Fergus.' Dave put a matey arm round Fergus's shoulder for a moment, and went on talking. Fergus felt the first warmth of human touch for four days. Dave didn't freak him out, so why should his way of earning cash? Fergus started asking himself: How weird can it be? How disgusting can it be? You can always walk out.

Dave bought another round. Fergus felt the blood leave his knees and go to his head – or perhaps it was the other way around. Anyway, the bar was lurching a bit and the lights became a smear of yellow, and the bass of the music was throbbing pleasantly up his spine. Dave was looking at him, eyes full of amusement. He was whispering in Fergus's ear about what he did. It was, he said, no different really from doing it on yourself at home.

Fergus stared down at the dead-man's trainers he was wearing. He hated them, and he certainly wasn't going to get back on the bus home wearing them, a failure. What was the point in coming down here if he didn't experience all the possibilities?

'Well, I do want tae get some high-top Nikes . . .' he began.

'That'll cost you an arm and a leg. Or a hand job?' They laughed, Fergus shaky with the knowledge that he'd agreed to go ahead. They drank to it.

Just after eleven, Dave picked up the men, two of his regulars from the city in well-cut suits. The slightly balding one with elephants on his silk tie went into the Gents with Fergus. The encounter was almost silent. It was not as if Fergus hadn't practised the art many times. The yuppie's veiny little penis was erect before the man even unzipped his fly. Fergus grabbed it and thought of England, of new Nikes. He could hear Dave doing the same in the fourth cubicle along. Fergus wondered for a second if the punter was thinking of him, or of happy days at his public school. Anyway, it was mechanical, quick, practical, except that the man was sort of half hugging him and staring at the ceiling. He came. Fergus averted his eyes, handed him some bog roll and kept his mind on the Nikes. The man handed him a crisp twenty-pound note.

Fergus felt simultaneously rich and queasy. He was very relieved that nothing had gone wrong. Dave was waiting for him slouched against the photo booth outside, his eyebrows raised.

'All right?'

Fergus nodded, embarrassed and also flushed with success and alcohol. The catchphrase from *Mastermind* on the telly was going through his head: 'I've started, so I'll finish . . .' he said to Dave.

Fergus pocketed another twenty quid from a weasely estate agent in a striped shirt who asked longingly – before heading off to his wife in Croydon – if Fergus would be there again. Then they loitered by the photo booth with Gary until Dave said the last trains were leaving and they'd call it a day. It was the easiest, fastest money Fergus had ever made in his life. Gary walked off to meet some guy at his flat, and Dave shrugged: 'C'mon. I don't ever go home with strangers like that. It's his funeral.'

They walked out of the station into the night and the neon of Victoria. Fergus was still addled by the drink and flashbacks of the weird experience in the fluorescent-lit toilets.

He was talking full speed and giggling complicitly with Dave, before he noticed they were heading towards the river.

'Thought we were going for some chips,' said Fergus. 'But where's—'

'We're going home. I'm knackered. And you're weird,' said Dave. 'But you can sleep on my floor.'

'Aw, thanks. I wondered.' They walked along into the empty sidestreets of Pimlico, down towards Vauxhall Bridge, watching the warm lights go off in fancy houses with thick swagged curtains, fine wallpapers and chandeliers.

'Just the one night, mate. Then you're on your own. Anyway, you're set up with that forty quid, and there's more where that came from.'

'I'm not sure if I want to do that again . . .'

'Even with me?' Dave had his hand on Fergus's jeans beneath the backpack. They stopped against a curlicued wrought-iron fence. Dave kissed him. Fergus wondered what he'd said or done, what signal he'd given Dave, other than desperation. But in some ways Fergus liked it, this odd sensation of hard skin and stubble, of kissing someone as strong as yourself. There was the unexpectedness of the smell of aftershave and the feel of muscle as Dave lifted off his backpack and pulled him close. There. Fergus had a hard-on too, which he hadn't come anywhere near before with the ugly weirdos in the Gents, and it surprised him. It was worth investigating. In his new life, Fergus wasn't going to exclude any possibility, however peculiar. The physical warmth was intensely comforting in the vastness of the city and the night. Fergus and Dave wrapped their seventeen-year-old arms round each other, and basked in the reflected light from the arched Georgian window above, where a man smoked a cigar, oblivious to them.

By the time they walked across the lamplit river into the tangled streets of Vauxhall, Fergus's heart was beating so hard he could feel it bulging the skin of his chest. As Dave stopped at last before the boarded-up, graffiti-sprayed door of a tall house with the stucco peeling leprotically away, it occurred, rather late, to Fergus that he might be raped, robbed or drugged, or perhaps all three. But he was also desperately excited.

'C'mon,' said Dave cheerfully opening the door into a black hole. 'My room's right at the top.' Going upstairs was easier said than done, because part of the banister was missing, and the treads were rotten, barely illuminated by a weak, bare bulb. Fergus had the uneasy feeling he'd seen a live chicken go into one of the shadowy rooms on the rubbish-strewn ground floor, but he thought it best not to mention it. The words 'voodoo sacrifice' kept going through his mind. The smell was not great either. Fergus detected damp, fried food, mouldering socks, nail-varnish remover, sweat and paint. Dave unlocked a padlock on the door to his bedroom, and switched on a small, dim lamp. His shirts and trousers hung carefully pressed on a clothes rail. There was a portable television with a wire coat-hanger as an aerial, a hairdryer, and on the bare floorboards, a double mattress neatly made up.

'I don't know if . . .' said Fergus.

'I won't do anything you don't want to,' said Dave, and he started unzipping Fergus's jeans.

'Can we switch out the light?' asked Fergus.

He awoke sprawled diagonally across the bed, staring up at a high white ceiling which featured plaster grapes and a worrying damp patch. It had begun to rain, a hot, heavy storm, and yellowish drips were forming on the damp. Dave had his eyes shut beneath long, dark eyelashes. Fergus tentatively touched his shoulder, and Dave stirred, smiling in his half-sleep. Fergus couldn't decide whether he was embarrassed or impressed by what he'd done.

But then, why did it matter anyway? He made the rules now.

'Thought you might have disappeared in the night,' said Dave, rolling over, awake. He reached out to grab Fergus. 'But you're still here, eh?' It was raining, just a little, indoors.

Fergus grinned. The whole situation was surreal. Dave suddenly leapt up, naked, and grabbed a large, black City gent's umbrella, which he unfurled upside down to catch the various drips from the ceiling. Then he threw himself back down on the bed. 'More?' he asked.

They got up sweatily around eleven. Dave stood in his boxers, carefully counting down his seven shirts on the rack and picking one. 'Do you know the theory of the half-life of shirts? A City gent told me it. For every day you wear a shirt without washing it, it has to rest two days on the hanger. Once you've worn a shirt twice, it needs to air four days, and so on. Works. Saves on the laundry.'

Fergus digested this useful information, and put on his only clean T-shirt. They went to find some breakfast. They passed an older white man with dreadlocks at the bottom of the precarious stairs, and Dave nodded to him. The man had reading glasses on and appeared, with some difficulty, to be sticking a long wire through a tiny hole into the glass dial of an electricity meter on the wall.

The kitchen of the squat was barely equipped, and fearsomely dirty. A loaf sat pale blue and furry on the breadboard, and the sink was filled with greasy brown water and mugs. But there was, miraculously, a frying pan, and the fridge threw up a half-open packet of bacon and some grubby-looking eggs.

'Are these still OK to use?' asked Fergus doubtfully.

'Oh they're fresh all right,' said Dave. 'Look out the back.' Where once there had been a manicured garden, there was now a ton of rusting junk, a decomposing salmon-pink mattress, an old bath, and a bunch of chickens pecking at the remains of the grass.

'Stef keeps 'em. The guy with the dreadlocks jamming the electric reading so we don't pay so much. You take the wire out when they come to read the meter. Anyway, Stef started the squat. You should ask him if a room's going. No one'll take the attic, see, with the damp. But in summer it might be OK. You have to make a donation to the SWP though.'

Fergus screwed up his nose, questioning, as he cooked.

'Socialist Workers' Party. He distributes their newspapers outside the tube.' Dave pointed to piles of neatly stacked and tied tabloids out in the hall. 'He doesn't bother us, but . . . I'm probably a Tory myself.'

'Right,' said Fergus, increasingly astounded. He couldn't think of what to say. The eggs were bright-yellow yolked and fresh. They finished up their plates.

'Shall I try to wash these?' he said tentatively, eyeing the evil sink.

'Nah, just throw them in there.' Dave joyfully aimed the dirty plates like flying saucers at an open binbag in the corner. 'We'll get Gary to get some more china today from Woolworths. He likes the challenge of it, stopping it clinking under his Barbour.'

'Barber?' asked Fergus, puzzled.

'Barbour jacket. He got it off some Sloaney John. Lots of pockets, see, so it's ideal for shoplifting.'

Fergus started laughing. While many normal people might have considered his present situation to be unfortunate, Fergus felt brilliant that morning as he walked out into the May sunlight, into the dregs of Vauxhall, to learn the name of his new street.

Chapter Eight

1989
'Pump Up the Jam':
Technotronic

On the nights when the squat went completely mental and smoking bodies were strewn all over the sticky, swirly carpets, Stef would sometimes hypnotise a chicken. As official squat-father, Stef would grandly announce the impending performance over the music, and a small procession would follow him with the nervous brown bird clamped tight under his arm. Stef's girlfriend would then hold the bird, while Stef stared at it deeply, eye-to-eye, his matted dreadlocks trailing on the floor. Then Stef would take a handful of sand from his pocket, and slowly trickle it out in a thin line, away from the chicken. The chicken would freeze and stare at the line on the ground, mesmerised. It would stay there for hours. It made you question your sanity, or perhaps the reliability of your dealer, but it was a natural phenomenon.

On mornings after, when Fergus could remember nothing but his name, the hypnotic image of the chicken would be there, pecking at his brains. He also suffered earworms, an endless loop of Technotronic or Inspiral Carpets thrumming painfully and repetitively in his head. Fergus would emerge gingerly from the duvet, reassure himself that there was no one else on his saggy mattress, check for empty bottles, condoms and discarded pharmaceuticals, and note that he had bolted the inside of his door, which was always a sign that the party had been on the excessive side. Sometimes the blackout moments were retrievable from his camera, if not his memory: photographs of pompadours and peroxide; goths and junkies; leather queens and campy royalists; and, inevitably, Stef's mates, dull crusties with dogs on strings. Fergus's acquaintances were wide, although not select.

Over the months, Fergus's lens focused tightly on the changing cast and dramas of the squat, although his social life ranged increasingly wider: to warehouse parties in Shacklewell Lane and Dalston in the East End, Trip City at the Elephant and Castle, and the raves in the railway vaults by Vauxhall Bridge. He hitched lifts with brand-new friends to barns in Oxfordshire and fields behind the Heston Services for outdoor raves where he melted with women and men into a fluid, chemical happiness which went on until sunrise. He had had no idea before of how much he liked dancing.

Fergus, and sometimes Dave, followed the growing and increasingly smiley e-crowd from party to party, from Labyrinth to Sunrise and Biology. Dave and Fergus's physical relationship had lasted a matter of days, but their friendship had endured. Fergus's curiosity was sated by the experience but Dave was quite insatiable, and his companions, both paying and free, changed weekly if not nightly. Fergus observed it all; he peered over the edge of that world and pulled back. He worried about Dave and the constant shadow of AIDS and the warnings which screamed from newspapers and billboards.

But the party had to go on, and Fergus came home so often at dawn that he entered his own timezone, rising at two in the afternoon, and walking endlessly around the streets of London until he went to work in the evenings at the Black Prince pub near the squat, where he'd found a part-time job. The hours suited his after-hours social life, but the money didn't. Meanwhile Dave was raking it in: 'Why do you work in a pub for peanuts when you could make mad money?' he always said, and Fergus would shrug and explain that nowadays he preferred cash-in-hand to dick-in-hand, that was all, nothing personal. Fergus didn't admit that he was scared and uncomfortable with that kind of work unless he was drunk or stoned. Besides, advised by Stef who was an expert on all things anarchist, Fergus was signing on as well as doing the casual shifts in the pub.

Dave seemed very comfortable with his lifestyle. 'Prostitution allows you to meet classy people that you wouldn't otherwise meet,' he explained one night as Fergus cooked chicken curry for him in the squat kitchen. 'Is this one of Stef's?' said Dave, poking at the meat in the korma with a wooden spoon.

'It was looking a bit peaky. I put it out of its misery.' Fergus laughed. 'It was a fucker to pluck, though. I'm never doing that again.'

They sat down to eat together, a contrasting pair. Fergus was pallid and skeletal, while Dave rolled up his

155

sleeves to display his pumped-up arms and sunbed tan, carefully matched by blond streaks in his hair. 'This is good,' he said, scooping up the chicken korma (which had once been called Henrietta). 'I'm thinking of renting a flat,' he said. 'You could come in with me if you got a better job.' But Fergus knew he couldn't afford it, and suddenly felt leaden and cold at the thought of being alone in the squat without Dave, who'd become, over the months, his pseudo-family. Dave had a deal with some fancy escort agency now (which had resulted in the useful installation of a payphone in the squat), but it was hard to tell where business ended and pleasure began. Fergus supposed that was a sign of a fulfilling job. On the other hand, Dave would sometimes arrive home, looking furtive and upset after a dingo date. He explained it thus to Fergus: 'A dingo date is when you wake up in the morning, you're in bed with someone dead ugly, you can't remember their name, or what you've done. Worse still, they're asleep and *lying on your arm*. More than anything, you don't want to speak to them. So like a dingo in a trap, you chew your own arm off and leave it behind, rather than wake them up.'

Dingos, chickens, snakes: there was a surprising amount of fauna for Central London. The snakes – pythons belonging to the customers – were to be found at the Black Prince, a spit and sawdust pub which served a number of the local Vauxhall estates, and kept its dusty Christmas tinsel up all year to save the bother. The owner had given Fergus the job on the grounds that he sounded hard, 'although you look like a fucking poofter'. Last orders, drink-up time, and altercations outside all went smoothly the minute Fergus opened his mouth. If there was a fight in the Gents, Fergus would go in, hand two towelling bar mats to the participants, and advise them in his finest Gorbals to mop their gore-spattered brows and get out. 'It's a bleeding miracle, mate,' said the owner, delighted. 'Can't remember the last time someone got glassed on your shift.' He was also impressed with Fergus's sleight of hand when sneakily serving beer slops, one of the bar's specialities, and with his timekeeping. Despite his dedication to partying, the Protestant work ethic remained immoveable in Fergus; he was, for only a few hours a day, a reliable employee in the bar. His mother's favourite word 'respectable' still dogged him in work if not in play.

He often thought of Isla when he was talking in the bar to the wifies – as Fergus codenamed them – the lovely, big, boob-tubed, hoop-earringed, pasty-fat, run-down, motherly women from the estates who called Fergus 'love', and were always buying him a pint and a bag of crisps to fatten him up. He missed Isla's warmth, but not enough to return home.

One evening, one of Fergus's regular wifies came in with a mottled brown scarf round her neck. As she ordered her Baileys at the bar, the scarf lifted its head and flicked out its pink forked tongue. Fergus dropped the glass and backed into a wall of spirit bottles.

'S'awright, love, she's harmless. Just a python,' said the woman. 'We breed 'em. Give us some ice in it, eh?'

Fergus was worried the python might squeeze someone – him, for instance. He pointed weakly to the 'No Dogs' sign on the open door, for once lost for words. The regulars at the bar looked up with amused interest, hoping for an argument. Clearly the python was a regular too. The customers had seen Fergus punt obstreperous drunks out into the street, but a boa constrictor was beyond his capabilities.

'Suzy – Fergus, Fergus – Suzy,' said the woman introducing the reptile. 'She's just a baby, only a couple of feet long,' and like a baby the snake settled back down to sleep, drooping like any casual neckscarf. Fergus poured the Baileys with a shaking hand and pushed it across the counter, staying as far back as possible. Thereafter Suzy and her owner came in regularly, as did the snake-woman's husband.

'I've got a little corn snake in me pocket,' the snake-man told Fergus cheerfully one evening, wiggling a zip on his black anorak. 'D'y want a butchers?' Fergus declined. He became used to Suzy, though, almost fond of her. Occasionally, when the Black Prince was quiet in the afternoons, he allowed her a dignified slalom along the bar, in and out of the beer pumps. He took her portrait with her owner. Tentatively, he touched her skin, and her scales were dry and warm, not wet and slimy like he expected. Suzy's owners bred pet snakes in glass tanks all over their flat in one of the high-rises. The snake-man was the scarier of the two, and often would get rat-arsed in the pub with a younger – though no less painted – woman, who was clearly his girlfriend. Then one day the girlfriend disappeared, and the snake-man staggered up to the bar, alone, demanding a double vodka and some sympathy.

'She got me – Suzy fuckin' got me,' he said, taking his

red, swollen hand from his pocket and displaying it for all to see. On the palm and on the back of his hand, there were deep double-fang bites.

'At least a python's not poisonous,' said Fergus, trying to perk him up.

The snake man shook his head, despairing. 'The wife says if we have another fight that Suzy's going to squeeze me. She's gone ballistic.'

'Wife found out about the girlfriend?' said Fergus, raising his eyebrows.

'Yeah. That snake, she's loyal to her owner, see, like, like, I dunno – a Rottweiler or a bull terrier. Protective.'

'Women, eh?' said Fergus, since he knew this was the sort of thing barmen said.

Women. There were women in Fergus's life too, but no one permanent. He couldn't face possession by girlfriends with handbags, lingering perfume and keys after escaping them so recently. Jennifer was a weight off his mind, off his body. And men required no follow up, no commitment, sometimes no names. When the nights swayed and exploded and burst into colour, Fergus ranged across the genders – once, to his surprise, in between them – and chased fantastical creatures and sensations, just to see what would happen.

In comparison, Burnoch had faded into dull monochrome. The weeks passed, and then a year, then two, and there was no going back, no reason. In a lockup in his mind, his conscience occasionally whispered thoughts of abandonment and betrayal, but what could he do? A few weeks after he'd arrived in London, he'd written a long, apologetic letter to Jennifer, but now he could hardly remember what she looked like. He couldn't remember anything interesting she'd said. He thought about Karen too. He owed her, but he had no idea how to repay the debt.

The only person he really missed was Al, and it was hard to keep in touch long distance. Fergus had also phoned Sam Green, rather tardily, to resign. 'Don't tell me anything,' Sam had said cheerfully. 'I know, it was you in that car, and you're out of here. Hope it's working out. There's always a job here for you if for any reason your tail ends up between your legs.'

Fergus occasionally called his mother on Sundays when he knew Stuart would be out playing golf (possibly Stuart's only endearing trait was his joy in golfing in rodding rain, or among vampiric midges). Fergus tried to communicate with Isla; about his job, his friends, her life, but it all seemed to drain away into small talk; she took the jewels he offered up of his new life and coated them with disdain and banality. Nothing was going to go well, ever, she seemed to say. He wasn't sure, but he sometimes wondered if she was just jealous that he had escaped Burnoch at the very age she'd been trapped by it.

Her negativity was all-embracing. Fergus rang her, euphoric, the night after the Berlin Wall came down. 'Have you seen it on telly? The people dancing, chipping chunks off the wall? There's this guy driving a red BMW filled with flowers and girls back and forth through Checkpoint Charlie? The Brandenburg Gate? I wish I was there.' Fergus sighed. He could almost hear Isla's lips pursing.

There was an intake of breath. 'It'll all end badly, you know,' she said. 'Always does in those communist places.'

Sometimes it did end badly around Fergus, but somehow he mostly avoided trouble, as though he'd already had his share. Stuff happened, though: one night when Fergus came round the corner from the pub, he saw two police cars outside the graffitied door, raiding the squat, so he diverted to an all-night club and arrived calmly the next morning, about the same time as Stef was returning from the cells for possession (fortunately nothing worse. Stef had slipped his stash into a loose drainpipe by his window and had to dismantle half the plumbing to get it out later).

Fergus went mental, though, when someone broke into his room and stole his 35mm Nikon and lenses, worth hundreds of pounds, worth hours of his labour in the deli. He was livid that he had been stripped of his eye, his viewpoint, his pleasure, his obsession. He realised how naked he felt without the camera, at once a weapon and a shield. Grimly, he worked double shifts at the pub and lived off bread and pasta and Dave until he earned enough for a secondhand camera and some new equipment. But the loss rankled. He was angry and filled with a bitter determination to push on, to make money, to secure material goods and hold them tight.

He also wanted to kill the main suspect in the crime: Gary, the little punk from the station, always in need of a sub. But there was no sign of him after the camera was stolen. Gary had slipped in and out of their lives and had become increasingly unreliable, gaunt and pale until he faded away completely into rehab – or death. No one knew which. Dave wandered their old haunts looking for Gary for a few weeks, but no one had phone numbers or addresses. People passed through the squat all the time, without ties, and after two years, Fergus became part of the squat's old guard. Friendship was a loose, temporary connection for those who had unhitched themselves from family and history to float freely. Fergus was aware that he, too, could disappear unnoticed any time.

Often he had a lightheaded feeling that he barely existed. He would observe the world from its edges, in silence, not speaking except when necessary until he arrived for the evening shift in the noisy pub. He was trained in the art of enjoying emptiness and his own company, an only child schooled by long evenings in his Burnoch bedroom beyond the trapdoor. Fergus paced the surface of London, sometimes clocking up ten miles a day on his now-filthy Nike high-tops, and observed. All the while, though, he was aware that he was pursuing something, a vision, a way of seeing. He did the obvious: watched afternoon films alone (sometimes entirely so in the cinema) and spent whole days in London's great galleries and museums to get his money's worth. He gathered useful information: the importance of presentation, framing with the eye, and shocking with the new. At least, that's what it said in the glossy, grossly overweight books he read for free for hours in the museum shops. It was much better than lurking in the damp, cold squat with a feeble Dimplex.

Fergus took a particular liking to The Photographer's Gallery across from Leicester Square, and it was here that names like Salgado, Arbus, Mapplethorpe, Meiselas, WeeGee and Magnum came to mean something to him. They were mostly still in a monochrome world, while

Fergus – lacking a darkroom – only took colour now. Yet when he saw Martin Parr's acid-bright photographs of the working classes at play in New Brighton, he thought: Yes! I can do that. I already do that. But how do I make sure people see it? The adrenaline of ambition ripped through him. Fergus became aware of some inexplicable chess move that had to be made, which would take him from the floor of the galleries to the walls. It involved chutzpah, he knew, and a portfolio, which required printing and a huge amount of money in a professional lab. It involved *knowing the right people.*

Fergus began his quest in what he thought would be the right place: Clerkenwell. The run-down, dusty streets were just beginning their revival; warehouses were being rescued by architects and clubs and bars were spreading out to Smithfields, Old Street, and along to Hoxton, like a fashionable stain. Fergus could smell it: the shifting, the success. He took a series of negatives to a long, loftlike building in Clerkenwell, with the words Urban Imaging written in over-trendy lettering outside. He chatted up the girl at the desk, in between her swearing at motorbike couriers in leather jackets, selling film, and reading her horoscope. He liked the atmosphere of urgency, the anxious pacing of the customers, the cocky news photographers in multi-pocketed, military-style jackets, the smell of strong potions and chemicals, the sound of machines printing, and the bright, desperate lights. On his second visit, the girl allowed him in to see his prints being processed, and a spotty geek named Brian (whose skin lived in eternal fluorescent light or darkness) let Fergus adjust the colour on one print, until it was saturated and screamed artificiality.

'That's what I want!' said Fergus, having a eureka moment as the photo emerged from the bath of developer. 'That's what I always wanted.'

'Ewww. Makes that snake look unreal, like a toy or a scarf or something.' Brian-the-geek held it up in disgust.

'Precisely,' said Fergus. 'Can I buy you a pint, Brian?'

Such offers were rare for Brian, and later when he emerged – horribly – into the daylight, Fergus took full advantage of him, pumping him for information about the business, the clientele, the galleries, the newspapers. Brian was a proper drone, however. He knew little, but he knew there were jobs going in the ever-expanding business. Fergus took one: part courier, part processor, part slave. He left his job in the pub.

It was fortunate that Urban Imaging was open until eleven at night, and when it was quiet Fergus stayed on late to experiment in the empty lab, until his eyes were red and his brain light with chemicals. Brian sometimes stayed too, for he had nowhere else to go. Fergus wanted to strangle him, so boring and halitotic was he. But Fergus soon picked up the necessary skills and eclipsed Brian to become the lab manager's choice for the most exacting pieces of printing: the advertising shoots, the glossy magazine work, and the huge prints for galleries. For Fergus, anyone who entered the building was a potential contact or conduit to something better. He chatted to everyone: the photographers, the artists, the curators, gleaning and storing information, making new friends. He took his mixed portfolio – spanning his photographs from Burnoch to

London – round a few galleries, but no one bit. They took one glance at Fergus in his battered leather jacket clutching his portfolio, and dismissed him: a skinny teenager, not a heavyweight. He hardly looked his nineteen years. The rejections infuriated him. He became more determined to get noticed.

One winter afternoon, Fergus was sitting on the high stool at the front counter fending off the motorcycle messengers wanting films developed right this minute, mate, when a man came in who seemed to be from another time and place. Among the Clerkenwell media-types in sloganed T-shirts, piercings and drainpipes, or architects in slick black tailoring, this chap (he was definitely a chap, thought Fergus) stuck out. He was about six feet four, gussied up in a crisp pink shirt with cufflinks, and a dark green corduroy suit, and somehow he resembled a young Labrador. His fair hair was already thinning, but he retained the flushed cheeks of youth, the sort which might turn into the red-veined ones of alcoholic excess later. Toff, thought Fergus. Gay? Maybe. Public school type, definitely. His name, Fergus noted from the invoice, was Charles Wentworth.

So Fergus was not inclined to be particularly charming to this Sloaney buffoon, until he saw the photographs he was handling for his gallery, Flow in Clerkenwell. The photographs stopped Fergus short, made him revise his instant opinion of the man. The images were unlike anything else around. They were disgusting and wonderful, moving and upsetting at the same time. Some were inexplicable and others corny and porny. They were nothing like the work anyone else was handling. They were the sort of powerful photographs that get banned, or merit a bashing in *The Sun*. Photographs that sell.

Fergus introduced himself to Charles, chatted, flirted a little, and hung round to watch the developing and editing. He observed Charles's incredible self confidence, his physical bulk, his silky public school manner. Yet there also was something different about him, something that had made him abandon Chelsea and follow the money and inspiration flooding into the EC1 postcode. The next time Charles came in, Fergus was ready.

In the chemical fug of the lab, Fergus was rolling a door-sized matt print off one of the machines. It was one in a series Charles was having printed up of ordinary people holding up signs revealing their innermost thoughts. This one was of a besuited businesswoman clutching a neatly handwritten sign which said 'I'm desperate'.

'I can do better than this,' Fergus said to Charles, as their heads bent together over the print.

'That's pretty good quality. I want that bit of graininess. I'm happy with that.'

'No, no. *I* can do better. I'm a photographer too. By night.'

'Everyone's a photographer round here,' said Charles dismissively, squinting into a magnifier above a contact sheet.

Fergus whipped the contact sheet out from under his nose, and opened his portfolio out on the table instead. Charles glared at him. Fergus grinned and spread out his wares. There were just twelve enormous colour prints, selected from thousands.

'Take you two minutes to say yes or no to me,' said

Fergus, winningly. Charles looked puzzled, unsure what sort of offer was being made.

But once he studied the photographs, Charles took a great deal longer than that. Conflicting expressions crossed his face as he sifted through the pictures. Fergus, because he was fond of labelling, had given each print a one-word title: *Norman*, *Nikes*, *Lube*, *Gymbag*, *Prong*, *Victoria*, *Quentin*, *Martyr*, *Punter*, *Hen*, *Ashtray* and *Suzy*. Charles made no comment on the work, but fired a thousand questions at Fergus.

'How did you get this kind of access? Those men allowed you to . . . they're smiling at you. Some of them are asleep. It's very intimate.'

'Well, sometimes it's my friend Dave, or his boyfriends, and then it's other folk in the squat or the pub, but over two years. It's taken a while to get exactly what I wanted. The lighting was always a struggle until I got my camera stuff nicked and bought a ring flash instead.'

Charles nodded. 'You're saying you actually live in this place, this squat, among these junkies and weirdos?' He was looking carefully at Fergus's forearms in his white T-shirt, as though track marks might suddenly pop out on his skin.

'Yeah. So?'

'Mmmm.' Charles clearly liked this backstory, although perhaps he found it all too gritty. 'I see. You've had room to express yourself. Time. Freedom from responsibility. I suppose living in a squat rent free is rather decadent, like having a private income, isn't it?'

'I don't know what the hell you're talking about,' Fergus answered. Charles sat back and narrowed his eyes, looked Fergus up and down. A huge smile came across his face. Fergus had a doubtful moment, convinced that Charles was more interested in him than his photographs.

'I'll do you a favour. A week's exhibition. We've an empty slot next month. And we'll give you thirty per cent if we sell anything.'

'Fifty,' said Fergus. 'I heard fifty per cent's the going rate.'

'You are in no position to negotiate, young man. I'd have to talk to the owner anyway.'

Fergus shrugged and snapped his portfolio closed. His heart was thumping.

'Damn it,' said Charles, not usually given to swearing or indeed any form of violent expression. Fergus's confidence had thrown him, somehow. 'Fifty then.'

A few days later, Charles took Fergus out to discuss their deal. He seemed to take an almost voyeuristic pleasure in Fergus's stories, and he suggested they went for sushi in one of the first Japanese places that had opened in London, between two dreary shops in the sleazy end of King's Cross.

'Raw fish? Like oysters?' asked Fergus. They were driving down there in Charles's convertible black Golf Gti with radial tyres and cream upholstery.

'No, sliced. You'll like it.'

He loved it: raw yellowtail and eel and urchin roe and fatty tuna. Charles traded these strange foods for Fergus's tales of strangeness from the lurid planet of the squat. Charles was only twenty-four, it turned out, but he had the gravitas of twice that age. Fergus thought they might have nothing in common, nothing to say, but instead he was having the conversation he'd been having in his head for months, aloud: about images and meaning and techniques, about the truth and falsity of the photograph. Charles challenged him, explained, and listened. It was exhilarating. Going home, Fergus wished he could remain in Charles's world. He also felt a sick rush of envy, an aching inequality, as he sat in the leather seat of the poncy, va-va-voom car. He'd forgotten how much he missed engines, oil smells, revs, specs and Uncle Jim. He'd forgotten how much missed good food. He suddenly ached to own a car, a flat, flash clothes, all the expensive temptations he had been without for so long.

'I live in Battersea, or Chelsea South as people now prefer to call it,' said Charles, 'so I'll run you home on the way.' His face was a joy to behold as he stopped for about two seconds outside the squat, as though its grafitti and metal-gridded windows might contaminate him. Gritty pictures were one thing; the reality quite another.

'Want to come in for a drink?' asked Fergus, genuinely hopeful.

'No. No thank you,' said Charles. 'Absolutely not. They'd slash off my roof in five minutes out here.'

Charles never did enter the squat, but after he and Fergus became friends as well as colleagues – Fergus's exhibition at Charles's Flow Gallery sold out, and he went from risky proposition to solid investment – Fergus often visited Charles's apartment in a converted warehouse over-looking the wrong side of the Thames. It was dead yuppie, the décor dead obvious, but at the time Fergus could dream of nothing more exquisite than the Le Corbusier-style black leather sofa with steel frame, the glass coffee table, the huge black-and-white art photos everywhere, the stripped, polished floorboards, and the fuck-off Bang and Olufsen stereo with four speakers.

Charles's flat was a hard place to quit for the increasingly dismal squat, which Dave had now left for better accommodation. One exceptionally hot early-summer night, Fergus came back to Vauxhall from the urbane world of Charles's apartment and his fancy friends who always brought round 'a couple of bottles of really good claret'. On the second flight of stairs in the squat, he found a dead chicken.

Fergus kicked it out of the way and it hit the landing with a wet thud. A nauseating smell rose from the corpse.

'Fuckit!' he shouted. 'Stef, why'd you let the fucking bird cark it on the stair? And then leave it there to rot all day?'

Stef poked his head woozily out of the room he shared with his girlfriend.

'Just chill, Fergus, yeah?'

'Christ,' muttered Fergus, going up to his room. As he unlocked the padlock, he thought it would be pleasant to live without locks. His room, under the eaves, was filled with hot, fetid air. He lay down on his mattress on the floor, and imagined owning a huge Sleepeezee pocket-sprung bed. He listened to the sirens and polluting traffic outside, and thought of the waves on Macrihanish beach. He stripped off to his boxers and looked at his grey, slightly unwashed skin. He had become a troglodyte, taking the tube every day between Vauxhall and Farringdon, working long hours in the lab's searing artificial light, and only breathing the air when it was dark. He went to the payphone, thinking it would be nice to have a normal phone, found fifty pence, and called Al in Scotland to say yes to his recent proposition.

Kate Muir

THE CORRESPONDENT
March 11, 1990

Other exhibitions worth noting:

At the **Flow Gallery** in Clerkenwell, a small exhibition by newcomer **Fergus MacFarlane** has the stench of the early Martin Parr about it, with its use of hyper-real colour and ring flash lighting, yet unlike Parr, MacFarlane brings a softness and intimacy to these portraits, which appear to have been taken in bedsits or perhaps a male brothel in Vauxhall.

It's all here: the hairy backs, appendix scars, the drag queens, the sad droopy penises, track marks, and Mapplethorpe-style homoerotic musculature of anonymous men. Often they smile at the camera, welcoming the intrusion. This is not about voyeurism; we sense the photographer's intimacy with the milieu.

This type of image has been endlessly essayed in black and white, but this is saturated, tropical colour. London some-times seems like a foreign resort, with the gents' toilets of Victoria Station filled with jolly fellow travellers; the talismanic appearances of live chickens and voodoo snakes; and the parties . . . well, the parties look absolutely terrific. There is a tenderness in this work that balances the grunginess. There is no judgement.

The catalogue reveals that MacFarlane is only 19, and this shows in his repetitive, slightly clichéd, tight cropping, imitating the limited field of a Polaroid. On the other hand, these images are instant, about living in the moment. We assume junkies and male prostitutes are having the worst time imaginable, but this is art predicated on the possibility of pleasure.

Fergus MacFarlane, Vauxhall Viva, at Flow, Clerkenwell Green, EC1, until 17 March.

Chapter Nine

1990

I Know Where I'm Going: Powell and Pressburger

After three years down south, Fergus felt the scales falling from his eyes and the pollution dripping off his once-grey skin into the clean salty water. He could see clearly now into the distance where mottled seals slobbed around on rocks and the spray shimmered in the morning light off the island of Jura. He felt relieved to escape the myopic night-life and walled-in world of London, but it was equally unnerving to be back in Scotland. He was a stranger here too; he noticed his accent had softened and his expectations of people had hardened.

When Al had called, a month ago, offering him a summer job cooking for the boat charters he was running out of Oban, Fergus knew he would not refuse. He physically ached for the views without end, for the emptiness of the landscape. At last he was floating beneath the Paps of Jura, the undulating brown hills that poked like a dinosaur's spine out of the water. He wanted to be here, where the weather mattered, where a storm meant life or death, rather than unfurling a brolly. He'd also missed Al deeply, missed the straightforwardness and honesty of their friendship.

Thus began a brilliant summer working on the open seas, landing on islands Fergus had read about but never seen, having languid picnics on beaches where no one had been for months, walking alone across steaming moors at dawn, and drinking in the rodding rain in isolated pubs with crump-faced locals. Fergus had no idea in London of how much he'd simply missed being outdoors. The photo lab didn't really need him in the lull of summer, so he took temporary leave and returned to his homeland, to the West Coast. But not to Burnoch.

Al was cool to work with: he now knew the coast instinctively and he could smell when the weather was turning. Al had failed every possible test at school, but had sailed through the Royal Yachting Association exams for offshore skippering and navigation. Plus his weight gave him dignity and solidity which reassured the guests on the boat. He also made Fergus relaxed in a way his friends in London, with their constant pursuit of decadence, did not. Besides, for the first time in many years Fergus was healthy: no drugs except for the occasional joint, and steady physical work hauling ropes, picnics and diving paraphernalia for the rich. He was muscled and his T-shirts were sunbleached. He stretched along on the bench seat at the back of the boat and was dangling his head over the water looking for crabs by the pier when he was interrupted by a thud.

'Pluck those pheasants, would you, there's a good fellow. We can have them tomorrow.' Roderick tossed three shot-infested corpses proudly on the deck, and gestured grandly at Fergus. Roderick was one of the eight hunting-shooting-sailing guests Fergus was cooking for this week.

Fergus peered up at the rugby-player bulk blotting out the sun with his gun looming menacingly, and decided you had to draw the line somewhere. Fergus wasn't going to do Roderick's dirty work. He shook his head sadly: 'Sorry, no' on the boat, mate. Skipper doesn't allow it – too much mess. Anyway, don't you want to hang them until they're properly honking?' Fergus stood up and smiled helpfully. 'I'll store them in a big Co-op bag in the larder for you. No problemo.' Roderick wasn't sure whether he'd been dissed or not. He stomped down to his cabin.

'There is a kind of posh Scot that should be lined up in front of his own twelve-bore shotgun and totally peppered,' whispered Fergus to Al in the wheelhouse after Roderick had gone.

'Not if they're paying your wages, you tosser,' said Al.

'Yeah, but they're a pernickety bunch. They all want their pheasants plucked or their eggs done all fluffy with an extra white, or fried sunnyside up, or softboiled to match their soft constitutions.'

Al growled at him. 'That's your bloody job. You're a fine short-order chef, Fergus, but you're rubbish at being diplomatic.' He set course for the short hop across to Gigha.

Fergus was still narked off because yesterday, their first day, the guest yachties had started braying for olive Martinis and Kir Royales in the late afternoon and he'd been at a loss. Edward, the guy who had rented the yacht and its crew, had come to lecture Fergus patronisingly on cocktail mixtures unknown in the Black Prince. Then Fergus and Fat Al had to schlep in the dinghy across to the hotel to beg a bag of ice, and buy bottles of gin, Martini and cassis. They found a tin of out-of-date olives at the Post Office shop. Fergus prided himself on provisioning well, with good food and cans of lager, heavy, and some nice white wine for the ladies, but these guys weren't like the down-to-earth divers he'd been cooking for on previous charters.

The itinerary was better with this lot, though: they were on a week's trip out of Crinan Harbour to Islay, Jura, Scarba, Gigha, Colonsay and Luing, with the guests taking in stops at one or two grand houseparties on islands, a spot of shooting and fishing, and the Oban summer ball along the way. Along with their spanking-new waterproofs, the guests had arrived with kilts and ballgowns which barely squeezed into the tiny cupboards in the cabins of the motor cruiser. Roderick had brought his shotguns in a metal lock-box, which lay temptingly beneath his bunk.

'Prizewinning bunch you've got us this week, Al,' said Fergus, spitting into the water. 'Could've guessed it when I saw their names.'

Roderick, Orlando, Tamsin, Sarah, George (female), Edward, Athene and Duncan had been at Edinburgh University together. They were jolly, and jolly well-connected Anglo-Scots. The haves and the have-yachts. Fergus was irritated by them on sight.

'Well, I love them because they paid us shitloads,' said Al. 'We're earning twice what we did on the dive charters, you know. Just smile nicely, Fergus, because we're providing quality service this time: you're the butler, cook and cleaning lady. Plus the cabin boy.'

'Die, motherfucker,' said Fergus happily. He didn't really care. Indeed he felt carefree. The only shadow looming over him was the knowledge that he had to visit Isla and Stuart sometime soon. In the meantime, he couldn't complain. The cruiser was forty-five feet long and less a gin palace than a seagoing tank: a big white comfy thing built in the seventies with five cabins, fake teak inside, and now-dingy cream leather upholstery. They anchored just off Gigha, a thin, pretty island, only seven miles long. The boat was in the lee of Eilean Garbh or rough rock, which was attached to Gigha by two glorious twin sandy beaches and a ridge of dunes, running up to electric green hills. Fergus and Al started cleaning up after breakfast while the guests went for a walk on the hill above the double bays, to see the views both ways to the Mull of Kintyre and Jura. Al had a cigarette and they sat on the deck, Fergus peeling a bucket of potatoes. The water was turquoise beneath them, perfect but for a few August jellyfish bobbing in the bay. The beach was deserted, except for flying black-and-white oyster-catchers.

'If you were marooned, right, on a remote Scottish island, which one of those lovely, toffy-nosed lassies would you give a good seeing to?' Al gestured at their guests walking on the fields above the beach. The two couples were holding hands, and the other four were straggling behind. 'I like that big Tamsin myself, lovely pair, she'd give you a great time, definitely. The ginger one, Athene, is single though, and George in the hotpants . . . maybe I'm in with a chance with her.'

'Al,' said Fergus strictly. 'You're supposed to be working, not shagging.'

The boat was throbbing white in the sun, and Fergus stripped off his T-shirt, rolled up his jeans, and stretched out on one of the desk cushions, thinking. He would like to be working boat charters all the time, but Al said there was only enough business in July and August.

'Maybe you could pay your way through the winter if you took photographs of cute seals in tartan and hairy cows in misty glens and sold them in galleries,' said Al, laughing.

Fergus snorted. 'And Highland weddings? You're talking to an artist here, you know, not a snapper.' He was joking, and also deadly serious. He knew his career was just beginning in London, and that Charles (when he got back from the villa in Tuscany) would get him more exposure and work. This was really a holiday, and for the moment, Fergus was manic with summer, with the long, light, beautiful days which would be replaced with winter depression and the dark grip of boredom if he stayed on in Scotland.

Suddenly, the peace was disturbed. Someone was calling his name. Two of the female guests were coming down the hill, one waving wildly. Fergus watched. The red-haired one in a sort of white shift (a cutty sark, thought Fergus) was strolling, but the blonde one in cut-off denim shorts called George was running and shouting at him to pick them up in the dinghy. Fergus did all the ferrying. He was a strong, efficient rower and Al was too lazy. Fergus could tell by George's hysterical voice that she'd probably seen an adder sunning itself on the rocks. He rowed slowly out to the beach. He'd hoped they would stay away for longer and give him some peace.

'We saw an adder! On the rocks!' said George getting into the dinghy.

'Really. A big one?' said Fergus calmly.

'Oh my God, at least four feet!'

'I don't think they grow to quite that size . . .' said Fergus. He grinned conspiratorially at Athene, the red-haired one, who seemed less bothered.

'More like two feet,' Athene said from beneath her huge straw hat. 'I don't mind them as much as George, but then I've been to India a lot. Seen many snakes of different lengths and strengths.' She gave Fergus an ironic look, and he wondered if she was flirting with him. He rowed on with his cargo of beautiful women, aware of the tattooed muscles in his arms and his brown back flexing pleasingly as he pulled on the oars. There were definitely worse jobs.

Fergus chatted to Athene – the women didn't seem to be quite so snobbish or worried about the crew knowing their place as the yachtie men did. He was curious to know all about travelling in India in case he ever had the dosh to go there one day. Athene had some kind of business in London where she imported Indian arty stuff. They discussed the adder population and he told her and George the full story of the Revenge of Suzy the Feminist Python. Athene roared with laughter. Fergus decided he quite liked this one.

'Spent my gap year in India,' continued Athene. A gap year, Fergus had recently discovered, was an upper-class codeword for an awfully long late-pubescent holiday. In Burnoch, the only gap years had been on the dole. 'I go to Delhi all the time to get jewellery for my shop in Camden,' continued Athene. 'So it's nice to be somewhere cold for a change.'

'No, this is hot,' said Fergus, gesturing at the sky. 'Too hot at sea for a paleskin like you.' Athene was so pale her eyelids were translucent pink, like the inside of a shell. She would be interesting to photograph close up.

Athene smiled. 'Sunscreen everywhere, large hat always.' Fergus handed her up on to the boat's ladder, holding her white, freckled fingers for just a moment longer than necessary. He let George scramble up by herself.

'Ahoy there, me shipmates!' bellowed an English accent from shore. It was Edward. Fergus rowed resignedly over and picked up the dull couples, Edward-and-Tamsin, and Duncan-and-Sarah. The little dinghy was full and the single males, Orlando and Roderick – who were the sort of men who wore rugby shirts all the time even though they were becoming flabby bankers – were about to be left on the shore.

'Do you not fancy swimming out to the boat?' shouted Fergus, trying to save himself the bother of another trip. 'I'll take your shoes and shirts. And watches.' The young men thought this a top-notch idea, and they piled into the cool, clear water, attempting an ostentatious Tarzan-style crawl to impress the women. Halfway out, Orlando was stung on the back by a jellyfish and crawled whimpering into the boat. Fergus hummed to himself and went down to the galley to get the vinegar to neutralise the sting. Orlando was suitably grateful.

'Full of danger here unless you know what you're doing, isn't it?' said Al with a too-hearty laugh that only Fergus noticed.

Al started the engine. Fergus cooked lunch. A few hours later, as the boat came round the headland towards Burnoch and the horseshoe harbour opened out before them, Fergus felt an icy shiver cross his broiled back. His mood blackened. His thoughts turned muddy and incomprehensible.

'Oh that's a cute fishing village!' squealed George who was sitting with the crowd on deck. 'I love the way they've painted all the shops and houses different colours all round the harbour! What's it called?'

'Burnoch,' said Fergus.

'Burrr-noch, och aye!' said Roderick, imitating Fergus's rolling 'r'. Fergus glowered at him.

'It's where we come from. Me and Al.'

Athene perked up at this. 'You grew up here? It's beautiful.'

'Not so much if you're living there. Mostly it's small. And small minded. And dark as death in winter.'

Fergus stared up at his old four-storey sandstone tenement, looming increasingly large over the water. You couldn't see *Marbella* from here, but you could feel it lurking. He sighed beneath the weight of it all.

'Are you all right?' said Athene quietly to him at the bow. 'You look rather green.'

'I'm going back to see my mum. For the first time in three years since I walked out.'

'Oh, I see,' said Athene gently, perhaps expecting more information, but none came. Fergus stomped off below to check his provisions and write a shopping list for the Co-op.

*

Half an hour later, Fergus had dropped off the Co-op bags at the boat and begun the march up the hill. He felt the sinking suffocation return the minute he rang the trilling bell of the bungalow and stood waiting by the twirly *Marbella* nameplate. His mum came to the door in fluffy pink high-heeled mules and her housecoat – even though he'd rung from Gigha to say he was coming early that evening – and just stood there at first saying: 'Oh my God, Fergus, oh my God, I can't believe it's you.' They hugged, and Fergus wondered if they were both going to burst into tears, when Stuart appeared at Isla's shoulder saying: 'Well, well, look what the cat dragged in. London town not good enough for you now, eh?'

'London's fine, Stuart. I'm just visiting my mum.' Fergus felt his jaw tightening and his head starting to throb.

'The prodigal son, eh?' Stuart said, pretending to give him a friendly clap on the back. 'Short of a few readies, are you?' He stared down at Fergus's fashionably ripped jeans and trainers.

Isla looked like she might skin Stuart alive. Her voice sounded tight: 'Make us a nice cup of tea, would you, Stuart, we've a lot of catching up to do.' Fergus wondered at this point why they both seemed to speak entirely in clichés. Perhaps Stuart's habit was infectious.

The living room was unexpectedly tiny with the half-circle of bile-green rug in front of the fireplace, and the low ceiling pressing down on his head. The telly was blaring in the background and his mum didn't bother to turn it off.

'Sit yourself down, son,' Isla said warmly, and then

launched her interrogation. But his answers to her questions were never good enough. Working in a lab and taking photographs was not, in his mother's opinion, 'a decent job with a decent wage'. He would never get any-where in London, apparently. Fergus got the impression that he shouldn't hope for too much, or be too ambitious in case *things went wrong*. London was expensive, extravagant, and it worried Isla. Presbyterian caution and hard work ran through her veins; there was none of this business of running away to try your luck. Fergus could sense the undercurrents: his mum was angry, ashamed that he'd disappeared.

'Look,' Isla continued, 'all your old friends are doing awfy well. Roddie's at college taking accounting, you know, Kenny's with the forestry, Jennifer's a nurse – lovely girl. I don't know why you . . .' Fergus glared at her, and Isla went swiftly on: 'And Karen's away doing history at Glasgow uni, although she's been home to see her family for Christmas every year, by the way.' The words 'unlike you' went unsaid.

Fergus leaned his head back on the settee and shut his eyes, drunk with the punches.

'Is she here the now?'

'Yes, Jennifer's still with her parents . . .'

'No, I mean Karen.'

But Karen was spending the holidays working in Glasgow, apparently. Fergus felt relieved, and then disappointed. Karen had replied to his letter long ago after the accident, but he felt their conversation – or rather his apology – was unfinished.

Auntie Margaret and Uncle Jim were always asking after

him, Isla said, but Margaret had a bit of angina. As for living in a squat! That wasn't *respectable*, although Fergus was not sure what was so respectable about having a baby at seventeen and then shagging your boss from the shop, but he didn't say anything.

'Squat?' Stuart said sharply, arriving in a sickening cloud of aftershave with the tea and a biscuit tin of Rover Assortment. 'A squat, is it now?' He looked smug and aggressive. 'Druggies and immigrants in the next door room, I'll bet? I don't call that a proper roof over your head. I hope you've thought about the criminal consequences of that, young man.'

'The police aren't after me, if that's what you think, Stuart.' Fergus turned away, ignoring him. 'Mum,' he began, 'I've got to—'

'Oh yes,' she interrupted, a little desperately. 'I need to get your bed ready for you, see, Stuart's been using that room as a sort of office, to store stuff . . .' Fergus preferred not to imagine what stuff Stuart was storing up.

'I can't stay, Mum, I'm working tonight with Al on this charter boat. I've got to cook dinner for half eight and I'm dropping in at the pub to see Uncle Jim.'

A wavering look crossed Isla's face which Fergus couldn't fathom: maybe relief, maybe disappointment that he couldn't stay. Stuart came and sat by Isla on the sofa and patted her proprietorially on the leg, eyeing the high-heeled mules. Sleazebag, thought Fergus, surprised that the sight still made him angry. His mum looked much older than women of thirty-seven did in London: any softness that remained was gone, her hair was lank, she seemed tired, and her fingertips – and, bizarrely, her toes –

appeared to be yellow from cigarettes. The sight made him melancholy; he felt a stomach-dropping sense that he'd lost all connection to her.

'What exactly are you doing on the boat, son?'

'It's a big motor cruiser. I'm cooking and doing everything else Al can't be arsed to do.'

'The ship's cook . . .' She had nodded a lot to herself, rocking weirdly on the sofa. 'Is that your ambition?'

'It's not my "ambition", Mum. It's a few weeks' work. I'm not going to become a fisherman or something. There's no money in it.'

Isla looked hurt. Fergus stormed off upstairs to fetch a bag of books and photographs from his room, and tried not to care about the whitewashing of his black walls and the replacement of his pictures with Thailand tourist posters. How could he have lived in this poky hole under the bungalow's eaves? The squat seemed grand in comparison.

'Look, I'll come by and see you next time I'm up, Mum.' He resolutely ignored Stuart. 'And you've got my number.'

'I think the problem is we don't have your *number*, son,' Stuart said, raising his eyebrows as though he'd been very clever. His glasses glinted. 'We just don't know what you're up to . . .'

'We've had some very odd people answering that phone of yours in London,' interrupted Isla. 'I never know whether to leave a message . . .' She looked like she was about to cry this time. Fergus knew he had to get out of the house. He had to drag himself away from the magnetic field of their negativity.

Kate Muir

'I'm away then,' Fergus said. Stuart nodded and immediately turned up the television, crossed his ankles on the pouffe, and settled back on the grey leatherette sofa.

Isla showed her son to the door, in tears now, speechless. 'Fergus . . . I . . . I . . .'

'I know, Mum. I'll keep in touch this time.' And then he quickly kissed her and left.

Fergus ran down the hill, each step away from *Marbella* becoming lighter. He was simultaneously sad and furious; he knew he'd said the wrong things, failed to connect, but perhaps there were no right things to say. When he saw Uncle Jim sitting on the sea wall outside the Hop and Anchor, with Sam Green having a pint beside him, he suddenly felt euphoric. 'Fergus! You wee bugger,' said Jim as Fergus ran up to him. 'By God you've changed, son. Got some muscle on you at last.' Jim squeezed his arm like a vice.

'Next time don't make it three years till you turn up,' said Sam, hopping up and down and grinning.

Fergus hugged them both, which they found slightly embarrassing. He could see them thinking that he'd picked up strange London ways. But they were full of encouragement, and jokes, and delight at seeing him. And as he left clutching a large wheel of Brie de Meaux – 'it was about to go too runny so you might as well have it' said Sam generously – Fergus thought with relief that he felt truly at home with people like Jim and Sam and Al.

Fergus's memories of the visit clung to him, the way smoke or bacon grease clings to your clothing, giving unexpected, sickening whiffs of the past. The next day, the sky darkened to fit his mood as they motored in to anchor just

186

off Bowmore on Islay. A cloud like an enormous grey cow-pat settled flatly over the island, and refused to budge. In the penetrating, permanent rain, the yachties went on a debilitating tour of the island's eight distilleries, from Lagavulin to Laphroaig. Al, who was in many ways becoming a master tour operator, had arranged for their visit to coincide with a showing of *I Know Where I'm Going* at seven in the Bowmore Hall. Fergus had never seen the 1945 film, a camp classic famous in these parts because of the scenes with Wendy Hiller and Roger Livesey on the nearby Corryvreckan Whirlpool off Jura. Hiller is a sharp-witted English girl who intends to marry an older man for money, Livesey is a penniless young naval officer who turns out to be a Scottish lord, and the Corryvreckan is its ravenous self.

While Al stayed on the boat, Fergus went to Bowmore's village hall-cum-cinema with the worn badminton court markings on the floor. There was a smell of ancient gym shoe, and he sat in the back row of rackety chairs listening to the rain on the roof, away from the now rather drunken yacht guests. Roderick was trying to paw Athene, and Orlando was sitting too close to George. The other couples lolled on one another, the different whiskies fighting each other in their veins. Fergus ignored them all and luxuriated in the film's moody black-and-white photography, the mist, and the cut-glass accent of Hiller, the heroine.

'People around here are very poor I suppose,' Hiller says to the penniless local laird. 'Not poor,' he says, 'they just haven't got money.'

'That's the same thing,' she says. 'Oh no, it's something quite different,' he answers.

The star of the show was the whirlpool, of course; a black, greasy, mass of water circling down a giant plughole. Fergus had never seen the Corryvreckan. According to Al, when Fergus got back on the boat, the plughole photograph was rubbish, and the film had been taken at the less dangerous side of Scarba. The Corryvreckan, said Al, is much more complicated than that, a whole series of unpredictable vortices, tidal rushes and standing waves that they were going to visit on the way back from Oban after the ball. 'Save the best till last.' Al had run summer day trips to the whirlpool all last year, until he'd upgraded to fancy charters.

Fergus had heard tales of the Oban Ball, the Argyllshire Summer Gathering, since he was a kid. The gentry danced all night in kilts and long dresses with tartan sashes, and ate a full Scottish breakfast at dawn, all in that dreary overlit hall. A few days later, Al docked at Oban harbour with hours to spare before the ball, but the women wanted to go into the ladies' powder room at the hotel to fix their evening dresses and their make-up. There was not a big enough mirror at sea, apparently. The gents were getting into their kilts on board. Fergus had never owned a kilt – proper ones were dead expensive. Edward's tartan gave off a strong stench of mothballs, and Roderick appeared to have attached the head of a rotting badger to his crotch area.

'Is that yer sporran?' roared Al. 'Did you shoot it yourself?'

'No, but my grandfather did,' said Roderick, insulted. His slack cheeks flushed in anger.

'This lot? They're beyond parody, aren't they?'

whispered Fergus to Al. 'If this is the Argyllshire Summer Gathering, how come the whole of Argyllshire's going but no' you and me?' he asked, mocking.

'You mean you didn't get an invite from the ball committee? The MacFarlanes of Burnoch are not one of Argyll's top families?' laughed Al. 'Oh dear. Well, you'll have to come down the pub the night. There's loads of folk we know in town.'

But Fergus wanted some time alone, and the boat would be empty all evening. Much as he loved Al, sharing a twin cabin with his every thought and the fleshy vibrato of his snores was hard to bear. Instead, he went for a long walk up the hills to stretch his legs and lose the strange tension that sometimes built up in him at sea. He returned at eight o'clock when it was still light. He settled on the aft deck with a chilled bottle of Furstenberg lager, which he had been saving for this moment, and his book. The dockside was quiet now, but for a few people drinking and laughing outside the pubs in the warm evening. Fergus lay on his back and took a couple of photographs as he stared up at the stone Coliseum glowing in the evening light. Well, it wasn't really the Coliseum but from here, up there astride the hill above Oban, McCaig's Tower looked Roman. In fact, the golden arches of the giant nineteenth-century folly had been built by a local philanthropist and nutter to keep the local stonemasons in work.

As the sky went postcard pink, Fergus read the short stories of Edgar Allan Poe. He'd taken the collection from his old bookshelf back in Burnoch, because he remembered it had a story about the Maëlstrom, the world's largest whirlpool off Norway. Poe would get him in the mood for the world's second largest, the Corryvreckan, which they were sailing to the next day. The story was a Gothic, hysterical description of a man whose hair turned overnight from black to white after he'd clung on to a barrel and survived the ravages of the whirlpool. The book had a pleasant, damp, secondhand smell.

'I became aware of a loud and gradually increasing sound, like the moaning of a vast herd of buffaloes upon an American prairie . . .' wrote Poe of the Maëlstrom. Fergus slugged some beer and continued: 'Here the vast bed of the waters, seamed and scarred into a thousand conflicting channels, burst suddenly into frenzied convulsion – heaving, boiling, hissing – gyrating in gigantic and innumerable vortices . . .'

Fergus was engrossed until he heard a series of wolf whistles far along the dock. In the distance, Athene was attracting unwanted local attention by marching barefoot in her evening dress towards the boat, carrying her satin stilettos. She had obviously walked all the way from the dance hall. Fergus stared as she crossed the industrial landscape of the harbour. Her dark coppery hair flowed behind, matching the corroded oil drums and bollards on the dock, and her iridescent blue dress mimicked the inky sea. Fergus lifted his camera and took a whole series of rust-and-ink photographs of the scene as she came closer. Suddenly Athene was scowling close up through the lens.

'What's the matter?' he said, putting down the camera and handing her on to the boat. 'Did you mind me taking a picture?'

'No, that's not it. I'm really pissed off,' said Athene. 'Those pompous wankers.'

'Who?' Fergus waited. Somehow he wanted to laugh.

'This old harridan in charge of the ball tried to staple napkins to the bottom of my dress *because I was showing too much leg*. It's a handkerchief hem, for God's sake. And very delicate Indian silk. So I said no way and she wouldn't let me into the hall. Jesus!'

Fergus tried to keep a straight face. 'You're telling me that in 1990 the Argyllshire Gathering still insists that ladies have to cover their ankles? For modesty?' He bent down and made a show of carefully examining Athene's hem, which went into points rather like a witch's dress. She did have very good ankles.

'So I walked out. Anyway, I don't know half the dances – that Reel of the 51st one, where they all link arms like teapots, and Hamilton House, never can do that.'

'But were you not trained from birth to—' Fergus was grinning.

Athene looked annoyed. 'I come from Hampshire. You make a lot of assumptions, don't you? Actually, I live in London now. And just because I went to university up here doesn't mean I can dance the fucking Highland fling.' She threw her shoes on the deck and flopped sulkily on to a cushion.

'I'm sorry,' said Fergus. 'You'll be needing a drink, then.'

He opened another beer and handed it to her. They drank in silence for a while, employer and employee suddenly forced to be companions. They were also aware that a conversation alone together was very different from the sort of banter they'd been indulging in all week.

'So what're you reading, Fergus?' said Athene, after

some time. Fergus explained about Poe, the Corryvreckan and the Maëlstrom. 'Go on, then, read me some now,' she said, curling up with her legs under her. 'I like the way your accent sounds.' He hesitated. 'Go on!' she said.

He began in a tentative voice, which became louder as he relaxed into the story and slid into the vortex of the whirlpool. 'The mouth of the terrific funnel, whose interior, as far as the eye could fathom it, was a smooth, shining and jet-black wall of water, inclined to the horizon at an angle of some forty-five degrees, speeding dizzily round and round with a swaying and sweltering motion, and sending forth to the winds an appalling voice, half shriek, half roar.'

'Where did *you* learn about Poe? I've never read any and I studied English.'

'You mean *me*, the simple deckhand? Like you said, you make a lot of assumptions.'

She squirmed, as far as he could see in the twilight. 'I'm sorry, I didn't mean that. I just didn't realise . . .'

'You're right.' He smiled. 'I'm really a photographer, not a deckhand. But here's my further education so far: the secondhand bookshop in Oban where I got this ages ago, and the school of hard drugs and knocks in London. Now let me finish this bit.' Athene looked embarrassed. She was also shivering. He gave her his sweatshirt and read on. 'The vortices or pits are of such an extent or depth, that if a ship comes within its attraction, it is inevitably absorbed and carried down to the bottom, and there beat to pieces against the rocks, and when the water relaxes, the fragments thereof are thrown up again.'

Fergus immediately had a horrible vision of his father's

body being bent and battered and carried to the bottom of the sea. He felt like a pornographer caught in the act, obsessed, indulging in twisted fantasies of the power of the ocean, of drowning and disaster. He shook his head to shift the image, and busied himself taking two more beers from the cooler.

'It's too dark to read now,' he said, his voice flat, cracking. He put the book down and folded his arms against the cold, against the hurt.

'Fergus?' Athene asked softly. 'Is something wrong?'

'No. Yes.' The sympathy in her voice burst open a vein of repressed emotion. 'I suddenly got to thinking about my dad and how he died. He died in a storm at sea, carried down to the bottom like that.'

'Was it recently?'

'When I was eight.'

Athene stretched out her hand and held his, and he told her the story of his fisherman father, his lost love for his mother, his wicked stepfather and his escape from Burnoch. In the darkness it was easy to speak, to explain things to himself as much as to her. And it was good talking properly to a woman, with her different understanding. All he could hear were her quiet questions, the waves licking the boat, and the distant sounds of the revelling town. She was a good listener. He wanted to lie in her arms, to smell the sea air on her skin, to feel secure at last, but a whole set of complexities lay between them. Athene was older; they came from different worlds, different classes. She was like Wendy Hiller in the Corryvreckan film, the heroine from the south with the cut-glass accent. She stayed with him until just before midnight when Al came swaggering along the quay and broke the spell of their intimacy. She quickly stood up to go down to her cabin.

'I don't want you to go,' whispered Fergus. 'I've told you everything and I don't know anything about you . . .'

'There'll be time,' said Athene, confidently.

The other ball-goers were not in good shape the next morning when the cruiser weighed anchor at Oban. Although the boat was being followed by a school of harbour porpoises, leaping and messing about, Edward and Tamsin were so hungover they were unable to leave their cabin, and Orlando kept vomiting discreetly over the side. Al suggested they all go back to bed and not rise until Fergus, now fully apprised of cocktail recipes, made Bloody Marys at noon. (It was important that everything went well on the last day of a charter, so the tips would be generous.) The sea was a little rough, and a wind was coming from the west. 'Perfect for the Corryvreckan,' said Al cheerfully.

Al gave the guests his spiel as they motored past the Garvellachs towards the whirlpool between Jura and Scarba. Like any showman, he liked the crowd nicely warmed up before the main act. Corryvreckan or Coire Bhreacan meant 'speckled cauldron' in Gaelic, but Al said he himself preferred the story of the Norwegian Prince Breakan who had to prove himself to the Scottish princess he loved by anchoring his boat for three days and nights in the whirlpool. Prince Breakan brought three ropes from Norway: one of hemp, one of wool, and one wound of women's hair, 'willingly cut off in purity and innocence', said Al, tapping the side of his nose. Fergus rolled his eyes at Athene and she giggled. Roderick stared suspiciously at them.

Prince Breakan's ropes broke, of course, until only the one of women's hair remained. Then that unravelled too, because one of the virgins was not entirely innocent. The boat was sucked into the whirlpool, Breakan's body was rescued by his dutiful dog, and it now rests in a cave somewhere on Jura.

'Does it surprise you at all that they blamed a woman?' asked Athene.

'No. That's traditional,' said Al. 'Now all of youse get back behind the cabin, because we're going in and the boat may spin.'

Fergus had seen the film, read the book, and now was going to have the thrilling fairground ride. Al had told him that he took tourists to the edge of the vortices off Scarba, and then switched off the engine, letting the boat literally be sucked in by the whirlpool tide at seven knots.

'It's classed by the Royal Navy as un-navigable,' said Al, as the engine went dead. The women squealed in excitement. Bubbles rose mysteriously, sudden patches of flat, calm water, blue-green from the oxygen. The boat slid terrifyingly close to sharp salami-slices of rock at the north of Jura, and then drunkenly over to the vicious meringue points off Scarba, the island at the other side of the whirlpool. Then they began turning in circles. Tamsin and Sarah started screaming. Behind them, a huge standing wave formed, and began, impossibly, to pursue the boat. Al revved the engine to full throttle, and for a moment there was a horrible, grinding sensation of going backwards and forwards at once, until he hauled the boat out to the gentle waters beyond.

In the calm, it was time for another Bloody Mary for all the guests, except Orlando who had sensibly taken to his bunk. Al finished his lecture, explaining that the vortices and waves are caused by tides that turn earlier outside Jura than within the narrow Sound. Beneath the Corryvreckan, there are huge rock pinnacles and deep undersea shelves which force the water to suddenly plunge. 'Of course you sometimes see deer swimming across and those sea-kayakers sometimes paddle through. Depends on your luck and the tide. And your level of insanity,' said Al, stubbing out his cigarette. 'Fergus, for instance, is a good rower. He could probably do it if he fancied.'

Edward put down his drink, excited, and pointed at Fergus. He liked the idea of some local sport. 'I say, I'll give you a hundred pounds, young man, if you row across the Corryvreckan, from here to over there,' he said. Fergus's head jerked up and he stared at Edward. Stuart had called him 'young man', too. Fergus curled his lip. He was infuriated enough to show off.

'Maybe . . .' he said. Fergus and Al held a whispered consultation on the possibilities. 'Tide's turned and it's calming down,' said Al, plotting. 'You'd be improving your week's wages, and if I drop you at that far side, the tide'll sweep you through fast and we'll pick you up, no bother at all.'

Edward, regarding them, thought they hadn't offered enough. 'What about two hundred? How does that sound?' he shouted.

'Two-fifty!'

The last voice was Roderick, who was obviously most keen to see Fergus go down the plughole.

'Done!' said Fergus, digging out one of the new, compact life jackets, just in case. The men were all shouting enthusiastically, but Athene was looking like thunder.

'Stop it. You're so stupid, all of you. And *you* of all people . . .' she snapped in Fergus's face.

The others didn't know what she meant, but Fergus did.

'Me of all people,' he said, staring levelly at her. 'Exactly. I've got to overcome that Mafia death threat hanging over me: "You'll swim with the fishes", haven't I?' Athene turned away in disgust and sat alone on the foredeck, hugging her knees, the hood of her sweatshirt hiding her face.

Fergus had, he realised, been waiting to prove that the sea was governable, biddable, beatable – in the right tide, though. He was so overloaded with the fiction of the whirlpool, the imaginary violence, the howlings and bellowings from fruitless struggles, that the reality seemed mundane. It was less scary than jumping on a rope over a burn, stealing a car, running away, or selling your services for the first time. He waited for the adrenaline hit and then climbed down the ladder into the dinghy.

Al had plotted a line for him, and he stuck to it, running on a green shoulder of wave at the side of the still-bubbling vortex. Fergus even played with the currents, spun the front of the dinghy a little, getting a feel of the powerful forces waiting if he edged further in. He rowed quickly on and it was almost an anticlimax as he was pushed safely through the channel by the tide. There were shouts and cheers from everyone on the boat. Fergus felt an exhilarating rush of confidence: the sea had given him something back. He'd beaten it.

Athene was still sitting silently at the front of the boat, watching through narrowed eyes as a very cross Roderick wrote Fergus a large cheque from Coutts bank. Fergus tucked it in his back pocket and went down into the galley to cook dinner. A while later, Athene left the others on deck and came down to stand by the galley door. Her arms were folded.

'Hello,' said Fergus. 'I thought you weren't speaking to me.'

'I'm not. I thought you were smarter than that.'

'It wasn't really dangerous, Athene,' said Fergus.

'I saw that. But not at first.' She gave an upside-down, awkward smile. Fergus considered the previously impossible: asking for her phone number in London. He took off his apron, folded it, and stood in the doorway so close to Athene he could see himself reflected in her eyes.

'Kir Royales all round to celebrate the end of a great trip!' boomed Roderick popping his head down from the deck. 'Can you serve them up pronto, Fergus?'

Chapter Ten

1991
The Electric Chair:
Andy Warhol

Six months after the boat trip down the West Coast, Athene still kept an amusing group photograph of her friends and the crew above the desk in her purple-painted shop in Camden. The Corryvreckan snap was pinned casually among bills, fire regulations and postcards; no one would have guessed how often she glanced up at the face of the fifth man along, the ship's cook. She was still obsessed by memories of the evening floating in the dark harbour at Oban, by Fergus's lack of convention and his recklessness. She imagined a variety of endings for his story. But he'd slipped away as he cast off the boat's ropes, leaving no trace.

It was sleeting outside, and visitors to *Athene Arbuthnot* with its funky silver sign and psychedelic window display were few. Athene had the heating up full, and felt asphyxiated among the patchouli oil, joss sticks and badly cured leather. She stood on a ladder trying to stack teetering piles of punched-tin lanterns, and wondered if the place was becoming more a soup than a souk with its orange and red silks and encroaching clutter. Her assistant was off with the flu again and Athene felt trapped. A dithering woman came in and insisted on seeing three different sizes of wooden elephants from high shelves, before plumping for the cheapest. Athene's profit margins were huge, given that costs in Asia were so low, but one wooden animal wouldn't pay the rent. The woman insisted on fancy wrap and a ribbon. Athene was just finishing up when an icy gust came through the front door and a dark hooded figure with too many bags entangled itself in the glass-bead curtain. Athene glanced up and dropped the scissors on her foot.

'Fuck!' she said. 'Fergus?'

Fergus's camera bags became snarled with the customer as she left, and he knocked down a stand of shell necklaces. He was flustered.

'Shit. I'm really sorry. I'll help you pick up the . . . I've just been photographing a band up the road at the Camden Palace and I saw . . . so I thought it might be you . . .'

'It is.' Shells crunched beneath their feet. 'Well, I'm very pleased to see you again. Amazed, actually.' She kissed him on both cheeks. Fergus was pale, dressed in black, the ghost of his summer self.

'Um. Great shop,' said Fergus awkwardly. He seemed to be addressing all his remarks directly to the thin kaftan top she'd made the mistake of wearing in mid-winter. 'How's business?'

'Terrible today.' Athene looked out into the empty street. The snow was getting heavier, muting the traffic, sealing them off. 'Have you time for a coffee?'

They sat talking on stools in the back shop with mugs of Nescafé and bags of unspoken tension. Then Fergus spotted the holiday snap on the noticeboard. 'There we all are. Did you go out with him in the end, then?' he asked, pointing at Roderick. 'You went off in his Porsche . . .'

'Ewww, no way,' said Athene. She was horrified he'd even considered that. 'Roderick just gave me a lift. I wasn't interested in him at all. I was more interested . . .' She blushed. 'I was more interested in you.' I can't believe I told him that, she thought.

'And now?' asked Fergus, his eyes bright, anxious, but giving nothing away.

She shrugged, digging herself in deeper. 'Nothing's changed.'

Fergus slid off his stool. He kissed her. 'You might have said.'

'You might have asked.'

On the shop door they hung the sign which said 'Closed for Lunch' and went to bed for a month. In Athene's flat in a dilapidated building in Camden Square, nights slid into days, and days into nights, and sometimes they were not sure whether the grey February light was dawn or dusk. A war in the desert came and went while they were between the sheets, but they hardly noticed. They lived in bed on wine and dried Serrano ham in wax paper from the Spanish delicatessen down the road, and grew thin with hunger to be with one another.

Athene's shop suffered appalling neglect: her assistant was grumpy, her regulars missed her, stock ran out, and she only made it in late in the afternoon, pallid as a life prisoner from time indoors, and shaking with the exhaustion of being constantly in love. Fergus was working as a freelance photographer now, but he temporarily stopped taking assignments and checking in with Charles who'd become his agent at the gallery. Of course, Fergus was still preoccupied with apertures and lenses and film speeds and light, but he had only one subject: Athene. Once he spent a week just taking close-ups of her white freckled arms and shoulders, the next week her lips, the next her spiralling hair, all in the winter half-light that filtered through the attic window. He often worked when she was sleeping, but if she was awake the slow exposure required Athene to stay deathly still, which made her hysterical with laughter. In those moments Fergus loved her so much he could not focus on the living whole without overloading; he had to separate her into manageable body parts like the dead relics of saints, and his photographs took on an uncanny, religious quality.

He worshipped Athene, letting no detail pass him by. He knew how many flecks of brown there were in her green irises, and that one fleck was crescent shaped. With his finger he drew imaginary star signs and constellations – Gemini, Aquarius, Pegasus, the Great Bear and whatnot – between the freckles on her shoulders. No one had ever paid attention to the soles of Athene's feet, but Fergus knew them with the expertise of a reflexologist. Despite his corporeal obsession, he believed their relationship was metaphysical, unlike any of the mechanical ones that had come before.

Athene was astounded by the speed and intensity of it all. She kept thinking about the tiny wax-paper packets of Japanese paper flowers she sold in the shop. You could keep the flat, dry, coiled discs for years, until you dropped them in water, and they expanded exponentially into huge, mad, gloriously coloured blooms.

Her passion crushed her conventional side. Having tried to be Bohemian in a quietly commercial sort of way, she was now really living a life where money, connections, appointments, jobs and even family no longer mattered. Fergus's unswerving dedication to being in the moment infected her. The telephone rang, the answering machine filled, and no one cared. Every glass was used up, so they drank wine from the bottle and each other's mouths. Their clothes were dirty, so they wore none.

Fergus had a thousand questions to ask her, a whole life to catch up on: epic, biographical pillow talk. Athene often thought she had no story; among her kind she was average, one of three sisters raised by a gentleman-farmer and his horsey wife in Hampshire. Athene, sent off to boarding school at eleven, had developed the emotional detachment of those who raise themselves among semi-strangers. Perhaps this detachment was why she empathised so strongly with Fergus, a detachment that fed a ravenous attachment.

'What I like best is the idea of you at Cheltenham Ladies' College. In fact, I get excited by the mere words "Cheltenham Ladies' College", and the green uniform of course . . .' said Fergus, looking through her photo album. 'What did you get expelled for? Cat fighting on the lacrosse pitch?'

'You like a cliché, don't you? No, it was drugs. Some very dull drugs. And then I stayed here in this flat with my big sister and went for the last year to Camden School for

Girls, where drugs were compulsory at A-level.' She smiled, but Fergus could tell it hadn't been that funny.

His wounds were easier to see, on the surface. Below his eye was a short, clean scar which in certain lights looked like a tear. 'Someone glassed me in an argument when I worked in a pub a couple of years ago.' Until Fergus explained, Athene didn't know the term 'glassed' – glasses were *raised* in her circles, not smashed and deployed as weapons. Then there was the long, shiny burn on his forearm. He told her how he came by it, on the hill above Burnoch, on the lookout point where the Scots lit bonfires to warn of approaching Viking raiders, and how he had come home to discover a different kind of raid by a man in slip-on shoes from Stornoway. Then Athene looked tearful. Fergus was touched. No one had ever cried for him before except his mother, and he could barely remember that.

Fergus's tattoos were unlike anything Athene had seen before, even in Camden. The primitive, blue lines seemed to have been chiselled rather than etched with a needle. Between his shoulder blades was a circle with a triple spiral in it, which Fergus said showed the waxing, waning and full moon. Celtic knots wound in a narrow band round his bicep. On the other arm was a clockwise spiral. 'That one represents the sun and the idea of growth and energy . . . well, it depends . . .' Fergus lowered his voice dramatically: 'Near where I lived there are great sloping stones grooved with these spirals. They're prehistoric cup-and-ring marks that let the blood from sacrifices run round and round and then down into the earth.' Athene snorted and traced the pattern on his skin. Men with cup-and-ring marks were a bracing change from men in cashmere.

Fergus had read a book about Celtic symbols, researched what was written on his body beforehand. 'What they mean is fluid. It depends on where you are at the time. Like the swastika, for instance – you'd never have that now, but before the Nazis stole it, it was used across the Celtic world as a cross.'

'It's a sacred symbol for the Hindus, too, which means let good prevail,' said Athene, crossing her legs into a complicated yoga pose that make her look like a naked white Buddha. Then she put her agile legs round his neck. It was the seventy-first time they had made love that month. Fergus had – childishly, he admitted – been keeping a tally.

When Athene had her period, she threw him out into the streets for a day, though he was keen to pursue her anyway. It was strange re-entering the real world after their fantasy in the joss-sticked feminine fug of Athene's flat, packed to the ceiling with ethnic jewellery, swathes of sequinned cloth, batiks and leather pouffes which smelled slightly rancid. Athene made a couple of Indian trips every year. She was a tough bargainer, shipped loads of junk, and also returned with three fat suitcases full of dirt-cheap trinkets, jewellery and bales of silk which often passed through customs as her own. Everyone found her eclectic sense of taste rather loveable, though Fergus privately wondered if the economics for the producers were as charming. Her friends featured pretty little objects from the shop in round-ups for *Harpers* or *Elle Decoration*.

While Athene went back to the shop, her days soundtracked by Bollywood music, Fergus returned to the squat in Vauxhall. He took an earful of friendly abuse from Stef about disappearing without a word. He felt a bit guilty and disloyal, until he noticed someone else's duvet on his bed, and an unprecedented tidiness about the damp room. Stef shrugged. He had already handed it over to one of his mates with dogs on strings. Fergus's unworldly goods were in two black binbags in a locked cupboard, and his photographs neatly rolled in cardboard tubes or stacked in boxes.

'I thought you were going to move on,' said Stef. 'And they're about to serve a repossession order. I had Dave all ready to come and pick up your stuff and keep it at his place. We're taking over an empty church in Brixton now. With a nice garden for the chickens.'

There was an ease of acceptance and departure about the squat; it was a place that celebrated impermanent, risk-filled lives, and Fergus no longer fitted in. He gave Stef Athene's phone number, knowing he would never use it.

Fergus took a taxi over to Clerkenwell to Charles's gallery to drop off his portfolio in the basement. Charles was running his own business now, part photo agency, part swanky gallery.

'Where the hell have you been?' said Charles. He was sitting grumpily at a Perspex table, wearing two scarves round his throat and drinking Lemsip.

'I fell in love. It was completely debilitating.' Fergus could not have looked more cheerful.

'Debilitating?' Charles sighed. 'Debilitating for me, more like. Do you know the number of calls we've fielded? The number of jobs you've missed since that shoot appeared last month in *The Face*? It's not like you're bloody Juergen Teller and can pick and choose.'

Fergus shuffled and stared at his feet. He had an up-before-the-headmaster feeling, which Charles did well, having attended Harrow.

'Now take up your portfolio and walk. I've got you an appointment down at the *Observer* colour magazine. Today. Now. Immediately.' Then Charles relented. 'So who is she? Or is it a he?'

Charles did some therapeutic coughing while Fergus explained.

'Is she Hubert Arbuthnot's daughter?' said Charles. 'Ariadne's sister? I've been to stay with their neighbours in Hampshire. Nice pile they have.'

'I've never seen their *pile*, except in pictures.' Fergus shrugged. 'Or her sister.' He was astounded by the way posh people in England all seemed to know one another. Charles had called a minicab, obviously worried that Fergus, a potential source of income, was going to disappear again.

At the *Observer*, Fergus handed in his portfolio and waited in the fancy foyer. Half an hour later, a wild-haired man with spectacles and cigarette-yellowed fingers appeared, said: 'You're bloody young, aren't you?', and commissioned him to do a story about skinheads and ska music in Bradford. Later that week, with his short hair and a Ben Sherman shirt, Fergus blended nicely into the Bradford night, and slid in for the kill, close up.

One good thing leads to another. Photographs sell themselves in a second – or not – and there was something sufficiently weird and new about Fergus's portraits that meant he kept getting repeat work from two Sunday magazines. He was amazed to be paid in hundreds instead of tenners, in cheques instead of cash, although Charles always took his ten per cent cut. 'You're a loss at the moment really, and a nightmare to administer, but you're also an investment,' said Charles, his eyes glinting.

When Fergus showed him the winter-lit photographs of the dislocated parts of Athene, over four hundred of them, Charles went into overdrive. 'These are superb. If I liked this sort of thing, I would be in heaven right now. Your dedication to the job, as such, is exemplary,' said Charles, as he trawled through mountains of left breasts, freckled arms goosepimpled with golden hairs, and a dozen curving spines. The photographs were beautiful, the colour so muted it was almost black and white. But there was also something macabre about them: the viewer was never sure if the doll-like model was asleep or dead. Athene's eyes never opened.

'Triptychs,' said Charles. 'Big blow-ups.'

'Uh?' said Fergus.

'That's what we'll do. That's what collectors want. A statement.'

And they did, a great deal. Fergus was a little squeamish about hanging his girlfriend a few months later on the walls of the Space Camden gallery (Charles's own gallery, Flow, was full for the year. 'Nothing wrong with spreading yourself around,' he said). When Fergus saw Athene, poster size, everywhere, he felt he had shares in that body; part ownership. Athene was delighted.

'I'm mysterious, unidentifiable, unless someone made an enormous jigsaw. And I love them. It's the first time I've ever felt happy about seeing myself in a photograph.'

Red 'sold' dots appeared under every triptych, and Fergus's confidence grew as the cheques came in. Who exactly was exploiting who anyway? Athene was pleased; she thought at last she had done something edgy and radical – when, in fact, she'd mostly been asleep. Equally, Athene wanted to display Fergus, her new acquisition, not just to her close friends but to London society. Fergus's first outing as a debutant, she decided, would be to a dinner party at Athene's godfather's house.

On the night of the dinner, they took a taxi to Little Venice. 'Well, it's a hell of a house,' said Fergus, standing gobsmacked before the glowing semi-palace, the uplighters in the garden illuminating the pale pink stucco. The building looked serenely over its electric gates and pollarded trees on to the canal filled with shifting reflections from the sodium lights and painted houseboats.

'Cost a fortune,' said Athene, opening the gate, watching him ingest the grandeur. 'But it's worth a lot more now.'

'Uh huh. You can see they've got that kind of money, because they must employ a full-time midget with nail scissors to go round trimming these dinky wee topiaries here.' Fergus poked his foot in the box balls, in five graded Toytown sizes, and also the fleur de lys-pattern hedge, surrounded by clipped mini lavender. He was nervous. He had a terrible urge to take a piss on the topiary. Instead, he pulled a lavender stalk and crushed the smell into his hand.

'Reminds me of Provence,' he said, sardonic. Athene giggled and towed him by the hand up the marble steps. The front door seemed to open by itself, and a short woman in a white apron appeared. Fergus shook the woman's hand cheerily and introduced himself.

'Pleased to meet you. I'm Constanzia,' she said smiling. 'May I take your coat, sir?'

'That's the maid, silly,' hissed Athene.

Fergus immediately knew worse was to come. The hall – which was the size of the whole of *Marbella* – had absolutely nothing in it except an endless black-and-white marble chequered floor and a life-sized sculpture of a running male nude – barrel-chested with long legs and a pitted surface – which, from his endless afternoons in galleries, Fergus instantly knew was an Elisabeth Frink. Big money. They passed other art he felt he ought to recognise, and then a Lucian Freud painting of some businessman, possibly their host, on the landing. Fergus felt intimidated, and slightly aggressive.

'We could have a quick one on their super-king-size bed, and then do a runner with the Freud over there, if that's what it is,' he whispered to Athene, biting her earlobe on the stairs. She giggled, worried about what Fergus might say or, worse, do. But she also wanted everyone to see this creature she'd captured, this visionary stranger with scars beneath his black T-shirt and narrow-cut deadman's suit from Oxfam.

They entered an enormous space filled with braying people and brocaded furniture. The ballroom? wondered Fergus. Do big London houses have ballrooms? Athene spun him round playfully. 'Come on, I want you to meet everyone.' In such fine company, Athene seemed to grow taller and grander. Her bias-cut silk dress rippled as she crossed the room, greeting everyone, air kissing like an espresso machine. Fergus was sure her voice had become posher, horsier, more likely to say 'hyme cyntehs' than home counties. He was sore afraid. He needed a drink. Someone in an apron, this time male, stuck a tray with glasses of pink champagne under his nose.

'Thanks,' said Fergus. 'I need that. I'm Fergus. And you'll be?'

'Ronaldo, sir.'

'Thanks, Ronaldo,' whispered Fergus, feeling he had an ally. Ronaldo, his humanity at last recognised by someone, pursued Fergus's glass all evening, refilling it gratefully. The results of this were ugly.

While Athene chattered, Fergus stood silently beside her occasionally nodding and staring up at the walls. Over the white fireplace hung one of Warhol's canvases of the electric chair. Fergus was awed by it, and impressed that the family wanted to live with it daily. Sometime soon Fergus was being sent to photograph Death Row in Texas. He had applied for his first passport only today. He wondered how his magazine pictures could compete with this icon, the dark blood-red photo-print of the electric chair with its black leather straps dangling, wires, and welcoming arms? It made him almost dizzy, the huge emptiness of the concrete execution chamber with the chair sitting way back, waiting.

Fergus swayed a little. A tiny, barrel-shaped, highly perfumed man had taken Fergus's hand between both of his and crushed it in an alpha male way. 'We are delighted to have you here this evening. Lots of the younger generation are here tonight, including you. We heard about the exhibition at Space Camden and Athene says . . .' It was Lucas Koons, their host, the famous advertising mogul and art collector, and Athene's godfather. (He turned out to be one of her many well-connected godfathers, including the one in The Lords, and the Sainsbury.)

A column of purple velvet interrupted and bent down to shake his hand. At about six foot three in her heels, she was the tallest woman Fergus had ever seen, a species apart. 'We saw the reviews and we're just dying to see your exhibition! I'm Annabel Koons, so pleased to meet you . . .' and so it went on – Fergus meeting one person after another, Ronaldo pursuing him doggedly with the champagne.

Fergus realised these people were made of different stuff, Teflon-coated with money against age and wear and tear. In Burnoch, older people wrinkled and their teeth fell out. Here they grew blandly smooth, and their teeth whiter. He began chatting to a funny flapper-type, a performance artist, and then realised only by her references to historical events that she could easily be his mother. But she looked in her twenties, like him. Not a wrinkle on her bare golden shoulders, skin soft as . . .

'Fer-gus!' Athene was alert to any encroachment on her territory. 'Come over here and meet Harry, he's an old mucker from Edinburgh. Deals in antiques.' Athene left them as Harry enquired as to Fergus's roots.

'Burnoch? Oh yes, some top-class shooting round there, isn't there?'

Fergus nodded, finished his glass, snarfed a lot of passing foie gras (which he hadn't tasted since scraping the tins out in the deli in Burnoch), and stared bemused at Harry, wondering why on earth a grown man would wear mustard-yellow trousers. With a red silk patterned waistcoat. Like Rupert Bear.

Harry said, politely: 'Yes, yes, it's coming back to me, the Frazers – you know, the Kensington Frazers – have a marvellous estate round there with that tiny castle, well, it's really a manor house with pretensions, frankly, some very good furniture though, and they have those extraordinary black sheep.'

'Black sheep in the family?' asked Fergus.

'No, no, vanity sheep: "*pour animer le paysage*".'

'You what?' Fergus scratched his balls. The Oxfam suit could have done with a clean.

'*Pour animer le paysage*. To animate the landscape. The black sheep look amazing dotted around when you go up their drive.'

'Does no one here have just the one house, then?' Fergus started to stir it. He couldn't help himself. The guy reminded him of Roderick on the boat.

'I'm sorry?'

'Does everyone have second homes? You must be very thankful they're not in Wales, then. They still say "Come home to a real fire", don't they, when the nationalists torch them? Is that a worry?'

Harry looked round desperately. 'This is not quite the place for that, old chap. Ah, there's Eugenia.' He leapt away, bellowing 'Eugenia!' across the room.

'Cheerio, Rupert,' growled Fergus, aware he'd gone too far.

'That's not Rupert, that's Harry,' said Athene. 'Rupert's over there.'

'I know it's Harry, but he is in fact dressed as Rupert Bear. Anyone could make the mistake.' Fergus was trying to suppress his laughter. It all seemed absurd.

'Anyway, we're going through to dinner,' said Athene, pushing him towards the door. 'You've done well, you've got Annabel Koons, I just peeked at the *placement*.'

'Why is everyone speaking French?' asked Fergus.

'Stop teasing,' said Athene. 'I've got my eye on you. Do you know how important Lucas Koons is in the art world?' Fergus shrugged, but she had a point. She was whisked away into the dining room by a young Thatcherite MP with foppish hair and a pinstriped suit, waffling on about the great, egalitarian leap forward of the poll tax.

Fergus followed them through, thinking it best not to discuss the poll tax here, that his mum and Stuart paid much the same tax for their bungalow as the Koons did for a palace. Their first-floor dining room overlooked the moonlit canal and the table was a stage set, glistening with silver and crystal in the candlelight, and scattered with pink cabbage roses which gave off an overblown, end-of-summer smell. When he'd lived in the squat, Fergus had stared through windows like this at night and seen the glow of the rich partying; it was surreal to be at the other side of the glass.

There were twenty places with name cards written in silver copperplate, and to make it more complicated, Koons announced that the men would all move two seats down after each course. Fergus wondered if you carried your own cutlery around. An exquisitely beautiful woman, maybe a model, was leaning across Fergus talking to Annabel Koons. Fergus noted with amusement that her artificial breasts stood out like two newly baked brown baps.

'Anyway, we just came on tonight from the *Vanity Fair*

Bafta party and Alice T. said: "I can't believe you've got somewhere better to go than this", so I just smiled enigmatically. I didn't say it was you, Annabel – then she'd have been insulted not to have been invited.'

Fergus nodded cheerily and said nothing. Dead good seared scallops, though. Maybe even wee queenies that had come from Loch Fyne. Suddenly Fergus felt very far from home in a way he hadn't in the squat or alone with Athene. He shouldn't be among these people at all.

Eugenia, who was sitting opposite – (and had previously been described to him by Athene as 'a rattling bag of calcium dripped into a dress') – enquired politely as to how he knew the Arbuthnots. 'I met Athene on a yacht in Scotland,' said Fergus vaguely. He could hear his accent softening, his words sounding clearer, more English. He was slightly ashamed. Ronaldo was there at his shoulder again, faithfully tanking up his wine glass.

'And what do you do?' Fergus said politely, noticing the extraordinary length of Eugenia's pale pink-lacquered nails, a handicap for manual labour.

'Ooh, busy, busy, this and that, though it's been a hard month for me because my daughter insisted, just insisted at thirteen, on going off to boarding school. I was devastated, of course, but she couldn't be happier, though the regime's not quite as lax as she'd like it. Ha ha. No, Bedales is marvellous, they let her keep her pony down there, and she can hop on the train to London for the weekend.'

Fergus pulled on his ear and tried to think of what knowledge he could offer in this area. 'Yes, we had boarders from the islands at Burnoch Academy, and the social services put them in a sort of bed and breakfast, so it was pure brilliant because they could go out on the town all weekend and get bevvied and their parents never knew. Plus they could smoke whenever they wanted. We were dead jealous. I can see why your daughter fancies it.'

Wrong, wrong, wrong. Eugenia's mouth was hanging wide open, and Fergus stopped speaking. It was puzzling how rich people had no fillings. Eugenia ended the conversation swiftly, leaving him with a view of her bony shoulders, and focused her whole attention on her dinner companion at the other side. He wondered if she didn't understand his accent. If they'd talked about art, or photography or even books, he'd have had something to say, but boarding schools that took horses were beyond him.

Fergus watched all the faces blur, feeling the wine inside him, and just sat listening to the tinkle of crystal and cutlery, and the cut-glass accents criss-crossing, leaving sentences in the air.

'. . . wanted to be a sculptor but I was drawn back to the estate when my mother died; it was almost a visceral thing and it had been so badly run for so long. I hardly have time for my work now, especially with the sculpture garden,' sighed a man's voice, which segued into someone else saying: 'There's nothing worse than a family fight about property, is there? You can see the point of primogeniture after a while, can't you?'

And from the elongated, glittering woman opposite him, whose body swam in and out of focus: '. . . having a Range Rover. People are always teasing me about my car, my armoured car, my armoured life and it makes me sooo cross. But buses? Buses are full of germs and I'm absolutely phobic about going underground, darling.'

Yet Koons was interesting. Koons was talking about Cindy Sherman and other photographers in New York, but Fergus was too far away to join in. He was rescued when the seating swap came round for the sweet course – or pudding, as Athene preferred to call it. He staggered round the table and was sandwiched between two beautiful twentysomethings, one of whom had designed the Koons's front garden below.

'D'ye make much money doing that?' enquired Fergus, practically. 'D'ye come and do all the trimming of those wee box balls yourself?'

'No, I design. I don't do aftercare.' She looked rather disdainful.

The other woman joined in. 'I started this little course at Chelsea Physic Garden and I've realised I love plantsmanship. I've just done up our garden, took me months, and Edward' – she nodded over at this point to a sleek, balding man twice her age, smoking a cigar – 'Edward was so pleased he said I should think of doing it professionally . . . but, you know, how would I manage the houses and the dogs?'

The words 'sell 'em and shoot 'em' were on Fergus's tongue, but he choked them back. He was thinking how much more at home he'd been dancing to ska music among the skinheads of Bradford the other night.

'So did you come down from Edinburgh with Athene last year?'

'No, I came down from Glasgow on the bus.'

The two women smiled patronisingly, as though he'd missed the meaning of something.

'And how did you end up becoming a photographer?'

Fergus, garrulous and increasingly reverting to his native tones, proudly told them the story. In full Technicolor, from Victoria Station to Space Camden. He covered squats, drugs, raves, rent boys, chickens, pythons, old Harrovians in Clerkenwell and his luck at meeting his latest subject, Athene.

The women looked disbelieving and utterly fascinated. 'You worked with rent boys? Prostitutes?'

Fergus thought he'd better be discreet. 'Aye. Well, when you're young and fresh faced you get a lot of offers – from older women, too, by the way – so my mates made a bit of money here and there. Why not?' He smiled charmingly at them.

By now the women were way out of their comfort zone, unsure whether they were being offered something, or whether the mickey was being taken. Athene had been watching the deteriorating scene from across the table, and announced, like some Victorian heroine, that she felt faint and needed a little air. She thanked the Koonses and signalled desperately to Fergus to come with her. He did. She ran down to the front door and slammed it behind them outside.

'How *could* you?' she screeched.

'How could *you* have made me miss that big strawberry meringue thing they were having?' said Fergus. Athene looked furious. 'Could what?' he asked, sheepish.

'Get so pissed. And start talking about Ruperts and rent boys at the table. We're leaving.'

'I didn't say I did it, you know. I kept it vague. Anyway, they were a bunch of snobs.' Ronaldo popped out with Athene's coat.

'Hope to see you again, sir,' he said, smiling.

'Definitely. Definitely, Ronaldo my man,' said Fergus, slapping him on the back.

'What will people think? I feel so ashamed.' Athene had little pink spots of anger glowing on her cheeks, and her eyes were livid and bright.

'Ashamed of what? Ashamed of me? What do you think I am? I can't turn into someone else. I had nothing to talk to those women about.' He waved down a taxi and they got in. He tried to take Athene's hand in the back, but she slid across the seat and jammed herself up against the window, silent.

'Well, if you won't speak I will,' Fergus burst out, almost yelling. The taxi driver turned round to enjoy the moment and almost crashed into a BMW ahead. 'I'll tell you, I've been with some useless wankers in my time, but this lot are in a different league. They're all unemployed, aren't they? All those so-called artists and gardeners and wives. They're all sponging off inherited money. Apart from the ones who've made their fortune exploiting halfwits with advertising. You've got to respect that, at least.' He punched hard down on the seat between them.

Athene sounded like she might cry. 'If you don't like all my friends that means . . .'

'I don't like you? That's not true. You know that.' Fergus stuck his head in his hands. 'Look, I'm sorry.'

'Why are you so angry?' asked Athene. 'You're always angry.' The taxi driver ostentatiously switched off the intercom, though he was still listening through a crack in the window.

'Oh come here.' He pulled her into his arms and he

could feel her tension deflating. 'I don't mean to be like that . . . it just builds up sometimes. Anyway, it's not you, it's them. I like your other friends, your mates, just not "society", as you would say. I kept thinking: these are not my people, I don't belong here. They were so old, even the young ones. Anyway, what can you know of anyone in one evening?' Athene nodded.

'Actually, you can know something,' continued Fergus. 'Eugenia was, as you predicted, "a rattling bag of calcium dripped into a dress". What a nightmare.' Athene was laughing now. 'I'm sorry you got a bad scene from *Pygmalion*,' said Fergus.

'You know a lot more than you let on, don't you?' said Athene.

Fergus grinned and didn't answer. The taxi pulled up outside the flat and they slammed the door and walked up the path. Fergus held Athene in her silk dress against the peeling paint of the communal stairwell and began to kiss her, too desperate to walk four flights up to the flat.

Chapter Eleven

1992
'Drop-kick Me, Jesus, Through the Goalposts of Life': Bobby Bare

Fergus was sweating nervously, shiftily eyeing the security guards. Not that he'd done anything wrong yet – it was just the first time he'd ever been in an airport, his first flight on a plane, aged twenty-two. How ridiculous, he thought. Even bloody Stuart Meek's been on a plane. Yet words like 'visa waiver form' induced a mild panic, and he nearly threw a tantrum when they tried to put his new film through the X-ray machine. A sniffer dog found him very attractive, perhaps detecting ancient traces of drugs on his backpack. Steady, laddie, he told himself. His heart palpitated as if it was on amyl nitrate. Just follow the signs, just follow the Departure signs, and no one will notice you're a total numptie. For God's sake, there were toddlers with roll-along pink Barbie suitcases who were world-weary travellers compared to him. Fergus lined up at the gate for Houston, Texas, his mind and stomach churning in purgatory between exhilaration and fear.

The fact that Fergus had not been on a transatlantic flight so far was obviously a tribute to early poverty, but also to his recent success. He'd been working almost non-stop in London for *I-D*, and a new magazine called *Dazed and Confused*, as well as *The Face*. He was riding the wave of grunge, as one of the portrait photographers who instantly conferred 'junkie chic' as the critics put it. Rather than glossy studios, he photographed models and rockstars in shabby bed and breakfasts in Kilburn; therefore he was not travelling to Caribbean beaches for the weekend. And now he was being rewarded by the *Observer* with a trip to Death Row.

Once Fergus was in the air he was fine, flying to America, the United States of America, to the great open land of his imagination peopled by Kerouac, Joseph Heller, Tom Wolfe. And all the films he'd ever loved: *Paris, Texas*; *The Godfather*; *Psycho*. Plus the great photographers: Cindy Sherman, Diane Arbus, Gary Winogrand, Dorothea Lange, Ansel Adams. He looked down upon the Atlantic from the ice-blue empty skies and understood the sea in a different way. He was no longer a surface creature, a fisherman. His point of view was that of a god. He felt the dead weight of his culture and history melting away, to be replaced by a heady anticipation of freedom. He wondered if some of his ancestors, the poverty-ravaged MacFarlanes who went across this same ocean to America after the Highland clearances, had felt the same.

After a Taco Bell dinner and a feverish night in a plastic airport motel, Fergus cruised out of Houston in a big Ford Thunderbird sedan, almost unflummoxed by driving on the opposite side of the road – around Burnoch the roads were mostly single track, with no proper sides to be taken. Roundabouts were very disturbing – a vortex swirling the wrong way – but he liked the way the traffic lights swung on wires in the endless sky. The maps were simple in this spacious, recently designed country. No poky, wee corners, so there was no getting lost, and soon he rolled off the freeway near Huntsville and stopped in front of a long, low, red-brick building, identifiable by its guard towers. The whole package was wrapped around with barbed wire. At the entrance, the Stars and Stripes and the Lone Star flag flew together.

As a first experience of America, it was beyond bizarre. His assignment was a photo essay on the first factory on Death Row. The factory was a sort of sweatshop, a tailoring department for new prison uniforms, in which trusty mass-murderers awaiting execution were allowed to play with enormous scissors – and supposedly no one got hurt. As Fergus walked down the rows of metal cells to the factory, a roar followed his progress. He was fresh meat, amusement for those who spent twenty-two hours a day caged. Great bears of men offered to fuck his sweet ass, and other more exotic propositions. The aggression was palpable and the smell of contained male animal was enough to make him gag. The convicts' bunks were within two feet of the cell toilets. 'Smell builds up over the years,' said the warder, shrugging. He held up a Perspex riot shield as they walked the gauntlet. 'You don't wanna get spat on,' he added cheerfully.

On the day Fergus arrived, there were over three

hundred prisoners on Texas's death row, the biggest in America. There were serial killers, violent rapists, murdering paedophiles and innocents. Fergus knew there had to be one or two innocent men: the slow, inarticulate ones with useless state-supplied lawyers; the ones who had been misjudged or framed. Whatever their crime, they were going to fry – or, rather, die by lethal injection, strapped to a hospital trolley, which he'd see later. Here, the electric chair of Warhol's day had been declared too erratic and gruesome for modern tastes. Fergus was relieved – for purely artistic reasons. He didn't have to battle with Warhol's image in his head.

A prisoner in a white boiler suit was coming along the corridor, handcuffed and flanked by two guards. He lunged at Fergus and the warden as they passed, growling. Fergus slid by against the wall. It was strange that he'd been more nervous getting on a United Airlines jet than he was photographing killers in a state penitentiary. Once Fergus was working, his mind shifted off into another plane: non judgemental until afterwards. When interaction with the subject was required, he became a malleable everyman, a chameleon to suit all tastes. He reduced himself to a ruthlessly efficient eye.

Through the security window, the sweatshop looked oddly normal: the whirring sewing machines and the black, white and Latino men bustling back and forth with patterns and bolts of cloth. Some were trimming thread with giant tailor's scissors, others finishing seams, or lurking by the coffee machine. In the middle of the room, one sad-looking man was imprisoned in a zoolike glass cage, a sort of office, while around him everyone moved freely. 'That's the guard,' explained Fergus's warden. 'But it's safe to go in. No injuries yet, and just a couple of fights that the prisoners broke up themselves.' Fergus smiled weakly, and hefted his cameras. His own guard was packing what looked like a Taser stun gun, and he remained beside Fergus like a stick-on Peter Pan shadow as they entered the factory. Fergus felt some relief at this: close up, the convicts, with their tattoos and aggressively shaven heads or scars, looked like the sort of people who might, at any moment, cut off your balls with pinking sheers and stuff them in your mouth.

They had nothing to lose. Yet the factory manager appeared at Fergus's side to say production was up, amazing considering the labour was unpaid. 'They do it for the privileges, to get out of their cells,' he said. He seemed a little irked that in the last few years he'd lost twenty-one of his best tailors to lethal injection with potassium chloride. All that training gone to waste.

Fergus put down his cameras and wandered over to one of the workbenches, sat down on an empty chair (perhaps a recently dead man's chair, he thought) and started talking to the men. The guard hovered at his elbow.

But the men were keen for any available distraction, desperate to tell him stories, enlist his help with appeals, to conjecture about the contents of last suppers, and to discuss where, exactly, Scotland might be. They could not have been more forthcoming, and there began a comparison of prison tattoos. Lots of the men had one blue teardrop tattooed below their eyes – they explained it was to mark a death in the family while they were in prison. Others had Crips gang insignia, and many forearms were tattooed with a giant intertwined T and S, for Texas Syndicate, one of the oldest prison gangs. Yet more had white supremacist signs, swastikas, which they showed unworriedly among brown-skinned fellow tailors. Clearly the factory was a neutral zone.

Fergus joined in, took off his shirt to display his Celtic tattoos, and one of the convicts did the same. Then another. 'Can I photograph that?' said Fergus, poring over a back matted with symbols, made at great risk by artist-convicts with a homemade tattoo gun.

'You don't want to be caught with a tattoo gun in a cell shakedown,' said a serial killer helpfully.

Soon a picture began to emerge: the bare skin of lost men bearing the names of lost women; the white prison uniforms, the colour of mourning in the Far East. The practical tools of the trade, the comedy-sized scissors, the gang insignia juxtaposed with the womanliness of neat sewing stitches. The tidy, orderly, TCI logo – Texas Correctional Industries – and the tidy, orderly waiting for death. 'When someone is executed that morning, we ask for a moment of silence,' said the manager. 'Then we switch on the machines again.'

The production line of death, thought Fergus, as he drove to the Walls Unit in the centre of Huntsville, where the executions took place. It was a red-brick building with guard towers opposite the Dairy Queen. A huge white clock on the front told the time of death, exactly. Inside, another guard took him through to the final holding cells, with their Day-Glo orange bars. Beyond that was the death chamber with a hospital trolley bolted to a white pedestal on the floor. Alone, Fergus worked the room. Fat, tan leather straps lay across the padded bed, waiting to hold a man still as he receives the slow intravenous drip of death. Fergus lay down on the bed and took pictures from the prisoner's point of view: the ceiling, the fluorescent lights, the tubes, the drips. A shiver of horror passed through him.

Released into the humid, eighty-degree sunshine, he realised he was shaking with the intensity of the experience, and the lack of food. He wandered over to the Dairy Queen and sat on a stool up at the counter. The white-bread waitress with her ponytail and her pert little Dairy Queen uniform was just like every waitress in every American movie. Fergus smiled familiarly at her, because she was familiar, and ordered a quarter pounder bacon cheddar grillburger basket with fries, and a creamy DQ strawberry soft-serve milkshake. They were mighty good, he thought, his head filling with the vernacular. So he got to talking with the waitress, who had a plastic badge with the word 'Loretta' on her breast. Her father worked in the 'correctional business', but so did everyone in town.

'Hey, even the Dairy Queen sometimes does last orders,' said Loretta. 'For the prisoners. You know what I mean?' Fergus nodded. 'That grillburger basket you're having is popular. And sometimes they'll order three flavours of milkshake before they go . . . well, why not?'

And then an idea came to Fergus, as he remembered all the talk among the convicts about their final meals. He went to the phone by the restrooms and called the press guy at the prison to ask for information on last suppers. Fergus found it slightly creepy that they actually kept a list of the meals. 'We have to. For the costings,' said the press guy. He was, given his job, very helpful and upbeat, and said he'd photocopy the information on the meals of thirty dead prisoners, and leave it at the gate in half an hour. 'Most of 'em like to order in from local restaurants,' said the officer. 'Makes a change from prison food.'

So it was that Fergus toured the gastronomic hotspots of Huntsville: Domino's Pizza, Taco Bell, Popeye's, KFC, Jack-in-the-Box Drive Thru, Schlotzskys, and asked them each to provide, precisely, the contents of the last suppers. He laid the food out like a Dutch still life, and photographed the meals carefully with a garish flash and reflectors that he knew would make everything look brightly toxic. Then he neatly wrote out each dead man's name with his chosen menu: 'Cheeseburger (extra cheese, pickles, onion, lettuce and salad dressing), tray of French fries, bottle of ketchup, twenty-five fried breaded shrimps, four cans of pineapple juice, two banana splits, bottle of Hershey's syrup, and one jar of apple butter jam.' Or 'double-meat cheeseburger (with jalapenos and trimmings on the side), vanilla malt, French fries, onion rings, ketchup, hot picante sauce, vanilla ice cream, two Cokes, two Dr Peppers, and a chicken fried steak sandwich with cheese pickles, lettuce, tomatoes and salad dressing.'

Someone else had ordered 'nothing', so he photographed that. Another wanted 'one cup of hot tea (from tea bags) and six chocolate chip cookies'.

Exhausted, Fergus ate and drank the contents of the last photograph – a family-sized deep-pan four-cheese pizza with hot pepperoni and extra mushrooms, with a sixteen-ounce green Gatorade – and got into the car. He knew he had two stories, one for the magazine on the factory, and one for himself on the garish horror of the last suppers.

Blown up big, on a white wall, with the contents neatly listed.

Fergus felt an intense relief as he left Huntsville, not merely because of the citizens' smug comfort with execution, but because it had in an odd way the same stultifying, small-town feel of Burnoch, except that here there was no escape out to sea. No breath of wind, but, instead, flat land that went on for ever, and trees that suffocated cars in green tunnels. He had hours to kill before he had to be at the airport, and hours more to hanker for Athene, to suffer the continuing withdrawal and the anticipation of reunion. The rented Thunderbird had a swampy suspension and steering that made him feel he was driving a waterbed. But there was still the thrill of the open road. He would go the long way round to Houston airport. In Huntsville, he saw signs to Crabbs Prairie and Galilee. They seemed as good places to go as any – they had great names. He took Route 1791 and shot through the nothingness of the suburbs, everything low, mean and jerry-built as though crushed flat by the hand of a malevolent god.

But then the road ran wide, straight, and invitingly empty through the woods. Fergus felt a rush of pleasure, lay back in his seat, pressed hard on the accelerator, and flicked through stations on the radio. He landed on what must have been a Christian-cowboy channel: 'Drop-kick Me, Jesus, Through the Goalposts of Life', was the song, by Bobby Bare. Fergus was overjoyed. He picked the chorus up immediately and sang along with the righteous brothers and sisters in Christ. He turned on to Route 1375, and the road sped out of the forest on to a bridge across a huge loch. Lake Conroe, said the sign, next to one advertising: 'Waterside Condos: Cissy Pillow Realtors – a Truly Personal Service!' The water stretched blue for miles down in the direction of Houston. Fergus drove on the pontoons across the lake, walking on water.

He flicked the radio tuner and spotted something on a classical station. He knew nothing about classical music but he recognised the Hovis theme tune from the telly; that advert where a little boy walks down a northern terraced street. But the notes went on, and on, deeper and more complicated, minute after minute of trumpets and horns, all seemingly celebrating in victorious crescendos the expansiveness of America and the open road, and the words of Kerouac came back to him from the bungalow's attic in Burnoch and he at last understood them fully. He truly sensed 'all that raw land that rolls in one unbelievable huge bulge over to the West Coast, and all that road going, all the people dreaming in the immensity of it'.

Fergus felt his throat tighten up with happiness. He was free of the final holding cell of his past. He existed only in the immense future.

'That was Dvořák's Symphony No 9, op 95, *From The New World*', said the radio. Of course it was. It had to be. Fergus grinned. The Thunderbird was straining to go, and he let the speedometer hit a hundred miles an hour, across his new world.

Chapter Twelve

1994
Trainspotting: Irvine Welsh

'As Thomas Hoving, director of the Metropolitan Museum in New York, once said: "Art is sexy! Art is money-sexy! Art is money-sexy-social-climbing-fantastic!" ' Charles whispered at the gallery door, incandescent with delight. His face and his tie were pink and shiny, but his suit was cut with an awesome sharpness. 'Come in, come in! Look around you, Fergus.'

The place was hoaching. Maybe two hundred people were packed into the Flux Warehouse in Hoxton, part of Charles's expanding gallery empire. The conversation crashed over Fergus, the great living hum, hubbub and intermittent flashes of a party at its peak. And although it was his exhibition opening, Fergus looked round with a sense of total dislocation. Who on earth were all these over-perfumed, over-confident, older people? Why were they here? And, more worryingly, was it necessary to wear a lobster hat like that indoors?

He felt like an actor dropped into the wrong scene. Where was Athene? Where were his friends? He folded beneath the force of the crowd's strident sociability, the nakedness of the networking, the power of money. Invisible in black jeans and a black T-shirt, he could feel himself shrinking to the size of a small dot on a screen before it switches off and disconnects.

'Come on. Spurf up!' ordered Charles. 'It's your big moment, and you're an hour late. Although it is amusing to make an entrance. Ta dah!' He propelled Fergus into the room. As they walked in, Charles's height and bearing drew attention to them both, and a quiver went through the crowd. It parted, Red-Sea style, to let them pass, and then congealed around Fergus, greeting, touching, kissing, desperately connecting with his access to *the thing*, whatever the thing was, that was now.

In an out-of-body moment, Fergus could imagine what the party would look like from above, the waves of people parting before him, and then whirlpooling round him. His photographic memory dredged up the human patterns and trails in the slow-exposure shots he'd once taken above the concourse of Victoria Station. That was seven years ago, another life, but Fergus felt he was still the same man, the same boy. He ached to disappear, to be behind his camera: a watcher, not a participant. He stared, half fascinated, half horrified, at the way the gathering focused in on him, and not on what was on the walls: his photographs.

Did they know these were Iris prints on 100.5 cm × 154.8cm Somerset Velvet paper? Did they know each one cost a bomb to make? That he had spent night after night fiddling with the colours so they would come out in these old-masterish subdued browns, dingy reds, greys, off-whites and lemons? That he'd paid each prostitute, upfront, the going rate for half an hour, and contained his photo-shoot to exactly that time, no more, no less, just like a punter? That during the months he'd taken this series of pictures, he'd thought constantly about his own few, desperate weeks in that world of paid-for pleasure in the station, of the uncomfortable feelings he grew to have about himself, his knowledge of physical mechanics and the sheer, humbling weakness and desperation on both sides? No. They just knew Fergus MacFarlane was a 'now' designer label. Dirty and edgy, but designer. The 'sold' dots by almost all the prints proved this.

It had been a simple idea. One winter day, with nothing better to do, he'd gathered all those prostitutes' cards and stickers from red phone boxes around King's Cross and Camden. Dozens of them. Each a perfect fantasy advertisement, with tacky typefaces and tiny glossy photos of Madame Sabrina Your Dominatrix; English Rose; Naughty Charlotte; or traditional offers of Two-Way Corrective Massage and Lesbian Babes. He phoned and turned up at the door of each girl, offering to pay for photographs instead of sex. Sometimes pimps turned him away, but lots of the girls were bored, up for it.

Naturally, no one looked at all like their calling card, which often showed women of a different nationality or skin colour, or were photocopied from porn mags. The blonde English Rose, for instance, had a strong Polish accent that day, although the other Roses on other shifts were, she said, proper Cockneys. 'The punters don't come to chat much, so it doesn't matter,' she added helpfully. So Fergus showed the prostitutes Polaroids to reassure them as he went along and took sympathetic, near-sepia portraits of thin, lost women on old floral bedspreads;

dominatrices too tired to whip; and garishly made-up girls that might have been thirty or thirteen. The prostitutes chose how they wanted to be photographed – naked or clothed, parodying their advertisements or denying them. He used the same upright format as their cards, and blew the original adverts up, glossy and blurred, so that they were as huge as his photographs. Side by side he displayed the fuzzy fantasy and the high-definition seedy, proud, reality. 'Broken Promise' became the title of the exhibition.

The heat and the gushing were incredible. Fergus only felt safe once he'd downed two caipirinhas. Charles was operating at his shoulder, like a royal courtier, introducing him, moving him on, hissing names in his ear as each guest approached.

'The Guggenheim Foundation's director of corporate development. Kiss ass now,' whispered Charles. 'A whacked-out last year's model – watch, don't pose with her for the photographers.' Then, 'Hoving in at the left in the white dress, the editor of *Vogue*, ooh look, with a Saatchi. Smile, Fergus. Two for the price of one.' There were photography critics that Fergus actually wanted to meet, an arts presenter from late-night television, a batch of junior Freuds, a Greek shipping billionaire now shopping, artists from Brick Lane, and a rockstar couple from Notting Hill whom Fergus recognised from the papers, carrying a trophy baby in a leather marsupial-pouch. Oddly enough, on first acquaintance, they all *adored* his work. And said so, breathily.

After a while, it became pleasurable to ride the great wave of adulation. Fergus felt completely warm and wanted in a way he hadn't felt since his early childhood, except with Athene. He drank more and more and wondered: if you can't be appreciated and loved by your parents, then maybe you want to be loved by everybody. And guess what? You don't have to love them all back.

At last Athene appeared by his side, basking in his glow, draped in a gold lamé number that only she was aristocratic enough to pull off without looking like one of the whores on the walls. He held her cool hand. Fergus felt the room rearrange itself around them, and more flashbulbs went off, capturing the couple together. 'Charming. Bit of quality, bit of rough,' said Charles, watching. 'Can't go wrong with that.'

Fergus scowled at him. 'It's not about bloody photographs of me and Athene. It's about the photographs I've taken.'

'Yes, of course. I don't know what made you think otherwise.' Charles slipped shiftily away.

At last Fergus found his friends by the bar: other photographers, colleagues from *The Face*, the *Observer* and the *Sunday Times* mag, a couple of students from Goldsmiths, a guy from Urban Imaging, and Dave, resplendent in a slick suit with Brian, his toy-boy turned barrow-boy turned city-gent partner. Fergus hugged Dave, feeling a relief that earthed him back in the squat, in his history, himself. Dave's blond highlights were particularly resplendent, and his partner was well impressed by the big price tags on Fergus's work, and said so. Fergus grinned. He liked the direct approach. Ten grand was ten grand, after all.

In the background, Fergus could hear Charles, chatting up the editor of *Vogue*, 'Britain has only really recently become fascinated by contemporary photography as an investment, and it still doesn't quite know how to handle it. We shouldn't be wondering how prices connect to value – we should be celebrating this extraordinary outburst of creativity in this part of London. Fergus has a vision and perceptions quite unlike . . .'

The *Vogue* editor interrupted: 'Yes, there's something of the inside job about the access he gets in these pictures. Is it true that MacFarlane once earned his living as a rent boy? I think his story's utterly fascinating. Gritty.'

'Well, you'd have to ask him that, of course,' said Charles, giving her the nod.

Behind Athene, out of the corner of his eye, Fergus saw the tall, looming, purple form of Annabel Koons, and he knew Lucas, her tiny powerball of a husband, would not be far behind. He remembered the dinner party three years earlier when he'd been so gauche and terrified of everyone. Koons pumped his hand, booming: 'Congratulations. I've bought four for my private gallery. The quality of light is exceptional. They're like Vermeers.'

Fergus felt an incredible hit of adrenaline, of ambition fulfilled, delicious as a drug.

'Um, thanks,' he said.

'You see,' said Koons, drawing him aside, 'photography is the easiest art, which perhaps makes it the hardest.'

'Absolutely true!' said Charles, magically appearing between them, alerted by his radar for connection and advancement. 'Of course, Fergus is an autodidact, so in many ways he is not constrained by the images of the past, by a visual library.' Koons nodded, as though this was profound.

'How do you bloody know?' said Fergus, feeling patronised. 'How do you know everything I've seen and read? I'm not some kind of naïve—'

Athene was tugging on Fergus's arm, dragging him away from Charles and Koons. 'Just chill. So what if Charles comes over all Svengali sometimes – he's doing a great job building up your profile. You should be grateful.'

'I know, I know, he's a genius at this. But sometimes I think that in another life he'd have been an estate agent,' said Fergus, grinning.

The crowd was thinning out and she persuaded him to the door with a pack of his friends who wanted to go clubbing. They left Charles fluttering around anxiously saying the right thing, holding the party like a baby. Fergus squeezed five people into his new baby, a black BMW, and the rest followed by taxi, running for cover in the darkness and house music of a club in an old bus garage in the East End. Fergus and Athene danced until three on ecstasy, mostly of the natural sort.

AMAZED AND CONFUSED

TEN QUESTIONS

This month: Grunge photographer Fergus MacFarlane, whose double-take on prostitution is showing at Flux Warehouse, Hoxton until July.

Age? 24
Born? Burnoch, Scotland
Influences? Arbus, Argos
Music? Kurt Cobain, The Corries
Food? Oysters, Caramac
Book? *Trainspotting*, Birdwatching
Drug? Alcohol
Hon or Rebel? Mongrel
Dreams? Fewer nightmares
Colour? Technicolor

Exhibitions:
Broken Promises, 1994, Flux Warehouse
Last Supper, 1992, Amnesty International, London
Deathly Still, 1991, Space, Camden
Viva Vauxhall, 1990, Flow Gallery

Chapter Thirteen

1996
A Midsummer Night's Dream,
incidental music, Op. 61,
Wedding March:
Felix Mendelssohn

'She's up to high doh,' said Fergus, pointing across the lawn at Athene who was bellowing at someone at the ribbon-draped door of a tent she had described as the 'chill-out yurt'.

'I'm sorry, sir?' said the caterer.

'She's up to high doh. You know, she's havering, dangerous. I'd stay well clear, if I were you, until that tent's up the way she wants it, or she'll bite your head off. I'm away to hide down the pub in the village.'

'Ah,' said the caterer, not sure if the bridegroom was joking about his beautiful bride-to-be. 'Right you are, sir.'

Fergus thought it best to have as little to do with the wedding set-up as possible. Marriage he wanted, party he wanted, but Indian-themed Raj-throwback reception for three hundred people he could do without. Athene, like all women just before their wedding day, had turned into Bridezilla. Getting this right was one of the most important moments in her life. Fergus understood this, but her attention to detail was psychotic, plus her nerves were so highly strung he swore he could hear a twanging noise every time she talked to him. To make matters worse, Athene was in league with her friend, a bossy blancmange of a woman called Lucinda Ebert, who was going into business as a wedding planner and wanted this to be her showpiece. Every time he saw Lucinda rolling into view, wearing yellow rubber gloves and neighing at a band of Sloaney debutante-types who worked for her, Fergus immediately thought of two lines from a poem he knew which went, 'O why do you walk through the fields in gloves ... O fat white woman whom nobody loves'. That was Lucinda: always the bridal organiser, never the bride.

Fergus dodged Lucinda and the Debutantes carrying giant red and orange silk cushions and kilims in to deck the chill-out and bar tents. The wedding looked like an outpost of Athene's shop, he thought, as he headed through the Arbuthnot family's ancestral grounds to the one-time gardener's cottage where Al was billeted for the wedding. Al – the best man – was already in his kilt, and totally on for partying. 'Nice joint they've got, eh? Like a fuckin' scene from *Four Weddings and a Funeral*,' he laughed. 'But even wackier. All that posh tottie. Pure dead brilliant. And I'm hearing about an elephant . . .'

Fergus growled at Al, and then recruited him for a trip down to the village pub. He wanted to have a word with him before Karen MacKay arrived, to check that everything was going to be OK. He had enough worries on his wedding day without past crimes being exhumed.

'When I invited you to be my best man a few months ago, Al, it didn't remotely occur to me that you would suddenly start going out with Karen MacKay, you total shagger,' said Fergus. 'I thought she didn't even live in Burnoch any more.'

'She's working at the archaeology department in Glasgow, but she still comes up for weekends to hang out with me on the boat. Not sure which she likes best – me or the sailing. Maybe it's to get away from all those up-their-own-arse intellectuals.' Al shrugged. He seemed slightly surprised by the quality of his conquest.

Fergus knew he'd have to talk to Karen about the accident in the stolen car, and would have to thank her face to face for keeping silent; the whole thing still made him squirm with deep-seated guilt.

'Don't think she cares,' said Al. 'If she did, she wouldn't be here. You can ask her yourself. She's coming off the twelve o'clock flight at Heathrow.'

They got their pints lined up on the ancient oak bar, and Fergus felt calmer.

'Champagne and curry? You're giving the guests curry?' Al snorted.

'Well, all different kinds of curry – you know, tandooris, baltis, pakora, naan bread, and all that . . .' faltered Fergus.

'Curry sauce and chips after a bevvy session, yes,' said Al shaking his head. 'Curry at a wedding, no. You have smoked salmon at proper weddings and strawberries and cream. It's a bit late now, though. Imagine what your mum'll say . . .'

Fergus's mum and Stuart were staying in the village inn upstairs amid tasteful antiques, beams, copies of *Horse and Hound*, and lots of whining from Stuart that he couldn't get the world championship golf on the telly. Isla was simultaneously proud and hyperactively nervous. Fergus was marrying into 'a very good family', she said. Respectability was hers at last! She'd taken her outfit back to Marks and Spencer's in Glasgow three times before settling on it and getting the matching hat at Fraser's. Plus it was the first time she'd been to England. Spain was her only knowledge of foreign lands, and Hampshire was a great deal more alien than Marbella or Majorca, without the cheery comfort of sombreros and sangria.

Uncle Jim and Auntie Margaret were staying in the inn too, except Jim was deep in the reed beds by the river, pursuing the birdlife, and Margaret was at the village hairdresser having her hair set in a style unaltered from the seventies, with immoveable backcombing that would last all day and perhaps for ever.

A dishevelled pensioner came in to the pub, wearing a floppy green hat and baggy shorts that displayed his gnarled knees, and carrying a bag that smelled of rotting fish. He seemed delighted to see Fergus. 'I say, getting some Dutch courage, are you? Mind if I join you? I'll just have a pre-prandial sherry.' He headed off to the bar.

'Who is that doatery old geezer? A poacher?' asked Al.

'No. That's my future father-in-law.'

'Fuck me.'

'No, he's brilliant. Mad as a cut snake.'

Hubert Arbuthnot was an obsessive, explained Fergus. 'With the advice of his dear friend Prince Charles . . .' – he paused to let Al snort – 'Hubert's got these Byzantine plans to turn the ancient family lands over to organic farming – you know, no chemical fertiliser. So now all his farmworkers hate him – you should hear them in the pub here at night. Their vegetables are full of slugs, and their cattle and sheep keep carking it from diseases which could easily be prevented by a good dose of dip and antibiotics.'

Al nodded – he was the son of a farmer himself – and in his easy, sociable way, launched into the topic of sheep diseases when Hubert plonked his sherry on their table. The group's conversation ran for some time, with particular reference to ovine foot rot and the art of keeping urban chickens in squats, before Hubert sighed, 'I must get back to dress before the Valkyries start looking for me. They're quite mad at the moment.' The poor man – a former classics scholar – was henpecked by his alabaster-chiselled wife Catherine and their three daughters. Athene's sisters were, predictably, called Ariadne and Artemis, explained Fergus to Al. The eldest, Ariadne, was a super-socialite in the wholesale pashmina import business, which had gained her the title of the Pashmina Queen of London, and a new entry in *Debrett's People of Today*. Ariadne was rather prominently displaying her peach pashmina over her bridesmaid's dress, hoping for sales. Artemis ran a riding stable in Buckinghamshire and the local branch of the Pony Club. 'They give me the heebie jeebies,' said Fergus. 'They're not like Athene.'

*

Later, as Fergus got ready, he watched Catherine, Athene's mother, from his mullioned bedroom window. He was never sure if she was intelligent, or just relied on grandeur to cloak her general ignorance. Down below, in a high-necked, bejewelled dress, with her red hair scraped up in a bun, she looked as severe as Queen Elizabeth I. Fergus saw her glide regally across the lawn as though she were on castors, ordering servants here and there and beheading dead flowers. Fergus slowly wrapped his brand new MacFarlane tartan kilt around himself, feeling the smooth expense of the expanse of woollen cloth on his bare legs. There was a time in Scotland, he remembered, when only twee teuchters and posh people wore kilts, but since *Braveheart* everyone had to do the step-we-gaily thing. He debated whether or not to wear his boxers. WWWWD? What would William Wallace do? It was probably OK now, even liberating, to dangle freely in church. He'd try to make sure his future mother-in-law got wind of it. Polite and welcoming as Catherine Arbuthnot was, Fergus knew she would much rather her daughter had married a Rupert in a stiff suit.

And now here he was, at the church, with less than an hour to go. Mind you, parts of his own family were nothing to write home about, Fergus had to admit, as his stepfather hove menacingly into view. Stuart was wearing a brown suit with a lilac shirt and a purple velvet bow tie, an outfit which had a terrible stench of the seventies about it. One got the impression he certainly hadn't gone shopping before his stepson's wedding. His tinted aviator glasses glinted, and he seemed to be staring at the gaggle of flower girls, which was fortunate, because Fergus couldn't even bear to make eye contact with him. 'Hi, Stuart,' he mumbled. 'How's it going?' Stuart was still worrying about the golf results.

'Is there a television somewhere in the big house?' he asked casually.

Isla was looking nice, though, in a green coatdress with matching Saxon court shoes. She looked at Fergus peculiarly when he asked her the name and number of her shoes, for old time's sake. 'Tania, if you must know,' she said, 'in 07 patent leather.' She was all flushed and in a kerfuffle, because she couldn't find her gloves.

'Don't worry, no one wears gloves to weddings any more. You're looking great,' said Fergus, hugging her before he led her to the front pew.

'I'm very happy for you, son. She's a lovely girl,' Isla said, flushed with the embarrassment of saying the right thing. But then she clocked the exquisite orchids draping the altar, and he could see the numbers totting up. She was off: 'I said to your Auntie Margaret, what can all this be costing, would they not be better putting down a deposit on a house if we're talking this kind of money? Still, we're here now, eh? Might as well enjoy ourselves.' Fergus nodded resignedly. Sometimes nothing changed.

Burnoch people kept arriving, and now Auntie Margaret was crushing him to her ever-larger chest, which reminded Fergus for a glancing moment of his father's funeral, except that now it was he that towered over her hat. He was suddenly aware that, at twenty-six, he was getting married at the same age his dad had been when he died. The melancholy feeling passed as Uncle Jim slapped him on the shoulders, genuinely proud. 'Well done, Fergus.

I'm dead proud of you. And it looks like we're on for a gallus party.'

Al and Fergus stood up at the altar waiting in their kilts. 'I feel like a right numptie,' said Al. 'Moss Bros rented me the wrong tartan. This is Stewart, but then no one here will know.'

Then Karen MacKay slipped into the church, almost late, disappearing into a side pew like a ghost, which, from Fergus's point of view, she was. He watched her. She turned, gave a huge smile and waved to them both at the front. She had bobbed dark hair now and was wearing a brown asymmetric dress – not Al's usual type at all. Fergus was somehow reassured by her presence: more supporters were here now from the away team.

He stared up into a stained-glass window, lost in the psychedelic colours and conflicting thoughts. The estate's fifteenth-century chapel was hewn from local stone, which glowed apricot in the sun. Like many churches, in Fergus's experience, it had that creepy, dusty smell which made him think of desiccated holy bones wrapped in rotting linen. There were also wafts of damp, mushroomy old hymn books, disturbing in some way to a non-believer like himself. By the font there was a medieval tomb of carved stone, showing a knight in armour – who must have been barely five foot – and his lady. A marriage that ended well, in a double stone coffin.

It was cool in the chapel, even in July, and Fergus shook with nerves. He could feel his balls shrivelling. He moved nearer to Al, who kept sympathetically whispering, 'Steady, Big Man' as the organist played classical music neither of them knew. The church filled to bursting with the Great and the Good, and Fergus's less-salubrious friends and relations. Perhaps all weddings had their own apartheid, but when he compared the groom's side of the church to the bride's, it was clear each was from a different race of people. On Fergus's side, his relations were looking homely, dowdy, or trying-too-hard, and towards the back, the crowd grew weird and arty, sporting a diverse range of body piercings. Everyone seemed slightly pasty; Charles was the only aberration. But on Athene's side, the women's golden skin glowed and there were so many enormous hats it looked like a scene from Ascot. Fergus wondered if marrying would unite his two existences, whether he and Athene could heal the nagging schizophrenia of then and now, north and south.

He felt incredibly serious about the marriage. He knew that without Athene, he would collapse, truly homeless. To Fergus it seemed that Athene was impossibly beautiful, impossibly perfect, impossibly good, and that she had completely filled the black hole of need in him. His only fear was whether or not, with all his flaws, he could love her enough.

The trumpet voluntary began, followed by the wedding march. Athene was walking up to the altar on the arm of her father Hubert, who was grinning with joy like a mad old monkey stuffed in a penguin suit. Ariadne and Artemis were bridesmaids behind. After the panic of the morning, Athene seemed to have found sudden serenity. She appeared beside Fergus, pale and bright eyed, looking medieval herself, or certainly not of this century. Her red hair poured down her back with tiny white flowers twined in the waves, and she wore a gold-patterned dress of white Indian silk.

As Athene stopped beside him and looked up, luminous with emotion, Fergus had a curious out-of-body feeling, as though he were watching himself on film. He wondered: can this be possible? Am I allowed this happiness, this perfection? Is she now mine? And do I deserve her? Yet he could hear the rustle of her dress and smell the perfume of the lilies riding from her bouquet. Athene was real, flesh and blood, smiling a little anxiously. There was singing and the vicar was saying something in the distance, breaking into Fergus's swoon.

'I do' would be the right thing to say at the moment, Fergus realised. So he did. He kissed Athene. 'I love you, love you, love you. I also love you forever,' he whispered, just to make things clear. Fergus looked down at the gold band itching with newness on his finger, and was astounded.

Seeing stars from all the flash photography, the two of them wandered hand in hand through the crowds in the garden, Fergus smiling so unstoppably his jaw began to ache. Staff in Nehru jackets or saris brought canapés, and Bollywood music played in the main marquee. It was all flawless, as Athene had planned for so long. Across the lawn down towards the ha-ha ('which is a wee ditch and not funny, by the way', Fergus was telling Al) were gathered Athene's friends and relations, including Sir Lucas and Lady Koons, the Powells, and the Sainsburys. Athene introduced Fergus to the Guinnesses and Barbours. 'They're all named after products! Or two-for-the-price-of-one,' he whispered afterwards, and Athene giggled and nipped him. Soon, they were surrounded by the Corryvreckan crew: Orlando, Tamsin, Edward,

George, Duncan, Sarah, and the thwarted Roderick, to whom Fergus was wickedly gracious.

Athene was no more comfortable with Fergus's relations than he was with hers, though she tried. The Scottish contingent was behind, standing in the safety of a tight circle, especially when Dave and his partner Brian approached hand in hand in matching Paul Smith suits.

Stuart turned his back on a waiter proffering tiny samosas; 'Spicy food doesn't agree with me,' said Stuart nasally.

'That's odd, because you're off with your mates in Thailand every year, and the food must be pretty exotic there,' snapped Fergus.

'I'd be happy with just plain sandwiches,' he muttered, then necked some more pink champagne.

'Oh c'mon, Stuart. The food's magic. Get beasted in,' said Al, bearing a bursting plate of pakoras and hot sauce, his preferred after-bender foodstuff.

Al had made a brilliant best man's speech – he was popular as a compère among his friends in Burnoch. He told the story of how the groom rowed heroically across the Corryvreckan whirlpool, besting the elements and dicing with death, to claim his bride. Al had conveniently truncated the story to just the best parts.

'Ooh, he was really funny. He sounded just like Billy Connelly,' said Lucinda, tittering, gloves off for conversational battle.

'We all sound like Billy Connelly up there, you know, Lucinda,' said Fergus, 'whereas you all—' Athene gave him a stop-right-there look.

Isla had complaints about the content of the speech:

'Why did he have to mention that you were the cook on the yacht? Why couldn't he just say—'

'Because it was true, Mum. And who cares?' said Fergus. 'We don't.'

'Still, it's lovely to see Al here – and Karen,' said Isla, ignoring his reply. 'She's doing awfully well at the uni, you know. Oh!' She was staring round the door of the chill-out tent, where a number of guests were no longer upright.

Stuart's eyes were bulging: 'What are *those* people doing in there?'

'Come on, Stuart,' said Athene quickly. 'I'll find a waiter who can show you where the TV is inside the house in case you want to check the golf results.' She propelled Stuart on to someone, and then disappeared into the crowd. Fergus watched her go, simultaneously grateful and bereft.

Fergus, Isla, Auntie Margaret and Al were left in the mayhem of the chill-out tent, where Fergus's friends seemed to be doing everything, by the looks of their pinpoint pupils and extraordinary costumes. Charles was particularly full of energy, racing round like an automated greeter, pumping charm from every pore. He made Fergus want to laugh, but on the other hand that was why he needed a dealer: undiscriminating conviviality was not his major skill. Charles was talking animatedly to a woman wearing a silver chainmail dress, and Fergus could hear his name being repeatedly mentioned.

Charles spotted Fergus and his mother using his almost undetectable over-shoulder radar, and dashed over. 'Mrs MacFarlane, so marvellous to meet you at last!' said Charles sweetly, shaking Isla's hand. 'And do I recognise that green coat dress from this season's Yves St Laurent collection? Lovely. Lovely cut. And you must be so proud of Fergus . . .' He continued as Isla stood amazed in her M&S and Tania 07s. No one had ever been this nice to her, and she had no sense of whether Charles was sincere or not. She waited till he had gone, sucked down some more champagne, and let it all flow by.

'Does this really look like Yves St Laurent, then?' Isla asked Auntie Margaret and Fergus.

'Och no,' said Margaret. 'That's what they call being charming down here.'

'Oh,' said Isla.

Fergus wandered off. He just wanted to enjoy himself now, but he was being stalked by a photographer, snapping his every move. Asking a couple of his mates to take private wedding photos had perhaps been a mistake. His friend who usually worked as a paparazzo had taken, he could tell, shots of Athene from the leg up getting out of the car and had used a telephoto lens from the balcony of the church for a close-up of her cleavage. Meanwhile, the war photographer was behaving like a sniper, sneaking up on unwary guests through the bushes, filming the carnage on the floor of the chill-out tent. Still, at least the unwanted *Hello!* photographer had only managed to get a snap of them coming out of the church, which wasn't on private land. Fergus felt embarrassed that the only bit of the wedding he'd organised had turned out so peculiarly.

Across the rose garden, he spotted Karen talking animatedly to a sculptor whose speciality was making perfect Victorian-style statues on huge plinths of B-list ephemeral celebrities, and placing them by night, with his fork-lift truck, among the great sculptures of generals and admirals in places like Trafalgar Square or Hyde Park. Sometimes it took days for the celeb-impostors to be noticed.

Fergus swallowed a couple of times and walked over. He'd only kissed Karen on the greeting line, but they hadn't talked properly. 'She's had this brilliant idea of me making fake monoliths and standing stones,' said the sculptor. 'Stick 'em among the real ones, up near where you come from. And we can write false archaeological papers on them . . .'

'That's a lot of tonnes to drag over rough territory,' said Fergus, grinning at Karen. She had chipped green nail varnish and was wearing a Celtic cross. 'How are you?'

'Really fine.'

The sculptor's girlfriend, wearing a black hat largely made of an alarm clock, appeared and whisked him off to meet Lucas Koons, who was using the wedding to harpoon fresh artistic meat.

Fergus and Karen stood in embarrassed silence for a minute, and then Fergus began disjointedly: 'I'm sorry, I often think what might have happened . . . and you had to miss the exam, and maybe . . . anyway, I'm still grateful, because—'

'Oh, for Pete's sake. It was nothing, like I said when I wrote back to you. Missing that maths exam was really a godsend – it stopped me from being a doctor, and you've no idea how crap I'd have been. I had to go to the Hunterian Museum the other day – you know, all those creepy specimens in formaldehyde – and I had to leave because I thought I was going to faint.'

Fergus felt reassured. Karen continued, 'And if you hadn't had to run away to London, none of this would have happened.' She gestured round at the grandeur. 'Anyway, thanks for inviting me with Al at such short notice – you didn't need too.'

'I'm really glad you're here,' said Fergus. 'Honestly. I'm really glad you're going out with him. So's he.' They talked for a while. Karen had a cigarette behind the tent, smoking in the manner favoured by working men on a sneaky break, holding the cigarette between her finger and thumb, cupped in her hand. This somehow made Fergus nostalgic.

The baby elephant appeared round the corner, wearing an Indian headdress with tinkling bells, and chased by a flock of exquisitely dressed children. Karen stared and exhaled a long plume of smoke. 'Did you know—'

'That there's an elephant in the room? Believe me, it wasn't my idea. None of this was my idea, but Athene's the bride. I'm just loving, honouring and obeying.' He shrugged with a smile. The elephant shat prodigiously at the tent door. The waiters all magically disappeared. Soon Lucinda Ebert appeared in yellow rubber Marigolds, her regal breasts marching ahead of her. Fergus whispered the 'Oh why do you walk through the fields in gloves' poem to Karen, who started wheezing with suppressed laughter.

A slightly pissed man in full morning dress accosted Fergus, who had no idea who he was. 'Congratulations, old chap. Athene's a treasure, and I didn't know you knew Charles! I meant to ask, did you meet him at Cambridge?' asked the man.

'In a photo lab,' said Fergus.

'Oh, sorry,' said the guest. 'Got the wrong end of the

stick there.' He wandered off. Karen raised one eyebrow at Fergus. He'd forgotten, since the playground, how meanly she could do this.

Al arrived behind Karen and put his arms round her. 'C'mon and dance with me.'

The smell of hot crushed grass and bodies coming from the tent suddenly made Fergus feel lightheaded. He wandered off to look for Athene, but she had been sucked deep into the crowd somewhere. As he passed the study windows of the big house, he saw Stuart, glued to the golf on the telly, and best left that way. Fergus walked towards the ornamental lake behind the house, and found the Britart pack was already there, romping in the warm, muddy water. Fergus peered down in the gathering dusk from the hill above. Were they naked? Almost inevitably. The alarm-clock hat was abandoned on the shore, and so was the black-and-white minidress. He was torn between joining his friends and hoping that Athene's mother would not witness the sight. Oh and now a girl was screaming hysterically and sprinting out of the water. 'Something bit me! There's something in there!'

'Snapping turtles,' shouted Fergus helpfully from his vantage point. 'Totally harmless.' Mrs Arbuthnot rolled down to the lake, waving her arms in irritation. Fergus headed for the party tent. Athene was there, dancing with Lucas Koons, whose bald head came to the level of her chest. Fergus tapped Koons on the shoulder. 'My shot,' he said. 'My wife.' As he swept Athene up into his arms and kissed her, Uncle Jim skipped thunderously into his view, dancing with Isla, his kilt twirling close to exposure.

'It's a rare tear, this,' said Jim, now cheerfully blootered.

'What did he say?' whispered Athene.

'A rare tear. Rhymes. Means a good time.' Fergus
sighed.

WOW!
July 24, 1996

The aristo-boho set were out in force last Saturday at the exotic Eastern-style wedding of socialite Athene Arbuthnot and Fergus MacFarlane, the celebrated – and celebrity – photographer.

The happy couple chose the Arbuthnots' fifteenth-century country seat, Netherbourne Hall in Hampshire, for their star-studded nuptials, which took place in the family chapel and afterwards in a marquee in the grounds, bedecked with brightly coloured Indian silks and ribbons. The bride (above, leaving the church) wore a sari-inspired wedding dress in white, embroidered with tiny gold birds. The groom, who hails from Argyllshire, wore a MacFarlane tartan kilt and carried a Leica camera in his sporran. The couple met on a yacht touring Scotland.

Over 300 guests were seated on embroidered cushions round low tables on oriental rugs. The Asian theme continued with traditional music, the surprise appearance of a baby elephant, spicy Indian food – and pink champagne. 'The Arbuthnot family made their fortune long ago in the British East India Company – plus Athene runs a fantastic shop selling Asian objects d'art, so the theme just seemed to be right,' said Lucinda Ebert of the Bespoke Wedding Company of Fulham, which styled the event.

Chapter Fourteen

1997
'Becoming More Like Alfie':
The Divine Comedy

Today's grand work of portraiture: a wee blonde actress called Patty who was wearing nothing but the Union Jack. Which is nice, thought Fergus. He liked to photograph the ones that had just burst into celebrity, with that blaze of insane confidence that he sometimes felt, too, in those heady – and, as it turned out, extremely short – days of Cool Britannia. But if these were the It-girls and the Brit-boys of the early Blair regime, it was Fergus who bestowed the 'it' upon them with his camera and slid their gleaming, airbrushed bodies between the glossy covers of *Vanity Fair* and *Vogue*. His magazine photographs, said the critics, were 'so ravishing, so revealing, so *now*, that they make the words redundant'.

For such commercial portraits, the money was outstanding. The thought required was minimal. And the work and the invitations poured in, from that summer's celebrities, from Downing Street even, from Damien, Sarah, Angus, Sam and Jay; from the Sensation party at the

Royal Academy for those newly minted Young British Artists. Fergus tossed the thick cream envelopes unopened on his office floor, much to Athene's annoyance. 'We should go to these,' she said. 'It would be good for your career, never mind my amusement.' She opened them, jealous and thwarted. But she was so morning sick, afternoon sick, and evening sick for months on end, that parties became purgatory.

Fergus felt to blame: he was the devil out of *Rosemary's Baby* who had impregnated Athene with the spawn of evil, or at least Scottish working-class spawn that didn't agree with her at all. Like the fable of *The Princess and the Pea*, his tiny pod was causing untold damage to her delicate constitution. Yet he was so joyous about fatherhood. He felt it was a chance to heal and seal his past, to make good, to build something new, to make whole his half-family, but it was already way harder than he'd imagined.

The problem was that Athene was not up for it any more. In fact, she was dead against it, and Fergus now-adays found it hard to function without it, without some kind of release. His love for Athene came in wrenching waves. She was the only still point in this speeding, shifting world which made more and more demands on him. This week, for instance, Charles had him exhibiting in contemporary photography fairs in Basel and New York, and doing a shoot in Mexico, as well as the portrait in London. Charles fed his own bank balance and Fergus's ambition with choice morsels that he couldn't refuse. 'I want you to be on the rollcall of household names,' said Charles. He now managed a whole stable of photo-graphers. 'Now's your moment.' But this hyper-real life, strung out between timezones, left Fergus needing an outlet for the live wires coiled inside him, or his mind short circuited, went black and all creation stopped. At first, running obsessively helped him. Every morning, if he was in the country, he pounded all the polluted way from the flat in Camden to his studio behind Hoxton Square, and worked like a mad dog. But by evening his stomach was knotted, his nails bitten, his knuckles cracking, and there was no choice but to drink his way out of the corner.

That day after the shoot, the wee actress, Patty, showed no sign of wanting to go home (actually, she had no home to go to, because she was living in Claridges). She sat drinking beer with Fergus and his assistant, Blue. The studio was a cool place to hang out. It was the first building Fergus had owned, and he was fond of the razor wire round the walls, the clanging metal gates, the industrial warehouse exterior and his mint Toyota Land Cruiser with its blacked-out windows sitting in the yard. The place made Fergus feel he was in a KGB compound at the start of some ridiculous spy story. Besides, you'd be asking for trouble leaving a car like that out on the streets round here.

On the two floors of the warehouse there was endless space for shoots, sets, equipment, a couple of Jasper Morrison sofas from SCP round the corner and a job lot of stuffed creatures from a taxidermy shop that had recently gone out of business on Old Street. There were a dozen scabrous owls and birds of prey in glass bell-jars, a mangy stoat with one eye missing, a pike, and an eland that gave off a rank, musty smell. Scrutiny from the birds made everyone else nervous, but they reminded Fergus pleasantly of birdwatching in the hills around Burnoch, and were also useful as freakish props when the subject for portraiture was a stuffed shirt, or a dumb beauty with an unlived-in face. He also had a collection of broken dolls and mannequins' limbs, gathered by Blue from the dregs of Petticoat Lane Market, which performed the same purpose: making the photograph's object abject.

After a beer, Blue – who was, confusingly, black – went off to meet Charles somewhere. He was an exquisitely handsome twenty year old that Charles had taken a fancy to and set up as Fergus's personal assistant, fielder and catcher. Blue had turned out to be very sensible, but for his moniker. 'Who the hell's called Blue anyway?' growled Fergus as he shut the gates on him.

'You don't want to know my real name,' said Blue, darkly.

Patty suggested Fergus took more pictures of her, and he did, amused by her slightly cheesy performance naked beneath the flag. He talked soothingly to her as he worked. These shots were better than anything he already had in the can. Patty was sweet, though her head seemed huge like a shaggy lion's, with a childlike thin body below. She seemed to think that Fergus knew the rules of inter-celebrity-intercourse, written in stars' trailers from time immemorial: don't ask, don't tell, and don't waste time on polite preliminaries.

'Come on, then,' she said, flopping on the sofa and letting the flag fall to half-mast.

'Thanks, but I can't,' said Fergus. 'My wife, she's pregnant and—'

'Fine, then,' said Patty, quite unbowed. 'Are you sure you're sure?'

'Yes,' said Fergus. But he wasn't. He desperately wanted the escapism, the relief. Such moments were harder and harder to resist, and easy to come by. 'Another beer?' he said. He put on The Divine Comedy, Wildean masters of irony who sang 'Becoming More Like Alfie', which made Fergus laugh guiltily and puzzled Patty because she was too young and too desperately milking the present to have wasted time on an old Michael Caine film. But Fergus had shelves and shelves of videos in the studio: he played them into the night, succoured by images, until he was tired enough to go home and sleep without dreaming, without wanting anything else.

He made it up to Athene for such thought crimes and absences by cooking passionately for her. This was tricky, because in the throes of pregnancy, she only wanted to eat potatoes and rice, except when she had psychotic midnight cravings for lemons, which required raids on the all-night shop. Athene had never eaten much anyway, and now with the constant nausea battling with her growing belly, her body resembled a long sock with a tennis ball stuffed down it. Fergus wanted to make her rounded, rosy, healthy. He cooked for the future and for fecundity: he found tiny, nutty, thin-skinned new potatoes, fresh from their dusting of soil, and boiled them scattered with chopped thyme or mint leaves, or made a crush with olive oil and dollops of crème fraiche. From the pages of Nigel Slater, Fergus unearthed Tartafin: potatoes sliced thinly, no thicker than pound coins, cooked slowly in a covered pan with garlic and olive oil until fragrant and pale gold, soft and buttery. Then he sliced cheese on top – Taleggio, Reblochon or Gruyère – and let it melt under the grill. There was also pasta delicately flavoured with lemon, fresh mint and cream, and a slightly gooey lemon poppy-seed loaf recipe for emergency rations.

He fed Athene these exquisite things and felt her tight-banded belly with the solicitude, she complained, of the witch in 'Hansel and Gretel'. But Fergus was truly solicitous, feeling all-at-once proud and protective and stomach-churningly nervous. He was fascinated as he sat with a glass of wine on the chair in the bathroom, studying her blue-veined, eggshell-thin-skinned belly in a bath they could no longer share. He watched amazed as the globe-of-the-world curve was suddenly shattered by a hand or maybe a foot punching through the skin, bulging it like extruded dough, and then disappearing, leaving no trace. He longed to photograph those moments, but Son Number One – whose penis had shown up perkily on the ultrasound – was highly unpredictable.

Traditionally, a pregnant woman starts nesting towards the end of her confinement: cleaning furiously, pointlessly tidying cupboards, buying amusing baby hats with bunny ears, etc. In Athene's case, nesting became a sort of extreme sport involving a cast of hundreds and a cost of thousands. She decided to dedicate her pregnancy to totally gutting and rebuilding an old bed-and-breakfast hotel they'd bought in Belsize Park, and turning it into the perfect postmodern family home. The task was gargantuan: the stucco was falling from the brick like dandruff; there was a strong smell everywhere of cat piss 'or perhaps cat casserole', mused Fergus, and the interior was a brown study of stained carpets and pus-coloured wallpaper.

This was all good news for Fergus and Athene: there was nothing to save but the façade, so they ripped out floors and walls down to a skeleton and employed a well-known minimalist architect, who had designed both monasteries in Eastern Europe and stores on Fifth Avenue. He brought with him profound philosophy, and a huge cement mixer, which poured out acres of polished cream concrete, underpinning 'floating' walls, and flowing outside like smooth lava beneath the two-storey-high windows into the garden, so that interior and exterior were one. The polished concrete ended, swirling down into a plunge pool beneath instant apple trees. It seemed both exquisite, and horribly grown-up – Fergus was twenty-seven, Athene twenty-nine – and he sometimes felt the weight of the house pressing down on him, like the weight of stones on a medieval martyr.

Yet the time spent on this great aesthetic project, the hours spent drooling over blueprints and Japanese interiors magazines and catalogues of stainless-steel kitchen door handles also brought Fergus and Athene great joy: for once, they were working together, their minds at one, their artistic sensibilities on full alert. While Athene dreamed of wet-rooms, Fergus dreamed of inbuilt espresso machines and a library – proper houses had libraries – for his photography and art books, a place filled with proof of what he had become. He wasn't greedy in a crude way, but he was greedy for perfection. Aside from shelves, Fergus generally favoured absolutely nothing as much as possible, just empty space – he had, after all, lived in a bungalow with knitted poodle toilet-roll covers – while Athene was drawn to colours and – sinfully – clutter. The architect stamped on that immediately, and took her to the Milan furniture fair for the weekend to refine her taste.

As Athene expanded, so did the sense of panic and anticipation in the building site. The troops from Eastern Europe doubled, and were dragooned into working at the weekends by the site manager. There was a final paint crisis: Athene was torn between Farrow and Ball colours with names like 'grubby string', 'rotted parchment' and 'yellowing shirt armpit' – or so Fergus said – which were all versions of cream. The day the workmen finished painting the front door with three coats of 'lamp-room grey', Athene went into labour.

When Athene rang to tell him her waters had broken two weeks early, Fergus was in Brixton documenting the Alternative Miss World Competition with a curator from the Royal Academy, who was dressed as a newt in a bikini. He put his cameras into their steel cases and forced a taxi to drive at an arrestable pace up to the private hospital in St John's Wood, where Athene had already gone. She had planned a water birth with a personal midwife coach-cum-aromatherapist, in a dimly lit suite, with a background of soothing yogic music. Instead, she was in a curtained cubicle alone, under fluorescent strip lights, in labour and in tears.

'They're going to make me have a Caesarian . . . the baby's the wrong way round,' she wailed when Fergus walked in. Then she gasped and flipped back and forth in pain on the trolley, like a fish out of water, only to return to normal between contractions. Always pale, she was almost see-through in the harsh light. The veins in her temples seemed about to burst. Fergus held her, feeling completely helpless, shocked by the muscle-rippling strength of her contraction, the lack of control. She was possessed.

'Right then, Mrs MacFarlane, we'll just pop in the epidural,' said an Irish nurse with vast red hands and cheeks and a horse-sized syringe. 'Mr MacFarlane, the doctor will have a word with you outside.' It was, said the teenager in blue scrubs (surely wrongly labelled as a doctor), 'a footling breach'. Although Fergus understood that the baby was upside down with his foot in the exit, he liked the old-fashioned sound of the phrase 'footling breach'. But when it came to the operating theatre with its glinting scalpels and the arc lights and the tubes and drains suddenly emanating from his wife, Fergus freaked out. He thought about going to throw up in the day room. Of course, Fergus could actually see what was going on at the technical end behind a green cloth fence erected across Athene's chest. Athene was screened from the gory action and stoned on some floaty painkiller, so she had relaxed and was chatting away to the teenage-looking doctor. Fergus looked down at his metal equipment cases.

'Would it be OK . . .' began Fergus. 'Would it be OK if I took some photographs? Take my mind off . . .'

Athene smiled. 'Cool,' she said.

'Sure,' said the doctor.

Fergus opened his cases and got out his operating paraphernalia, took a light meter reading and readied two cameras. Once he had the tools of the trade in his hands, the tightness in his stomach dissolved and he stopped shaking. He had a job to do. He went in close as the scalpel came down hari-kiri style, and tracked the changing colours as the red burst through the white skin and fat layers. The slight tearing, squelching sound didn't bother him at all. But his other senses were still working. There was a new smell: yeasty, fresh, meaty. Fergus focused, forcing the fear back.

It happened fast. Soon the doctor had sliced through into the womb, and his gloved hand disappeared into Athene, fishing around. Then something soft and dark and round appeared in his fist, and there was a yanking movement, a sucking sound, and what looked like a couple of pounds of raw Toulouse sausages appeared before Fergus's clicking lens. Then the bright-red thing opened its mouth and eyes, and made a small discomfited noise. His mouth was a neat black hole in the red mist. He was angry, not drowning but waving, little limbs cycling in the air. Suddenly there were people in scrubs blocking Fergus's view and he was back at the top of the bed holding Athene's hand and yelling: 'Yes! Yes! And it's definitely a boy!'

They mopped up the baby, wrapped him in what appeared to be a white dishtowel, and laid him beside Athene on the pillow. She turned her face to the baby's and they stared at each other, with the same mildly surprised expression. Fergus took the first picture of them in profile, nose to nose, their relationship one-minute old and already earthshattering.

They called him Raphael, and then Athene suddenly fell asleep, her son in a sort of fish tank on wheels beside her bed. For a long time, Fergus stared at them both with an aching tenderness in his throat. Then he went out to the visitors' room and started calling friends and relatives. Soon his phone was buzzing back like an excited hamster in his pocket. After he called Charles, he rang his mother to tell her the news: 'I'll get in some blue wool for a wee jacket then – I didn't want to go do it before and end up with the wrong colour – and we'll have a look at the timetable for trains from Central when the shop's not so busy,' she said, which was code for 'congratulations'.

Then Fergus called Al. 'The ball's in the back of the net! I'm over the moon, Brian! A son, eight pounds, looks dead Scottish. In fact – hey, I'll send you a photo – he could be yours with that red hair and the scrunched-up face.'

But the time of jubilation was all too short: Fergus slipped away into the obsessive and insane world of new parenthood, where a hiccup can cause a virtual inquisition, sleeping babies must be woken to check their vital signs, and a slightly runny nose means a trip to Emergency. They were always busy, doing what Fergus wasn't quite sure. All he knew was that work was like a balm to him, a place where he could get his thoughts in order, although he hated being sent abroad. That was like losing a limb.

Fergus and Athene's new house became something between an interior design show and a school nativity play, as friends and relatives came bearing gifts, and then took a tour of the minimalist polished concrete interiors, with a mandatory stop-off at the slate wet-room with double-power shower and sliding glass roof which opened to the stars or the summer rain. Athene received visitors in the living room, where she remained on the Antonio Citterio sofa, feeding the demanding Raphael from her beautiful blue-veined breasts. She took motherhood and its dramas far more seriously than she'd ever taken her own career. Phalanxes of Ruperts and Sophies, the Koons, artists and photographers all paid court. An old American student friend of Athene's called Henry Molton, whom Fergus had never met before, rolled smoothly in. Henry brought Raph a ride-on polished oak model Spitfire, which Fergus thought was a bit excessive. He kept tripping over it in Raph's room. Nearly everyone else brought tasteful French clothing or tiny cashmere jumpers for the baby to vomit on before handwashing.

All this silly luxury caused no improvement, however, in their sleep patterns. Fergus was astounded to be under the control of a quixotic dictator, when all his life, *he*'d made the decisions. Athene had refused the services of a maternity nurse, and Raphael ruled through fear and lung power, like any normal first baby. Or, as Fergus said to Charles, 'It's imposed upon you. You love it. But it's like suddenly being asked to wear a strange hat, day and night, for the rest of your life.'

'I guarantee it's harder for Athene,' said Charles, sympathetically taking Earl Grey and pastel-iced fairy cakes with her on the sofa. He was Raph's godfather.

'Of course Godfather also describes your day-to-day role anyway.' Fergus was vaguely but naggingly aware that the contracts he'd signed a few years ago with Flux, Charles's company, were extremely generous to his dealer. More generous than most. Which is perhaps why Charles on his second visit to Raph had carefully brought a blue box from Tiffany's – for Athene, not the baby – and a bottle of Laphroaig for Fergus. 'Children get far too much attention, from the start,' said Charles. 'They should know their place.'

Raphael's place was perhaps too central to their lives. If he was home, Fergus took a photograph of his son's face every day, in the same position, from the same distance, in natural light, as the baby lay looking up on the blue changing mat. At first Raph was a crumpled, wizened, blotched pensioner with constant worries. Occasionally he screamed. Then at about a month, he smiled for the camera. A few days later, he was bright red all over with anger, then white. Hands started to wave in the pictures. His face widened, until his cheeks looked almost edible, like those recipes for 'cheeks of cod with lemon and capers'. By six months, Raphael's legs – not featured in the shots – resembled pink salami, tied with string, so deep were the layers of fat meeting at his knees.

At just over a year, Raph began to speak. He was funny. When Fergus changed a stinker of a nappy, he would often say 'not too bad' to himself in courageous tones. Soon Raph was smiling up at him from the changing table and saying his first phrase 'not too bad?' in hope.

Fergus went on photographing the face of this walking, talking creature, every day unless he was abroad working. The changes were imperceptible, day by day, but week by week, month by month, they were extraordinary, a miracle of metamorphosis. Fergus was fascinated by the collected works of his son; Athene was fascinated by her son, and her own role. Her interest in Fergus was limited. Fergus felt almost jealous, excluded from Athene's affections, and very often excluded from their bed by the amazing night contortions of Raph, who always slept with them. Diagonally. Across most of the bed.

Sometime Raph would have to leave his mother's bed as Fergus had left Isla's, and Fergus knew it wouldn't be pretty.

*

One day, when Fergus was playing with Raph on the slide in Primrose Hill, on one of the rare weekends he was home, Al rang from Scotland.

'Hey, how are you? Long time no speak,' said Fergus. 'I'm in the park with Raph. He's running rampant on the slide. Mad as a cut snake.'

'Oh. Right,' said Al, but his voice had gone flat. Fergus knew every tone of his friend's conversation, and something was wrong. Al had broken up with Karen a few months ago, but Fergus had thought he was over it. They talked, but every subject came to a dead end.

'Are y'alright? Is something the matter?'

Al sounded shaky. 'I just wanted to tell you, I suppose. I've been meaning to tell you for ages. I could've been there with you, but she wouldn't have it. She wanted to get rid of it.'

'Who? What?'

'Karen. I got her pregnant. By mistake.'

'Is that why you broke up with her?' Fergus felt awful to have been so out of touch, so distant. 'You never explained why. Why didn't you tell me? I'm your best friend for God's sake.'

'She said she didn't want anyone to know. I wasn't going to tell you, but every time you talk about Raph and that . . .'

'I'm sorry, Al, I wish I'd—'

'Karen said that we weren't right for each other, and a baby wasn't going to make it better. She said it would make it worse. She didn't want to settle down, she didn't want to leave Glasgow. I always knew deep down that she thought she was too fucking good for—'

'No, that's rubbish, Al. It's shit, though.'

'She's gone dead weird. None of her friends have seen her.' He went silent. 'Fergus, why do women get to decide these things and we don't? Like it wasn't my baby at all?'

Fergus thought this was not a conversation for the phone. 'Look, we need to talk properly. Get a flight. Come down here for the weekend, let it go, get away from everything. We'll go out on the ran dan.'

London Evening News
February 16, 2000

WOMAN FOILS PARK RAPIST ATTACK

By Aileen Collins

A woman foiled another attack yesterday by the man suspected of being the London park rapist. Police say the incident, on Hampstead Health, bears all the hallmarks of the man who has previously assaulted women on London Fields and Finsbury Park.

A 32-year-old woman from Belsize Park was attacked by a man wielding a knife as she jogged in broad daylight at 10 a.m. on the Eastern side of the Heath. The victim has not been named, but it is understood that she fought back when assaulted by the man.

Police are examining the crime scene and the knife, which was dropped by the attacker as he ran away. They described the man as white, in his thirties, with medium build and short dark hair. He was wearing a grey hooded top.

The Hampstead attack follows the rape of a woman jogger at knifepoint in Finsbury Park last month, and a sexual assault of another woman who was walking her dog in London Fields in November.

Chapter Fifteen

2001
The Contented Toddler Years:
Gina Ford

Sometimes Athene imagined she and Fergus were like vast continents. Long ago, they'd been joined together, like America and Europe once were before the dawn of history. But then huge tectonic shifts took place and slowly the continents, the solid rock, split and moved apart. The continental drift seemed so unlikely and happened so slowly that it was invisible to the naked eye, until one day an ocean appeared between the two.

Athene first realised how far she and Fergus had drifted apart on the day, over a year ago, that she'd been attacked in the park. Her aggression towards her attacker, that disgusting little man, had been fuelled by a horrible, repressed aggression towards Fergus. Or so her therapist said. The therapist had also pointed out the healthiness of Athene's reaction at the time in the park; that she'd done something positive and powerful. Athene was over the attack; she didn't have nightmares any more, but it had opened her eyes to the obvious. She had put many of their stresses down to having babies, broken nights and Fergus's insane work schedule, but then she went to search for a number on his mobile phone, and found messages from a dozen different women. She wasn't stupid. Plus all those weekends when Al had come down from Scotland, and they'd gone out 'on the tear'. For God's sake, you only needed to look in the gossip pages of the papers sometimes, to see Fergus exiting this party or that with his groupies. Perhaps she had always known. Charles and his boyfriend Blue were in league with Fergus and always keen for a nightcap, an after-party. Charles justified the endless excess, the publicity, saying: 'Athene, you've got to understand the value of a high public profile for those considering investing in a nebulous market. It's an anti-elitist strategy. I want his photographs to be seen by the most people possible.'

Fergus rocketed from wild revelry to a sober, workaholic disappearance for days on end. His family had to squeeze into the space between. It was all or nothing for Fergus. Work, drugs and alcohol all got the same on-off treatment from him. Fergus had once quoted Athene a line from the poet Edwin Muir who said, 'Scottish people drink spasmodically and intensely, for the sake of a momentary but complete release, whereas the English like to bathe and paddle about bucolically in a mild puddle of beer.'

So it was, for momentary but complete release, that Fergus was opening a bottle of 1985 Chateau Talbot from his cellar, and pushing a glass across to Athene. At least he's home on Friday evening for once, she thought. The nanny had gone off to her separate flat in the basement and they'd put the kids to bed – Hannah fighting back against sleep all the way, as usual. Then Fergus and Athene sat across the kitchen table, with absolutely nothing to say to each other.

Athene stared vaguely at the glass, and left her hands flaccid on her lap. She felt like crying, for no particular reason. She turned away to look out through the huge plate-glass windows at the apple tree illuminated in the garden lights, the rotting, abandoned fruit all round its roots. Of course everyone felt a similar fear and melancholia just after 9/11, but this was about them, too. The poisonous dust that shrouded downtown New York had permeated the cracks in their lives far away.

'What's wrong?' asked Fergus.

'I don't know. I feel it's all pointless.'

He obviously thought she was referring to the attack on the towers, which they'd been discussing earlier. 'I know, I feel that too. I'm eaten up by frustration and inadequacy – there's only one subject now. I'm feeling fucking useless.'

'No, I didn't mean just that. I mean us. It feels pointless, empty,' said Athene. Fergus looked shocked.

'Oh come on,' said Fergus. 'I've done my best, ever since you accused me last year of "sucking life out of you and pumping lives into you, and not giving anything back".' He was imitating her voice. 'And I've stayed faithful to you.' Athene realised this was a confession that he'd been unfaithful before.

'And I do try to help with the kids, if I'm not away, but you're the one who sleeps so lightly you hear Hannah's slightest squeak. She's eighteen months now – she should be able to get through the night. She's not a baby. And you're the one the children run to when something goes wrong because you're there. And you've got staff coming out of your ears. Is there really that much to complain about?' He knocked back another glass of wine.

'Yes,' said Athene. 'What about the way you abandon me, us. The way you don't talk to me any more, about anything. The way we keep being invited to Sunday lunch at other normal families' houses, and they ask: "Where's Fergus?" And I say you're working. Again.'

'This is a pivotal point in my career, here and in America, and in Germany. I've got to travel. It matters. I'm involved right now in that exhibition I told you about with Gillian Wearing, Jurgen Teller, Sarah Lucas, Martin Parr . . . everyone. I've got to get it right.'

Athene could feel herself going livid red and she was shaking. 'You can't be reasoned with, can you? Let me put it more simply for you: you're not a proper father.'

She watched Fergus wince as he took the bullet right in his stomach. He couldn't shake words off, with their gangrenous stink of the truth. He fought back because he was cornered.

'Oh let me see now, I can't be a father because I never had one properly, and you're fucked up because Mummy and Daddy sent you to boarding school and you had it so easy you never had to struggle and it all came on a plate, so you're what? A tiny bit bored? A tiny bit tired having to get up at night? Trying to compete too hard with those pointless blonde yoga-mummies, with their personally trained buttocks like twin uplifted cherries, their self-reverential conversations, their houses that are shrines to cleanliness, their minds that are empty, their—'

'I'm not like that,' said Athene flatly.

But Fergus was on a roll. 'Well, why don't you *do* something, instead of being a yummy mummy and leaving that shop to run itself in your name. Oh, and on that subject, why don't you pay those fucking peasants in India a bit more? It's called fair trade.' He poured out more of his £40 bottle of wine.

Athene reached for a physical weapon. *The Contented Toddler Years* hit Fergus hard on the side of the head, leaving an oozing cut.

'Fuck,' he said. 'Why'd you fucking do that?'

Athene shrugged. 'I'm sorry.' Their anger had been deflated by the violence. Fergus went across to the bathroom to find a tissue. He shut the door and sat down on the seat, his head in his hands.

Athene leaned her hot cheek against the door. She was crying. 'I'm sorry. I just feel you're distant. It's so different from the way it was ten years ago when we first met. Now I feel your absence even when you're in the room sometimes, when everyone, my friends, our friends are around, and you're not there mentally.'

'I get distracted,' said Fergus emerging. 'I've got a lot to think about right now.'

He walked over and put his arms tentatively round her. 'Come to bed,' he said. They lay there talking, two separate lost continents in a king-sized ocean of Frette sheets. They needed something more than temporary reconciliation. 'Why don't you come to my therapist,' she said.

Fergus cracked his knuckles. 'What can you possibly say in there about yourself, us, hour after hour, week after week? I can't do it, Athene. I don't want my privacy invaded. I've always managed, over the years, to haul all my broken parts together and march on. I'm not going to let some privileged Hampstead shrink prod me for cracks.'

'Fine,' said Athene, turning away and trying to sleep. She was shattered in both senses.

Fergus wanted to make amends somehow, though, and a week later, he appeared in the early evening outside the house, sitting in the cream leather bucket seat of a red convertible BMW roadster. Athene thought it was for him, until she saw the numberplate: ATH 3NE. It was a love token; a wheeled apology. He obviously felt the car would be a more effective tool in healing their rift than marriage therapy. He jumped out, dangling the keys, a huge grin across his face.

'I've brought you a present!' He opened the door of the shiny, ostentatiously labelled machine.

'Oh. Oh my God! You bought that thing for me, with the name on it? But I've already got a people carrier, I mean I . . .'

'Go on! Try it,' said Fergus, so boyishly excited he didn't notice her hesitation.

Athene fumbled her way into the car and spent a lot of time nervously adjusting the mirror, the seat and the belt. At last she jerked the engine into action, and the car shot off like a rat up a drainpipe. She could tell that Fergus was trying not to grimace as she inexpertly braked and revved all the way round the block.

'Thank you,' Athene said when they had parked with some difficulty outside the house. 'Thank you so much. You're so sweet. It's a wonderful car. I love it, and, um, the

ATH 3NE numberplate . . . the numberplate is very special.' Athene laughed brightly, but there was an undertone in her voice which only the long-married can hear. Fergus heard it, and looked across quizzically.

'Is there something wrong? Did you . . .' But by then the children had rushed madly down the front steps to run around the new toy. Raphael wanted to sit in the driving seat and hoot the horn, while Hannah, like her father, was pressing all the buttons to see what they would do.

Fergus slid four-year-old Raph on to his lap, switched on the engine and lights, and let him pretend to steer. Athene thought there was something delicious about his little legs in shorts dangling, and his utter determination to drive. Raph yanked the steering wheel from side to side, shouting: 'Make it go, Daddy, make it go!' When Fergus explained they weren't leaving the parking spot, Raph started yelling angrily. Fergus got out of the car, lifted him up, then dumped him on the pavement and shut the door. He threw the keys at Athene, and turned to his son.

'You should never scream like that. Stop it right now.' But Raph went right on screaming, down on the ground, kicking his heels like a tantruming toddler even though he was four. He continued at full pitch for some minutes, a noise which caused the neighbours to appear at their doors.

'What's up with you, Raph, for God's sake?' Fergus asked. 'Can't you do something about him?' he said to Athene.

'Why don't *you* do something?'

'I've got to go. I've a meeting at the Ivy in an hour. I just came back to drop off the car.'

'All right,' said Athene, feeling an uncontrollable anger building up. She pulled Raph off the ground, and gave Fergus a vicious stare.

'We could take the car back if you don't like it,' he said, abruptly.

'No. I like the car. I just don't like what it represents. Just because you didn't have any money when you grew up you think it solves everything, but it doesn't.'

She had a sudden idea. 'Why don't you find out what it's like. Here.' She threw Raph wailing into Fergus's arms, picked up her huge handbag and rummaged for the new car keys. She jumped into the car and drove off, leaving Fergus mouthing at her in the distance like a silent film.

Ninety minutes later – it was a nippy little car – Athene checked into a very fine boutique hotel on the seafront in Brighton. She booked a pedicure for Saturday morning, a massage for Sunday afternoon, and dinner that night. Then she took her shoes off and walked for a while along the dark pebbled beach, looking at the lights of the pier reflecting on the black water, feeling the wind blowing inside her head, her life suddenly, lusciously empty.

Back at home, Fergus was astounded, but he thought Athene would be back later. Probably she'd gone for some Ben and Jerry's Cherry Garcia frozen yogurt, which she often ate in time of need. He irritatedly cancelled his meeting at the Ivy. Then he put the children straight to bed. Cora the nanny was off, since it was Friday night. He sat at the kitchen table, drank a bottle of wine on an empty stomach, then staggered up to bed, mightily pissed off and exhausted.

He was woken before dawn on Saturday morning by a persistent hammering inside and outside his head. Raph was on the bottom of the bed, dressed in pyjamas and a pirate hat, and was employing the plastic hammer and chisel from his Bob the Builder toolkit on Athene's mother-of-pearl inlaid jewellery box.

'Dad! I want to get the treasure, but it won't open.' In the light from the door, he stood up and took a heavier swing. A shard of mother-of-pearl flew up.

'Stop. Stop it now!' shouted Fergus 'What the . . . what the hell do you think you're doing? It's five thirty,' he said, peering in shock at the clock. 'It's still dark outside. And that's your mother's, so leave it alone.' Fergus persuaded Raph not to commit further disturbance in his room, and lay back down to grapple for more sleep. But the noise had woken Hannah up, and she was blaring, 'Mama! Mama!' like a foghorn. 'Jesus,' said Fergus. Why couldn't Athene deal with this? He staggered into the spare room, but the bed was crisply made up. Athene wasn't there.

He picked Hannah out of her cot, and brought her into bed with him. She seemed warm, friendly and relatively silent, but she did smell a little ripe. In fact, she needed changing. He headed through to the nursery and sorted her out.

'Breakfast, then?' Fergus said mock-cheerily to the children, while trying to call Athene. She had her bloody phone turned off. He rang down to the nanny in her flat, but got no reply there either. He put Hannah in her ergonomic wooden high chair and tried to feed her some Cheerios and milk. She shook her head and kept her mouth resolutely shut, except to enquire 'Where Mama?' now and then in a small, sad voice. Exasperated, Fergus put some dry Cheerios on her tray. Hannah flung them, one by one, on to the floor, where Raph went round woofing like a dog and eating them. They both laughed. Fergus did not. He stashed the kids in front of *Balamory*, and they stared dumbly at the simple joys of Scottish seaside life in the cute, Fisher-Price-coloured village.

Fergus drank three cups of black coffee, read the sports section, and gnawed at the skin round his nails. He tried texting Athene, to no avail. He was suddenly worried she'd crashed the car, but surely the police would have rung him? He had a photoshoot later in the day, with a band, so he couldn't take the kids. He stormed down to the nanny's flat to ask for help. Cora emerged from her bathroom wearing a large cream hat and a silk suit with a cream rose in the lapel. Her sister's wedding. He'd forgotten, but he suddenly suspected Athene had not. Cora was busy all day, all night, and wouldn't be back until Sunday evening. Fergus smiled inanely at Cora, wished her sister the best, and then went upstairs to grind his teeth.

It was one of the longest mornings of his life. Hannah wouldn't get into the Bugaboo Frog – he felt like a prison guard strapping her in – and then she wouldn't get out either. Any change seemed to fill her with horror, and she hadn't eaten anything yet. Somehow, when Athene was there, everything flowed, stuff got scheduled with the kids, but here he was sitting in the Primrose Hill playpark with all the other hungover Saturday fathers, waiting for the minutes to go by. Hannah wanted to do impossibly dangerous stunts that her walking and balancing skills did not allow, and Raph got sand in his eyes in a fight with a three year old in an Arsenal strip. Fergus sat with Raph on his knee and tried Athene again. 'I'm by the seaside,' her text came back.

'When R U back? I've got to work.'

'Back Monday p.m. Have a great weekend with the kids.'

He tried to ring Athene properly, but her phone immediately turned off.

Fergus called two nanny agencies, which were closed on Saturdays. Then he tried Blue, his assistant: 'No, you just have to hang on to them for an hour, Blue, while I do the shoot. Take them for an ice cream or something . . . What d'you mean, you're not paid to . . . No, no nappies, I guarantee. I'll pay you danger money . . .'

Fergus cooked bacon and eggs and beans for his and Raph's lunch, but Hannah was still on hunger strike. She had a will of iron. 'Maybe she's ill,' said Fergus to Raph, who was rapidly having to become his confidant.

'No, she likes mushy stuff,' said Raph knowledgeably. Fergus offered her apple puree and Hannah rubbed it in her hair and started crying. 'Maybe a Smartie?' said Raph, pointing hopefully to the high shelf where sweets and evil mood-swinging items with E-numbers were kept out of reach.

'You're right, my man.' Fergus scattered the Smarties on the high-chair tray, and Hannah ate them all happily. Which meant she was on a psychotic chocolate-covered sugar high when he handed her at the studio to Blue, who looked absolutely horrified. 'This is an Alexander McQueen jacket,' he said. 'Wool-cashmere blend. This season. And if she puts her hands anywhere . . .'

'I'm washing them,' said Fergus, his voice cracking with stress. 'I'm washing her hands now.' Blue, with a pained expression on his face, loaded the kids back into the car, and drove off. He circled the studio block five times, until Hannah threw up, whereupon Blue reappeared at the door, alongside the band awaiting their photoshoot for the cover of *Esquire*.

'Jesus wept,' said Fergus, staring at the mess. 'Just try to contain them in front of the telly.' He handed Blue the babywipes, closed the door of the back room of the studio, and pretended to the band that nothing was happening. He kept hearing Hannah crying in the background. It was the worst shoot he'd ever done. Not that anyone noticed. He stuck the band members among some stuffed stags from the good old taxidermy collection, and everyone was highly impressed.

'A thousand pounds,' whispered Blue angrily afterwards. 'That's what you owe me if the dry cleaning doesn't work.' He stuck his chin in the air defiantly. 'I let Raph play with your laptop, by the way, but the screen's frozen now.'

Fergus drove Hannah and Raph back home in the stinking car, as they gratingly sang 'The Wheels on the Bus Go Round and Round' together, fifteen times in a row, each one more out of tune. Raph ate a huge dinner, but Hannah would only drink a bottle of milk. Fergus made many offerings to her: bread, cereal, fruit, raisins, but all were ignored or tossed aside. After fifteen minutes of struggle, he pushed a yoghurt-covered spoon into her mouth, and she started wailing: 'Want Mama, want Mama!'

'Oh come on, it's yummy strawberry,' said Fergus in a bright voice, laced with dread.

But Hannah would not negotiate. She moved into full-on hysterical screaming. Fergus felt ready to scream himself. In his head, Hannah became this huge powerful force, a monster that couldn't be denied, a giant baby that was a noise machine with an open mouth and boiling emotions that wound Fergus right up. He picked up last week's weapon, *The Contented Toddler Years*, from the kitchen table, and began reading the chapter on food. Everything he was doing was wrong. Fergus started to worry, and then he suddenly realised something: children can't tell the time! He could put them to bed at six o'clock, and they'd think it was seven thirty. Genius! He did Hannah's bath, and went to get a nappy. There were none.

Sighing, he loaded the kids into the car and drove to the corner shop. He carried Hannah in. She was floppy and exhausted, giving sudden little shivers, the aftermath of crying so hard. 'Mini, midi, maxi nappies or pull-ups, Pampers or Huggies?' said the shop owner enthusiastically.

Fergus was stymied. 'Just give me whatever. Kind of medium. And a bottle of tequila and six limes.' The shop owner looked at him askance, as though he might report the alcoholic fathering to the social services, and took his platinum credit card. Fergus felt his hip getting slightly damp where Hannah was perched, nappyless, in her pyjamas. He sighed. It couldn't possibly get any worse. Hannah crashed out in the car on the way home, and she stayed virtually asleep as he changed her and put her in her cot, where she lay breathing gently, suddenly pink and angelic. He kissed her resignedly. He put Raph in bed too, opened the Tequila, made a jug of Margaritas, and turned on the football highlights. Soon he felt much, much better.

At three in the morning, Fergus felt much worse when Hannah awoke, yowling wildly with hunger. He went down to the kitchen and got a bottle of milk, and on re-entering her room, he stood on a sharp piece of Raph's Duplo. His foot began to bleed on the white carpet.

At dawn, everyone was up again for a brand new day. Fergus looked at the bags under his eyes, the red veins in them, last week's *Contented Toddler*-induced scar on his forehead, and the plaster on his foot, and felt that full-time motherhood was perhaps not for him. He wandered down to the kitchen and arrested Raph who was inside the fridge testing the remains of his Margarita.

'It's like a lime ice lolly, Dad,' observed Raph, before returning a little unsteadily to his Duplo.

Fergus guiltily made porridge with maple syrup, which everyone ate, and then tried to work at the kitchen table while the kids played together on the floor. Raph was making repetitive 'neeawww-boom!' noises behind the sofa, and Hannah was humming tunelessly.

On his computer – once he'd fixed it – Fergus went through a series of photographs he was editing for an exhibition in Berlin. He became completely absorbed in the scenes, which looked as though they had come from some film noir, although in fact each had been carefully staged. There was a woman's hair spread out in the corner of the frame, as though she'd been dragged across thick red carpet, and the theatrical style created a nightmarish sense of foreboding – and maybe thinly veiled violence. Fergus had used cinematic devices, manipulating the camera angle and depth of field. There were cruel close-ups and sharply cropped figures standing at the edge of the frame, which heightened the atmosphere. When Fergus had been shooting the series, he'd thought about the old grainy videos they used to watch in the squat of *Carrie*, *All About Eve*, and *The Exorcist*. The women in his pictures were surreal and uncanny dolls, or just disembodied legs in white tights, strange arms, the rest off screen. He marked the places where Blue needed to crop or Photoshop an image. He wondered how badly these objectified women would go down with Athene's therapist, and he shrugged. He wasn't ashamed of using photography as a place to play around with his psyche.

'Neeawww-boom!' said Raph.

Fergus suddenly saw that Raph had built two tall, multi-coloured towers with his cubes of Duplo, and was ramming a Duplo plane, piloted by a white plastic cat, into one tower, and then the next. All the bricks fell down in a pile, then Raph built them up again, ready for the kamikaze cat to attack.

Fergus closed his laptop, chilled. 'What're you doing, son?'

'This big plane goes into the tower and boom! It all falls down. There's a fire too, so I got a fire engine coming. Nee naw! Nee naw!'

'Where d'you see that?'

'It was on telly again this morning, when you was upstairs with Hannah. It's amazing! Neeawww-boom!'

Fergus shook his head and wondered what he had wrought.

The hours passed slowly and they reminded Fergus of what he used to call cabbage time back in Burnoch, where nothing of consequence was said or done. When Cora the nanny came back on Sunday evening, he was ecstatic. 'I love you, Cora,' he said to her on the doorstep. 'How was the wedding? Do you want a raise? What does Athene pay you? I think you deserve a raise.'

Fergus made his victorious escape to the Compton Club in Soho, a warren of a place where decadence is concealed in the dark, and a sort of omerta seals the lips of its celebrity clientele. He met up with Charles and Blue, plus a random selection of BritArt types who constantly hung out there in the rooftop bar. There was also a girl in a Viktor and Rolf asymmetric top, who represented beauty, and an architect in black who represented money. They fitted together in a perfect equation.

Charles was enthroned in a huge cracked-leather armchair, looking like the Godfather he was to all of them, his wallet fat from their artistic portfolios, his credit card powdery with joy. 'Marvellous to be in civilised company, marvellous,' he was saying. 'Had such a dull weekend in the Cotswolds with horrid couples who kept shooting things. And I missed you,' he said, turning to Blue, who looked back at him lovingly.

They were ordering champagne by the bucket. Charles was plotting with Blue to invest in a restaurant. There was talk of Asian fusion. 'No, no,' said Fergus, 'make it Scottish. Why don't the Scots make sushi? Why, with all that seaweed and fresh fish and shellfish all year round in globally warming waters are they not intelligent enough to make people pay through the nose for a sliver of scallop dumped on a hummock of rice?'

'Not a ridiculous idea,' said Charles. 'But what matters most in a restaurant now is not just the food but the right designer, the right paintings or installations on the walls, the right people. It's all about aura.'

Fergus looked down and noticed a glop of baby rice on his jacket, which was not contributing to his aura at all. As Fergus washed his sleeve in the Gents, some kid from St Martin's recognised him and offered him a line. Fergus took it. 'Thanks. That'll help. I tell you, the E-numbers in a can of Fanta would send me doo-lally tonight after what I've been through.' The student laughed. Fergus ordered grapefruit-flavoured vodka: fine, crisp, unsticky and 'quaffable in large quantities', according to Charles. Fergus imbibed large quantities. Time now passed like a torpedo, an unsettling change of rhythm.

Blue was talking to a bodily fluid sculptor about *Les Fleurs du Mal*. 'According to Nietzsche,' announced Blue, 'decadence is not to be fought but is absolutely necessary.'

Fergus thought Blue was learning a lot at Charles's knee, so to speak, just as Fergus had. He wondered if he ought to warn Blue before it all went too far. But Charles was whispering bitchily in his ear: 'That sculptor there has brought *his biographer* with him to see the Sunday-night action.' They laughed. Meanwhile, the biographer occasionally scribbled in a little black Moleskine notebook.

'Decay and decadence are natural excretory functions,' continued the sculptor, who was known for his works in shit. *Of* shit, thought Fergus. 'Natural excretory function,' repeated the sculptor, sipping champagne. 'It's the decomposition of society, but in the end it provides a healthy balance: the twin towers fall, wars begin, death annihilates life in order to make room for more life, death consumes life's excess . . .'

Fergus felt a surge of anger. 'You are so fucking pretentious, talking in a language you don't even understand. No, you're just heartless and stupid. You're so closeted into your tiny world, playing with shit and blood like they're Play Doh, that you think mass death is just another fun subject for your art. Well, you're wrong.'

He jabbed his finger in the sculptor's face. 'Gentlemen, gentlemen!' admonished Charles.

A painter interrupted, trying to side with the sculptor. Fergus had been boiling up with anger since Friday, and the painter got the brunt of it: 'You're a visual artist, that's why you should fucking shut up. Don't justify what you do in words, or they'll find out how shallow you really are.'

And then Fergus sat morosely knocking back vodkas for an hour, moaning to Blue about how depressed he felt about the state of the art world, which was code for himself. Ethan Erikson, a video artist, sat down at their table. Fergus perked up and told him exactly how crap his million-dollar installations of time-lapse gay hot-tub scenes were.

'Actually, they're very funny in a Chaplin-in-chaps kind of way,' said Charles. 'Now can you chill out, Fergus?'

'If they were heterosexual and slowed down they'd be middlebrow porn, Ethan. Why don't you do something that matters? At least one of us should stop producing crap, or little plastic soldiers, or grubby laundry, or creatures in formaldehyde, or damning photographs of B-list celebrities (my own little vice) and calling it art. These people can't be duped by you for fucking ever, can they, Charles?'

'Fergus, shut up, you're roaring drunk,' said Charles.

'Drunk? No, no, no, no, this is art. Film me, Ethan. Film me on your new five-hundred-quid mini camera. Come on, look.'

And Fergus ripped off his shirt so the buttons popped off in the manner of the Incredible Hulk transforming, and with shaking hands he pulled down his trousers and jumped up naked on to the bar. He had to stoop a little to keep his head from touching the ceiling. He spread his legs wide and shouted slurred encouragement to the crowd. 'Look! Take me!'

There was an embarrassed rumble round the room and people turned away whispering, concentrating hard on their cocktails.

'Cock!' shouted Fergus. 'Not cocktails! Cock! Look at it, the wee flaccid thing! What can this display's inner meaning be, art lovers? Shall I piss to bring some movement to the installation? Let me see, is it abject? Is it criticising existing norms, challenging received opinions? Yes it is!'

The artists started muttering and leaving for the big bar downstairs. The barman grabbed Fergus's leg and hauled him off balance until he fell on to Charles who was purple with embarrassment. 'Stop it,' he growled. 'Just pull yourself together.'

Fergus gestured for Ethan to follow him. 'Come on, big

man, it's the Emperor's New Clothes installation. Come and see the bollocks!'

And Fergus strode regally out of the bar into the stairwell, where he passed many surprised-looking club members and headed on, directly through the private cinema room filled with Sony executives, making an amusing shadow dance as he crossed stark bollock naked in front of the screen. He went on to the downstairs lounge bar and paraded through it, unstoppable, Charles shouting behind him, until he was outside and the cool dark shocked him into knowledge of what he was doing. Still, he couldn't pause now. He had to finish the transgressive act, take it to its logical end. Girls were squealing and laughing in the street. Men were saying 'Get a grip, mate!' A waiter offered him a white tablecloth for modesty, but he refused and marched on down Old Compton Street until he fell into the arms of a policeman, who escorted him from the area.

Fergus was booked for indecent exposure and public nuisance at Bow Street magistrates. His single call was to Cora, to offer her double time for babysitting all night, while he had a good, uninterrupted sleep in a solitary police cell.

The ensuing, amusing publicity almost doubled the expected price of a series of Fergus's photographs at an auction in Sotheby's to just over a million pounds. But ten days later the full, glorious, stupidity of his act rebounded on him as he was walking across the Millennium Bridge after a meeting at the Tate Modern, and got the call to go on *Celebrity Big Brother* for Comic Relief.

'You're fucking joking,' he said.

'No,' said the *Big Brother* researcher.

Fergus threw his phone in the Thames. He felt a sudden rush of shame.

Kate Muir

ARTCRUSH
Autumn 2001

Marcus Anhelm assesses the use of intimacy and voyeurism in the work of photographer Fergus MacFarlane

MacFarlane's images offer a different way of negotiating subjectivity; decoding his insider-outsider viewpoint is the key to comprehending his work. MacFarlane attempts to distance the viewer from identification with the autobiographical content of his work, yet this is simultaneously contradicted by his control of the narrative and intensely personal style.

Although MacFarlane's photography fits the so-called Young British Artist matrix, defining the world in terms of a shared consumption of mass culture, it also confounds it with what some critics have decried as 'dated sympathy and intimacy'. He is an autodidact, and thus refreshingly free of the norms of textbook photography.

John Roberts suggests that one key change in the art of the 1990s was its 'loss of guilt in front of popular culture'. He argues that the 'bad behaviour' of the Young British Artists should be read as neither apolitical, nor merely infantile, but as 'a celebration of aesthetically despised categories of popular language and culture in deliberate reaction to theory-led, deconstructive art practices of the 1980s.'

MacFarlane's 'Trash' photography series exemplifies this, emphasising the vulnerability of body and mind to damage and scarring of the most banal sort. But his newer work – such as the video installation *Maw* – exhibits fragile traces of memory and articulates a sense of otherness, of the familiar becoming strange, of the strange becoming familiar.

The influences are obvious: declining industrial working-class Scotland, a fine awareness of poverty and its degradations, yet a perverse joy in what is immediately available. It is MacFarlane's photo collages of the upper classes at play which are most disturbing, and reveal a real class hatred, a product of his damaged past. This proletarian-philistine reflex is not noticeable in his earlier work (Vauxhall Viva, see Flow catalogue, 1990) and the initial, iconic portraits of his wife, Athene Arbuthnot (Unknown Territory, Taschen, 1992). When MacFarlane is on form, consistently focused on the body, on the domestic, on skin, on texture, he seems . . . continued pp. 17–22

294

London Evening News

Soho Streaker

Some said it was performance art when celebrity photographer Fergus MacFarlane streaked through Soho last night. The whole of Old Compton Street was treated to the sight of MacFarlane – dazed, confused and stark naked. MacFarlane had been carousing with his BritArt cronies in the Compton Club, and was arrested for indecent exposure just before he reached Shaftesbury Avenue. His multimillionaire dealer, Charles Wentworth, refused to comment.

Chapter Sixteen

2004
'We Laugh Indoors':
Death Cab for Cutie

Fergus drove his Land Cruiser past Jerk Chicken, Cheap and Eazi International Shipping, Aladin Gents Hairstylist, and the Just Brother café. The streets of Hackney were busy with drug dealers' dogs, orange onion sacks, screaming offers of phonecards for Pakistan, Bangladesh and Afghanistan, okra and Toilet Duck, and Stop the War posters. Plus the multilingual graffiti that indicated this was the sorting depot of London. A place of change, not always for the best, but change nonetheless. Fergus was here to make a still-life of this moment of flux, of the traces left behind by the pioneers and the failures. Once again, he turned off the High Street into an elephant-grey council estate of four-storey flats, some boarded up with metal screens on the windows, some with carefully tended spider plants and ornaments, all facing on to long concrete balconies which funnelled crime and wind and threat.

Surrounded by the low-rise estate was one thirty-storey

tower, standing out like a sore thumb (as Fergus's mum would say), and zoned for demolition. The doors were boarded, and yellow tape marked the site as dangerous and unstable. The high flats were ugly pebbledashed stacking cubes, the quality of the building materials was shoddy, and fingers of green damp crawled up from the earth. The top floor was rumoured to move up to three feet in a sidewind, and great cracks had appeared in the walls. It ought, thought Fergus, to be exploded, a cardstack of concrete falling into a pile of dust. He used to like to watch those demolition shots on film with Raph when he was a toddler obsessed with diggers and destruction, especially when they ran the film backwards and all was magically restored. But while it awaited the wrecking ball or the dynamite, the building still held the stories of its tenants.

Fergus took out the yellow hard hat and fluorescent waistcoat he kept in his car for moments like this, and slipped through a hole he'd cut in the wire fence last time. He lifted a board off the service door and climbed up slowly through the piss-perfumed hallways filled with crunchy broken glass, blood-stained mattresses, and discarded prams. The doors of most of the flats were already open, kicked in by local gangs, already scavenged. He reached the twenty-first floor, where his work would begin. His cameras weighed heavily upon him.

Now Fergus was alone in the great creaking tower, sure that he could feel it sway, leaning right out of the smashed high corridor window over the dog-shitty playpark way below, and wondering what the suicide rate was from such places. He stopped himself hanging out and got on with the work of portraying ordinary lives passing. He had one hundred and seventy-two pictures to take, one of each sixteen by twelve feet low-ceilinged box, which had once been someone's living room.

He was two thirds of the way through the project now, and what astounded him as he set up his tripod, battery lights and reflectors, was the range of the traces on the walls: from purple flock wallpaper, to Socialist Worker posters, from the colours of the Orient to the blandness of British magnolia, from Arabic graffiti to a plate of the Pope on the wall that no one even wanted to nick. Some of his photographs were plain yellow Mondrian squares, others reddish Rothkos, and one was old Anaglypta wallpaper painted bubblegum-pink with orange, red and blue spots, as good as a Damien Hirst. Often the view included a dead ironing board, a burst couch, newspapers, or broken toys. Some of the flats contained scenes petrified in time – tables overturned, coffee mugs on the floor, as though they had been raided, and refugees had run away with their belongings on their backs. Probably some of the council tenants were indeed refugees, with last-minute habits that died hard once the eviction order came.

By taking the same shot towards the back wall, at the same height, with the same exposure, Fergus imposed a uniformity which allowed the individuality, the perverse diversity, the battle of cultures, centre stage. He had pierced the blank concrete exterior of the tower, opened its heart. He would blow perhaps a hundred of the photographs up to metre-squared size, and display them all in a fine London gallery far from here in every sense.

Fergus was passing the fourteenth floor, using a torch to

find his way down the dark stairwell, when he heard voices below him, structural engineers checking the options for demolition. He walked by the men, holding his metal case and tripod, like any surveyor, and gave them a friendly, fellow-worker's nod.

Back in the safety of the car – which he'd paid a gang of small boys to guard – Fergus sat back, queasily aware of the contrasting leathery luxury around him, and in his head he saw a loop of memory from his childhood, his mother possessed as she stripped the new wallpaper off their living-room wall, with Abba blasting out, as the layers of previous tenants reappeared. He wanted to ask his mother why she'd done that, why she buried all traces of his dad, wiped him from their lives, never talked about him, and replaced him with . . . he wasn't going to even bother going there. Fergus revved the car up and got out of the estate.

He headed for the studio, his mobile throbbing constantly in the car cradle: a commercial agency wanting him to photograph two household gods from Arsenal for an advertising campaign for watches. Another message from a woman who was pursuing him. He didn't bother to call either back. He could see no reason now. He was working hard on his own obsessions, so hard he was sleeping only four or five hours a night, and his veins ran with Red Bull and espresso, when they weren't channelling vodka. Yet his skin was papery, his eyes were sunken and sullen, and his ribs were showing in the same way they had long ago in the squat. He wore the straggly remains of a brown beard. What was the point in shaving?

Fergus wondered why he wasn't happier, because he

had been released from many onerous bonds: his marriage, and the business of airbrushing celebrity egos for cash. Fergus could not complain of the management genius that had now entirely liberated him from the need to make money. He was thirty-four and worth many millions of pounds, most of which lay dormant in art warehouses. This was surprising. Until he'd had to go to the divorce lawyers, Fergus hadn't properly been unaware of his net worth. Now it allowed him, at least, to be gracious.

He'd just signed the house over to Athene and the kids. But he'd kept the half-finished barn they'd bought together in Scotland, which Athene had never been keen on. But he'd sloughed off the Belsize Park house like the big white albatross it was. He'd felt a weird lightness when he'd gone round with the removal company to pick up his books, photographs and clothes, and realised what little he possessed – ten years of marriage and all he had to show for it was a half-full Transit. He'd left Athene buried under all the tonnes of polished concrete, Italian marble, range cookers and bright Fisher-Price plastic.

Athene had the kids most of the time, though, and Fergus found being deprived of daily contact felt like living with an unhealed sore. Picking at it, he was so aware, when he had Raph and Hannah on those two weekends a month in his child-unfriendly loft next to the studio in Hoxton, of his non-presence during their week. He found himself searching for clues to their lives, their needs, following up missing links in their conversation, second-guessing. At seven and, particularly, four, they had no real ability to recount troubles and successes of the previous days: they lived in the present, and he was always in the wrong place, at the wrong time. As he stood on the sidelines at school concerts and sports days, he had a freakish sense that he was merely acting the part of 'Dad' as Raph and Hannah ran to the more familiar person they called Mummy. Worse still, Athene was sometimes accompanied by her new lover, her American old friend Henry, a sleek master of the universe who towered over Fergus and stank of entitlement.

Fergus minded that the boyfriend got to play a fathering role, but his feelings for Athene were cauterised. The relationship was now practical and civilised. How could their relationship be so utterly empty when once it had been full? He tried to explain it to Charles, who had always been fond of Athene, and still went round to see her and the kids.

'I loved her, of course I did, but I also wonder if I loved her for being an antidote to my past, for being as far from Burnoch as possible?'

Charles looked unconvinced. 'Or it just might be that she's beautiful, and your instinct is to be deeply influenced by images and surfaces. But she's a good person, too. And that Henry is a total dick. He has a Humvee,' he added helpfully.

Fergus wasn't going to go there. 'Yes, but in the end with us there was never that thing I see in other couples, like you and Blue, for God's sake: you are real best friends, intellectual companions.'

He knew, at heart, that he'd been a wrong turning for Athene, and now she was back on track and had solidified into the charming socialite she'd always been: warm and a bit superficial. He could think that now. Yet long ago her social carapace, her education, her confidence had camouflaged her failings. And his failings, which were a great deal worse.

Half the time, the kids could barely fit him into their busy schedule of schoolfriends' birthday parties and sports. Fergus stood watching Raph play football on Saturday morning on Primrose Hill, with over-equipped children who played like a bunch of padded-up nancys. They were rubbish, pure rubbish, because they didn't put in the time in alleyways after school slamming the ball against the wall, again and again. They only worked with professional trainers, and they didn't fight for the ball. Fergus despaired, tried to get Raph going himself, but his son got bored after half an hour with him on the pitch. Indeed, Raph wasn't even that interested in watching the match on Saturday afternoon, although he pretended to, and he had to have the latest Arsenal strip each year and hundreds of pounds' worth of collectable football cards in some book. Fergus didn't get it.

Still, Hannah's social events were worse: Fergus found his job on the weekends was to provide a sort of chauffeur service to take Hannah to eat leatherette pizza while watching some crap clown with her peers, or to arrive in some indoor soft-play hell filled with screaming spoilt children and snot-covered plastic balls and slides. Equally irritating were the green families who served organic tofu cake and carrot sticks to a table of sad, hungry four-year-old faces. Once, when Fergus took some photographs of Hannah's friends at the execrable soft-play centre, a manager came running up to him screaming that he had to get signed permission from each parent, as though he were some kind of pervert. This was not the way quality time should be used, thought Fergus.

He became slippery about taking them to parties, and instead made them scooter for miles as he ran through the park, or else they'd hang out in Hoxton, or go round grand art galleries with Charles and Blue, who liked children who knew their place – in small doses. What Hannah had to say, sitting on your shoulders, about the Picasso or the Saatchi collection was often similar, and certainly funnier, than the average punter's reaction. Raph would spend hours staring at Jake and Dinos Chapman's 'Hell', the landscape of carnage peopled by toy soldiers. It was probably unhealthy, but it wasn't dull.

Fergus soon found he needed to make his own version of hell, to work on something that mattered. His obsession began when he was visiting his Glaswegian friend Marty who was a photo editor on the *Sunday Times*, late one night in the office. (Long ago, Marty had been the paparazzo at his wedding.) Fergus waited by the picture desk until Marty was ready for a drink, and meanwhile saw onscreen, and in blurred black-and-white printouts, all the discarded photographs from that evening's suicide bombing: the ones that were too gory and distressing over readers' breakfasts in Tunbridge Wells. He stared at a teenage girl with her face missing, and a market with bodies, black-charred flesh and fruit flung indiscriminately. Women were running, mouths dark and wide with screams, holding flowered shower curtains to collect the remains. 'Oh Jesus,' Fergus said. 'How do you pick when . . . oh my God.'

'We don't pick,' Marty said. 'We spike. You can't use this

stuff. Maybe a bloodstain on a wall, or a child's body from a distance, or an iconic lost sandal. We use a lot of iconic lost sandals. We imply. And it doesn't make the front page any more, anywhere but Iraq.' He sighed. They went drinking, Scottish style.

Fergus remained preoccupied with the aftermath of the bombs in Iraq and thought: if people do not care to see the reality of Iraq as news, maybe they will accept it as art. So a few weeks later, he arranged to go into Baghdad in the reassuring company of a war-jaded correspondent from the *Sunday Times*. Athene was incandescent: 'What if you die out there? What if you're kidnapped? What will I tell the children? That their father doesn't care? That he'll risk—'

Fergus interrupted. 'I need to go. I have to.' For a moment Fergus wondered what was wrong with him, that he placed so little value on his own life. He couldn't bear to think about Raph and Hannah; he had to blank them out to do his job. And he could see a point to going to Iraq, while his life here at home seemed to be increasingly flat and pointless.

He took a flight with the journalist from Amman on a Royal Jordanian aircraft piloted and crewed by crazed South Africans, who flew at high altitude and did a stomach-churning corkscrew landing for safety. At the first checkpoint just outside the airport complex, two dusty, banged-up Mercedes were waiting for them with drivers and armed bodyguards. Baghdad looked pretty rough after years of battering. That there were still palm trees waving among the debris seemed extraordinary. Fergus stayed with the other correspondents – who weren't embedded with the Americans – at the rundown Hamra Hotel, a ten-storey seventies' concrete building with terrible food, protected by a ring of blast-proof concrete walls and patrolled by Iraqi and British security guards.

From the rooftop of the Hamra there was a panoramic view of Baghdad. Fergus learned to read the signs in the sky before he grabbed his camera and rushed out in one of the two old Mercs.

'The biggest bombs are obvious,' said the *Sunday Times* journalist. 'You hear the bang and feel the windows rattle – or even break, if it's close by. For the others, you'll see the puff of white smoke from here, made by the explosives, then the billowing black smoke of fires from cars, petrol, buildings, whatever.'

Sometimes there was the distant crackling of small arms. The journalists Fergus was with were keen to avoid the locals' wrath at foreigners and possible kidnapping. 'I'm a firm believer in the fifteen-minute in-and-out job,' said the *Sunday Times* guy. 'Before they spot what you're doing.' Two highly paid gunmen shadowed them every tense second they were on the streets.

The first time Fergus went out to an attack, just outside a mosque, he was terrified by the chaos and madness, people running everywhere shouting incomprehensibly. Then in front of his trainers, he saw a burned, severed hand lying like a black glove on the pavement, and he thought: 'Oh, I'll just take a picture of that glove.' He was working away from all angles, concentrating for some two minutes before his brain contacted his body with the truth, and in the heat and the stench, he vomited into the gutter.

That had been nothing. Had he known what was to come, he would have saved his bile.

They tended to arrive at the scenes of carnage along with half of Baghdad: first the Iraqi police in blue shirts, and armed with pistols and AK47s, walking around flapping their arms; then the old red fire trucks and ambulances; then crowds of worried civilians; then a convoy of unhelpful Americans in Humvees, only interested in taking bodyparts for DNA-testing if there'd been a suicide bomb.

Fergus stayed in Baghdad for a month, photographing fresh bombsites or the hospitals by day and observing the psychotic jollity and boorishness of the safe Green Zone by night. As usual, the camera protected him and let him detach from the present while capturing it for the future. A tiny digital Leica let him operate almost unnoticed on the run – and sometimes he had to run away – and it was accurate. He worked surreptitiously, at incredible speed, but even then the bodyguards sometimes had to drag him away. The other journalists, who were pretty reckless themselves, thought he had a death wish. Or that he was just stupid.

'No,' said Fergus, over a beer. 'But you have to understand, I've got to be there at the very second it happens. The best shots are often just when you think it's all over. And there's something about the Leica that gets me going. You know, Henri Cartier-Bresson said the Leica feels "like a big warm kiss, like a shot from a revolver, and like the psychoanalyst's couch". The last two are very useful here.'

Fergus had never felt such adrenaline and fear, coupled

with an aching disgust and disbelief. Now he could understand the addiction and attraction for the war correspondents around him: after all, what else mattered? Fergus's sleep was a slide show of carnage, yet in the Green Zone, if he visited in the evenings, there was beer and skittles, laughing American soldiers round the pool, the PX general store filled with Reese's Peanut Butter Cups. Fergus took photographs of this too, the garish schizophrenic carnival world of comfort and safety. His Iraq exhibition would be one of contrasts.

Back in his studio in London, Fergus sat drinking coffee and spooling through the thousands of images from Baghdad on his laptop, cropping away the clichés, making them lean with the intensity of silence. Marty had collected a series of the unpublishable photographs from news services like Agence France Presse and Reuters, and Fergus wanted to display his large photographs alongside those instant grainy printouts with their bare-knuckle captions: 'An explosion outside the western mosque killed twelve people and left thirty-five injured. Local media said the bomb was triggered by a home-made device using a mobile phone and washing-machine motor attached to a gas cylinder. A witness reported seeing nails scattered before the area was cleared by local security forces.' Then there would be Fergus's prints, of the surreal things that happen after a bomb: people praying prone in the dust; a man's torn shirt suspended on the telephone wires; on the canopy above a bread shop, a leg still wearing a Nike shoe . . . and then the boarders, sweepers, glaziers and business as usual.

At night, when he went out, he felt London was the surreal place, not Baghdad. Everything at home seemed so blinging, so super-rich for a country still fighting a conflict. In the booming economy, Charles had diversified and, together with Blue, plus a heavyweight backer, had opened a Scottish seafood restaurant called Alba, which he used as a base for all operations. Fergus walked into Alba one evening to discuss plans with Charles for his Iraq exhibition. Charles sucked his teeth and said: 'Everyone will come to that and of course no one will buy anything, apart from institutions.' Fergus shrugged. The permanent collections of MOMA and the Met in New York, the Tate Modern and the Stedelijk Museum in Amsterdam had all bought his work already.

'As a boost for your reputation, though, it's brilliant,' added Charles.

'I didn't do it for a "boost". I did it because I had to.' Fergus felt Charles was belittling him.

'Exactly,' said Charles. 'That's why you are the talent and I am the management.'

Alba was a light and fascinating distraction for Fergus during what turned out to be a dark year. He liked to go behind the scenes in the kitchen, watching and learning from the chefs, and occasionally killing lobsters with the same enthusiasm he had long ago in the deli in Burnoch. Alba took no reservations – you just turned up, drank at the hundred-foot long zinc counter in the former car showroom, and waited for a table. Economically, it was a brilliant move: the restaurant was never empty. There were, of course, huge MacFarlane prints on the walls, as well as those of some other artists Charles represented, and the rest was decorated with fabrics by Timorous Beasties, the design company from Glasgow that specialised in *toile de Jouy* imitations charmingly picturing Glasgow's high flats, dreaming spires, homeless folk, drug addicts, and menacing seagulls.

In order to be achingly trendy, the restaurant was also organic, the whisky varieties were in the hundreds, and the seafood was trucked overnight from Scotland, the langoustines running live around the back of the van, oysters submerged in sacks, the lobsters sloshing in tanks, the razor clams clattering on the M6. The sushi was thrillingly fresh, and Fergus's contribution to the menu turned out to be the best seller: the Scallop Buttie – something he and Sam Green had invented long ago. This was a traditional soft Scottish bap containing two scallops marinated with a little olive oil and garlic, barbecued for exactly thirty seconds on each side, and finished with a squirt of lemon. They sold hundreds a day, up at the bar. This was nothing to the profit they made on the porridge.

Charles was delighted to have created something himself, rather than selling the creativity of others. He had caused an atmosphere, he had caused a place to appear at the right moment, in the right place. Plus he was the man who invented the haggis seaweed roll, which people ordered once, and then never again. On the night Alba won the *Time Out* Best Newcomer of the Year restaurant award, Charles instituted a late-night lock in, and invited everyone who had supported the restaurant in its early days. To celebrate, there was champagne, bowls of langoustines (plus a tiny silver bowl of cocaine), and 'We Laugh Indoors' by that Seattle band, Death Cab for Cutie, was playing on the sound system – a system where any diner could plug in an iPod and entertain the whole restaurant, should they desire. And people did. They desired to dance, and they piled up the tables and chairs and opened the floor. Fergus shrugged off the weight that always seemed to be upon him now, and watched Charles (somewhat embarrassedly) and Blue (sinuously) dance themselves into a trance of pleasure.

Fergus left at two in the morning, his accumulated lack of sleep pulling him home. But home was this odd rented loft, empty of childish or human noise, with wonderful views round the skyline of London, and no soul. He hid himself under the covers, trying to escape the huge empty space. As he began to enter a feverish, desperate sleep, his mobile rang. Fergus leaned over and switched it off. Then the house phone rang. It was Blue.

'Fergus?'

'Hey, Blue, I'm asleep. Great party. But can you ring back tomorrow?'

'No. Listen, Charles has had a heart attack.'

'You're joking.' Fergus shot up in bed and felt dizzy. 'He can't have. Are you sure? He's forty, for God's sake. You don't—'

'Just come, Fergus. I didn't know who else to call. I don't know what to do. He's in St Mary's Paddington, cardiac intensive care.'

'Fuck. I'm coming.'

In the dimly lit ward, Charles was an unconscious mess

of wires and tubes. His skin was dead grey in the light from the green screen bleeping by his bed. A plastic tube was pumping oxygen into his nose. There was a drip going into his hand. His blond hair was flopping over one eye. Fergus gingerly pushed it back.

'Charles?' he said quietly, but there was no response.

'He blacked out while we were dancing. I thought he was having some kind of fit.' Blue's voice was strained, high. 'But once we got him here, his heart kept stopping. They shocked him twice, but now it's working again.' He paused. 'I'm so scared, Fergus.'

Fergus looked to the side of the bed and saw a grim trolley with steel plates and electric wires, the dramatic instruments of every hospital casualty film, where they shout 'Clear!' and then shoot a million volts through a corpse to make it rise from the dead. He somehow had never imagined such machines were really used. He wanted to retch. Instead, he put his arm round Blue, who was shaking.

'Did you call his parents?' said Fergus.

'I have. They'll be down here from Aldershot in an hour or so. They didn't know who I was, though. They thought I just worked with him, ran the restaurant. I thought he'd—'

Fergus rolled his eyes. 'Trust Charles. Always discreet and so bloody old fashioned.'

'Never mind,' said Blue, his eyes glinting with unshed tears. 'I don't understand why it's happened. I don't want it to happen to him again. He's not that unhealthy or anything. Do you think it was a bad hit or something?'

The duty doctor came in, a harsh-looking, grey-haired man with wire spectacles, and spoke to them.

'I think he'll be fine now, he's stabilised, but we need to monitor him carefully.' He looked askance at Fergus – still gaunt from Baghdad – and Blue in his designer hoodie, as though they might be candidates for an ASBO.

'Mr Wentworth appears to have had a cocaine-induced cardiac arrest. We just did a bloodtest. He takes cocaine, doesn't he?' The doctor looked steely.

'Very occasionally,' lied Fergus.

'Hmmm. Do you realise the seriousness of this? This is the third cardiac arrest of this kind I've seen in intensive care this year. One patient was in his thirties. You should know that over time, even taken *recreationally*, cocaine weakens the heart. Did Mr Wentworth ever have palpitations that you noticed?'

'Shit.' Blue gulped. 'But we never thought—'

'Well, he's got a second chance now, I hope.' The doctor clipped the board back on the end of the bed and walked briskly out.

'Christ,' said Fergus.

'He took a tiny line at the end of the night. He was too busy before. Too happy.' Blue's voice was getting more hysterical.

'Hold on, hold on. You need to calm down. Let's get a coffee. He's going to be knocked out for a while.'

One of the intensive-care nurses checking Charles's chart and the monitoring screens nodded sympathetically at them. 'He's stable now. His vital signs are normal, but he's heavily sedated. I'll be here. Why don't you both come back in half an hour?'

Fergus gestured at the waves evenly rising and falling on the green screen and steered Blue past the floral plastic curtains towards the visitors' room at the end of the ward. Blue sat weakly down on a hard plastic chair. By the time Fergus had put two pound coins into the vending machine and ordered two white coffees with sugar in polystyrene cups, Charles was dead.

London Evening News
LONDONER'S DIARY

The flame-haired socialite Athene Arbuthnot is back in her Manolos and on our pages again, seen here leaving Annabel's after a charity bash last night, on the arm of American hedge-fund manager Henry Molton III. The two new friends began the evening at Nobu with several of Molton's colleagues and several bottles of Cristale, then ended up in traditional Arbuthnot territory dancing at Annabel's, where they were picked up by a chauffeur in an armour-plated black Humvee – Molton's idea of a little city runaround.

Chapter 17

2005

These Demented Lands:
Alan Warner

It was one of those Scottish summer monsoons, perfectly calibrated to Fergus's mood, where it either sheeted, pished down, rained stair rods, turned dreich, or produced a fine, soft smirr. In whatever form, the heavens dumped on him, without pause. Camus once said that there are many injustices in this world, but one that is never mentioned is that of climate. Scots, thought Fergus, suffer this injustice more than most: not with newsworthy tempests and tornadoes, but with slow dripping water torture.

Trapped inside the stone-walled barn, Fergus's only compensation was watching the sea change over Islay and Jura from the picture window: mist slobbering over the morning or limp, short-lived rainbows. Then came the glowering sky, the roiling grey waves, the white spindrift, and the sulfurous studies before another storm. In the clouded blank of night, the weather reduced to sound instead of vision: sea slurps and wind screams and breakages on the beach far below. All Fergus could see in the dark was the green light warning intermittently of the rocks, a warning only heeded by the sleepless.

Fergus's barn was a perfect place to dash your insomniac head against stone, to swear and shout alone, to do penance, since the nearest habitation was a mile away. Here was emptiness and time for contemplation and self-loathing. Time for questions too: is this what a breakdown feels like? Is this what bereavement feels like? Is this what a break-up feels like? Is this what a broken man does? Does he literally bend in half with the pain? Does he crouch in a corner, pull his knees towards his crumpled forehead and lock his jaw? Coiled small in agony, in the enormous space, Fergus's lonely rocking form created a clear patch in the builders' dust still on the barn floorboards. In the night, he felt his demons watching through the vast windows and giving him the finger.

The shock of Charles's death opened a wound in Fergus that led to other troubles, an emotional MRSA which so poisoned him by the end of May that he could no longer work or even talk. His mind kept flashing back to the same themes: death, adultery, accidents, absent fathers, lost children. He came north to scream, but he couldn't cry: he never had since the night he left Burnoch for ever. So Fergus paced all day before the beautiful view with aching dry eyes and the mother of all headaches.

Although it was over half a year after Charles's death, Blue and Fergus still talked about him all the time on the phone; it helped them both.

Blue was still running Fergus's studio and business in London; he was too shaken to do it more than half-heartedly, but Fergus didn't care. He had an odd sense of relief, too, that he didn't admit to Blue, that Charles was no longer dragging him into the public eye, that he was no longer for sale. When Charles disappeared, his world went with him. Charles's newspaper obituary had said: 'If there is one thing that defines Wentworth, even more than the stable of New Establishment Photographers whom he has known and nurtured since the early nineties, it is parties.' In hindsight, Fergus thought his friendship with Charles had sometimes been unhealthy: that of father to son; sophisticate to neophyte; business to pleasure; packaging to product. But whatever its intricacies, psychological and social, it had stood solidly there for sixteen years, unchanging while the rest of Fergus's life swirled.

'I miss his unerring judgement, and his poncy corduroy trousers,' said Fergus.

'I wonder all the time,' said Blue. 'I wonder if Charles was just destined to die then, if he always had a badly plumbed heart, or if it would have made a difference if you or I had said something?'

'Don't feel guilty,' said Fergus. 'That careful use of coke, it was Charles's crutch – and it was probably the secret of his success you know. Come on, he was the uptight son of an Army major and he became a gay, celebrity art dealer. No wonder he needed chemical help to reconcile the two.'

Besides, Fergus had his own addictions. He was deprived of most of them here in the wilderness, apart from the drink. There was no work to obsess him, no women for miles, and running over the moor for an hour in the streaming rain, his feet leaden and claggy with mud, was hopeless. Living alone pressed much more heavily upon him here than when he was busily working in

London. After thirteen years with Athene, it was here that he most missed someone's warm presence, a body in the bed.

Over the weeks, as he had as a teenager, he read incessantly to escape. His choices were *The Man Who Walks* followed by *These Demented Lands*; bleak, difficult books that rose out of this landscape, and sucked him back with a negativity so deep it was funny. He inhabited a place of twisted triple meanings, unreliable narrators, and an underlying Presbyterianism that battled any decadence. Any analyst, thought Fergus, would tell him he suffered from the same conflict himself – driven simultaneously by the Protestant work ethic and the desire to be wildly degenerate. He desperately needed some company. He thought about Karen, but the only person he rang was Al. Then, after a few weeks, he called Karen's mother's house, for the hell of it. He still knew the number. He remembered everyone's number in Burnoch. He left a message.

Al was keen to escape for an evening from his new three-bed Barratt house in Oban which contained his six-month-old identical twins and his lovely wife Mairi.

'I like being with the babies, it's not that,' said Al, 'but Mairi's older sister's turned up to help for a month. Help? All she does is interfere and then she sits all night like a big puddin' in front of the telly complaining and eating chocolate Hobnobs.'

Fergus felt a deep relaxation go through his veins at the conversation: he was back in a world where the worst addictions were chocolate Hobnobs.

He poured Al some more wine into a tumbler – he'd not

yet properly equipped the barn. 'By the way, the Co-op's off-sales is brilliant now. I went in and almost missed the choice between Buckfast Tonic Wine and Piat d'Or of old.'

Al was stressed by doubly sleepless nights and the fact he'd also just invested in a massive island charter business. 'I've bought three B-class boats, and they're not just going to do island hopping. We're going to go right out into the Atlantic, going to take divers and birdwatchers right out to the Flannan Islands and St Kilda. But I have to spend a lot refurbishing the boats – they were commercial craft, and uncomfortable doesn't cover it. Plus they're plug ugly.'

'I'll invest in your business, Al,' said Fergus, cheered up by this thought.

'I don't want your charity.' Al looked annoyed. He didn't want to be patronised.

'It's not charity. We'll sign a contract. You can pay me back.'

'Serious?'

'Dead serious,' said Fergus. 'What else have I got to do with my money?'

Al grinned, shook his hand. 'Well,' he said, 'you could buy something less painful to sit on.' He gestured at the wooden table and chairs and the mattress on the floor. 'And a bath might be good. Have you smelled yourself recently?'

Fergus laughed. 'I'm not sure if I live here or I'm just visiting, like a Monopoly counter on the jail square. I like it like this. It's monastic. Nothing to worry about.'

He'd bought the vast shell of a barn, which was imaginatively called Stone Barn by the builders, when they went bankrupt four years ago. He was still married then, and

Fergus had been as excited as a small child showing a sandcastle, but Athene had visited the place for ten minutes, looked disgusted, shuddered in her fur coat in the cold, and then insisted that they drive an hour away to stay in a country house hotel with Reiki massages.

But the barn was Fergus's folly, and he loved it. It was thirty winding miles from Burnoch, and work had stopped after they'd put in the wiring and the glass wall of windows on the narrow gable end looking perilously off the cliff directly into the sea. A wooden stairway led up to the beams of a mezzanine floor that didn't yet exist.

Al looked around. The bathroom had nothing in it but the builders' toilet. 'My brother-in-law's a good plumber and he knows a plasterer.'

'I like the stone walls,' said Fergus.

'Oh that's very New York loft, isn't it?' said Al, in full deflationary mode. 'I tell you, Fergus, come winter up here, it'll freeze the balls off a brass monkey. You'll be wanting plaster and proper insulation.'

Fergus looked at his kitchen, which consisted of a sink, a kettle and two electric rings, and the rest of the barn with the bare bulbs dangling. It was untouched, a place waiting for a beginning.

When Al left, Fergus was alone for another week. He had no television, no broadband, no papers, no contact with the outside world. It was lovely. The weather improved, and he submerged himself in the landscape, the churning sea and the wind-slashed cliffs where flowers struggled and no trees would grow. This land had fathered him in a way no one else ever had, and remained constant, unchanging. These were the same cliffs he had walked birdwatching as a child, but they were far enough for safety from the world of Burnoch.

Or perhaps not. One day, there was a message on his phone. He went out on to the cliffs to get a signal.

'So I hear you've gone doo-lally and stopped washing, apparently,' began Karen. 'And grown a beard.' People in England, thought Fergus, were so much more polite.

'Have you been talking to Al? I didn't know you still spoke.'

'Yes, well, that was a long time ago, and as you well know, you can't help bumping into everyone up here. Eventually. Anyway, it's nice to have you back. If you are back.'

Karen was teaching archaeology at Glasgow, but was working with her students on an excavation project in the Kilmartin Valley during the summer. 'We're digging up at the hill fort of Dunadd, you know, the place where your beardy namesake Fergus Mor mac Erc rolled up in the sixth century from Ireland and made the kingdom of *Dalriada* . . .'

'*Dalriada*.' He was thinking suddenly about their fathers' boat, and not the kingdom.

'Oh. Right,' she said, realising the sense was different for him. *Dalriada* was a word she used almost every day at the moment, and it meant nothing to her. 'Have you been down to see your mum, then?'

'Uh huh.' Last week, he'd driven the sixty-mile round trip to Burnoch for a dull cup of tea with his mum. Stuart kept popping into the kitchen, and he and Isla hadn't got beyond platitudes as per usual. 'I'm waiting till Stuart goes away on his annual golfing fortnight so I can have a proper conversation with her.'

'So when are you going down to Burnoch?' asked Karen with what Fergus thought was some interest.

'I'm trying not to. I'll meet you for a drink in the pub in Kilmartin one day after work, if you'd like. I've got to go to the Co-op anyway.'

Supplies were very low when Fergus drove down to Kilmartin on the 9th of July. He'd made a bit of an effort, washed, and put on a clean T-shirt. He drove so fast on the dirt roads in the Land Cruiser (the four-wheel drive was at last coming in useful) that he still had an hour to kill after he'd been to the Co-op. He decided to get the paper and wait for Karen in the pub.

When he walked down to the shop in the village, he stood stunned, and then bought all the newspapers. He'd had no idea what had happened. The headlines were all about the carnage of 7 July, when fifty-two Londoners were killed in explosions on the tube and the bus. He staggered into the pub and laid the papers out on the table, looking for names and faces he knew. But of course someone would have left a message if a friend had died. He ploughed his way through the news, suddenly reconnected to the outside world and its grim rendering, questioning and blaming. Deep in the paper Fergus found a page of tributes from readers to relatives and friends. There were photographs, short obituaries, and this poem. An ordinary, unfancy poem written by an anonymous reader, who may or may not have lost someone in the bombs:

THE CORRESPONDENT
Friday July 9, 2005

Calm Chaos

Due to
A random
Act of cruelty
Tube and bus services
Are suspended
Until further notice.
You're left with a packed lunch
Made by your mother
Her last touch
Before her blood sprayed the walls
Of the British Medical Association
In Woburn Place.

No one comes to pick you up
Your father has no idea
Your mother's mobile is down
Whose wasn't?
So he didn't know
Her cause of death:
She'd gone to M&S
To buy Magic Knickers
Seen on Trinny and Susannah.

He doesn't know until
The school calls at four

323

And then he doesn't come
The neighbour does.

Your father walks
From tube to tube
Hospital to hospital
Calling out her name
Crying under his umbrella
Which shakes in his hand so much
The raindrops have no time to settle.

We live parallel lives
With the disappeared
The wrong bus
The wrong motorway
The wrong weather
Proof of death piles up
Our happiness when it comes
(And it still does)
Has a strange aftertaste.

There's constant pressure
To be at peace with the world
To have done the right thing
To have tied up loose ends
Because anything could happen
All is calm chaos
That very British 'Calm Chaos'
And you are a random particle.
However fond you are of them
However strong your grip

On your favourite random particles
One may spin off into the void.

So you won't feel the pain
Pray that it's you.

The reader's poem made Fergus painfully aware of his own selfishness and the need to live for now, and connect immediately with everyone: with Raph, with Hannah, with his mother, with his friends, with whatever remained. He was still shattered when Karen came through the door of the pub.

'Fergus!' she said bouncing over, and then she noticed what he was reading.

'I know. It's terrible. Did you know someone?'

'No. But you sort of feel you know them all, people our own age. And those injuries . . .' He knew what that sort of carnage was like – he'd seen it in Baghdad. 'But can I get you a drink? It'd be nice to talk about something else.'

He stared at Karen's face. She was still pretty, but there were lines around her mouth and her brown eyes, the lines that wait offstage throughout your twenties and suddenly pounce in your thirties, taking revenge. And that meant he must have the same lines; he was much older too. 'I haven't seen you since . . . since my wedding. Oh dear.'

She was wearing jeans and quite a cool T-shirt which said in black copperplate: 'En ma Fin gît mon Commencement.' Fergus couldn't think of what to say to her, so he asked what it meant.

'In my end is my beginning,' said Karen. 'It was

embroidered on Mary Queen of Scots' cloth of estate when she was imprisoned. The T-shirt's from a conference on feminist history and archaeology.'

'Ah,' said Fergus, slightly unnerved by the feminist aspect. 'Are you into all that, then?'

He wondered about the fact she'd never married; about her break-up with Al.

They set to talking, with many years and pints to work through, and Fergus eventually found himself telling Karen about his children. 'I sort of ache for them when I'm up here, but I've been so useless – I don't know, depressed, maybe just mad – that I couldn't face seeing them. And I don't see them enough, so I feel this, this physical and emotional distance.'

'Well you should so something about it,' said Karen, ever practical. 'Straightaway.'

'You're right,' said Fergus, 'but what do you do if your children are growing up in a different nation and class? Raphael and Hannah – listen to their names, names from elsewhere.' Increasingly, he felt his children were preserved in English aspic. But every time he saw them, their physical presence was such a pleasure, the size of their toes, their smooth rounded bellies, their expressions, but they were also a different species from him. 'Our own wild, dirty childhoods, they would terrify them.'

'It's different up here now too. All that freedom's illegal.' Karen shrugged. 'Nice as it's been doing the free counselling, it's last orders and I've got to go. Starting at seven tomorrow morning.'

Fergus stared, noticing three tiny holes in her ear and one in her nose that once held punkish studs and were now empty. He was suddenly interested in her history, all the missing parts.

'Shit. I'm sorry,' said Fergus. 'I just talked and talked, didn't I?'

'Yes, you did. Like an escaped hermit,' said Karen grinning. 'Me next time.' She kissed him on both cheeks, English-style, he noted, and walked out into the summer night.

Fergus took her advice about the children. He rang Athene to ask if Raph and Hannah could come to stay. She was taking Hannah to her grandmother's for the week, but she said Raph could come. 'I'll come down and drive him up,' said Fergus.

'That won't be necessary,' said Athene briskly. 'He can come up on Henry's plane, and you can pick him up in Glasgow airport.'

'Wow,' said Fergus. '*Henry's plane.*' Well, if ever there was a sign that Raph needed to come down to earth and be with his father, that was it. Fergus wanted to take Raph up on to the hills to look for sea eagles and stags, to look over the sea towards America. He wanted to read to him, and buy him a penknife, so he could whittle sticks and dissect beetles, and cut his finger and have the balls not to cry.

A week later, Fergus MacFarlane, the multi-millionaire, found himself desperately running round Braehead IKEA on the road to Glasgow airport, buying a flatpack bunkbed and quilt for Raph, and stuffing them into the back of the Land Cruiser. Fergus had the fortune, but he hadn't yet developed the organisational habits of the rich: Athene had always been better at delegation, retail and delivery.

When he got to Arrivals, Raph ran to him, jumped up, and clung to him like a red-haired monkey, and Fergus felt a great wrench of love for him. Raph was wildly excited: 'Hey, you've got a beard! I came by myself! I had a lemonade and two packs of Pringles. Don't tell Mummy. Did you see the plane? He had a Learjet but now he's got a Gulfstream, with bigger engines.'

Fergus sighed. 'I missed you, son,' said Fergus. 'I'm sorry I've been away for a month.'

In the car, Raph took off his brand new mini-Barbour, found the socket and plugged in his iPod to play Fergus something atrocious by a teen-band called Busted. 'This is my new iPod, the latest model, because Hannah stamped on the other one,' explained Raph.

Fergus wondered how he'd produced such clean, air-conditioned, centrally heated, allergy-tested, spoiled children. What was going on?

Yet when they got to the barn, with the wind whipping off the cliff across the moor, and a sharp sun pushing fingers of light down into the roaring ocean, Raph became as wild as the elements. He went far too close to the crumbling edge of the cliff, and Fergus raced beside him, catching his hand, and they ran together. Raph loved the huge space of the barn, sliding on the wooden floor in his socks from one end to the other, leaving tracks in the dust. Then he noticed something was missing. 'What do you mean, you don't have telly or a Playstation or an X-box? What do you do all day?' he asked, staring round. 'Oh, computer,' he said, relieved to see the laptop on the table.

Fergus sighed, forebore from telling Raph there was no broadband, and took him fishing before dinner in the lochan about half a mile up the hill. Raph was used to the instant gratification and death of the virtual-game world, and was very puzzled that after an hour they'd caught nothing.

'There are brown trout in there, you can see them jumping sometimes. Look, there, that circle forming on the water. It's just a question of stealth and patience,' said Fergus enthusiastically.

But Raph was tired and hungry. 'I want to go home, Daddy.' A fine drizzle had begun and the midges smelled new, young flesh. Raph was poxed and miserable by the time they got home. Fergus stuck him in front of the wood-burning stove, fed him some dinner and set to the unpleasant task of making the IKEA bunkbeds.

'I'm bored,' said Raph biting his nails. Fergus grunted, searching the floor for a lost bolt.

'Daddy! I'm bored,' he repeated. Fergus gave him a Harry Potter he'd bought in a rush at the airport bookshop, and added that there was nothing wrong with calling him just Dad. Fergus was beginning to get irritated with Raph, plus it was seven o'clock and he hadn't had a drink yet.

'I've seen all the Harry Potter films – so why do I need to read the books?' moaned Raph. Fergus actually growled.

'Well, get your lazy arse over here and help me build this, then.' Raph looked slightly nervous, but because he spent a lot of time with intricate Lego sets, he was good at reading diagrams, even Swedish ones. He held the slats in place while Fergus screwed them down and balanced the headboard and the ladder while minor adjustments were made with the Allen key. Half an hour later – having executed the modern bonding equivalent of barn-raising – they had a glorious father-and-son moment of victory.

'We have beaten the Vikings and their evil flatpacks!' announced Fergus.

Raph felt he should have the top bunk, 'in case Hannah falls out when she comes'. Then Fergus read aloud to Raph (to his initial puzzlement) the beginning of *To Kill a Mockingbird*, until he fell asleep. For the first time in months, Fergus went to bed sober.

It was not always plain sailing from there. For instance, Fergus, feeling nostalgic, cooked herring in oatmeal one night. Raph poked it with a knife and saw the bones. 'Ick. I am not touching that. There's a hairbrush inside it.'

Raph had packed his mobile phone, but not his wellies, and Fergus couldn't go to Burnoch for a pair, because that would have meant seeing Stuart in what was now Meek Shoes, bought out by Stuart when the Saxon chain collapsed. Instead, they drove to the chandlers in Kinloch for wellies and other supplies, including some strong rope which Fergus attached to the barn rafters so Raph could swing high across the room, from a launch pad on the sink draining board to the stairs that went nowhere. They also built a home-made outdoor shower – Raph's delight at the lack of a bath knew no bounds – from a metal bucket with holes punched in it, and a hose attached to the mixer tap on the sink. Until then, they'd been bathing by running in and out of the icy sea, which left them cleanish but crunchy. 'You're what they call a soapdogger,' explained Fergus. 'It means you hate washing. So then you get bowffin, mingin' or honkin', which are all words for smelly.' Raph nodded very seriously, as though he were learning school French.

They climbed down the cliffs to the beach every afternoon, and when Raph found an old blue trawler net among the driftwood, they brought it home and strung it up to make a hammock inside. As Fergus screwed metal rings into the walls to hold the net up, he found himself talking away to Raph about his grandfather, the fishing, prawns being nicknamed wombles, and the comeback of The Wombles in this recycling-conscious time. For the first time in months, Fergus felt really glad to be alive.

When Raph went back, Fergus felt the emptiness and isolation of the barn all the more. He travelled to London every fortnight to spend a weekend with the kids, afraid to let them slip away again, and when he came back, he began making small forays into the world. He took his clothes to the launderette. He shaved. He answered calls. He insulated the barn for winter. He walked the two miles down to the pub alone at night and talked to the barman and locals, and felt at ease. He saw Uncle Jim, and helped him in almost-silent communion for three hours to fix a gearbox. He bought a proper cooker, and invited Karen over for dinner. Not in a predatory way, because he didn't feel that. He didn't want anyone right now. Indeed, he wasn't sure what he felt, other than that he quite liked talking to her. And there weren't many other people to talk to out there. Or restaurants to go to.

*

The night before Karen drove her clapped-out VW Golf with one working headlight up the dirt track to visit Fergus, she dreamed that he walked all the way across the Kilmartin valley and the Great Moss in the darkness and came to lie beside her in bed. This was unexpected, to say the least. In the morning, she woke sweating, satiated, disturbed by the emptiness of the other pillow and the fullness of her mind. The embarrassing truth seemed to be that she had been stimulated by nothing more than the synapses of her brain, an unlikely feat. In the cold light of the winter dawn, she shook off the feeling. Fergus was damaged, not a reliable proposition at all, and anyway she had a boyfriend in Glasgow. Feeling sinful, or more sinned against, she took a cool shower. She dressed in baggy grey and black of all-enveloping invisibility, wanting to reveal nothing. But it was freakish, this possession by someone who, in many ways, she hardly knew.

Yet when Fergus opened the barn door that evening, Karen thought that she could see the knowledge of it in his face, his half-grin of recognition. She'd invited him in last night, after all. It was her choice. He was just doing his job. Then she pulled herself together. They were both spending too much time alone in isolated places, and it was evidently sending her crackers.

'I brought you some books,' she said, thrusting a teetering pile at him. 'Sort of educational ones.' Karen raised her eyebrows. 'I hear you're not working on anything yet.' She had meant to be kind, but she realised that sounded critical. She felt jumpy, alone with Fergus in the big, echoing barn with the waves crashing outside and the black expanse of the uncurtained windows.

'Do you ever feel scared here?'

'Only of myself,' said Fergus, making a monstrous face. He seemed to be slightly uncomfortable too. He faffed around finding plates and cutlery, dropping things. 'You're the first person I've cooked for, apart from Raph, in six months, so I'm out of practice. And I am working now, by the way. Huge landscapes like abstract paintings. The sea. No Heilan' cows, though.'

Karen noticed Fergus's native accent come back increasingly as he spoke to her. She realised how clean and almost English-sounding his voice was now. She grinned and didn't say anything. Instead, she yattered about her work, about the standing stones, the cists, the monuments fixing the cycles of the moon and sun, the places of sacrifice, and the moments, when it wasn't raining and cold, that she felt connected deep back into the earth and the past.

Fergus was listening, looking mesmerised. Karen addressed her next remarks to the fish stew he'd made. 'I sort of know what you've been through. It was like that for me after I broke up with Al . . . God, it was eight years ago. And after that I distracted myself by working and working, and got an assistant professorship and everything, but I'm not sure who I was proving myself to. It all comes back to feeling there's something missing, something not quite right. You know?' She looked up at him, wondering.

'Al told me about what happened. I'm sorry.'

'I didn't feel strong enough then, whole enough to be a mother. And it would have been so wrong with him. We were about to break up when it happened. And selfishly, I didn't want to come back here with Al and live that cloying small-town life. And a while after that I lost the grip altogether, and, well, we're not a nation that goes in for analysis and all that, so I talked to myself and read my way out of it, very slowly. But I stayed attached and rooted to here and to my friends in Glasgow and family, and you . . . you seem to be on your own here.'

'Not right now.' He had a huge smile.

'No.' Karen felt flustered herself now. 'Anyway, I brought you some of my old reading material, novels mostly, seeing as there's not much else to do here. You've always read your way through things, unless you've changed,' continued Karen. Then she snorted: 'Look what reading *On the Road* did for you.' Instinctively, she rubbed the old scar on her forehead under her fringe. Karen knew, without saying, that they were both thinking back to the surreal night of the crash.

'I'm heartily sick of things crashing and burning,' said Fergus. 'I have to put up with it every day at the moment. You know that early morning half-awake half-asleep moment, when you're vulnerable to all sorts of stuff?' Karen blushed and nodded vigorously. What was he going to say? 'Well, every morning for the last week, I've had an awful awakening. I'm sitting on that wooden chair at the door there, overlooking the sea, and one of those fucking Tornado fighters comes down low over the water – you know they can fly across Scotland from RAF Lossiemouth in a few minutes – and you see them before you hear them, they're faster than the speed of sound. So I see this black fighter jet swooping, and instead of lifting up into the hills at the last moment, it comes straight at the barn. Far behind, the sound follows it, a great thundering roar. I know I'm going to die, so I say "I love you" to someone, but there's no one there. That's what you're supposed to do when you're going to die. And then I'm blown away into huge coils of white and yellow fire, into nothingness, and then consciousness. That's how I wake up, dead, every morning.'

Karen studied Fergus in the light and shadow of the barn as he spoke. He looked much the same: sinewy, edgy, with piercing eyes, but now there was a deep groove between his eyebrows, shooting up to the middle of his forehead. It seemed carved like a rune in stone.

Karen put down her glass. 'You have to envision a future, Fergus,' she said quietly.

'I know.' He went silent. 'Anyway, I've been to the iron-mongers for a cafetière. No more Nescafé. Do you want a coffee?'

'Yeah, a quick one so I'm awake enough to drive in the dark.'

When she stood up to leave, Fergus dumped a heavy Steidl coffee-table book of his photographs in her arms. 'I feel I should give you some books back but I've only got this.'

Karen got in her Golf and it made a terrifying bronchial noise. She hummed as she started off down the dirt track in a sliver of silver light which came through the clouds.

'You need a bulb in that headlamp. And a new exhaust,' shouted Fergus, waving in the distance. 'Meet me down at Jim's garage on Saturday and we'll fix it for you.' It was an offer you couldn't refuse.

Chapter Eighteen

2006
Lanark: Alasdair Gray

Fergus had been running along the top of the cliffs, crushing the sea-pinks flowering beneath his trainers. When he came back he stood panting out on the hill behind the house, standing on the seismic cracks on the rocks, looking down on to the Paps of Jura. It was there that Vodafone sent him a rare and unexpected signal, rather like God pointing a huge gnarled, hairy Pythonesque finger at him from the sky.

'Yeah, Mum, what is it?' he said, laconic. He'd been ringing Isla now and then, especially while Stuart was away on a golfing trip in Thailand. They'd almost had proper conversations recently. But not quite.

But all he could hear was his mother gasping and crying – and swearing – and it took half a minute to get any sense out of her.

'You've got to come down here, Fergus, and see this. I need you to come down here right now.'

When Fergus had arrived at the bungalow, Isla didn't even hear him walking in. He found her sobbing, tearing the sheets off the bed, waving a bottle of bleach.

'I feel so soiled, Fergus. Oh my God.' She crumpled on to the bed and began to explain.

How predictable was it that Stuart's annual visits to Thailand were not golfing holidays? How predictable was it that, while he was away, Isla might one day look up new shoe styles for the shop online – in this case Lolita shoes in 00 patent leather with crossover straps – and come across the other, creepy Lolita-loving websites Stuart had been accessing all along? How predictable was it that he would have hidden file after file of his favourite underage porn and filthy shoe-fetish shots in a folder named 'Golfing Tips'?

As Fergus looked over her shoulder at the creepy files on the computer in his old loft bedroom, he wasn't wholly surprised. It confirmed everything he expected of his sleazebag stepfather, his instincts from the first. But Isla was in total shock. She'd gone white. 'I think I'm going to be sick.'

Fergus took her through to the kitchen and made hot, sweet tea, which is what he knew you did in these situations.

'I feel so stupid. So betrayed,' said Isla, tears pouring down her face. 'We've been married for twenty-five years, Fergus. How could I not have noticed the sort of man he was?'

Fergus couldn't think of a helpful thing to say at this point, so he said nothing and just held her hand.

'Oh my God!' she suddenly said with a sharp intake of breath. 'He didn't ever touch—'

'No, Mum. I think it's young girls that he likes. And maybe it's only fantasy,' he reassured her, while actually thinking about what the wanker of a man was probably doing this very second in Thailand. He wished so much he'd expressed his doubts to Isla long ago.

'I think we both need a proper drink.' He got out the Baileys Irish Cream for Isla and Stuart's whisky for himself. Isla poured it all out, her doubts and unhappiness, her husband's now-explicable weirdness and petty meanness. 'But I thought that was what marriages were like. It wasn't too bad. We were comfortable together.'

'I wish I'd let the fucker drown in his car in the harbour years ago,' said Fergus, angry.

Isla looked upset by that. 'I know you didn't always get on with him very well, Fergus, but I did my best for you. I wanted to give you stability, a man, a proper home. What else could I do? I always knew he wasn't Mr Right, but he wasn't always Mr Wrong either.'

'You didn't just do it for me,' he said. 'You did it for yourself mostly. You know that.'

Isla stopped crying and went red with anger. 'Do you fucking know what it's like having a baby at seventeen? Do you know what it's like to lose your freedom right there before you've even had time to taste it? Do you know what it's like to be a fucking widow at twenty-five? Oh, you've had it easy, son.'

Fergus felt breathless, unable to speak. He'd never really seen it from Isla's point of view. He'd never talked to her, adult to adult, until then. But she wasn't really much older than him, fifty-three to his thirty-six, barely a generation apart.

'I'm sorry, Mum. I'm sorry that all this has happened to you.'

*

Over the next week, Fergus found he was forced into the role of the adult in their relationship. Isla was keen to move out of the bungalow. 'I don't want to be anywhere there's even a trace of *him*,' she said in disgust, but Fergus explained to her that she owned half the house, and half the business she'd built up with Stuart. 'He owes you big time, he's not going to inconvenience you, and I'll buy him out of the other half of the business when he's in jail.'

'Jail?' Isla was horrified at the idea of giving the computer hard disc to the police; she didn't want to be the person who sent Stuart to prison. 'He hasn't actually done anything as far as we know,' she began. She somehow didn't think looking at underage porn led to paedophilia. After some argument, Fergus let her make the decision, but he took the hard disc home to his barn as ransom. 'Stuart won't bother you so long as he knows I've got the evidence. He'll be too scared.' He bought Isla a new, uncontaminated Apple laptop, and with some satisfaction began to plan their revenge on Stuart's return.

Fergus thought it was best that Isla wasn't there for the confrontation, so he persuaded her to let him pay for a week-long stay at a spa near Edinburgh with her best friend Kathy, the manageress at the fish factory. With Isla's help – his mum ostentatiously wearing rubber gloves – they packed Stuart's clothes and personal possessions into ten bin bags which they left outside the garage. Fergus changed all the house locks, and put new ones on the shop. Then Fergus sat distractedly watching Jeremy Clarkson on television, the curtains open, awaiting Stuart's car turning into the drive.

At the first crunch of the gravel, Fergus was out of the front door, slamming it behind him.

'Hello, Stuart,' he said, in a stabbing, icy voice.

Stuart looked irritated, then terrified.

'We've found all the child pornography on your computer. The *Golfing Tips* file,' said Fergus. A look of panic crossed Stuart's face, but then he tried to shrug it off.

'None of your fucking business,' he said, and pushed by Fergus to the front door, suddenly puzzled that his key wouldn't fit. 'This is my house, you fuckhead,' he screamed at Fergus. 'I've done nothing wrong.'

'Nothing wrong with ten-year-old girls naked in their mums' high heels? Or wearing leather? I don't think so. And God knows what filthy stuff you've been doing all these years in Thailand. So just take those bin bags and get the fuck out of my mum's life and out of Burnoch, or the hard disc goes to the police.' Fergus was shaking with anger. 'And her lawyer will be contacting you about her share of the house and the business.' Fergus gave him a nasty grin. He realised money was Stuart's breaking point. 'I know she doesn't really need the cash, but I want you to feel the pain.'

Stuart stepped aggressively right up to Fergus, right in his face. Fergus's hand shot up by itself, and he decked Stuart. Into Fergus's right hook, which looked fairly stand-ard, went decades of frustration. Everything that rankled, everything than remained unsaid and undone, was expunged in one simple, sincere gesture.

Fergus stood over the groaning, collapsed body, which looked empty, like a dead man's suit. Stuart's glasses were crushed into his face like rubber and his nose was trickling blood into the pebbled drive of *Marbella*. One punch was all it took. As his stepfather lay whimpering on the drive, Fergus placed the Glasgow divorce lawyer's card beside Stuart's mashed face. 'You'll need this. Don't ever come near us again.'

Fergus went into the house and watched from the window as Stuart crawled into the car and drove blindly off. Fergus phoned Isla at the spa to tell her it was done.

'Did you *have* to hit him?' she asked.

'Definitely,' said Fergus. 'Self-protection.'

'Oh. It was like that, was it? Well, thank you, son. Thank you for everything you've done. Your dad would have been proud of you,' she said. 'I've got a sauna and a massage booked, so I've got to go.'

Fergus shut the bungalow door with its shiny new brass lock, sighed a huge, tearing, relieved sigh, and drove off.

In the following months, Isla MacFarlane – no longer Meek or mild – blossomed. After the initial shock, she suddenly had the freedom she'd longed for before she became a teenage bride. She went to Glasgow and came back with a new wardrobe and hairstyle. Fergus paid for her to go on a Caribbean cruise with 'the girls' – all in their fifties from Burnoch – who were up for anything. She came up to the barn in the summer, and hung out with Fergus and her grandchildren on the beach.

Isla had always been a good businesswoman, and the shop acquired fresh white paint and a new name: The Burnoch Boot Store, for what else do people buy in the country? Isla stocked a wide range of climbing boots and cheap wellies for the locals and overpriced French ones for the yachties and tourists. She was on top of the latest trends: Crocs and Converse were seen in Burnoch for the first time; profits shot up. Her entrepreneurial nature was at last properly unleashed from Stuart's caution.

Helping his mother dragged Fergus back into the world. He needed to work properly again. The photographs he'd taken of the landscape around the Stone Barn were far too beautiful and simple to be displayed. People would think he had lost his edge. He hadn't. He planned to take on the uglier side of Scotland too.

To that end, in the autumn, Fergus was down in Glasgow hanging out in the cocktail lounge of some fancy beige boutique hotel in the Merchant City reading Alasdair Gray's novel *Lanark*. It was one of the books Karen had given him the previous year. The worn paperback had a Leviathan figure on the front, and below him, in obsessively etched detail, the central belt of Scotland, stretching from the Forth Road Bridge to the Clyde, the sky punctured by high-rise flats, industrial chimneys, Glasgow Cathedral and the Necropolis. Fergus was sitting at the bar decoding the book's cover and simultaneously texting analysis of the Arsenal score to Raph, when an arty-looking Goth girl came sidewinding up to him from the bar and asked if he didn't mind signing his autograph on a napkin. 'No bother at all,' said Fergus. 'But who on earth do you think I am?'

'You're Fergus MacFarlane,' she said. 'I saw your exhibition at the Tate Modern except you had one hand over your eye when they photographed you for the catalogue. And I've seen you in magazines.'

And who was she?

'I'm your waitress, on the next shift. We don't get grants at art school any more, you know, not like in your day.'

Another customer called her over to order a cocktail stupidly called the Waverly, or possibly the Wavery, and Fergus disappeared back into *Lanark*. It was an anarchic, fantastic, four-book epic, some of which Fergus found impenetrable, for which he blamed his lack of formal education rather than the author himself. But he could tell *Lanark* was a great novel, its story nominally the journey of an artist like himself, of Presbyterian predestination and pure hedonism, but also of the city of Glasgow and its dystopian twin Unthank. *Lanark* was published twenty-five years ago, when much of Glasgow was still on its post-industrial knees, half its literature had not yet been written, and its cocktail bars did not yet contain repro-Eames chairs in lime-green plastic.

In the book, one character says: 'Glasgow is a magnificent city . . . why do we hardly ever notice that?'

'Because nobody imagines living here,' says another. 'Think of Florence, Paris, London, New York. Nobody visiting them for the first time is a stranger because he's already visited them in paintings, novels, history books and films. But if a city hasn't been used by an artist, not even the inhabitants live there imaginatively.'

Now the city was being used and abused by artists and he was one of them. There were all those films too – *Red Road*, *My Name is Joe*, *Ae Fond Kiss*, *Young Adam* – none of them showing the dreamier side of the city. Nevermind. Fergus had come to Glasgow to take photographs of a similar nature, the ones that hadn't been taken by the newspapers of the inner-city neighbourhood of the Calton when it shot into the public – indeed international – eye that year for its record-breaking human degradation. He hauled his camera bag on to his shoulder and decided to walk to the Calton from his hotel in the Merchant City. The light was right at last, roaming in the gloaming and all that bollocks. It was no more than a mile from the Versace and Gucci in the hotel gift shop to the glorious grottiness of the Barras street market in the Calton with its fellaffalorry DVDs and chipped Teasmades and fake Chanel thongs for a pound.

Soon he came to that very street corner by the Barrowland Ballroom where almost twenty years ago he and Karen had seen Lloyd Cole and the Commotions. It was a strange, lurching then-and-now moment. In the dusk, he stood staring at the building just as the tacky orange Barrowland sign and neon stars began to glow on the concrete slab exterior, and wondered what would have happened if he and Karen had taken the last bus instead that night. She wouldn't have missed her Maths Higher, she'd have a different job, maybe, and he might have gone to Glasgow School of Art like that wee waitress, and probably would have a nice West End flat, and a flat, unambitious life.

Maybe he'd have lived in Bearsden. Bearsden is a tasteful, leafy Glasgow suburb with a life expectancy of over eighty, one of the best in the world. And a few miles away in grotty Calton, the survival rate was a good twenty-six years less. Here in the poor, cholesterol-rich, cancerous Calton, life expectancy for men was less than fifty-four. Fifty-four. Picture that. Worse than Iraq, or

Gaza. How do you picture that, anyway? Fergus had in his head the Walker Evans and Dorothea Lange photographs of rural poverty for the Farm Security Administration Survey in America. Yes, the black and white of such scenes had been done, as had the garish Martin Parr version, but there was a third way: wide screen, cinematic, painterly, using only the morning light and the dusk. Fergus was working his way through it, day by day, pub by pub, bookie by bookie, from the Cabin Bar to Baird's to Hielan Jessie to William Hill, via the TONGS, BLACK HAND, SHE TOI and GOVIE gang graffiti. Yet his eye wanted to make it more Vermeer than Hieronymous Bosch. He created exquisite portraits at night over a WKD Irn-Bru or a Bacardi Breezer with the prostitutes and addicts and single mums who'd left their children home alone because how else do you get out? In the landscape there were tenements and lesion-spawning tanning parlours and off-licences with more grids and irons than the Bar-L and beautiful lanky Nylon-clad boys chipping a ball around and dreaming of a trial with Celtic.

Almost everyone was on Incapacity Benefit, and drinking to remain incapacitated. On Wednesday morning, when the methadone prescriptions were filled, Fergus photographed just the shoes of the junkies waiting patiently in the massive queue outside Munro's chemist. Two had only one leg. Plus there was the heroic smoking by half the population . . . that was a thing of dying beauty in itself, the clouds and smirrs holding floating conversations outside the doors of every pub, now the law had banned cigarettes inside. And the newspaper articles: 'If you are born in the Calton, rather than Bearsden, you are three times more likely to have a heart attack, four times more likely to be hospitalised, and ten times more likely to grow up in a house where everyone is unemployed.' Close up, in lines and curlicues, in flowerings of red veins, the locals' faces expressed these facts, simply and clearly, without the need for statistics. Fergus talked away to them in the pubs, but inside he felt shock and shame that this had become the story of his own people.

By the time he got back to the hotel at almost ten o'clock, he was filled with something between an awakening of purpose and exhaustion. He felt he had no more strength to work that evening: all the colour had been sucked out of him. Everything was grey and excruciatingly lonely. He sat on the silk bedcover with the Frette linen sheets and opened *Lanark*. He read the plain dedication on the title page. 'To Fergus, from Karen.' And then the puzzling comment written by her below: 'As Alasdair Gray says, "Work as if you live in the early days of a better nation." '

This suddenly seemed the right thing for him to do – or perhaps he was already doing it. Of its own accord, Fergus's hand was scrolling for Karen's number on his mobile. He needed to talk to her. In fact, she was suddenly, clearly the only person anywhere he wanted to talk to. She was still in her office at the university. He imagined her beneath a desk of papers in the grim fluorescent lights, the radiators clanking as they cooled. What ancient archaeological emergencies can there be at ten on a Thursday night?

Karen didn't seem entirely surprised to hear from him, although they hadn't seen each other for a few months. He persuaded her to drive over to the hotel for a drink, and went down to the bar to wait. It was packed, at the peak of its curve of novelty in the city. He stood at the counter and began, with roaring hunger, to murder a dish of olives. The Goth waitress was hanging over the bar, her breasts too-obviously served up like little white doughballs in her shredded black top.

The waitress was very pleased to see him. 'Hello again, Fergus! What'll you be having?' There was a time when he might have considered . . . but not now, not any more. A group of art students suddenly converged on him, snapping pictures with their mobiles. He felt like a freak. Then he saw Karen watching the circus from the bar door, and pushed through the crowd towards her. He hugged her, forcing her to abandon her polite air-kiss.

'I thought you would call,' she observed tartly. 'When you were sorted.' She smiled.

'Don't look all enigmatic at me like that. It makes me nervous. What do you want to drink?'

Karen wanted a pint. The women he'd known in London never drank lager. Nor did they wear mud-spattered jeans and a fleece to a cocktail bar. She stripped down to her white T-shirt, which had green stains on the side.

'Is that better?' she said. 'I wasn't planning to go out.' She still smelled of fresh, damp grass.

'You've got lichen all over the back of your hair,' said Fergus, brushing it off her bob. 'You're a mess.' He felt suddenly very affectionate towards her.

'I've been mapping standing stones out in a bog near

Stirling today. That's why I'm so . . . droukit and mockit,' she said, slipping back into the language of their childhood, and by then the pint was mostly gone. Fergus grabbed two barstools as they were vacated, and kept an eye on Karen's reflection in the mirror, as though by tracking the double set of reactions, he might learn more.

'So why do you work so late all alone in that office? You work all the time,' said Fergus. He grinned. 'You don't happen to work as if you live in the early days of a better nation, do you? I've just been reading that.'

'I work all the time so I don't become a mad cat lady, or join another book group, obviously,' said Karen, deadpan. 'And you work all the time because . . . you want to be laid bare, you want to be understood. Cheers.'

'Christ,' said Fergus. 'I only asked you for a drink to perk me up. Not to poke around in my psyche.'

'Well, I just read your book. I mean, I looked at it properly. It was as revealing as a biography.' There was a silence.

'As for us both being workaholics,' said Fergus, 'did you read that quote from Bill Clinton the other day, talking about his father dying before he was born? I nearly emailed you it. He said: "I had the feeling that I had to live for two people, and that if I did well enough somehow I could make up for the life he should have had".'

Karen nodded. 'Also, who knows how flawed our dads were, but since we've nothing really to go on, we've made them icons. I've been thinking about all that recently, about my life and yours moving in parallel, mirroring, the lines crossing and moving away again.' She shrugged.

'Well, I'm no better than you – I'm still looking for explanations. I'm in the business of digging up the dead, aren't I? I'm never happier than when I'm pottering around alone in a tomb. My favourite place to be is walking the line of burial cairns along the Kilmartin valley. So is there something wrong with me?'

'Yes,' said Fergus happily. 'There definitely is. There is something wrong with us.'

They began to talk at such speed that Fergus felt the world around him was unravelling. They were grasping, gabbling, gasping for the next sentence. There was no time to be lost, because so much lay wasted behind them.

'You know, Fergus MacFarlane, since you reappeared this side of the border you have been taking up shedloads of my time when frankly I should be doing something more worthwhile,' said Karen suddenly, leaning close to him, confessing what was in the air. 'I was looking at those photos – the squat and the rent boys and then the ethereal wife and the skanky prostitutes . . .' she paused to find the words '. . . and there was something sympathetic about all of them. But then, in the next few years, something dead ugly happens: you get bitter and mean about those Tennent's Lager Lovelies and your barely hidden contempt for celebrity and those twisted, abused women like bad scenes out of a film noir.'

'Oh God,' said Fergus, distressed. 'Do you hate them? Do you hate me?'

'No. No, the opposite, really,' said Karen, unaware of what she'd implied. 'Those pictures were so troubled, yet now you're all grown up and there are these sad, empty flats and a bloodbath in Iraq. So I just wonder about someone that comfortable with war and death and sex and maiming and beauty all at once . . .'

Fergus was not merely lost for words: it appeared that his entire vocabulary had drained away. He wasn't sure if Karen was declaring something, or just offering uncomfortable analysis.

'I'm not asking you to explain, Fergus. I can see that something has tipped now, that your world has altered just a tiny fraction . . .' She was blushing now, but she was fearless. 'I don't think about you all the time, you know, but in waves that come and go. You're a recurring infection and fever, like malaria.'

'Malaria?' Now he had been compared to a plague he wanted to hold Karen, but he was horribly aware of the watchers with their camera phones behind, and also that his instincts might be quite wrong. Karen was very peculiar. Always had been. He watched Karen twining her legs nervously round the leather barstool, her eyes wide with exhilaration, her mouth part open. He reached out and took her hand. Her touch brought him to a terrifying halt: he saw blood running down the car window; he pressed her up against the wall of the close, kissed her inexpertly, and smelled the sea; he sat in front of the Gas Miser with her, holding his Tunnock's Caramel Wafer, miserable and melting.

Fergus mumbled, 'I don't want to stop talking like this.'

Karen's eyes looked shiny, as though there might be tears on the surface. Fergus continued. 'You know when we were little we all used to imagine we could buy an endless stick of Burnoch rock that would magically regenerate? I feel like that, that we could begin again where we started.' Because this is it, isn't it? thought Fergus. This is the one we are hardwired for, the one that altered our synapses early on, and nothing quite fits so perfectly in that slot again. He leaned over to kiss her.

'Maybe,' she said. She met his eye. 'Maybe we could try.'

'We could go upstairs, to my room, if you wanted . . . you could stay,' he said.

'No. I can't. Gavin'll be waiting up for me.'

Fergus's gut plunged.

'You've got a fucking Gavin? Waiting? Up? For you? Couldn't you have told me that?'

'You never asked.'

'I thought you were a mad, single, cat lady. You have to leave this Gavin. Immediately.'

'I will if you give me a good reason.'

Fergus was aroused and at the same time had an unexpected shaky feeling, his heart beating too fast. 'I'm always hungry for something. And I'm frightened of what might happen next. But I'm going to try my best. I'm going to tell you a story of what it might be like, if we're lucky. What we might do. And you must tell me what you want from me.'

So she told him the dark, indefinable secrets that women and men only tell themselves, indeed dare not speak because all remains unspoken in the night. Everyone has those secrets, the same and utterly different. And he whispered back, as intensely part of her imagined world as she was. He was good with pictures, after all. They talked, and talked, and talked until she was silent and he did all the talking up to a crescendo. To the drinkers around on the leather sofas, it almost looked like Karen was swooning. Her eyes stopped focusing, and turned inward, but that happens after a few drinks, doesn't it? Who would guess they had surrendered to each other in an unexpected leap of faith? The only evidence was that Karen's eyes were glistening, and that Fergus looked incredibly pleased with himself.

'I love you,' he said.

'You can't possibly say that after one evening,' said Karen.

'It's not one evening. It's my whole life.'

'Time, please,' said the waitress, looking jealously at Karen as she put on her fleece.

Fergus, in free-fall, staggered upstairs alone as the noise of the bar slowly drained away around him and a voice began to speak inside his head. Karen is much more than the sum of the compelling parts you just discovered again, it said. She is literally your other half. When you left Burnoch, you left your own history behind and her along with it. You rejected the dour. You rejected the small-mindedness of a stricken seaport. You rejected the rain. You rejected Irn Bru in babies' bottles. You rejected the crimes you committed. You rejected the half-light of the long summer nights. You rejected those who accepted that life was 'No' too bad, son'. You rejected the smell of boiled cabbage in the close. You rejected those who said 'That's too good for us, son'. You rejected being working class. You rejected your mother. You rejected the phosphorescence of mackerel on the water. You rejected your friends. And you rejected all the Karens, with their ordinary names and ordinary prospects. And if you'd gone out with her, no good would have come of it. And if she'd stayed with you, she would never have engaged with the world. But now, it has all changed. The question now is: can you find salvation in one person? No. Can you go back? Yes. Can you try?

Thank fuck you're not from Croydon, added the voice.

Kate Muir

Photography For
The Third Millennium

Catalogue Notes
Autumn 2006

Fergus MacFarlane

Of the ten photographers in this Tate Modern exhibition, Fergus MacFarlane provides the defining images of our image-drenched age. His shocking *Green and Red* series taken in the aftermath of atrocities in Baghdad uses both his own work – stomach-dropping, blood-draining, time-stopping reportage of horror – coupled with the instant press agency shots of disasters which were deemed too gruesome to use in the mainstream media. At the same time, MacFarlane enters the otherworld of Baghdad's Green Zone, and with a slow, sumptuous eye and rich colour, documents the incongruous Americana. This is more typical of the Scottish-born artist's recent work, in which modern photography takes on the weight of painting. This is exemplified in the lyrical but ultimately controlled *Refuge* series, of rooms in a comdemned tower block in Hackney. The photographs are dense with allusions, yet perfectly composed. The concrete cubes of rooms become abstract sentiments as the physical rhythms of landscape and architecture become psychological.

Chapter Nineteen

2007
A Voyage to St Kilda:
Martin Martin

St Kilda is an island on the edge of the world. It rises out of the Atlantic where the water is so deep it holds entire mountains, and this is the highest of them all. It is the westernmost inhabitable land in Scotland, but no one lives there permanently. The last thirty villagers were evicted with chests of drawers and china tea services on their backs in 1930. There is something both ghostly and thrawn about the place: it suffers the brunt of storms roaring across from Canada; it suffers unimaginable isolation and desolation, yet it is still one of the most beautiful sights on earth. When Fergus first sailed to St Kilda, it seemed to him that a dark volcano had erupted from the sea and been carpeted with green, and when his boat slid into the horseshoe-shaped bay, it was floating in the volcano's crater. Sharp black cliffs rose hundreds of feet out of the water, white with thousands upon thousands of fulmars, nesting on rocks iced with bird droppings. There were no trees on the two-mile-wide island, so the villagers used to

355

wait for driftwood to be washed up to make their coffins.

After eighteen hours at sea – sailing out from Oban through the Sound of Mull, past Canna and up the western side of Skye before crossing the Sound of Harris – they were now at anchor in Village Bay opposite the long, low, abandoned cottages along the grassy single street. Above them stretched St Kilda's slopes spotted with hundreds of pale grey cleits, domed stone stores from the days when the islanders lived on dried fulmar and puffin porridge. While everyone else was on deck mesmerised by the view, Fergus was down in the galley vigorously mushing fresh red chillis, garlic and root ginger in a pestle and mortar he'd brought specially with him. He added lemon juice and olive oil and the smell burst out the hatch on to the deck. He'd had a gut feeling that fresh crab meat would come his way on this journey, and he had prepared, even down to the linguine and the growing parsley. He was chopping the crab meat up, mixing brown flesh with white, when Karen appeared at the galley door. He wiped his hands on his apron and made a grab at her – the crossing had been so rough until now that they hadn't had a chance to do anything in their cabin except cling to the sides of their narrow bunks and pray they weren't going to throw up. But now the sea was glass-calm, and Fergus was cooking for all the extremely empty stomachs on the seventy-five foot steel-hulled Arctic rescue vessel – incorrectly described as a 'luxury cruiser' in Al's advertisements.

'Now give us a kiss,' said Fergus. Karen hung on to him, still finding her sea legs.

'I was more terrified by that gale we just passed through than I wanted to admit,' she said.

A few hours before reaching St Kilda, the sea had turned into a roiling grey soup, and the boat had rocked at a forty-five-degree angle, the sky swapping places with the sea. Greasy waves had crested over the deck, and hissing spray blanked the view. Al, at the wheel, had remained completely calm. Fergus knew his skippering of old, and he'd trusted the strong, thick metal of the boat. In the gale he'd been laughing, soaked, clinging on to the handrails at the front of the boat, clinging on to life, but Karen had been below deck, drowned in memories and fear. He held her, so she would shake off the memories.

Fergus had chartered the boat, but they were here in the Atlantic for many good reasons: Al and his crew were keen to test St Kilda as a tourist route for his charter cruises; Karen had brought four students out for an excavation on St Kilda, and Fergus was taking photographs free for a National Trust exhibition marking the island's status as World Heritage Site. He was also the ship's cook again after many years, producing the simple fresh crab linguine. It was too spicy for Uncle Jim – now sixty-six and birdwatching full time – who had come along for the ultimate twitcher's holiday. Now, however, Jim had seen an opportunity for a part-time job as Al's floating bird guide, lecturing the tourists. Jim ostentatiously took out a packet of Rennies as he sat on a pile of orange life rafts holding a bird book.

'On this island there are sixty-three thousand pairs of fulmars,' Jim read aloud excitedly through his bifocals, 'forty thousand pairs of puffins in burrows, and gannets and razorbills and skuas ... and one hell of a lot of birdshit.'

'Where would we be without your brilliant analysis,

Jim?' said Fergus once again thinking how pleased he was to have his uncle on board. They all took the dinghy on to shore and soon they passed the church, the manse, and the ghost town of Main Street, with its cottages, some roofless shells, others part restored. Further along were the ugly modern military barracks for the staff of the rocket-tracking station on the hill, and more importantly, their famous part-time pub, the Puff Inn. They left Karen and her students in the village and Al, Jim and Fergus climbed higher and higher, through the sea pinks and sorrel, through fields of cleits like beehives in the grass, and wild brown Soay sheep. They aimed for the high dip between the two peaks, and as they rose up they could hear invisible seabirds screaming somewhere. Great skuas – massive brownish birds with hooked beaks and with four-feet wingspans – flew overhead like pterodactyls, strafing them.

They reached the grassy top of the gap between the hills, and almost plunged off a sheer cliff, falling twelve hundred feet into the sea. Far below them, thousands of seabirds circled in the air, docking in and out of nests in crevices on the cliff. There had been a cartoonlike disappearing of the land: you could almost run suspended in mid-air before the fall. Jim lay shakily down on the grass a safe distance from the edge.

'Jings, crivens, help ma Boab,' he said, laughing. 'That was why we could hear the birds and no' see them.'

'This is so cool,' said Al, grinning across at Fergus. 'Take a picture for my website.' They stood near the edge with the strong wind holding them back from toppling and stared out to the view of the stacs, the rocks that shot five or six hundred feet out of the water. Stac Am Armin was like a witch's hat, and Stac Lee was white with thousands of gannets and their droppings. Further on there was the little island of Boreray, where the St Kildans had grazed their sheep.

Fergus leaned out to take the photograph, and was suddenly aware of how close to death the St Kildans must have been all the time, as they climbed barefoot up the sheer cliffs, killing birds and gathering their eggs to survive.

'Just as there's a species of St Kilda wren, a St Kilda mouse, so there's the St Kilda toe,' announced Jim.

'Toe?'

'Yes, apparently there was a genetic tendency to a huge big toe,' said Jim. 'A humungous, elongated toe that let the men cling more easily to the cracks in the rocks. On the other side of the island, there's the Mistress Stone, where the marriageable men had to balance on one leg – on the edge of a three-hundred-foot drop, mind – to prove their agility on the rocks and their ability to support a family.' They clung with one toe on to life, thought Fergus, and then passed the deformity on to the next generation.

'Watching someone else being bonxied from a distance is St Kilda's ultimate spectator sport,' continued Jim cheerfully, pointing down the hill at two pairs of birds circling. Fergus had never heard him so garrulous. The skuas were known here as bonxies. 'The missing link between gulls and buzzards,' said Jim ominously, sliding his jacket over his head as they came closer to the birds. Suddenly a set of claws whipped by Fergus's eyes and he felt the rush of wind from the huge bird.

'Shit!' He shouted. 'Duck, Al!' The next bird came close to ripping Al's red baseball cap off. Then another dive-bombed them, squawking angrily. 'It's like the fucking scene from *The Birds*.'

Uncle Jim was laughing fit to burst. He'd clearly been in the company of bonxies before. 'They're protecting their nests this time of year. They lay their eggs on the ground. Dead serious about parenting they are,' he said disappearing under his jacket again. 'The pair stay together their whole lives. They're monogamous. And furious,' he said, swotting one away with his bird book.

Al and Jim went off to pursue puffins, while Fergus sauntered along the grassy track through the village and looked up at a mackerel sky which passed from mood to mood above him, as though in a speeded-up film. He had a curious feeling that time could equally well be going backwards as well as forwards, and if he hurried a little, he would find round the corner of the next house those dour-faced children of St Kilda's photographs, dark-haired girls with centre partings and serious, frowning boys, clinging to their Presbyterianism in the wild.

Instead, he saw Karen kneeling in her jeans in the gritty yellow-brown soil of a shallow pit behind one of the black-houses, the wind blowing her hair wildly. A few geeky students surrounded her, staring at something held in her hand. In the distance, he could hear her voice '. . . pottery has no diagnostic features. It's just too small and abraded for thermoluminescence dating.'

To Fergus, the words thermoluminescence dating brought up pictures of strobe-lighted kids dancing on ecstasy, but the students were nodding at something else.

'The archaeology here's crazily layered,' she was saying. '*Now* and *then* have no meaning. Stones got reused a dozen times, and some cleits could have been made a hundred or a thousand years ago. No one knows.'

Fergus liked watching her lecture, the precise way her mouth moved, the tiny frown of concentration. She was rootling through a rubbish pit, behind the ancient, round-cornered blackhouse, carefully pulling out and noting shards of coarse, coiled pottery which could be from the Iron Age, and a few layers higher, a turquoise glass bottle from G. Foster Clark and Co., Maidstone. Another broken opaque bottle had the words Eiffel Tower Fruit Juices pressed into the glass, shipped all the way here after the tower was constructed for the World Fair in Paris. And then there were objects from the days when Martin Martin produced the first written account of visiting St Kilda in 1697.

While visitors came occasionally in the summer months, for thousands of years, it was the onslaught of late nineteenth-century tourism and trade that killed the St Kildans off, with city viruses and city vices. 'From these artefacts,' Karen said, now holding up a broken piece of paraffin lamp, 'you can see the impact the products of industrialised Britain had on a materially primitive society.' She saw Fergus out of the corner of her eye, and waved. She sighed and looked back at the students '. . . a primitive society that we complacently watched as it died.'

Fergus waved back, but he stood some distance from the site, and dug in his camera bag. How could you photograph the layers here? The volcano-island, the rocks, the deserted buildings, the skies were powerful in themselves, but he wanted more. There was the old-fashioned solution: a long exposure. In one of the ruined houses where the students were excavating, Fergus put a manual Leica R6 with a 60mm lens on a tripod, which he exposed for the floor in the centre, knowing that the rest would go into darkness, with the natural light burning a moving student who became an apparition, a mere trace in time. Inspired, Fergus took more images which were vague and atmospheric, sometimes chilling. They were stills from a film, the narrative lost but lurking insistently in the background. They were about what mattered to Fergus most: landscape and memory.

He had to find Karen so she understood what he was feeling. He took her hand and they walked up towards Conachair and Mullach Mor, the two highest mountains, which somehow created their own atmosphere, attracting individual perfect clouds to sit unmoving on the peaks. Even on this sunny day, the hilltops were still chopped off by the mist. But the weather systems had created an ethereal place, a place of half-light and half-truth, of streaks of sunlight at the edge of the mist. It was there that Karen and Fergus stood, mesmerised.

Down below, Village Bay was a perfect half-moon of turquoise, and the houses looked like stone hieroglyphics on the expanse of grass. Down below, all was solid, while Karen and Fergus floated above, on a level with the black silhouettes of seabirds rising and falling in the currents of warm air above the cliffs. It was a strange, heady atmosphere, adrift on a raft of fresh Atlantic oxygen, unpolluted by anything but history. Karen said she felt almost faint in the vastness of the space. Fergus was suspended between a growing happiness, and a weight of melancholy and loss:

his own, and the island's. Something caught in his throat.

There was still a soft wind, so they sat in the lee of a large cleit, their backs against its sun-warm stones. The mist stretched fingers towards them, but could not penetrate their pocket of brightness. They touched the stones. Close up, the cleit was a miracle of geometry, each dry stone interlocking with its neighbour, their union long sealed with a roof of moss and grass. There remained a sense that someone – a hundred or even a thousand years ago – thought very carefully about this cleit, perfected an important place of storage, of form and function, which might let him live through another winter on the edge of the world.

Fergus found he was crying. For the first time in twenty years. His eyes were shut against the tears silently making their way out. He tipped his head back against the ancient stones and let the compacted agony and shame run down with gravity. He wept for those he had lost, wronged, ignored and hurt. He wept for his children and for himself, for his aching need for a home, a purpose, an ending. At the same time, he knew that all this lay within himself, dormant and damaged. He could feel it unfurling. He just needed the strength to let it out, to remove his body armour. He had to make the leap from observer to participant. He had to take his painful place in this world and not slide along its surface. He was no longer an island.

Karen said nothing, but her arm slipped between Fergus and the stones, and she held him. Her fingers scooped the tears from his cheeks until there were none. Ten minutes went by, maybe more.

'I'm sorry,' he said, shaking still. 'I haven't . . .'

'I know,' said Karen. 'You don't need to tell me why. I know.'

Fergus understood then that in the last year Karen had breached his defences, wriggled her fingers between the carefully laid stones which had protected him and held him safe for so long. She understood him, as she understood herself. But she was stronger than he was and clearsighted. She was courageous and bore scars, while he had lived a life sheltered by the camera, through the cliché of a glass darkly.

They clung together. The mountain was empty of other humans; the Puff Inn would open at six o'clock and a few tiny figures moved magnetically towards it on the grass below them. The only sound came from the skuas, dive-bombing imaginary foes. Fergus tried to explain. He broke the silence but the waves of his thought were almost inexpressible. He went under in a torrent of words, which only sometimes made sense to Karen. When his words ran out, they touched. Behind the cleit, they slipped naked into the landscape, on to the rough grass. From above, from the point of view of the skuas, their pale flesh was all interlocking sinews, bodies entangled with the earth.

Fergus suddenly shook his head and smiled: 'I hate to say this – because you may remember there was a wee problem with this the first time we did this up the close – but in the backpack we have sticking plasters, water, a squashed Kit Kat, two cameras and the latest *Observer Book of Birds*, but no condom.'

They laughed. Karen slid on top.

'Is it safe to . . .?' asked Fergus.

'No. I'm feeling very fertile.'

'But . . .'

'You love me.' She looked determined and amused.

'Yes. Yes I do.' He smiled and threw his head back in delight.

Sometime later, Fergus and Karen walked hand in hand down to the Puff Inn, the most westerly bar in Scotland. Garish, childlike paintings of puffins covered the walls, military types played pool, and in the corner, a widescreen television incongruously showed cricket in the southern hemisphere. Through the window, there was still an endless stretch of clear blue water, and their boat rocking in the bay, awaiting their homecoming.

𝔅urnoch 𝔊a3ette

February 23, 2008

MacKay MacFarlane. To Karen MacKay and Fergus MacFarlane, of Stone Barn, near Kinloch, Argyll, a son, Robert, born at Kinloch Hospital on February 21, 2008.

ACKNOWLEDGEMENTS

I would like to thank my brilliant editor Harriet Evans, and my agent Gill Coleridge for her endless encouragement. The late Sir Tom Hopkinson was an inspiration long ago with his photography lectures. My thanks also go to: Rick Beeston for the Baghdad advice, Nadav and Nicole Kander for the photography, the Western Bar in Glasgow for the pythons, Mike Murray for the trips to the Corryvreckan, the British Library for shelter, Northern Light Charters for the voyage to St Kilda, Felicity Rubinstein for the Welsh writing-breaks, Magnus Macintyre for the zeitgeist, Robin Hunt for the tea and sympathy, Jagoda Scott for holding the fort, and Ben Macintyre for everything else.

KATE MUIR

Left Bank

'Hugely entertaining' *The Times*

YOU ARE INVITED

to lose yourself in the world of Olivier and Madison Malin, glamorous French philosopher and gorgeous American actress

AT HOME

In Paris's most exclusive neighbourhood, the Glittering. Stylish. Elegant.

LEFT BANK

Intrigue. Scandal. Drama. It's all here.

RSVP

'A seamless comedy of manners' *Independent*

'Addictive' *Easy Living*

'Magnifique!' *Company*

'The kind of novel you can really immerse yourself in' *Heat*

978 0 7553 2502 3

headline
review

CARRIE ADAMS

The Godmother

Tessa King is the Godmother.

And she's having the time of her life. Trouble is, she doesn't know it.

Sassy and solvent, Tessa King has nothing tying her down but her friends and her four godchildren. She could accept any invitation and go on any adventure. But she doesn't. She's idling in neutral, waiting for her own 'happy ever after'.

Then her wish for domestic bliss is granted. Marriage and motherhood could be hers if she wants them. But as ever, the devil's in the detail and Tessa soon discovers that 'happy ever after' is just the beginning of the story because some fairytales aren't fair.

Heart-warming, dark, funny and almost too true to bear, *The Godmother* is the antidote to chick-lit we've all been waiting for.

'I couldn't pull my nose out of this book – it's an emotional roller coaster. You must read it, your friends must read it. Everyone will relate to it and relate to each other so much more because of it' Adele Parks

978 0 7553 2954 0

headline
review

Now you can buy any of these other bestselling
books from your bookshop or
direct from the publisher.

FREE P&P AND UK DELIVERY
(Overseas and Ireland £3.50 per book)

Left Bank	Kate Muir	£6.99
The Stepmother	Carrie Adams	£6.99
The Lost Art of Keeping Secrets	Eva Rice	£6.99
The Sisterhood	Emily Barr	£6.99
A Perfect Life	Raffaella Barker	£6.99
Midnight Champagne	Manette Ansay	£7.99
The Island	Victoria Hislop	£6.99
The Consequences Of Marriage	Isla Dewar	£7.99
That Summer Affair	Sarah Challis	£6.99
The Vanishing Act of Esme Lennox	Maggie O'Farrell	£7.99
Bright Lights and Promises	Pauline McLynn	£6.99
Beautiful Strangers	Julie Highmore	£6.99

TO ORDER SIMPLY CALL THIS NUMBER

01235 400 414

or visit our website: www.headline.co.uk

Prices and availability subject to change without notice.